DEATH WISH

Singer turned his head to look at the vitos. As they parted the curtain of smoke, the voice in his head tempted him.

You don't need a gun anyway. Think about what you did to me. Why don't you just ask them nicely to go die?

"I won't do it," he whispered.

You could if you wanted to, said the voice.

"I can't. I won't try." But he was already trying, his mind reaching out for the pilots . . .

By Ann Tonsor Zeddies
Published by Ballantine Books:

DEATHGIFT

SKY ROAD

SKY ROAD

Ann Tonsor Zeddies

A Del Rey Book

BALLANTINE BOOKS • NEW YORK

A Del Rey Book
Published by Ballantine Books

Copyright © 1992 by Ann Tonsor Zeddies

All rights reserved under International and Pan-American Copyright Conventions. Published in the United States of America by Ballantine Books, a division of Random House, Inc., New York, and simultaneously in Canada by Random House of Canada Limited, Toronto.

Library of Congress Catalog Card Number: 92-97049

ISBN 0-345-37865-2

Manufactured in the United States of America

First Edition: February 1993

For the tibe of my youth:
Stephen John, Claire, Margaret Grace

SKY ROAD

Dave M. Kovack
Pontypool, Ont.   Feb. 14, 2012

I Weaving the Medicine Shirt

This is a very good story, not overly exciting but not boring, just a good read.

From the last quarter of this story the "peace-maker" inserted a lot of foul profanity but the author is trying to show how we should live; and that will not work until the 2nd coming.

I read this in Apr + May 2012 — it is still good. I will try to get some other of her works.

P.K.

1

In the camp at the foot of the mountains the night fire twisted and tugged within its circle, then slept at last, like a watchdog whose vigilance had gone unrewarded. A reflection of the flames danced in the eyes of the man who watched from the hillside. He was drawn to the flame as the shadows of the unburied were drawn to the fires of the living. The scents of the camp were calling him home, yet he was a stranger there.

They are Thanha, he thought. The Free People. Riders. My people. He feared that the fire of longing in him would light him up like a torch for those below to see. He forced it back till it dimmed like a coal. He let the wind blow past him and over him as if he were just another tangle of dry branches.

He had left his own companions waiting behind him, safely out of reach. They had learned much in the long journey from the south, but he still could not trust them not to betray themselves. With their alien weapons, they could wreak havoc in the dark, killing indiscriminately. That was the one mistake they must avoid. It was important not to be discovered and captured, not to provoke a fight. He wanted to enter the camp peacefully, in his own way and time.

He had already pinpointed the positions of the guards. As they stepped in and out of the shadows, he kept track of them. He was preparing to make his move when sudden, familiar terror seized him by the throat. The air quivered with a sound that was still beyond the guards' hearing. Something deadly moved in the night. He knew that his companions felt the alarm, too, but the people in the camp below slept on. They had no way of knowing about the destruction that was coming.

3

He had only a few moments to decide what he would do. Warn them? If they saw him, they might take him for an enemy and try to kill him. He knew those people and their fierce thoughts. He knew them as he had once known his own people. Once. Before the terror in the night had taken them.

It took a painful wrench to shift his thoughts back to the strangerfolk language and speak to the others.

Air strike coming, he told them. *I have to warn them. Stay here. I don't want to see you killed by the Riders. That would be the last bad joke.*

He did not stop to listen to their confused protests. He sucked in a deep breath and screamed, the old battle yell he had learned from his foster father. Then he plunged downhill through the snowdrifts as arrows hissed past him toward the place where he had been.

He could hear the alarmed camp waking as he ran among the tents. Beyond their shouting, he heard the scream in the air that told of the fire-from-the-sky ships coming. These Riders would meet their fate on their feet, at least. They would not die sleeping, as his own people had. But once awake and armed, they would stand and fight, and he knew they must not.

He ran for the picket line, hoping to reach it before they did. The horses were already rearing and plunging, panicked by the unearthly roar in the sky. He slashed the ropes and scattered the horses just before the first fists of thunder plunged into the earth and hurled him off his feet.

He was shocked by the high, thin screaming that he heard in a momentary gap between bursts of thunder. Riders did not cry out in fear. There must have been children present—children too young to control their terror. He tried to locate that sound and head for it, dodging the warriors who ran past him toward the milling horses.

On the south side of the camp, the splattered snow was blackened with dirt and soot and the tents had caught fire. He ripped tent pegs out of the ground and lifted up the felt. The children ran to him, big ones carrying the little ones. They did not hang back from him as he had feared. They ignored his clothing and came to his voice. They did not stop to ask who he was.

"Run to the rocks," he ordered them. "Hide yourselves in the gullies and cover your heads. Stay there till someone comes for you."

The older warriors had rushed out to protect the little ones.

Confused, finding no enemy on the ground, some of them came running back to the burning tents.

"Take them to the rocks!" the man shouted. "Don't fight! Run! Go with the children!"

He could hear the flying fire ships coming back. The warriors gathered together, making a pathetic stand in the smoking circle of their tents.

"Don't fight!" he screamed. "Run!" The words came strangely to his lips. Those words, in that order, had never been spoken in the Riders' tongue. They could not hear him. They stood their ground, as they would stand to the end.

He shed his shirt, the remnant of his alien uniform, as he ran toward them. He had heard a Singer giving battle instructions to the Riders more than once. He summoned that carrying chant and called them again with all his force. They started to turn toward him, uncertain. They saw his bare chest and his flowing hair by the light of the fire. He looked like a Singer. They moved; they began to run. It was going to be too late; he could feel it. The fire ships closed rapidly on their second pass. Snow burst upward where the deadly metal from their guns ripped into the earth. He was caught in a nightmare memory of the night the fire had fallen on his home, obliterating his people forever. Still he ran and called.

Then, behind him, he heard his companions open fire. He had been entirely Rider since he had given the alarm—thinking in Thanha, lost in his memories. He snapped back to awareness of the present. Would his friends' weapons be enough to give them a chance? The flying machines were the small ones that sped close to the ground, not the steel spearheads that soared cloud-high. Even so, they were nearly invulnerable.

The flying thunder swerved away and up toward the ridge where his friends held their position. He swerved with the sound, fearing equally for the people so like his own and the strangers who had become his brothers. He spotted a flash from a new position below the crest of the hill and guessed what they were trying to do. The gunships made a tight turn to rake the flank of the hill, giving an expert eye at the highest point of the ridge a chance to hit them from their most vulnerable angle. It was the only way to stop the attack, but whoever was drawing the fire was in great danger.

Straining for some clue to what was happening, he thought he heard a change in pitch in the roar of the engines. He could not be sure. Then the first ship struck the ridge and broke up in cartwheeling chunks of burning metal. The other flying machines seemed to hesitate in midair, then pulled up and away. A sudden silence fell in which human voices could be heard again, sounding small and exposed. By then the laboring warriors had nearly reached the rocks. Behind them, dark shapes dotted the snow like bundles of rags cast aside in flight. Snow and sky glimmered an even gray. The moon had set, and dawn was coming.

The stranger pulled up with the rest of them and stood, panting. Out of the foggy afterimage of the explosion figures hurried down through the snow to join him, and he counted, dry-mouthed with fear. Four. They had all made it.

Something ran and tickled on the stranger's arm, and he slapped at it, half-dazedly thinking it was an insect. He was surprised to feel wetness. Blood ran from a dozen cuts. Flying bits of metal had grazed his shoulder. He recognized the sensation as pain, then ignored it again.

An older man limped toward him, leaning for support on the shoulder of a young one. The old man's hair was clubbed in a war knot and bound up with a gold-embroidered strip of silk. The stranger stood very still, arms spread as if he could shelter his friends behind them. He knew that several unseen arrows were trembling on the string, a breath away from his ribs. Deeply humiliated by an enemy too big to fight, the survivors might avenge themselves on any strangers if he gave them a reason to strike.

Drop your weapons, he said urgently to those behind him. *Drop them—now!*

Reluctantly they let the rifles, still warm, fall into the snow.

"I am Siri. I am Asharya here," the old man announced. "Who are you that takes it on himself to tell the Riders of the North Hills to run away? Who made you Singer for this people?"

"No one made me Singer," the stranger answered hoarsely. "But Singer is my name."

"Tell me no riddles, stranger," the old man said. "This is not a night for playing games."

"No riddle, Grandfather. My foster father gave me the name when I came to the Riders. I learned music from the true Singer of my people, but I never took his place. I was still young when they went where they had no need of me."

He raised his head. His voice was still low, but it carried. "My name is Singer, my people the Riders of the Rock. I bring you a song to save your lives or end them. Will you give me a welcome?"

Sunlight had been gathering at the horizon. It spilled over, dazzling him and touching him with welcome warmth. The Riders drew a quick breath, as if he had materialized from the shadows like a ghost. The bows trained on him were lowered. The Riders did not fear their dead, but they held them in awe.

"The Rock is no more, stranger," the Asharya said.

"It lives in me."

Slowly the Asharya limped closer and dared to touch the stranger's face. There was a collective sigh as they saw that he was flesh and blood, after all.

"I heard of the one they called Singer. They said he was tall, like you, and like you he had golden hair and sky-colored eyes. But the Singer they spoke of bore a scar like a death mark— from here to there." The old man's fingers traced a line across the stranger's face from the corner of his eye to his lip. Beneath a smear of blood, the stranger's skin was smooth and even.

"A healer took that scar from me."

The Asharya let disbelief show on his face. He had not yet called the stranger a liar, but he did not need to say the word aloud.

"I saw the place where the Rock once stood. All the gatherings of the People sent riders to witness that destruction when we heard the news. We saw a great wound in the earth. We saw many, many dead. It is not possible that one man lived through that. The Rock is no more."

"Still I live." The stranger held out his bloodied hands, palms up, in the formal gesture of greeting. "There is one way to know who I am," he said. His strange blue eyes locked with the old man's, and the Asharya was the first to look away. But the old man would not touch him. He stared over Singer's shoulder.

"Who are these others who come uninvited, hiding behind your shoulder? Why don't they name themselves?"

"They don't speak as we do," said the man who called himself Singer. "Nonetheless they are my hearth brothers." He beckoned them up where the old man could see them clearly.

"Zhanne," Singer said, nodding toward the smallest member of the group, who still came resolutely first. He repeated her name to himself in her own language, silently. *Captain Janet Logan, medical corps.*

Zhanne had the best grasp of the Riders' language. She understood what was being said, but she maintained a properly expressionless face.

His right-hand brother took back his usual place at Singer's shoulder, and it was good to have him there again.

"Palha." *Pablo Saldivar, Mobile Force.* Saldivar looked the most at home of any of them. Much of his strangerfolk clothing had worn out or been given to the others and had been replaced with whatever game they could skin and dress.

"Lyn." *Mellyn Greenway, pilot and mechanic.* She stepped forward with her hand automatically reaching for a firing button that was not there. She narrowed her gray eyes and shot the Asharya an evil look.

The last man in the group met the Asharya's eyes with quiet confidence, taking his measure.

"Makho." *General Marcus Aurelius Kruger, Mobile Force commander, forcibly retired.*

"These are not hearth brothers," the Asharya said. His voice was thick with suppressed anger. "They come wearing the clothing of our enemies and carrying weapons like those which have killed my people."

"Go look on the hillside for the enemies they killed for you," Singer said.

"Wolf kills wolf. Do I ask the victor to eat by my fire?" The Asharya stared him down while Singer held his tongue. He was afraid that if he argued, he would force the Asharya to order him away.

Janet stepped up to the old man before Singer could stop her. "Maybe I don't understand your ways," she said. "I am a healer, not a fighter, and I am young. But if I were Grandfather to this people, as you are, I'd be ashamed to hear my children crying with pain while I laid hard words on a man who had shed blood for them."

Her Thanha was nearly perfect. The Asharya blinked as if she had struck him, but Singer saw a grudging respect in his face. The People liked straight talk.

"The young one is right," the old man said. "Name yourself what you please. It's not our business. You have shed blood for us tonight. We must thank you for that. We have little to offer in return, however. You must forgive us if we take little pleasure in strangers these days. You have leave to sleep one night by our fire. Then take whatever provisions you need to set you on your journey and farewell." He turned away.

Singer knew then more than ever that something was badly

wrong. There should not have been a war camp in winter. Children should not have been brought into such danger. And never before had he known a leader of the People to deny the privilege of hospitality to strangers.

Lyn bent to pick up her weapon, brushing off the snow. "That's telling him, Janney," she muttered. "We nearly got blown to shit for him, the old fart. He could at least be polite."

She turned her attention to Singer. "And the same thing to you, chico. We've been humping through the snow for six weeks with you, and the minute we find these folks you've been looking for, you take off without so much as a high sign and leave us to cover your ass."

"It seemed the best thing at the time," Singer said wearily. "I was afraid for you." He wondered if he could find his shirt back there in the snow. He was cold. But the dead men were colder. He did not want to go back among them.

Kruger put a hand on Lyn's shoulder, silently warning her to ease up. "What happens now?" he asked Singer.

"You don't argue with the Asharya," Singer said. "He gave us one night; only deeds will change his mind. Those vitos—were they your people, Makho?"

Kruger shook his head. "No way. They were Deltans, of course, but I've never heard of Consorso forces this far north. We should go through the wreckage to make sure, but I'm certain those were New Peoples' Union vitos. According to the treaty, the Nupis don't belong up here, either. I can't figure what in hell they were doing."

"Will they come back?"

"Maybe tonight. They weren't expecting ground fire, or they wouldn't have pulled out so fast. We surprised them. When they decide what to do about it, they'll be back, but I doubt if they'll try it in the daytime."

"That was my thought, too," Singer said. "We need to move soon. If Siri has the head to be Asharya, he'll see that. But before he can move, they have to salvage the tents and catch the horses and take care of the wounded. If we can help, maybe he'll talk to us after."

"Speaking of the wounded," Janet said, touching his arm, "you need to get this fixed up."

He brushed her off. "This is nothing. I need to go after those horses. We can't move without them. You and Lyn can stay here—take care of the people who are really hurt. The old woman there will be the one in charge. Ask her what to do. Your Than-ha's good enough to get along without me for a couple of hours."

He walked away while she hesitated.

Lyn came up behind her as she stood looking after him.

"Are you going to let him walk away like that? What the fuck is smokin' him, anyway?"

"His Rock is gone," Janet said sadly. "He knows that. But still, in his heart, all the way up here he's been thinking that he's coming home. He just had his nose rubbed in it again. Cut him some slack, Lyn. There isn't much else we can do for him right now. He'll be back."

She blew on her numb fingers, trying to rub some sensitivity back into them.

"In the meantime we have work to do. I'm going to make a surgical tech out of you. One easy workshop, no money down, employment guaranteed."

The pale sun had passed its highest point by the time the riders came back with as many horses as they had been able to find. Saldivar rode behind Kruger on a recaptured bay stallion. Kruger had surprised everyone by remembering that he had once known how to ride. A boy came running to meet Singer as soon as he had dismounted.

"The healers want you," the boy said, half-shy of him, half-pleased to see the stranger up close. "The black-haired stranger woman is in their tent. She's asking for you."

Singer knew what waited for him in the tent and knew that he could not leave Janet alone there any longer. He followed the boy, making his way carefully among the wounded. The worst hurt had been lifted onto the sleeping ledge, where they could be as comfortable as possible. The warmth inside felt good to him, but the smell of blood was maddening. He saw one or two of the healers glance sharply at him. He was creating a disturbance. It was a relief to seek out Janet's familiar presence, though he knew at once that she wanted something from him.

"Where have you been?" she asked. She straightened up from her cramped position—she had been crouching over a body on the ledge—but she held her hands out stiffly in front of her, not touching him. They were sticky with blood.

"What's the problem?"

"Well, it could be worse," she said grimly. "These people are better medics than I would have imagined possible. Now I understand how you could survive with all those scars of yours.

They can set bones; they can stop some kinds of bleeding. But madre'dio, I don't have enough antiseptic, I don't have antibiotics, I don't have my flash sterilizer. I don't have enough gel or clips or even sutures. I've got people unpicking embroidery and boiling the silk for me. I'm using sterile saline—at least I hope it's sterile—and some kind of alcohol to cleanse and then sewing them up. But sometimes that just isn't good enough.''

She swallowed hard. "They have their own form of triage, it seems. Most of the people who got hit are either dead or ambulatory. Then there are the ones we'd be working hardest on if this were a Deltan field hospital—hurt bad but will live with care. Those are the ones they're treating like expectants. It's killing me because I know I could save them if I had my equipment. Without it—I don't know, but they won't even let me try. This one, for instance. They told me to get away from him. They were going to do something, some word I don't know, but I gathered the result would be death in short order. I told them to wait for you. They got angry and said, 'See for yourself, then'—some other word I don't know. They all backed off.'' One corner of her lip curled ruefully. "Just like a bunch of docs resigning from a case. So I shot him up heavily and waited. His chest is crushed—broken ribs and all kinds of internal injuries. I'd have to open him up to have even a chance of helping him, but they won't let me cut him.''

Don't ask me to do this, he thought, but he could not get the words out. Instead he followed her to the ledge where the man lay. He was unconscious. Singer could feel the absence, deeper than sleep. Blood bubbled at torn lips with every breath. Pain coiled in the damaged body like a snake hiding. To touch the man would be like allowing the snake to sink its fangs into him.

"Is there someone here who knows this man?'' he asked.

"He is our brother, stranger,'' one of the healers said, offended.

"Someone who loved him more than most.''

There was silence. Finally one of the other wounded spoke.

"Is Kata still living? Kata knew him well.''

One of the old people hurried out, returning in a few minutes with a thin, black-haired young man. The old one murmured a quick explanation to him. Kata glanced shyly at the strangers and crouched down by the wounded man, not meeting their eyes.

"This is Herat,'' he said softly. "He had hearth friends, but they are mostly gone now. He had a partner. She got sick and died before we left our home. He was a good friend to me. He was herdmaster since I was a boy, and I worked the herds with him. He taught me everything, just like a foster father.'' He stole another look at Singer and Janet. There was a faint flicker of hope in his dark eyes. ''Can you help him? I thought he would die.''

Singer extended a hand in the Thanha way, silently asking permission to touch, and the young man clasped hands with him.

''After the flying people took our herds away, he was the first to say we should go after them,'' Kata said. ''He dressed himself for the war road, but I think he set his face toward the Road to the North, the Sky Road. Toward death.''

The young man choked on tears he would not shed and fell silent, but Singer had a clear picture of the man who lay broken. Despair had stolen Herat's strength before the fire ships had come. Singer felt it touch him, too, cold and treacherous as ice that would split rock with its unseen probing fingers. He wished that Janet had not brought him there, but he could not delay any longer. He was causing more hurt to the living and to the dying one. The Riders could deal with death when it came, but the pain of waiting and not knowing was hard for them to bear.

He took a deep breath and laid his hands on Herat's chest. The pain struck into him like venom. He felt sweat spring out on his face. He felt himself swaying and felt Janet steady him. Then he lost track of his own body in the awareness of the other. Herat was mangled internally by fragments of his own bones, splintered by the force of the blow he had taken. The flesh was cut and swollen. Blood seeped into torn lungs, into places where it was not meant to go. Singer had no words to analyze this ruin. It overwhelmed and sickened him.

Again he felt Janet steadying him. She had names for each fiber. He could hear her at the back of his mind, calmly analyzing the damage. He left that task to her and went on, searching beyond drugs and shock for the man himself.

What he found was like darkness at first. He moved through it as gently and quietly as he could. Someone was there, waiting, like a herd guard in winter waiting for the dawn. There was no thought in that half consciousness but a dull wonder that night could last so long. The numbness that wrapped him meant death, but it protected him from pain he could no longer bear. To stir him and ask him to fight for his life would be recalling him to a hopeless battle.

Singer disengaged himself carefully, enough to look back at Janet and see that her healing ways had no help for these wounds, either. He found that the eldest of the healers had drawn near, as well.

Is your stranger friend satisfied now? Have you kept him in his pain long enough? The question came into his mind forcefully but silently and left a bitter taste. She was angry.

Yes, barasha, he answered humbly. *We are satisfied.* He was ready to let go now, to let her do whatever else could be done. But she cut him off.

You took this on yourself. Now it is your responsibility to see him through it.

Singer wanted to run again, but he was too deeply entangled with the wounded man. He could feel that the drugs were not as strong anymore. If he pulled himself away, he risked shocking Herat awake. He turned his back on the others, on praise and blame alike, and went back into the darkness.

Go on, brother, he whispered to the one who waited for him there. *Kata sends you his love. There's nothing more to wait for.*

The dying man moved farther on his trackless way without waking. Singer took the pain of that leave-taking on himself. He felt that body losing its hold on life, like lights going out one by one in a great city, like stars fading from a sky that would never know dawn. He had never known this man, but he knew him now, and cherished him, and was torn by his passing. He reached for the last trace of him and reached farther, until he was lost in the winter beyond the stars.

Living hands shook him back to awareness, and that hurt, too.

"Fool!" the old woman said aloud. "You want to play at being a healer? You want to interfere? Then take the full weight of it! Go down the road with them and see how it feels!"

Singer could not stop shivering. His hands felt like ice. He looked down at the old woman from what seemed a great distance. She was punishing him relentlessly for being a stranger. He was too tired to make her see otherwise. Herat lay between them, dead, with young Kata weeping quietly at his feet.

Janet was not paying any attention to the old woman. She had already moved on to the next. She looked back impatiently when she noticed that Singer was not right behind her.

"Get moving. They don't have much time," she said, and he followed her.

* * *

A lifetime later he moved to find the next moaning, bloody body and found that there was no next. He straightened up. It had become quiet in the tent. He could hear the hiss of snow against the smoke flap, the crackle of the small fire. His hands had touched raw flesh and burns and broken bones. Now he was numb and felt nothing, not even Janet's hand on his arm.

"Don't quit yet. There's someone else," she said, stiff-lipped. When Singer looked at her, she flinched but stood her ground. She pointed. A woman was rocking herself to and fro beside a small, blanket-wrapped bundle.

Oh, Hesukristo and all the other gods of the strangerfolk, not a child, Singer prayed silently. He reached back through his time with the strangerfolk soldiers for all the foul words they had taught him, but the bundle was still there.

"What happened?" he asked.

Janet turned back the wrappings carefully. "She got hit in the belly. I sewed up the artery so she's not bleeding to death, and I cleaned up as well as I could. But she's got a puncture wound right through into the liver, and I can't fix it, and I'm afraid to close up without fixing it. The boss old lady was hung up between fascination and outrage. She thought sewing people up was a max idea but thinks I'm making a hell of a botch of it, and she's right about that. If you can't help, I'll cut the damaged tissue out of the liver and close it as best I can, and then she'll probably either bleed to death internally or die of infection."

She explained stolidly, gazing at the gaping wound in the child's abdomen without flinching. She was as ruthless in her own way as any warrior, Singer thought.

"Give her to me," he said.

Janet really looked at him and hesitated for the first time. "You can't move her," she protested.

"Give her to me!"

He sat cross-legged on the ledge, cradling the child in his arms. She whimpered but stayed limp. Janet had given her too much of the strangers' medicine in her attempt to still the pain. Herat had welcomed that stupor, but the child fought it as a child would struggle to kick off an entangling blanket.

Fight, little one, fight! Singer encouraged her. He warmed himself at her small, sturdy spirit as if at a glowing ember. There was no poisonous flavor of despair in her thoughts. They were simple and clean. She wanted to get up. She wanted to live. He felt her legs tremble as she tried to kick and soothed her hastily. In her dream she was still running, reaching for her mother.

Singer reached to reassure her, but she whimpered in her sleep again, trying to get away. He was a stranger.

He started to weave a net for her in her dreams, like the game called "pathways" that Thanha children played with a string twisted around their fingers. His fingers twitched, wanting the strings of his *thamla*, but there was a strange weight on his arms. He would have to weave a pattern without his instrument.

It was moonlight he wove, the moonlight that trickled like lines of ice over the rocks where a boy her age had waited alone in a night as frosty cold as this one. He did not call for his mother. He had forgotten her face and her name. No one was coming to rescue him. Only a handful of notes from a half-remembered song stood between him and the fear of the dark. The boy sang for himself alone, but the child heard him. She was not afraid of him. She paused in her flight and followed the silver pattern of his song, and her pain and panic faded. Under cover of the music, he breathed on the embers of her strength till they glowed bright. Her heart beat faster, her blood raced, the insulted tissues reached and wove themselves together. He did not have Janet's skill, but the Delh'tani medic had already mended much of what was broken. The child's body found its own wisdom for rebuilding the rest.

Silence fell in the tent when he started to sing. It was a simple song, a child's song for the Lady of the Fountains. The voice was hushed and hoarse but woke echoes in their hearts. They were all alone with the cold and the sound of their own breath for company. They listened for another voice to answer them and feared that it would never come. Their hope was as fragile as a child's breath and as slender as a harp string, but still it sang in the night, weaving them together into the pattern.

Imperceptibly the tune changed, warming and rocking them. It resolved into words again, into a Thanha sleep song, reassuring and well remembered as their mothers' arms.

> You will ride the wind,
> You will track a star;
> You will catch a dream,
> You will travel far.

Janet awoke suddenly from a drowsy warmth of well-being and scolded herself vigorously. Madre'dio, what am I doing? she thought. This is no time to nod off! She saw that Singer's arms had loosened around the child and sprang to catch her before she could fall from his lap. Singer did not move; he seemed to have fallen asleep. Carefully she gathered up the little girl and laid her back in bed. She turned back the dressings to make sure that the handling had not damaged any of her delicate work.

The gaping incision had closed. A shallow, scabbed crescent scarred the child's belly, but the wound was gone.

2

Singer struggled back to consciousness as she took the child from him.

"No, not this one," he said.

"It's all right," Janet said. "She's all right."

The woman who had been watching by the child's bed looked from them to the child in stunned disbelief. She saw that the girl was sleeping peacefully and burst into tears of joy that called the Thanha healers immediately to her side.

"Is that the end?" Singer asked Janet. He had lost track. He remembered that many people had been hurt, but he could not clearly remember what he had done. He was so cold that his whole body ached. He had stopped shivering a long time before.

"What about you?" Janet asked. "You look as if you need a rest."

He shook his head. Thoughts came slowly, but there was an urgency somewhere in his mind. "We have to move the tents now. There can't be much daylight left."

"At least put on something warm. You'll freeze to death."

That touched his pride. Long before, he had been taught not

to feel the cold. He should have been able to summon the warmth he needed, but he was too tired.

Someone laid the warm weight of a sheepskin cloak around his shoulders. The old woman came to him with a bowl in her hands. His stomach knotted at the thought of food, but she did not ask if he wanted it. She pushed a lump of honey between his lips.

"Eat, *barasheli*, young brother. You need the strength."

When he looked at her, startled, she shoved the bowl against his chest so he had to take it.

"My name is Morne. You and your friend are honored guests of my hearth now, as long as you choose to stay with us."

"But Siri—" Singer said.

"Siri will say nothing."

She touched Janet's lips with honey, as well.

"I have worked beside this woman," she said. "I have seen her take the blood of my people on her hands. Her heart is Thanha. How does this happen? She comes from beyond the lands we know, farther even than the cityfolk. How can she be one of us?"

"Singer brought me to the Riders," Janet said. "Just as he was brought in his time. I want only truth between us, however, so I must tell you that I still have a heart for my own people. They drove me away, so I came to the Riders, but I do not want any harm to come to them."

The old woman nodded. "You speak as a healer. You have the wish for peace with all people. Since you carry weapons, I think you have learned that the healer's wish must sometimes be set aside so her own people can live."

Janet lowered her eyes. "I have killed with my own hands. I killed for the sake of my friends, but it has been sorrow to my heart that I did it."

Morne looked from one to the other. "You are *kamarh*?"

"All of us are kamarh," Singer answered. "All of us are bound together. Our lives are one; our hearts are one. If you want Zhanne and me, you must accept all of us."

"Five of you? I have heard of three binding themselves in this way but never so many." Morne looked deep into Singer's eyes. "I knew Hilurin, who once was Singer for the Rock. He spoke of a young brother who would be the best Singer in memory if he lived. He said this boy had the feeling-for-the-People more strongly than anyone he had known in his long years. This boy could touch the hearts and thoughts of his people even from far away. He could move them by his songs, and he could speak clearly to them—not just feelings sent from one to another, as a handclasp is passed along, but clear words, as clear as speech, but silent.''

I have heard you speak to my heart. You are that boy. She finished her speech silently.

I was that boy. Now I have nothing but my hearth brothers. I have no People unless you will let me travel with you awhile.

She felt the strength of his plea. ''I felt your sister here. She speaks clearly, as you do, and her heart is strong for healing. Are all of your kamarh like you?''

Singer shrugged. ''I have not the wisdom to judge that, bar-asha. They come from the strangerfolk, without training, without brothers around them. Who can say what they would have been? I have felt Zhanne and Lyn speak words to me from far away. I think their gift is as strong as any among our people. Palha and Makho have hearts deep and strong, though their skill for this may be less. Makho was an Asharya among his own folk.''

Morne raised her eyebrows. ''Then where are his children? Even among the strangers, surely an Asharya would never leave his own, whatever the reason.''

''Death took them from his hand. Palha and I are the last of them. If not for us, he would now be on the Heroes' Road with the others. He understands your sorrows.''

Morne nodded slowly. ''You see how few we are,'' she said in a low voice. ''You see how few children are left. Wounds I can deal with, and the sickness of the old and weak, but this year I saw the children who should have been strong dying of fever, dying even of coughing sickness. Never in my long years have I seen the children of the North Hills losing their lives because they were too hungry and weak to fight. It is a shame that is very bitter to me. Today you saved lives that were doubly dear because they were all we had left. You and your kamarh are welcome at my hearth. Siri will not speak against it.''

She strode away with her head high.

''I didn't understand all of that,'' Janet said, dipping hungrily into the bowl. It held boiled grain sweetened with more honey. Singer took a mouthful and found that he was wolf-hungry.

''What was that thing she said they died of?''

''Coughing sickness.'' Singer translated for her. ''Everybody gets it when they're babies. Cityfolk die of it pretty often, I guess. My brother had it as a child and nearly died. But it is the pride of the Riders that we survive things that kill others. We may die young from the wounds of war, but our children are well fed and well cared for, so they don't die of the little sicknesses of children, as it happens in the cities. When something like that carries off our young ones, we feel very ashamed.''

"Now I understand. That's exactly how I felt when I saw civilian kids dying of river fever. One shot in time would have stopped it, and clean water would have prevented it. It was a disgrace. I like the way Morne thinks. I wish I could hang around her for a while. I might learn something.''

Singer gulped the last of the grain. "Oh, we'll stay. She has decided.''

"I thought Siri was the heavy here.''

"He won't go against his healer. You'll see.''

While they ate, the Riders had been taking the tent down around them. They shared out the bread and dried meat with everyone in the tent so they would all have enough food for a day or two if they were lost or separated on the trail.

Singer polished the bowl clean with his fingers and handed it back to one of the children who was stowing the cooking gear. Others had rolled the felt side panels of the tent and bundled the pole framework and were loading those things on horse drags. The wounded were back on their feet again, bundled in extra cloaks and blankets. Most of them were still pale and shaky.

"How strong are those people?'' Janet asked him privately.

"Don't know. You know I'm not a proper healer at all, and not a *medikh'* like you.'' He frowned, trying to recall how their bodies had felt from the inside. "The bones are joined, but they're not—they don't feel heavy like they were.''

"That's what I thought. Density. That's the word you want. They don't have it yet.''

"Rest and plenty of food's what they need, but they can't have it. At least they can go with us. If they're strong enough, they will recover. In time.''

"What would they have done if it hadn't worked?'' she asked. "Surely Siri wouldn't have left them here to die?''

"Their choice. If they could take the pain of riding, we'd take them if they had to be tied to the saddle. If they couldn't, or if they were already on the road, somebody would have made sure they died quickly.''

"I can't believe Morne would let that happen.''

"She'd do almost anything to avoid it. When your people have to give up, they give their wounded drugs and leave them to die alone. We can't do that. It's hard to let them go, hard to walk that road with them and come back alone, but we do it if we must. Need is an iron master.''

He pulled the cloak closer, but it did not help much. The deathly cold was in his bones.

By the time the tents were packed, the rest of the Riders were saddled up and ready. Those who had injured backs and hips rode in drags along with the baggage. Only ashes and trampled snow marked their camping place, and the wind was swiftly erasing those traces. The sun showed low and pale, fading behind the rolls of cloud that hurried down from the northwest.

"Looks like more snow," Kruger said. He and Saldivar shared a horse; they rode with Siri, among the remaining *pallantai*, the fighting strength of the Riders, those who were still strong enough to provide a defensive escort for the helpless. Janet was mounted on one of the pack animals that pulled a drag for the recovering wounded. Lyn walked beside her. Siri had offered Singer a horse to ride among the pallantai, but Singer would not take it.

"Horse would ask why I don't carry him with these long legs. I can get through the snow faster than he can."

They moved off at a trot, slowing only when they had to push through chest-high drifts. Siri would not retreat east toward the sheer mountain wall they called the Curtain but headed northwest into the last of the foothills, where they would have some chance to find shelter. Singer held to Kruger's stirrup leather and loped along beside their lean, ribby horse. Saldivar dismounted at intervals and ran on the other side to give the animal a rest and to pound some feeling back into his feet. As dark came down, the file of riders slowed to a weary walk. Singer hung more heavily on the stirrup. Saldivar tried to persuade him to change places, but he only shook his head without looking up. Saldivar stayed on the horse, huddling against Kruger, with his hands jammed through Kruger's belt. His fingers were too numb to hold on.

It was completely dark when they heard the hooves ahead of them clattering and sliding on rock. They found themselves slipping downward over gravel and ledges slick with ice. Below them lay a frozen river with a steep bluff beyond standing up black against the faintly glowing clouds. The river had narrowed in the dry season before winter, leaving a wide sandbank in the lee of the bluffs. They crossed over the ice and set up camp under the bluff, where wind had scoured away the snow. One of the horses fell through the ice, but the water was not deep, and the animal floundered to shore with the help of half a dozen Riders hauling on the lead rope. Icicles froze instantly on its shaggy winter coat.

The Riders had brought small bundles of dry, resinous wood with them and firehorns to start a new blaze quickly. The young ones dismounted, and as soon as they could force their stiff legs to obey them, they scavenged along the banks for more wood. By the time the tents were up, fires were ready to light.

Siri had sent a few of the able-bodied pallantai to find a quick path up the bluff in case the fire ships came back.

"You and your friends can get up there with your fire weapons and try to cover us as we scatter," he said to Singer.

"We might not have time," Singer protested. "We should camp up there, be ready as soon as we hear them. I should take the watch until dawn."

Siri made the hand sign for "silence!" and Singer stopped talking.

"Visit my sleeping place," Siri said. It was an order, not an invitation. He pushed through the door flap without waiting for them to accept.

They followed him to a curtained corner. A rug or two, mostly unburned, had been laid on the floor. The curtain helped keep out the draft, but it also blocked the heat of the fire. A brass pan of coals gave some warmth, but it was comfortable there only by contrast with the cold outside. Singer remembered, like something from another life, the first time he had ever seen the Grandmother of his own people. Her sleeping place had been rich with gold-embroidered weavings and precious furs. She had been attended by captains and weavers. She had wisely ruled a strong people. Now all that was gone, wiped out in an eyeblink by the strangers from beyond the sky.

Before his eyes was another Asharya, reduced to holding council in a smoky corner of a patched felt tent. He was attended by a handful of old people and first-year pallantai, with a half-grown boy to run his errands. Another trail of loss and destruction had brought the Riders to this camp.

The Asharya turned his situation into a grim joke. "I see you're overcome by the riches of my tent. You should be—I can tell you that every one of my people is as well cared for as I am. We're so rich, in fact, that we'd be ashamed to let strangers pass without accepting our hospitality."

The boy passed around cups with lumps of honey in the bottom, and Siri himself poured hot tea for them.

"Good against cold," he said, expertly swirling the melting sweetness. Finally he looked up and met Singer's eyes.

"Truth—you saved our lives, for one more day, at least. Still it goes hard to see my people run, and I cannot find it in my heart to thank you for it. The only thanks I can give is to say stay with us if you still want to. But I must tell you that this road has not been kind to us. Our hospitality may cost you something."

"You are Thanha and not fools," Singer said. "Only desperate need would drive you to this wolf's road in winter, and with little children. Tell us your need, and I swear by the Rock that was, we'll help you if we can."

Siri frowned, looking again over Singer's shoulder at his friends. "You are Thanha. I believe that, though I don't know who you are or what brought you here. But what about these? Will they be bound by your promise?"

Singer shrugged. "I told you once they were my brothers. If you think I'm lying, why should I say it again?"

"Why would they risk their lives in this fight, brothers or not? Why should you? Why would you survive the Rock to come and die in this place?"

"We didn't come here to die."

Siri laughed in his face. "What did you come for, then? We haven't got much else to offer you."

Singer knew what the Asharya was doing. He was goading, probing, trying to get them to betray the truth about themselves.

He stretched out his hands to the old man, palms up. It was a guileless gesture. That was what any well-mannered young man would do in greeting an elder.

Singer knew that the Asharya was afraid of him. To touch hands in the formal greeting meant to open his mind to the stranger. He feared even that limited contact. Singer also knew that the old man could not show fear before his captains. Singer's face and posture pleaded silently with the Asharya. *See how young I am, how harmless.* He saw annoyance cross the Asharya's face as the old man recognized how he was being pushed, but the persuasion worked. The Asharya touched palms with him.

Years of work with rein leather, sword hilt and knife hilt, herder's staff and hunter's bow had hardened and toughened the hands Singer held. The old man had served his people gladly all his life, but the new weight laid on his shoulders was crushing him to the ground. That much Singer sensed. Then the Asharya made contact, with clumsy power. Singer gritted his teeth, trying not to close himself to that painful inquest. He struggled to give the Asharya what he needed to know without opening any of the locked doors.

Siri touched the black night when fire from the sky had destroyed the Rock and recoiled from it as a finger skipped off scorching metal. He saw the hospital prison Janet had freed Singer from, and Singer's time as a soldier for Kruger, his stranger Asharya, but the only memory that made sense to the old man was Singer's leave-taking from the strangers. Singer felt him linger with pleasure on the rolling black smoke and fire filling the sky behind them as they left the strangers' city behind and fled north toward the plains. Sweat sprang out on Singer's face as though he were standing too close to that fire. Siri was forcing him too near the things he could not look at again.

He could bear no more and jerked his hands away, breaking off contact. How had this man ever become Asharya? If he handled a horse as he did humans, he would never have lived to wear his gray hair.

The old man had felt those discourteous thoughts before Singer backed away. His mouth set dourly.

"Yes, I have heavy hands," he said. "My herdmaster always said so. Yet I have found a horse or two who would carry me. That's no secret. Nor is it a secret that I would never have been Grandfather for this people if there were anyone living who could do it better. Now you know these things about me, and doubtless more besides, for you are quick to see. But what do I know about you? You come to me with open hands, but you slip away from me even as I touch you."

"It's the words, Grandfather, not just me," Singer said. "Too hard, giving you true talk about things I don't understand and you have never seen. After the Rock—I ran to Erech Tolanh, to the Iron City, to look for help. The city was destroyed. Loose in the ruins were strangers, and more strangers overhead, flying. I—made my way to their place, and I was a prisoner there. These friends of mine set me free and in doing so won the anger of their own kind. That is why they are with me now. Their people, fighting among themselves, destroyed both the Rock and the Iron City. They are still at war, and you are caught in the middle, it seems."

Siri brooded, looking at Singer's face. "Every word you speak has a shadow. You call yourself Singer, but you have another name that is hidden. There is a darkness in you that I fear. You are like the shadow of a great storm, running ahead of the lightning. I take my people under your shadow because I have no other shelter for them. Be careful how you deal with my children.''

Singer bowed his head, shaken. He had expected to win the old man's trust. He had not expected an Asharya's vision from him.

Behind him, Kruger cleared his throat and extended a hand to Siri as if he did this every day. Singer was grateful for the intervention, and amused. Kruger detested inefficiency, and this must have seemed to him a most inefficient way to come to an agreement.

''I ask for Singer to translate for us if I can't find the words,'' Kruger said. ''I learn your speech slowly. Tell me, why are you chasing the flying people? What is the enmity between you?''

The Asharya sighed. ''Our trouble began last year—not long after the Rock was destroyed. It was a bad summer. Since the Iron City burned, too, and Hadhla the City Master was dead, the other cities began to fight among each other again. At first we were happy. We thought there would be plenty of work for us that year, and indeed we were called by the City of Gulls to fight for them. When the pallantai rode out, they found themselves sent against helpless people—homeless fugitives from the wreck of the Iron City. City of Gulls wanted them killed so they would not come begging there.

''The pallantai were insulted. They wanted to destroy the city, but they were too few. Instead they left that service and rode to City of the Rivermouth. They had heard from the Tall Grass People that there was good fighting along the river.''

Pain slowed his words, and he closed his eyes for a moment. ''I wasn't with the war host. I had been the summer captain for many years. That year a younger man took the pallantai to war. Would that I had gone with them. Would that I were now on the Road to the North with my brothers. A few came back, too few to beat the drums. They said the cityfolk had weapons never seen before.'' He glared at Kruger. ''Weapons like those you carry! Weapons like those you saw last night—the fire from the sky. *Ayei!* My brothers stood their ground, and they died. There was no deathgift for them, no revenge to make their sleep sweet. Only the mourning. All winter we heard the winds grieving for them.

"Then, in wolf month, when the cold was deepest, the flying people found us again by our winter hearth. Their flying ships scattered the herds and ran them off. They carried away our *silangh* and most of the horses. For our honor and our very existence, we had to pursue our herds. I begged the Asharya, the true Asharya who was still living then, to let me take what was left of the pallantai. She refused. She said she'd had enough of hiding by the hearth while her children died. So we left those who were too old, too young, or too crippled to ride, and the rest of us set out on this trail. I begged, also, that the children stay behind. But none of us knew when we would be coming back. The mothers and fathers feared the children would starve while they were gone. The children had already lost so many who were dear to them. They didn't want us to leave them. So, in the end, only the very youngest stayed. The rest are with us, as you see.

"We lost our Singer on that journey. Our Asharya, too, died on the way. She didn't have to see the end of us. If I did not love and honor her name, I'd curse her for leaving us like this—with no better guide than me."

He bit off the last words and looked straight at Kruger. "Now you know what I know. Maybe you can tell me why there is enmity between your people and us. They steal from us. They shoot us like dogs, never showing us their faces. What have we done to them to be so despised?"

Kruger stood up. "Will you come outside with me? I'd like to show you something."

The Asharya followed him. Curious, some of the others in the tent trailed behind. Outside, the cold was sharp, but the wind had died and the sky was almost clear, with a few rolls of cloud off to the southeast. The starlight pierced Singer's heart with joy. Those were the stars of his boyhood, once again in their right places, telling him the way home. But he saw his friends' glances roving anxiously across the horizon. Since the strangers had come, even the sky harbored enemies. A new light there was not a wonder but a danger beacon.

"You know the stars better than I do," Kruger said to the Asharya. "You've lived here all your life. I've only been here fifteen years. What do you call the bright one there?"

"That is Shanyelos, the Bright Flower," Siri answered, though he seemed puzzled by the question. "We call it so because it has a red color like the crimsonvine. No other star has such a color."

"And that, low on the horizon?"

"That one is Yona, the Burning Coal."

"How are those two different from the other stars?"

"How can you be so ignorant, stranger? The other stars dance the same pattern, month by month, year by year. They change their time of rising but never their place in the pattern. Those two wander among the rest. They follow a path, but it is a lonely path. There are four others like them. We call them the Hunter Stars, because they follow a trail alone."

"That's correct," Kruger said. "They follow a different path among the stars because they are not stars. They are worlds like this one. They don't shine with their own light, like the stars. The light you see is the sun's light, reflecting from their faces. It shines on them when the face of your world is turned away from the sun, as now."

Siri gave Kruger his full attention. "How do you know this? Are you Somostai? They claim to know the secrets of heaven and earth."

Kruger grimaced. "No, I'm not Somostai, whatever that is. I don't know any secrets. I'm a plain soldier, like yourself." He saw that he had offended Siri and looked quickly to Singer for help.

"My friend means you are both pallantai," Singer said. "That word you used is offensive to the Free People," he explained to Kruger. "Means an armed man who works for one of the City Masters. Thanha serve no master."

"Interesting," Kruger said to Singer in Delteix. "That offensive word is the one I learned from you." He turned back to Siri. "Anyway, I'm not so sure I'm pallantai, either. All I meant to say was I make my living with my weapons and my wits, and what I know about the secrets of heaven is by plain observation. I was there."

Siri looked from Kruger to Singer. "Is he crazy?"

"Look, the Hunter Stars travel around," Kruger said. "Well, people can travel around the sky, too. Those flying things—we call them vitos—they go up off the earth and fly through the sky to another place on the same world. We have ships that will leave one world altogether and go to another."

Siri gazed out at the bright dots of light. "So the Hunter Stars are worlds," he said finally. "Which one did you come from?"

"None of them. This one is the only world of this sun where people like us can live. The Flower is too hot. The Coal is too cold. The others have something wrong with them, too. I've seen pictures.''

"Where, then?'' the Asharya demanded.

"Farther. Do you see that star just above the—'' He faltered.

"Horizon,'' Singer supplied.

"Yes. I can't be sure that's the one. I'm not much of an—*astronomer*,'' he said in Delteix. "Help me, Singer.''

"There's no word,'' Singer said. "Someone with learning about the stars.''

"Well, whatever the word, I'm not one. But I think that's it. Our star. Worlds circle it, like this one and the other Hunter Stars.''

The Asharya tried to consider it, then shook his head. "Impossible. It's too far away. You would have grown old and died before you got here.'' He shook his head again. "Is it far away? What do I know!''

"Yes, it's far.'' Kruger sighed. "It took about fifty years to get here. They put us to sleep for the journey, and we didn't get any older. Well, not much older.''

"These ships,'' Siri said suspiciously. "Where are they now?''

"The ships are big, big as a hill or the top of a mountain. We put in them all the things we thought we might need to live here. When we came close to your world, the machines we built woke up a few of us to guide the ship to its harbor, and those people woke the rest of us. The first ship was designed to be left high up, circling around your world, to be a haven for the others when they came. It's still there. We have a craft that could take you there—we call it a 'shuttle'—but you can't see it from the ground. The second ship and the third were sent back to our own place. Whether they ever arrived, I cannot say. The distance is too great for us to speak.''

Siri listened with fascinated attention, but it was clear that he still found the story hard to believe.

"Why? Why would you leave your home and travel so far? What did you hope to gain?''

"My people have an old story—that we came to our own place from still another star. Now we're traveling again, looking for our relatives. That's part of it. The other part of it is that we have cities just as you do, and they fight with each other. Two great cities made this journey, and now they're fighting over your world. We call our world Delta—that means a river mouth, or a three-sided shape, or the fourth one in a line. My city called itself the Consorso. It's a lot of cities in alliance, actually. The others call themselves the New Peoples' Union. I believe it was the Union that attacked you, but to be honest, it doesn't much matter. They made a private agreement—a 'treaty,' we call it— between themselves to carve you up and take your land. Singer thinks it was my people who destroyed the Rock.

"I did not know of this treaty. You must understand that most of my people do not even know that you exist. Their leaders have told them this is an empty world, theirs for the taking. The Consorso and Union leaders are enemies, but they agree on this one thing: They will work together to kill you all before the rest of their people find out you are there. They fear their people would not have the stomach for the slaughter if they knew."

"How do the cityfolk come into this?" Siri asked.

"I don't know for sure. I think it may be that the Union has decided that the cityfolk are more useful to them alive than dead. They may have broken their agreement with those who were my leaders. That could be why the Consorso attacked the Iron City— because they feared that Hadhla was helping their enemies.

"So that's your answer, or as much of one as I know. You're living in a place they want, and they'll run you off it if they can. It's nothing personal."

"Nothing personal, that's the true word," Singer said. His Thanha was soft and musical after Kruger's heavily accented, laboriously phrased speech. "These people love things, even more than the Somostai do. Things are their wisdom and their riches. We have nothing—no flying machines, no fire weapons, no ships to carry us between the worlds. Who has nothing is nothing. That's how they think. That's why they despise us."

"I understand," the Asharya said heavily. "You have shown me wonderful things tonight. Perhaps tomorrow you will show me another wonder—how to teach these flying people that the Riders cannot be bought and sold. Come inside."

Most of the Riders were asleep, but a couple of the captains were always awake. They poured tea and made a place for the strangers by the fire. Singer sipped at the tea and held it in his mouth till the warmth was gone. He was so sleepy, he kept forgetting to swallow, and finally the cup slipped from his fingers. He could feel the others longing for the black medicine drink they called coffee. Whenever they were too tired, they thought about it. Black. He was drinking in the blackness.

* * *

"Give him here," Saldivar said as simply as Singer had held out his arms for the child. He climbed up on the sleeping ledge, settled Singer against his shoulder, and put most of the blanket over him.

"He's out cold," Janet said. "And I mean cold. I'm worried about him. He's pushing it."

She put her wrist against his neck to test his temperature. Her hands were still too cold to feel anything. She pulled off his boots and rubbed his feet till they were just chilly and not ice-white. Then she did the same for Saldivar. She warmed their boot liners by the fire till they were nearly dry.

"Well, they don't smell any better, but they should feel better," she said, putting them back on.

Lyn and Kruger had been drying their own feet.

"Here, let me get your boots off," Lyn said to Janet. "How are you doing yourself?"

"Fine," Janet said automatically, but she let them wrap her in blankets. She stretched her feet luxuriously toward the fire. " 'Dio, that feels good. How long has it been since we took a break?"

Lyn calculated. "We must have walked twenty miles yesterday. Remember? Singer kept saying he smelled a camp. We found them after dark and staked them out, and then the attack and then moving here—it's been nearly forty-eight hours."

"Hard to believe. Hard to believe we really found them."

"Yeah, well, if these are Singer's Thanha, I'm not impressed," Saldivar said from the ledge above them. "They're ~~useless~~." troubled

"Voice of the wet blanket," Lyn said.

"Yeah, very funny. They look like a bunch of raggedy-ass refugees to me. No home, no food, too many casualties, and too dumb to run away. They're about to smoke it. One day we've been with them, and Singer's already killing himself trying to save their butts. I don't like that. He's no ~~fucking~~ good in the look-before-you-leap area. That's our responsibility. So think about it."

That was a long speech for Saldivar.

"Dakko, cofra. Tomorrow." That was patience, for Lyn.

Janet felt the sharpness of his concern. She wanted to speak to him, but she felt herself sinking into treacherous sleep. Her body was immobile, but her mind drifted through a night world where fearful thoughts of the past hours circled her like flocks of birds just at the edge of sight. She had forced the torn flesh and the pain of the wounded out of her mind while she dealt with their injuries. Now their cries haunted her. The thick smell of blood filled her nostrils. She reached out for Singer, but he was too far away, and the shadow strength of Saldivar was with him. She tried to speak to Lyn, but Lyn could not hear her, either. She wandered deeper into the night until suddenly she came to a place she had not been looking for.

She was still looking at shadows: thick, black patterned shadows like the inked blots and curves of a brush painting. Black against grainy gray. The shadows lay in even ripples till they were interrupted by an untidy heap that did not seem to belong there. She tried to go closer. That was when she realized that she was not seeing through her own eyes. It was someone else's dream, and he did not want to go near that place. *Madre'dio, no, it's more dead people.* The smell of blood clung even in the dream.

His shirt clung heavily, wet and soggy. The wetness showed up black in the spotlight. The smell of it reminded him of seawater—cold, salty, metallic, with a hint of muck or rot in it. His mouth was crusted with the same taste. He lay on the lee side of a dune, but the sand did not feel right. It was cold and powdery, and it looked rusty gray, not sparkling white. No, he felt sure he was not on the beach.

He frowned. Spotlight? That went with concrete and wire, not with powdery dust piled into rills by a cold wind. He rolled onto his back and looked up. What he had taken for a spotlight was the bright round face of a moon. He looked automatically for the second moon, but it was not there, and this one was too bright. *I'm not on Delta anymore. This is Nuvospera, New Hope. New home. New hole. New hell.*

But he still could not remember what he was doing here. *Dio,* how his head hurt. As if the moonlight were piercing his skull.

He looked back down the dune and saw the ruffled wake he had left in its smooth surface. He must have dragged himself up, but he had no memory of doing so. He must have been unconscious for a long time. He had crawled away from the bodies at the bottom of the hill. Bodies. *Kristo.* The patrol.

He was bending over marks in the sand. The marks had a hidden significance that he tried in vain to read. Mahmad and Garza argued hotly over details that were invisible to his eyes. There was a noise. Garza turned around, in front of him so he could not see over the big man's broad shoulders. He saw Garza raise the rifle. Then the earth heaved under them. He felt his feet leave the ground. Blinding light burst all around them, but he was partly shielded by Garza's body. Then something hit him in the head, and Garza fell on him like a wall collapsing. The sound of the explosion filled the world as he was crushed down into darkness.

He was back on the dune. He still could not remember how he had crawled from beneath the bodies. He did not want to go back down there, but he knew he had to. He slid and staggered part of the way down the slope, fell, and ended up crawling again. The patrol lay interlaced with each other, like a puzzle he did not really want to solve. He tried to count legs but could not make it come out even. He could not shift the bodies. They were too heavy. He had to crawl in among them and feel for a neck pulse. He had seen a lot of dead men, but he had never touched one. Not when they were cold and rubbery like a chicken just out of the cooler. He counted five, and that was everyone but Garza.

He saw that Garza lay faceup, chest ripped open and throat half-gone, on a circle of sand soaked black. He fumbled off his own sodden shirt and felt his chest. The skin was unbroken. *That's not my blood, it's his. He saved my life twice—once going down and once when someone came back to strip the weapons and left me for dead with the others.*

He sat in the sand, holding the damp and bloody rag that had been his shirt and trying to think. The tracks in the sand were spelling out another message for him, one that he could read without Mahmad's help: Run away! Where could he run? Moonlight winked off the mirrors sewn into the shirt. Something about a mirror, something about a message he wanted to leave for the one person who would be sure to get it. If they sent her the shirt—had he left her a message, or was that all part of the dream? She had come for him the last time he had been buried, the time of the spotlights and the wire. Kristo, how his head hurt.

Long fingers of shadow crept down the dune toward him, and when he looked up, he saw a dark frieze of armed men and animals—horses?—behind the two who stood over him, watching. The tall one wore a robe so dark that his pale face seemed to float in the air. The other had a dark beard and a chest plate and helmet that looked like flak armor but shone like metal.

He looked from one to the other, grasping for words, his only weapons. The one in black had clever, curious eyes and looked like someone he could talk to. Ordinarily he would have pitched to that man, but those clever eyes glittered like a snake's. The man in black was hungry, and that worried him.

"My name's Logan," he said deferentially to the soldier. "I'm a noncombatant. A video rep. I can show you ID if you'll give me permission to go into my pocket."

He recognized the glaze of total incomprehension. He was not going to be able to talk his way out of this one. The man in black bent and said something in the soldier's ear. As the shaven head moved, an earring caught the moonlight. It was shaped like a skull with a fanged, open mouth. *I knew I didn't like him.*

"You speak Spanya?" he asked, without hope. "Fokish? Ingleix? Nippo?"

The soldier cut him off with a harsh string of words. It was obviously a question, but the language was not even vaguely familiar.

"I'm sorry, I don't understand."

The soldier grabbed him by the hair and twisted. The pain in his head was so acute that he fell forward into the sand. He saw the boot coming in slow motion, with a feeling that this had all happened before. *Of course it has. I'm dreaming. I'd like to wake up now, please.*

At the last minute he forgot that it was not real. *Janney,* he called. Just as he had the first time. *Janney, are you there? Please, please come and get me. I'm lost.*

The dream broke up into darkness and bright flashes of pain just as Janet realized whose dream it was. Panicked, she tried to catch hold of the dreamer but could not move her arms and legs. They were heavy, heavy and cold as the dead, pinned down. She screamed *Jon, Jon, where are you?* but could not find his answer.

She gasped and sat up, shedding blankets and letting in a bitter swirl of cold. She opened her eyes to the firelit dark of the tent, not the white on black of moonlight in the Dust. She thought there had been a lot of noise, running feet and screaming, but the tent was silent.

Singer's eyes were open, but he held very still while he tried to figure out what had happened. He was disoriented. He had been so deeply asleep that he had not even been dreaming. Then that peace had been broken by the sight of a young, dark-haired man, shirtless in the cold. At first Singer had thought he was dreaming of the Mountain Spirit, who chose that shape often when he walked the earth. But the young man's chest was marked with blood, his hair was cut short in grief, and there was fear in his eyes. Just as Singer knew that he recognized those eyes, he saw the reason for the fear. Two men stood over the young man: a blackrobe and a captain of the cityfolk armed for war. Singer's own fearful memories of the cityfolk kicked him awake, and he heard his hearth friend crying out for help.

But the tent was silent. There had been danger, but in another place and time. He shifted cautiously to get Palha's knee out of his back and tried to slow down his heart.

"I saw my brother," Janet said, shivering. "He didn't die."

Singer nodded. "The cityfolk took him. There was a blackrobe, a Somostai, with them."

Janet's eyes widened. "I thought you were asleep. I couldn't find you."

"Woke up when they started to beat him. Such men beat me once." His shoulders twitched.

"He survived when the patrol was ambushed. That's why they never found his body. But how do I know he's still alive? What if those bastards killed him?"

"Think a minute, isé," Singer tried to calm her with his voice and eyes. He tasted the dream again. "He was remembering."

Her face cleared. "Yes. I wasn't dreaming about him. I was in his dream. He kept trying to wake up. So he must have survived what I saw. But if he's alive, why can't I find him now?"

"I don't know, isé. Sometimes between waking and sleeping, the heart goes traveling. When day comes, distances fall between us again."

Janet bit her thumbnail. "He was calling for me. When they sent me his shirt and declared him dead with the others, I didn't believe it. I knew he was alive. Now I really know it. That wasn't his blood. I saw him take the shirt off. I have to find him, Singer."

"I wish I could promise you, Zhanne-iao," he said softly. "He is my brother, too; that's all I can say." He felt the weight of her longing like a chain of gold lying heavy on his neck. "It may be he's still a captive of the cityfolk. If we follow Siri's will and pursue the flying people, we'll be traveling toward the city road. Maybe you will find him there."

Janet sighed and crept back between Lyn and Kruger. "I'm sorry I woke you up. You know, if we're going to start sharing our bad dreams, we have enough of them among us to make sure nobody ever sleeps through the night. And we keep piling up more. We have to stop this war, Singer, or none of us will ever sleep again.''

He leaned on Palha's shoulder again and caught a brief impression of big trees, dry leaves crunching underfoot, smell of ferns in the mist. He heard Jan say something, but he had already followed Palha gratefully back into sleep.

3

As soon as the sun was up, Siri ordered a hot meal cooked for everyone. The horses were carefully rubbed down to warm them and free their coats from ice and snow. The strong and nimble were sent to gather firewood, set snares, and scout for feed beneath the snow. A group of children ran back to camp with their snow-reddened hands full of *resh* beans. They had found a hillside overgrown with the tangled vines. They set to work shaking snow from the vines and harvesting them by the quick method, setting the vines on fire and gathering the charred pods out of the ashes. The children jumped and shouted, delighting in the warmth of the flames. The extra beans were a treasure, like gold beneath the snow. Roasted and pounded, they would stretch the Riders' meager rations to sufficiency.

Once the beans were gathered, it was time to move on, before the smoke drew unwanted attention. Siri chose an advance party to scout ahead for a good camping place and to try again to pick up the trail of the missing herd. He sent the strongest of the pallantai on the best horses: a small band of gaunt men and women on grass-bellied ponies with hooves worn nearly to the quick. Singer insisted on going with them.

"I have lived with your enemies, Grandfather. I wore their clothes and ate their food. I know their scent and their tracks."

Saldivar and Lyn volunteered, too, but Kruger urged them to stay with the main force.

"It's the only way to make sure they don't try to fight again," he said to them privately. "If it becomes necessary, you fight a rearguard action and chase the rest of them off. If they make another stand against vitos, they're cooked."

He confronted Siri, who leaned on his staff watching the scouts saddle up.

"Look, Siri," he said in his clumsy Thanha, "these are my children, understand? Like your pallantai. If I lend them to you to help you protect all your little ones and whatnot, you have to respect their knowledge. If they tell you to run, then go like a rabbit. Don't get in their way or they won't be able to do their job."

The Asharya paused. His face was like a crag, and it was impossible to tell if he was offended.

"Agreed," he said. "They shall be like my own. And in return, I lend you my children. I cannot risk my wise heads today. They are all weary or too hurt to travel. I ask you to go with your Singer, to ride with my scouts. Keep their reins in your hand and bring them back safely."

He caught the scouts' attention with a gesture and pointed Kruger out to them. "This is your captain today. He has wisdom for you. Follow it."

He dismissed them and limped back toward the tent.

Kruger kicked his horse up beside Singer's. "Did I impress him? Insult him? Or what? I don't understand the protocol around here."

Singer grinned at him. "You talk straight, and that's the main thing. You come close to insulting his honor, trying to tell him what to do, but he'll take that from his 'wise heads.' Someone like Morne can tell him to his face he's a fool, though I don't say you should try it. You were bold, so he replies boldly. He tests you. That's the Thanha way. Open your hand and we fill it. Then we see if you can carry what you take hold of."

"So what did he mean, 'This is your captain'?"

"What he says. He puts them in your hand. They'll do what you tell them. Use them well and Siri will go on using you."

Kruger snorted. "Good to know I can be trusted with a scout squad."

Singer shrugged, deliberately teasing. "That remains to be seen, Con-el."

At the top of the next ridge he paused to look down. From horizon to horizon the world stretched empty as far as he could see. The plains rolled from the desert to the foot of the mountains, a patchwork of white and dun where the wind had piled snow high or swept the earth bare. Blowing snow trailed from the crest of the ridge like smoke. Kruger had told him that the strangerfolk had left an eye in the sky, revolving sleeplessly over the world below. Such an eye, Singer thought, might have noticed a motorized convoy or a troop of marching men. It might even have spotted their track in the snow, though the wind erased such markings quickly. But a handful of travelers cloaked in winter colors, huddled between the boulders, were surely too insignificant to be seen or to be noticed if they had been.

From such a height, perhaps even the flying machines of the enemy they hunted would look as small as flies. Singer wished he had eyes that could ride above the wind. For the wind brought him nothing. It was clean and cold as if it had touched nothing since it rushed down from the snowfields beyond Stormfather. If the flying people had allies on the ground, the wind had wiped out their tracks and their scent.

Young Kata pulled up beside Singer. "How do you track an enemy who can fly?"

"Use your head, not just your nose," Kruger said. "Reorient to where the camp was yesterday and see which direction the vitos headed when they flew away." He was not sure he could do it himself, but he counted on Singer's memory to retrace their travels.

Singer closed his eyes. His hands sketched a camp circle in empty air, then painted in moonglow and dawn.

"There," he said, pointing. The other pallantai had been watching closely, and at his gesture they nodded with the quick upward toss of the head that meant "clear!" in Thanha.

"North-northwest, or just about," Kruger said. "We should turn north a little."

"Yes, and come down off the hilltops," Singer said. "If they were running herds from the air, they would not be able to force them uphill. The horses would take the easiest way, through the valleys."

Again the Riders nodded approval, but they did not move. They all looked to Kruger. He was their captain. He kicked his horse and plunged awkwardly through the drifts below the ridge, and they followed.

He did not have to order them to spread out into a well-spaced search pattern. They worked well together, and silently, using hand signals and whistled calls.

"Those calls would fool nobody on a day like this," Singer told Kruger. "With such a wind, the small birds don't fly. But maybe your people wouldn't know that." He rode beside Kruger and explained the Riders' signals with a word or two, so unobtrusively that Kruger did not realize he was being educated.

They headed slowly north, casting back and forth across the valleys. Coming down a steep draw, they found ice where the low ground had been damp before the snow had come. A couple of the Riders slid off their horses and scuffed the snow aside where it was least deep. The ice beneath was shattered and churned into fragments. The Riders nodded to each other without saying anything. Singer watched Kruger with barely concealed amusement. Makho expected them to report their findings, and they were courteously waiting for him to state the obvious.

"They came this way," Kruger said finally.

"Truly," Singer agreed.

"What the hell are you waiting for now?" Kruger said.

"For you, Makho."

Kruger belatedly kicked his horse forward again. The animal humped its back, though it was too tired to buck, and Singer thought Makho would need some advice about horses, too.

They rode a couple of miles down the draw, pushing through snowdrifts and floundering from one drift to the next across the treacherous ice. Looking ahead, they could see that the draw deepened into a ravine too steep for the horses. They followed the frozen trail up again, out of the draw and across another hillside piled deep with snow. On the other side of the hill the slope ran down into the plains again. The ground had frozen hard long before the raiders had passed by. It was impossible to tell which way they had gone once they had reached the wide-open plains.

Singer found a spot where the snow was packed close to the ground and lay down full-length, pressing his ear to the ground. He listened for a long time while the cold seeped into him, but he felt only confused and distant rumors in the earth. Finally he pulled himself to his feet and leaned against his horse's shoulder to warm himself.

"Long gone," he said. The wind whistled in from the frozen sea of grass. Up here there was some faint flavor to it that he had not been able to catch back in camp. He tasted again, but the air was too cold. The elusive scent had vanished.

Down on the open plains there was no cover for the camp. Kruger sent back messengers to guide the rest of the Riders to a sheltered place behind the ridge. The advance party continued to search the plains as long as the light served them but found no trail.

The sun had faded to a pale disk behind blowing clouds, so feeble that they could look at it without blinking. The scouts eyed the horizon and pulled their cloaks tighter around their shoulders. Their thoughts turned toward camp. Kruger had not yet noticed the sinking sun or the scouts' unease. Eyes narrowed against the wind, he stared out at the plain as if he could reason a path through that blank whiteness.

Singer remounted and rode close to him, breaking his concentration.

"You're about to tell me it's late," Kruger growled. "I know that. I hate like hell to leave without finding the trail, though. It'll be that much colder tomorrow." He raised an arm to wave the Riders back, then hesitated, realizing he did not know how to command them. The raised arm was enough. Before he said a word, they were back on their horses and following him down into the draw.

"Tell me something, Singer," he said in Delteix. "When Siri tells us to be home by dark, is that an order? What about these people here? Am I in command, or am I offering suggestions?"

Singer tried to shape a good answer but failed. Kruger kept making distinctions between things that should have shared a unity. "If your father asks you, 'Catch my horse for me,' is that an order?"

"That's not a good example," Kruger said grimly. "Most people would agree that I never had a father."

"Everyone has a father," Singer said. Then he understood that Kruger was making a Delh'tani joke.

"So they do," Kruger said. "Even you. Who was he? I never asked." As Singer hesitated, he added, "I don't mean your foster father with the Riders. I mean your real father."

"My foster father was my real father. Deronh was the only father I had. I was not born till he brought me home to the Riders. The other one bred me as they breed cattle—for use or for slaughter. He was the City Master of Erech Tolanh. First he tried to kill me, then he tried to sell me. Long after, he tried to buy me back, but it was too late. By then he had struck himself a bargain he couldn't twist out of. Your people buried him in the ruins of his city, just as Deronh died when you struck the Rock.''

"No love lost between you, then.''

Singer laughed shortly. "Love? People were tools to him. If he loved anyone, it was my half brother Dona. Dona was his chosen son. Our father used him up and brought him to a bitter death. Dona had cause to hate if anyone did. But Dona hated no one.

"When I first knew Dona, he was angry. But I saw him put away anger and fear so he could learn. Over and over again. He wanted understanding more than anything. More than power or revenge. Zhanne is like him. I loved him, but I'm not like him. I think maybe he was wiser than I—but what good did it do him? He was too easy to kill. *Ai!*''

He switched from Delteix into Thanha and from speech into song. Kruger understood enough to know that it was a lament.

> Proud head and ready hand
> We gave to the hungry sand,
> And we'll never see his like again—
> *Ai, aiya, ai!*

The Riders behind pressed up closer to him and sang with him. Kruger could not catch all the words, but he heard the longing in their cold-roughened voices. He heard, also, how Singer worked them as he sang. Even while Singer freed his own grief, he kept the music in his hands as a rider kept the feel of the reins. He pulled in one and urged another on till the Riders fell into stride like a well-matched team. Their rough harmonies evened out and ran true. Kruger felt something in himself ease, as if Singer had untied knots he had not known were there. He jogged along with them, listening, as the light faded.

They found the camp easily in the dusk by the sounds of children's voices and the smells of smoke and food. The Riders unsaddled. Singer took hold of Kruger's rein.

"Give me the horse. You go in and get warm.''

A young woman tried to get the honor of taking the horses from him, but he waved her off. He wanted time to think. He rubbed their steaming sides till they were dry, checked their hooves, and turned them out to scout for grass under the snow crust. He called a boy and instructed him to give them a precious measure of feed after they had grazed awhile.

Then he cared for the tack—rubbed the bits clean with a handful of snow, checked the girths, and dried the leather with a clean rag. The work gave him an aching pleasure. He tended to it as carefully as if Deronh would come along in a few minutes to help him finish up. Speaking the names to Kruger had called up shadows in his mind, and he could almost see them waiting for him at the edge of camp. Dona stood high-headed and arrogant as he had when he had first come to the Riders, but his dark curls had grown long, Rider fashion, and his face was quick with curiosity to see the strangers from beyond the stars.

The old grief tore at Singer's heart, but he smiled. It was good to remember Dona as he had lived. For so long Singer had seen him only in his death.

"Ah, brother," he whispered. "I'd be where you are now if I hadn't made you that promise. You made me swear I'd live till I found out why they killed you, why our people died. I've lived, and I've found the strangers, but even now I don't know why."

Beside him Singer imagined a slighter shape: a small, dark-haired man smelling of saddle leather and horses and the herbs that horses loved. His habitually somber face lit up with love for the tall son he had snatched from the mountainside one bitter-cold night. That was Deronh; Singer felt him very close as he lingered over the tasks they had shared so many times. He closed his eyes and only saw Deronh more clearly.

But who was the other one? Behind Deronh there was a darker shadow, face turned away from him. A feeling of cold breathed toward him from that shape. The shadow was intimately known to him but not a friend—no, not a friend. In a moment it would turn toward him and speak. He did not want to see its eyes.

He flinched like an untrained child. But the shadow that touched his arm was only Janet.

"What was that?" she said, frowning.

He shook himself, slung the two bridles over his shoulder, and turned with her toward the tent.

"Thinking about Deronh," he said. " 'It's hard—I come home, but still they're not here.' That's what he said, almost the first thing I ever heard him say. He was grieving when he found me, for his partner. She died before I came to the Rock. I used to wonder why he couldn't forget her, be happy with his other friends who loved him."

Janet hugged him as far up as she could reach. "I know,"

she said softly. "But come in with me now, isé. Pablo has been chewing his tether over you."

The light and warmth inside dazzled him. It had grown darker than he thought outside. Saldivar did not admit to worrying, but Singer leaned against him and drank from his cup and felt him relax.

"No fear, *paliao*," Singer said. "No enemy, no danger, nothing. Boring, it was. And here?"

Saldivar handed him a dish of stew. "Nothing here, either. Just the way I like it."

"You really didn't find anything?" Lyn asked. "Mack is reporting to the Asharya now. He must be talking an awful lot of nothing."

"We found some traces, but they were stone cold. They trailed off into the plains like piss in a high wind. I thought there was something in the air, but I couldn't catch hold of it to find out what it was."

"That's not good," Jan said soberly. "Siri is hell-bent on catching the raiders, getting his herds back. It's the only thing that's giving them any kind of hope."

Siri and Kruger came out of the Asharya's sleeping place, still conferring, and sat down to eat together. People around the fire looked up expectantly but soon went back to their business. There was no need to ask if the search had been successful. Siri would have announced it if he had had good news.

Singer put down his empty dish. "I heard an interesting dream last night," he said. His voice was conversational, but people nearby leaned closer to listen. Morne came forward into the group around him, and the Riders moved back to give her a position of honor.

"It has been too long since we talked about dreams," she said. "Maybe the nights have been too full of sorrow. But now we have to seek a path wherever we can, even in the dark of night. Tell me about this dream, young brother. I would like to hear it."

Singer told them Janet's dream. He made a good story of it, weaving in what he knew of her search from the time before he had met her. He led her on with questions till she had searched out every detail of the dream. The Riders listened closely. A quest for a lost brother drew their full sympathy. When the story was over, several of them shyly offered comments.

"If you share a dream with him, he must be very near."

"He has a strong heart to have lived so long among the city-folk. Surely he will find his way back to you."

"Even in dreams it's very rare to touch another from so far. How does it happen that a stranger, not even Thanha, has that gift? The cityfolk can't do it. Are all the strangers like us?"

"No!" Janet denied that quickly. "Most of them wouldn't even believe it could happen. I learned it from Singer. Am still learning."

"They're twin-born," someone else said. "That makes the feeling-for-each-other stronger."

At that, someone spilled *chah*, the powerful drink of the Riders, into the fire and called out "Light on the road!" as blue flames jumped up. It sounded like an invocation.

"He calls on the Moon Woman and her brother, the Mountain Spirit," Singer murmured in Jan's ear. "Windrider and Lady of the Fountains—they are brother and sister, born at the same time. They think you are lucky because you, too, have a like-brother."

A woman who looked familiar spoke up. "This healer saved lives that are dear to us. I say we have a debt to pay. When we get the rest of our horses back, we should find her brother and save his life from cityfolk. Blood for blood and honor where honor is due." She lifted her head defiantly, and Janet recognized her. It was the woman who had been watching with the wounded child.

"Yes, and when I get out of here, I'll learn to fly, as the rabbit said in the soup pot," the Asharya said with heavy irony. "Ilyun speaks like a true Rider, but it's too soon to say *when*. Come to me when fresh horses are grazing around our camp, and we'll talk then."

Ilyun accepted the rebuke, but the child who had been sitting within her cloak stirred and scrambled to her feet.

"I am Roishe, born to the *barhedoni* of the Flint," she announced. "I have a dream to tell. But first I want to thank the stranger healers. Yesterday I was on the Road to the North. Today I can take the road with my people. See!" She stretched out her arms proudly.

Stepping among the seated Riders, she came face-to-face with Singer. She looked him over intently. "Where did he go—that boy who sang for me?" She touched his face. "That was you, wasn't it?"

He nodded. "Disappointed?"

"Yes. I wish you were my age. Grown people are not much good to play with. But you could sing for me again sometime."

She scraped her boot toe against the packed earth of the floor, gathering courage for one more question. "Did she ever come back? His mother?"

Singer met her eyes. "No. She never did."

Roishe sighed, accepting. "Is she dead?"

Singer shrugged. "Don't know. Guess so."

"Mine is. But I still dream she comes back sometimes." She lifted her chin. "But that's not the dream I wanted to tell."

She raised her voice so other people could hear. "I dreamed of a star of iron that fell down to earth. It was gray and hard at first, but as it fell, it glowed hot and hotter, till it was white and it ran like water. It ran into shapes in the sand and cooled, and the shapes rose up like strange animals made of iron. They roared and puffed out smoke and steam, and the children of the iron star ran among them, feeding them. They took the iron animals down under the earth, where they dug burrows to hide in, and the iron animals ate the rocks from the dark tunnels."

She looked around the gathering. "I don't understand this dream, but it was a true one—as true as seeing the boy who sang. I heard the stranger captain tell that the Hunter Stars are worlds. I think the strangers came from a star of iron, and somewhere they are doing all the things I saw."

"Iron smelting. Mining," Kruger said slowly in Delteix. He had no idea what the words for those things were in Thanha. "That's what it sounds like. It's uncanny. How would the child know?"

"Think carefully, isé," Singer urged the child. "When you saw the star fall, where did it come to earth?"

She did not hesitate. "North and west—toward the seaward side of the mountains. It fell among the rocks of the mountains."

"Grandfather, if your legs can hold out, we'll catch them. What good will it do them to hide their tracks if we can track them in our dreams?"

"You pack a heavy load on a child's dream," Siri said.

"If we go northwest to the place she spoke of, we will find them. This morning there was a scent in the wind, elusive as a pinch of dust cast on running water. At that time I could not recognize it, but now I know it for the breath of burning metal, the scent that goes with the strangerfolk wherever they go. We will find them—if that is truly your wish."

The Asharya grunted and handed his cup to one of the pallantai. "My wish now is to sleep. Tomorrow we will consider our road."

4

Siri did not lead the Riders directly northwest. For a few miles he followed the trail Kruger had found, but before they reached the plains, he turned south a little.

"What are you looking for, Grandfather?" Singer asked.

"You'll see it."

When Siri reined in his horse on a hilltop, Singer looked down.

"There's a road down there," Singer said. Kruger caught the overtones of disgust and fear in his voice, as if he had said "There's a snake down there" or "There's a corpse." Kruger, expecting a flat, obvious surface, saw nothing at first. Then he spotted what the Riders were seeing: a narrow linear depression beneath the snow. To Singer's eyes the road looped like a snare wire around the base of the hill, a trap waiting to be sprung. The road ran roughly north and south: south into the plains, northwest along the seaward edge of the mountains.

Siri shouldered his way to the front and looked down. The Riders leaned into the updraft from the valley, snuffing at the wind like their ponies. Siri waved a couple of the best trackers down toward the road. The rest moved back behind the hill to get out of the wind. Soon the trackers whistled from below. They waved toward the south; they had found traces running down toward the plains.

"Jon is *that* way," Janet said clearly. She pointed north with her chin.

Siri said one word: "South." The troop wheeled to follow him, paralleling the road, within bowshot of it. They could have doubled their speed on the road, but no Riders would trust themselves to a way built by strangers. There was a saying: "Lowland road, lowland promises." Both tempted with their smooth ease, and both led to nothing but trouble in the end.

Singer missed Janet, who had been riding close to him, and looked back. She had let the troop go by, leaving her alone on the ridge. Her horse tried to follow, and she pulled him in till he reared in protest, neighing. Her hair was growing long; it whipped around her as she wheeled the horse on his haunches. To argue with the Asharya was not done, but she had found a Thanha way to make her protest. Only Singer knew how strongly she was called to the north. Like her plunging horse, she was caught between an undeniable call and an equally unbreakable binding. Singer whistled through his teeth, the shrill cry of the valley hawk stooping: "Follow me down, down. Follow me!" She gave the horse his head at last and surged down, scattering snow.

"We're turning our backs on him," she said as she caught up with Singer.

"The brother has kept hold of his life without our help," he said. "These people can't."

Bitter words formed in her mind, words about choosing between her brother and a ragged band who did not even want them.

Before she could speak, he lunged out and caught her horse's bridle. He clung to his own seat by a hairbreadth balance while he drove both horses into a gallop. Janet's mount started to buck in outrage, and both of them were nearly spilled into the snow before Singer let go and swayed back into his saddle.

"What do you think you're doing?" she protested when she got her breath back. "Kindly remember I wasn't nursed by a mare, like you."

She saw by his face that he had not been joking. His eyes were as dark as the sea in winter.

"I can't choose," he said. "I'm caught, like that. Like you. Two horses, and I have to ride them both. I have to save them all, Zhanne. All the brothers."

Or die trying, she finished for him. The hard words died in her throat. Instead she said: " 'Two horses, one rope.' Thanha have a saying for everything, don't they? So what's the solution to that one?"

He shrugged. "Cut loose if you have any sense. Or you move fast and hang on like a fool's hope."

He quickened his pace, moving ahead of her to break a path. She was too quick to understand, and he did not want her to know just how desperate he was. Maybe it would have been better to leave her angry. It would have distracted her attention.

They rode till nightfall and set up camp in the dark again. The clouds had cleared away, and there was no snow falling to cover them. They were far enough out into the plains that there was little cover of any kind. They built a very small fire of dry wood, enough to boil a little water for tea and resh, and huddled around it in the cold. Still Singer was uneasy.

Siri scoffed at him. "You're superstitious about these people, boy," he said. "You've been among them too long. It's made you fearful as no good Thanha should be. Even if they see in the dark like owls, they'd have a hard time finding us. The tents are well banked with snow, and there's no smoke."

"They have eyes that can see the heat of your breath," Singer said. "They have weapons you can't imagine."

"Since when have the Riders spent their time imagining things to fear?" Siri asked.

Stung with insults, Singer rose to his feet. "Choose your witnesses, Grandfather," he said. "I am a Rider, and I imagine nothing. I regret that I expressed myself so badly that you could not hear me clearly. Send others and hear the news from them."

"Easy, easy, young one," Siri grumbled.

Singer did not sit down, and the Asharya saw that he was serious.

"Well, then, tell me again. I'm listening."

"There are enemies near here. I feel it. I smelled their smoke on the wind again today, and the tracks we follow are clear. Send scouts with me. Someone you will believe when they return to tell you these enemies are like none you ever faced before."

All over the tent people watched Singer challenge the Asharya.

Siri could not let it pass. He lurched painfully to his feet. "If the matter is so urgent, I will see to it myself."

There was a stir and a murmur in the tent. Scouting by night was unusual enough, but this time the Asharya was going, too. A couple of lucky young ones were shaken awake and sent out into the cold to fetch the horses while Siri chose his party. Young

Kata was summoned for his skill as a tracker. Kruger also insisted on joining the group.

"Take a young one to watch the horses," Singer suggested. "We will not be riding up to the front gate."

"Are you sure you can do this?" Kruger asked quietly as they were saddling up.

"Yes, Makho, I am sure. There are a large number of Delh'tani—they are Nupis, not your kind—not more than a fistful of miles from here."

"Singer, how can you possibly know that?"

It seemed so perfectly clear, yet when Singer tried to explain how he had found that knowledge, the explanations drained away from him into emptiness. He turned toward Kruger with a blind, baffled look that made the hairs on Kruger's neck rise.

"I *know.*"

He felt Makho's reaction, and it echoed something deep inside himself. The knowledge had something to do with a cold shadow whose eyes he could not see. The shadow had whispered to him that the camp would be there—not in words but on a cold breath like the wind. The shadow slipped knowledge that he did not want into his mind. It drew him on when all he wanted to do was turn and run.

Singer found the place as easily as if he had a map. When he signed for a stop and dismounted on an empty, snow-covered ridge, Siri looked at him as if he had gone crazy. They crossed the ridge on foot. Beyond it, Singer pointed silently to a glow in the sky ahead.

For the first time Siri's confidence that they would find nothing seemed shaken. "What is that?"

"The strangers."

Kata kept testing the air as they walked. "And our herds," he said finally. "Or I have lost my senses."

A thin bleating echoed his words. They leapt for cover at the first sound of it, then rose up, dusting the snow off and laughing. It was a weanling kid, its hooves so balled with packed snow that it could only hobble away from them, calling frantically for help. One of the pallantai reached for his bow, but Singer restrained him.

"Catch it."

Feinting with cloaks and lead ropes, they tackled the kid at last, hogtied it, and wrapped a strip of cloth around its muzzle to stop the bleating. Kata knocked the ice away from its hooves and slung it over his shoulder.

"What is this?" Kruger asked Singer, examining the little animal. "This isn't a sheep. It's not a goat, either. I don't know exactly what it is."

"Silangh," Singer said. "Has horns, hair, and hooves, but it's small. Not like the cattle of the lowlanders. We eat their meat, drink their milk, make clothes from their hair and skins."

When they came in sight of the herd, Singer made them crawl through the snow for the last few hundred yards. They stopped at the top of a long shallow slope. Below them stood a group of buildings, a guard tower, and a small landing pad. There was a flat area beyond the buildings that might have been an airstrip but was covered with snow.

"I wouldn't have believed it," Kruger said, gazing down at the wire fence and the glaring lights. "What are the Nupis doing here?"

"They have a pool of daylight around themselves," Kata said. "How did they do that?"

"Are they gods?" one of the other pallantai asked. "The Lady of the Waters can make a light in the darkness."

"Don't talk like a fool," Siri said roughly. "It's just some kind of cityfolk trick."

"It's not a trick," Singer said. "It's true knowledge. They drive the sunlight into a maze, as we trap horses. Within their maze the sun dances for them all night long. It's not a trick. But neither are they gods. The sun shines for everyone, the good and the bad. To learn a new way of using it doesn't make them gods.

"They are people, just very smart, crooked people, like clever wild dogs. We must be very sharp if we would escape being torn to pieces."

"If they know so much, why haven't they seen us?" Siri asked. His words exploded into the cold air like puffs of smoke.

"They aren't looking," Singer said. "It's our only advantage so far. They despise us. That's our good luck."

"Then let's take the herd and run before they take notice."

"Have you not seen, Grandfather? Down below are the flying machines that attacked us before. This time they would destroy us certainly."

"Then let us attack and destroy them before they can fly."

In answer Singer beckoned Kata to bring the kid. Kata crawled over, dragging the bound animal with difficulty, scuffling up the snow as it struggled. Snow crusted his face from lips to eyebrows; he did not have a free hand to wipe it away.

"Turn it loose," Singer said.

Kata slipped the knot that held the ropes tight. The kid kicked free of the loosened coils, stood trembling for an instant, then leapt away from them, downhill. It seemed barely to print the snow with its delicate hooves—once, twice, three times. It was halfway to the lit fence in seconds.

"Waste of a good meal," Siri grumbled. "Why are we sending them meat?"

A flash of light slapped their eyes, and the kid vanished. After the light came the sound and the smoke. A rain of small fragments pitted the snow, along with hot ashes, melting a small crater where the delicate hooves had touched.

Kata cried out and instantly clapped his hand over his mouth. The younger pallantai pressed themselves into the snow as if they would have liked to vanish.

Singer made the hand sign for silence. He caught a glimpse of figures moving down below—not covering themselves very well, he thought. There was an exchange of voices; he could not make out the words. They were not shouting and did not seem alarmed. A spotlight traveled slowly across the snow beyond the fence, paused at the crater, and retreated. The voices were quiet again.

"You endangered us," Siri said.

"He's right," Kruger said. "If I were in control of that camp, I would have wondered what spooked a wild animal into our minefield in the middle of the night. I'd have sent someone out to look." He used Thanha so Siri could understand him. He had taken to speaking Thanha most of the time, and when he came to a word like "minefield," he would simply give up and use Delteix.

"If their commanders were all like you, Makho, we'd have no chance at all," Singer said. "I sent our little four-legged brother out there for you, Grandfather. I wanted you to see for yourself what happens when we attack them."

"You could have told me."

Singer shrugged. "I heard it said that Riders did not imagine such things. So I thought it best to show you."

"Withdraw," Siri said heavily. They observed silence until they were close to the tents again. Their clothes were stiff with frost; the small fire gave so little heat that they could not retreat to the Asharya's corner for a conference. They huddled next to the coals. The other Thanha brought them blankets and tea and moved respectfully to the other side of the hearth to let them talk.

"What's to be done?" Siri said. "Do we have enough lives to buy a way through that field? Advise me."

Singer held back, hoping someone else would take his part. Kata bent to touch Siri's knee in supplication. "Grandfather, if you choose that path, I pray you put me in the front rank. I want to die first, before I watch my brothers and sisters cracked like lice in the fire." His face was very calm; his eyes looked on ruin.

"What would you have me do?" Siri said. His voice was the bellow of a baited bull. Faces across the fire turned toward him fearfully before he brought himself under control.

"Would you wish to lie down in the snow and be eaten by the foxes? I am Thanha. I must fight till I die, bare hands against blades if that is all I have left. Better to die face-to-face with an enemy than to be strangled in the night by starvation and cold unseen. If there is another choice, *advise me*!"

"When I was a boy," Singer said, "they taught me *never accept the enemy's choice of weapons*. One day we may beat them at their own game. Not today. Think, brothers. They have great and subtle knowledge, and thus we are destroyed. Where can we strike back with knowledge they do not have?"

Kata's face changed as if he had stepped back from the edge of a cliff. "The herds! They don't know silangh, or they would never try to drive them from the air with flying machines. When spring comes, that herd won't hold for a day. They'll be scattered all over the plains." He looked confused again. "But how does that serve us?"

"Bodies," Kruger said. "My first war I fought in the jungles." The word was not Thanha; he paused and looked to Singer for a translation.

"Hot, wet forests where the leaves are thick as thorns and the ground and treetops are full of creatures," Singer explained.

"Yes. Ants live there and march like armies. When they come to a river, they leap boldly in. The first rank drowns, and the second. But after many deaths the last rank marches over on the bodies of its brothers. That's all right for ants, not for humans. But picture those silangh stampeding down the hillside where that one kid went. The defenses are limited. The herd will buy a way through the field for us if you have the skill to drive them there."

The Asharya reached out and clasped hands with Kruger. He

grinned. "I see it, and what I see is good." He looked around the circle of advisers for approval. "Eh?"

They reached in, adding their grip to his till they were all handfasted.

"Best to go in at night," Siri added. "Unless you think otherwise."

"Night is best," Kruger agreed.

"Right. We're taking a chance by waiting one more day, but we'll trust our luck that long. Tomorrow we rest. Come nightfall, we'll stake out the herd and move."

Word spread around the tent in a soft murmur to all who were still awake. They slept late that morning. Siri told them to cook and eat their fill.

"We'll take no rations, no baggage with us. We bet all on one throw."

Grim faces broke into smiles as the word was passed. The fire could not be built up for fear of discovery, but the last of their stores simmered over the coals, sending out good smells: dried meat cooked hot and tender with spices after weeks of chewing it cold and tough and porridge sweetened with scarce honey and nuts. Children laughed and played games again, relaxing as they felt the happy excitement of their elders. The pallantai checked and cleaned their gear, and from age-softened skin packages they unwrapped their jewels and ornaments. The ragged band was dressed as if for a celebration by the time the food was ready to eat.

Kata and Ilyun shyly offered gifts to the strangers.

"We carry many ornaments for the dead," Ilyun said. "I would share with you the honors of my partner, mother of the child you saved. Tonight we make her a deathgift."

"These are the jewels my foster father won while he lived," Kata echoed. "Honor us by wearing them."

Singer bowed his head to accept a necklace of amber, a chain of silver flowers.

"It's been a long time," he said softly. "A long time since I went to war clothed in honor." He let the bright links slide through his scarred hands. They were as heavy as always, the weight of a life on every chain.

The others accepted arm rings, pendants, jeweled belts—all but Janet.

"I can't. It's against my—it's not for my honor. Singer, tell them."

"My sister is a healer," Singer said gently. "She will not take a life for the pride of it. Only in necessity."

Ilyun unwound a chain of silver as fine as spiderweb from one of her braids and hung it around Janet's neck and kissed her. "Then take this and wear it for luck. It's mine: no deathgift, just something from a friend. Even a healer shouldn't go to war undressed."

The Riders also found better clothes for them, something for each: a fine silk headcloth, a vest embroidered thickly with bright flowers, a scarlet cloak. Kruger shook his head, looking down at himself, and Lyn grinned broadly.

"On you it looks good, Kamerad," she said.

Singer stepped behind him and adjusted the knot in his headcloth. "When I was your soldier, I wore those ░░░░░░░ boots for you, Makho. Now you wear gold chains for me. Fair deal, no?"

"Doesn't seem like a good idea to have all this junk rattling and flashing," Saldivar said.

"It's for their pride. Maybe in a better year Siri would tell them to leave their ornaments at home, but not this time. We'll keep it quiet till we snatch the herd, though." He showed them how to wind the chains with lengths of black silk to muffle them.

They ate and slept for a couple of hours. As the sun went down, they said farewells to the children who were too young to ride with them. Those young ones would stay with Morne and a few of the wounded whose hurts were still healing. If they had no message from the pallantai the next day, they would have to go on alone.

"If we don't come back," Singer said to Morne, "keep going south. It gets warmer."

"If you don't come back, I think we will meet on the Road to the North, young one."

"Not me, barasha!" The child Roishe showed Singer her clenched fist. "I'm strong now, Singer. Strong enough to ride with the pallantai, but they won't take me. But if you don't come back, I'll come to get you myself."

Morne made a disapproving noise. "The child has a big mouth," she said.

Singer bent to embrace Roishe. "It's all right, barasha. She knew me when I was a boy."

5

The herd showed as a dark, moving mass against the snow. They could hear the animals snorting as they pushed against each other for warmth and the rattle of hooves on snow crust. From time to time a gleam of embers showed where the guards were sitting around their fire.

Siri started to point them out for the archers, but Singer put a hand on his arm to restrain him. He wanted the stampede to look completely spontaneous. He feared that the guards would have a radio or some way to send an alarm to the outpost. There was no need to kill them now, and it might even be dangerous.

Siri shook him off and gestured decisively to his pallantai. They had their bows bent in seconds.

When Kruger realized what they were trying to do, he was alarmed enough to risk a loud whisper. "They're going to shoot them in the dark? With *arrows*?"

Singer could only shrug in frustration. He could not argue with the Asharya. Siri had taken all the advice he wanted.

It was a difficult shot, with only the dim fireglow to reveal the shapes of their targets. Two of the men dropped without a sound. The third yelled and tried to get up before he was silenced by another arrow. There was a fourth man. They saw him only as a shadow slipping away from the fire. He froze like a rabbit. If he had kept his cover, he would have been hard to find. One of the archers started toward the place where he had vanished, stepping silently as a cat. Then the stranger made his mistake: He fired.

The horses jumped at a sound like the crack of a lightning-struck tree. They heard a singing in the air as something like a

53

hornet passed them by. But the stranger missed in the dark. The archer, seasoned in many an ambush and wolf hunt, loosed to the sound without needing to aim and heard his prey fall and lie still.

Siri sent the archers to make sure the guards were really dead.

"That's done it," Singer said to the Asharya, no longer troubling to keep his voice down. "They'll have heard that shot in the camp and be wondering why. We have to move the herd down now."

"We move when I'm ready, boy," Siri said. But he gave the signal to the youngest of the archers to put up their bows and start slinging pebbles into the flanks of the packed animals.

The silangh on the near edge of the herd began to bleat and mill around, tossing their heads. Kata unstrapped something from behind his saddle. He shook it out, and it unrolled like a pennon.

"Our secret weapon," he said. It smelled rank even to human noses. "Uncured wolf hides. We had enough to share with all my hearth brothers."

A dozen pallantai trotted forward with him, their wolfskin pennants flapping ahead of them in the wind. The herd animals tossed their horned heads. They faced toward the newcomers in threat. But when the beast smell kept coming, they broke and ran away from the smells of wolf and dead meat. They stampeded downhill toward the lights of the outpost.

Under the spotlights the herd was a brindled wave crested with tossing heads and horns. Its sound was muffled drums and bleating pipes, like a comic war host in a joke. After the first explosion the bleating rose to a frantic chorus. The buried devices in the field popped like nuts roasting in the coals. Sometimes the animals were annihilated like the first one; sometimes a torn half beast fell to earth to writhe under the hooves of its fellows.

The Riders watched in horror and amazement, fighting their horses, which were frantic at the noise and smell. Some of the Riders, too, gagged on the stench of scorched flesh. The animals at the forefront of the stampede would have turned back, but the panic behind them swept them on and pressed them against the fence. The first to hit the fence died convulsing as the current swept through them. Sparks and smoke eddied around their bodies. More and more of the animals piled up against the fence. The sound of the camp alarms shrilled above the screams of the dying animals. The wire gave under the pressure; the fence leaned inward and fell. Hot wires sparked and writhed. The lights flickered and went out as the surviving animals thundered into the compound.

That was the moment for the Riders. They thundered down along with the herd, their hoofbeats lost in the drumming of the others, crouched low to their horses' backs to seem like another herd of animals. They poured in through the gap. Their bows were back in their cases behind the saddle; in their hands they carried weapons for close fighting: swift javelins, broad-headed spears, and the long swords that cleaved heads like lightning parting the clouds.

Singer reined back from the dark and noisy chaos that raged among the strangers' buildings. He had seen Lyn and Saldivar go by, neck and neck, with their rifles clasped to their sides; Lyn was screaming with joy as if she had been born to the pallantai. Janet still rode behind him, her knife and handgun still at her belt. He did not want to lose sight of her. Kruger was armed but had not joined in the fighting. Soldiers ran between long low buildings like the ones Singer had seen in camps before. Something about these buildings struck him as wrong, and he willed a moment of calm for himself to consider why.

The buildings were big enough to hold many soldiers—enough to overwhelm this little band even in hand-to-hand fighting, where the strangerfolk weapons lost their advantage. But the doors were shut. No reinforcements poured from them. Kruger's horse crowded against him, and he knew before the Con-el spoke that he had seen the same thing. Singer wheeled sideways to avoid a bawling silangh and two-stepped along the side of the building, leaning out with one hand to test the shutters along the sides. Pounding vigorous enough to be heard above the din answered from within.

"They're locked in," Kruger shouted. "Prisoners!"

Singer grabbed his wrist, pulling their horses together till his stirrup clashed against Kruger's.

Sure? what if—and a picture of the door unlocked, more gray-clad Union soldiers boiling out.

Angry certainty from Kruger. "And ~~goddamn it,~~ don't do that!"

But Singer was already calling for Saldivar.

Pablo had been at the other end of the compound, but he arrived before Singer had time to speak again to Kruger. Singer felt Saldivar's fear arrive before the man himself came tearing around the building on his wild-eyed horse. Lyn pulled up in his wake.

Easy, easy. I'm all right. Singer tried to calm him, realizing too late that Palha had thought he was calling for help.

"You son of a bitch," Lyn cried. "I thought you were getting killed. Next time you pull this, I'll ▓▓▓▓▓ kill you myself."

Singer badly wanted the word Palha used when he wanted someone to stop talking, but it had slipped his mind. Instead, he made the Thanha gesture for silence emphatically and repeatedly.

"Makho wants to open this door, but we don't know who's inside. I need you and Lyn with your weapons to hold the door while he talks to them."

They stood one on each side, on guard, while Kruger knocked the locks off the door.

The men inside who had been pushing to get out backed off when the door actually opened. They wore green Consorso uniforms or Dust camouflage in various stages of decay.

"I'm Marcus Kruger, late commander of the First Mobile Force. Who all is in here?"

A voice in the crowd called incredulously, "Marcus?" The front row parted to let the speaker through. He stood staring at Kruger for a minute; then he grabbed Kruger by the shoulders and shook him joyfully.

"Detrik!" Kruger exclaimed. "You were reported dead. Your plane went down."

"Sure did. Went straight to hell, but die I didn't." Detrik turned and shouted back to the men inside. "All smooth, they're on our side. El Cuchillo's here, the Mother jefe. I know him."

A hoarse yell went up from inside, followed by renewed shoving.

"Quiet!" he roared, and they subsided.

He still clasped Kruger's shoulders. "Is this a rescue? Did you bring the Mothers up here? And what's up with the costumes?"

"Friends," Kruger said. "Look—this is not an official rescue. There's no ride home. But we are here to take this base. A handful of us from the Mobile Force but mostly Thanha. The horseback people. They live here. I'll explain later."

"I don't give a fuck who they are if they're here to help us kill Nupis."

"They are here to help, but all they've got is bows and arrows."

We need you to show us where to find weapons, show us their comm center and power lines."

Detrik grinned. "We'll do better than that if you'll let us the hell out of here."

At Kruger's order, Lyn and Saldivar lowered their weapons and stood back. Another ragged band poured through the doors: laughing, yelling, some of them stumbling and crying, all of their faces wild with surprise and question.

The man called Detrik was their leader, Singer saw. He had done a good job; the prisoners broke into squads automatically and looked to him for an explanation.

"They're here to get us out; that's all you need to know right now," Detrik announced. "You all know what we planned on if a chance like this came along. Well, it's here. We'll need to take the guardhouse, get weapons. First thing: get tools and break the chains off the chicos who are still in there. Second thing: get to the punishment cells and let them out. Third thing: anyone on horseback or wearing strange clothes is a friendly. Got that? Let's go." He told off small groups to free the remaining prisoners, and the rest of the troop headed for the guardhouse, with Lyn and Saldivar trotting alongside. Detrik swung awkwardly up to ride behind Kruger.

Janet turned to go with the group headed for the punishment cells. Singer hesitated. His heart was afire for the fight, but he did not want Janet to go unprotected in this turmoil.

Don't worry, I have my bodyguard, she assured him. He saw Ilyun pushing through the stream of prisoners to get to Janet's side.

We're going after the vito, hit them from the air. Watch Marcus! That was Lyn. She had a large group of young pallantai with her, and she was right—his place was with Kruger. He turned and galloped off after the main force.

He had a horse under him and a sword in his hand again. Pleasure as intense as water after long thirst coursed through him. He let go of planning and debating and sank into the fierce lights and deep shadows, the twist and sway of bodies, like a swimmer into a swift, familiar river.

He pushed his horse forward into the scuffle. It leapt and kicked at the sound of gunfire but bent to his asking and pressed on. The sword moved like a part of him, a part he had been missing for a long time. Most of the enemy had only handguns, but in the corner of a building he spotted the slender, deadly shape of a gun like Lyn's. He stung the pony next to him with the point of his sword to make it jump. He could not hear the sound of the shot, but blood exploded from the horse's neck. The rider was unhurt, but the pony had not moved fast enough. He wrenched his own mount around by brute force and surged through a hole in the crowd toward the building. The enemy, still aiming at the group, did not see him coming till it was too late. Singer felt the breath of the hot metal on his face as the shots passed, missing him. The gunner raised his weapon again, not to fire but as a desperate barrier between his face and Singer's descending blade. The sword met the smooth not-metal they called *pahlastika* and cleaved it, as a moment later it cleaved the bone of the stranger's skull.

Some stray gleam of light had shown Singer the face of his enemy in the moment before death: grimacing, pale, eyes vacant with fear. Singer bared his teeth in anger as he turned the horse away from the light-colored building that would make a target silhouette of a mounted man. The man was afraid, he thought. With a weapon that could kill me ten times in the space of a breath, he's afraid. He's used to killing at a distance, seeing targets—not hooves and teeth and two ironweight of razor-edged metal coming down on him.

He ground his teeth again, this time not at the strangers but at Siri. I know what he's doing. He isn't going for the guns, going for weapons to match them. He's riding them down, chasing them, enjoying himself. As I did. But soon some of these rabbits will resist the fear of us long enough to learn that we can be killed, and then we're dead. We're losing more horses already.

It was one of the first things they had taught him when he was a boy going out with the pallantai for the first time: never get off the horse! But he leapt from the saddle anyway, looped the reins over the horn, and beat the bewildered horse away from him, back into the safety of the dark. Then he ran after Kruger and his friends.

"Where have you been?" Kruger asked when he felt Singer grasp his stirrup leather.

"Learning something," Singer said. He was running to keep up. The Riders were ahead of them, gathering speed. They were headed for the buildings at the far corner of the fence, with Siri in the front line.

"He's crazy," Kruger said. "He's going to charge them. Shit!"

Singer knew that the charge would break at the center and

sweep to both sides in an encircling movement. But they went faster, closer. "Break, break," he pleaded with Siri, though he knew the Asharya could not hear him.

"Get off the horse," he said suddenly.

"What?"

Singer yanked Kruger's foot out of the stirrup and pulled him backward out of the saddle. Detrik lost his balance along with them and slid off over the horse's rump, narrowly missing getting kicked in the head. Singer crashed to the ground with Kruger on top of him.

"Goddamit!" Kruger yelled.

The charging Riders wheeled aside just as the guards holed up in their armory finally opened fire. Horses shrieked and tumbled in the front ranks, tripping those who followed. Siri galloped straight up the rising ground toward the building, sword upraised. Bullets tore up the ground around him, but he was not hit. For a moment he seemed truly invulnerable.

Then something slammed into the horse's chest, throwing horse and rider into the air. They seemed to hang suspended for an instant, keeping a semblance of their shapes, before they crashed entangled to the ground. The Riders had shot the tower gunner on the way in, but in the confusion another Nupi had climbed up to replace him.

"Da, daon," Singer whispered.

Kruger heard him in Delteix, in his head, screaming. *No! NO!*

Singer was calling for Janet before the sound of the explosion died. He knew she was coming as fast as she could, but he kept calling. He ran to the place where the Asharya had fallen. Siri's head and chest were still recognizable. Blood was everywhere, and Singer did not know how to stop it without stopping the heart from beating.

Grandfather, hold on. The healer is coming. He forced memories on the wounded man, memories of Janet and Lyn frantically working over his torn, limp body. *I was hurt this badly and I lived. They can fix it.* But he was lying, and the Asharya knew it.

Singer groped into the Asharya's consciousness brutally and awkwardly, searching for control of his failing body. He could stop the blood flowing to the ruined legs. They were beyond saving.

"Stop. I forbid—" Blood bubbled from Siri's lips, stopping the rest of his words, but Singer understood him.

I forbid it. No healer. Get Makho. Your Asharya. In agony, choking, the old man clung to Singer. *Hold me, one more breath. Hold me.*

Blind to his surroundings, Singer held him and cried out for Kruger.

"I'm right here, son. What is it?"

Siri's lips strained again. He was beyond speaking, but Singer hammered the words into Kruger's mind.

Take them. I give you my children.

"Tell him yes," Singer cried. "Tell him!" He fought for breath as he struggled to keep Siri breathing through lungs that were burned and filling with blood.

A shadow of that shared agony fell across Kruger. *He's dying,* he thought, *and he's leaving his troops with nothing. I remember how that was. God help me, I remember.*

He took the old man's hand. "I'll do the best I can for them," he said.

He felt Siri die.

Singer threw back his head and screamed like a wild animal.

He surged to his feet, and Kruger grabbed him, expecting him to charge wildly after the other Riders, seeking revenge for their leader. The pod gun fired again from the tower, sending up fountains of dirt and knocking over another handful of Riders. The survivors of the broken charge turned toward the tower. They hung on the far side of their mounts, to swing off and away when the horses were shot down. They ran between the horses. They crawled on their bellies through the cross fire. But none of them had reached the tower when Singer heard the cough and roar of engines that told him Lyn had reached the vito pad. The pod gun could bring down a vito at that range easily. Singer checked Makho for the ghost of an idea and found nothing. He raged at himself even while he ranged his eyes over the compound again, looking for a way out. *Stupid! They got the jump on us. They'll always win when it happens this way.*

The vito started to rise slowly from the pad. The guns were still live. Singer could feel the heat of the barrel as if he held it in his hands. It scorched him, burned him. Propellant in the cartridges, oil, the explosive packed in metal fists—all these would burn, but where was the spark to light them? Chemical ignition shells—that did him no good; the fire was buried too deep for him to find. Somewhere he could feel the restless bits of light he had learned to know, the same that danced in wires and tubes, that writhed in the broken fence. In a moment the fire would be seeking Lyn and Palha.

Something like a shadow fell across his mind, a finger of cold that pointed to knowledge he needed. Delayed ignition, that was the word. If he could set that free, it would light the shell by itself. He drew the line of fire while Kruger wrestled with him, tried to pull him down. He no longer felt himself standing on the same ground with Kruger. He was lost in a dance of patterns that hurt him with their complexity. If he could only grasp the smallest fragments of that dance—just enough to turn it, send the sparks leaping along the path already laid out for them.

A shriek from the tower, as the charge exploded in the magazine, was cut off suddenly as the other charges ignited and the tower went up in a ball of flame. Shrapnel whined in all directions, and the vito lifted to avoid the flame cloud.

Singer heard Lyn berating him.

How many times do I have to tell you, don't do that when I'm flying! Keep those buttheads away from the building. We're going for it.

She was safe, and he felt Palha with her, riding guns. He let Makho pull him down to shelter behind the body of a dead horse. He felt as if he had been dropped from a great height. He had fallen from a clean sparkling darkness into the slimy dirt of the battlefield. He dragged himself a little farther from Siri's body.

"You're the heavy now, Makho. Tell them what to do."

He pushed his face into the dirt as the vito roared over the building and blew the front wall out. The freed prisoners swarmed into the opening and dragged out any guards who were still alive. The guards bled from noses and ears, half-stunned by the concussion. The prisoners jumped them with improvised weapons or with their bare hands. Singer felt it happening. He felt how good it had been when his sword had leapt out like a live thing and came back bloody. The feeling was no longer clean and exhilarating like a drink of water. It felt like swallowing blood. He pulled himself upright and staggered toward them, stumbling over the bodies on the ground.

Kruger was ahead of him.

"Stop it!" Kruger roared, seizing the shoulders of the nearest prisoners to pull them off their prey. He finally attracted enough attention for one man to turn and ask, "Who the hell are you?"

"I'm your commanding officer, and I'm ordering you to back off."

The man shook Kruger off. The rest of the mob continued, oblivious to Kruger's orders.

The vito sank slowly lower till it hovered directly above them, the blast kicking up a choking dust and threatening to rip the rags off the prisoners' bodies. Lyn turned on the outside speakers.

"Stop!" they blared. "~~God damn it~~, quit! Don't kill the prisoners!"

The orders had no effect, but the wind from the vito was like cold water thrown over fighting dogs. They backed off, turning their eyes away from what they had been doing. For the first time since the attack had begun it was quiet in the compound, except for the sobbing of one of the beaten guards.

"Medical officer, take charge of the prisoners," Kruger said.

Jan was already on the ground with them. "Medical officer!" she repeated in disgust. "I'm not in your flaming forces anymore, Marcus. I deserted—remember?"

She had not intended to be heard, but in the silence her words rang out like an announcement. There was scattered applause.

She raised her voice. "I need help! Some of our own people are hurt worse than this. I need anybody who's been a para or scouts with field medical. If there's a clinic in this pit, I want to know where it is, and I want someone to go get a truck to take people there."

Kruger called for volunteers and sent them off with her. Some of the older Riders shifted their feet uneasily as Janet and her helpers carried away the ex-guards.

"What have Riders to do with prisoners?" they said.

"Where's the honor in killing a man who can't even stand up?" Kruger replied angrily.

The Rider who had spoken shrugged. "If they can't stand up, leave them lying. They can go where they please or die where they are. Makes no difference to me."

"That's where you're wrong. We want them for—oh, hell. What's the damn word for 'interrogation'?" he interrupted himself in Delteix. "To ask them questions, anyway. We're starving for knowledge. To kill them would be like—like wasting meat."

Singer had come up silently behind him and was standing at his shoulder. Singer said something in low, rapid Thanha.

The Rider lowered his eyes. "As you say, Grandfather."

"What did you say to him?" Kruger asked.

"I remind him that you are the Asharya now," Singer said. "I suggest he do what he's good at—taking care of horses, not arguing. Listen—Zhanne needs me now, I think. Word will get around that Siri has given them to you. Pick up the reins. If you need me, I will be with the healers. Kata is unhurt and rides well, so I told him to take a couple of friends and ride back for Morne and the children. That big man over there—the one you named Detrik—I hear them calling him Truck. The prisoners look to him. He and Palha can do whatever you want done while I am with Zhanne. Was this well done, my Grandfather?''

''You seem to have thought of everything,'' Kruger said. ''But I am not anyone's grandfather.''

''Maybe not now. You will become one.'' He loped away, leaving Kruger unwillingly in command.

6

The last time Singer had looked out from the door of the clinic, he had seen a dawn glow in the sky. At the time his only thought had been distaste for the color. It looked too much like a bruise. By the time Janet had finished with the last of the wounded and stepped back from the table, the glow had vanished. A plain, chalky light had taken its place. Early morning was cruel to the ugliness of the blasted field still littered with dead animals. The freed prisoners had repaired the electrical system, and the flood-lights left a stain on the fragile daylight.

He stumbled down the steps, rubbing dry, stinging eyes, and was intercepted by Saldivar.

''Heyo, cofra. You've been up all night, too? Can you stay up another hour? Mack wants you. Some of the prisoners are well enough to talk.''

Through his weariness, he heard the worry in Palha's voice. ''What are they doing to them?'' he asked.

"Nothing, yet. They're waiting on you."

"Who are they?"

"Mack is there. The big one they call Truck. He was the camp heavy while they were prisoners—kept them all together, and they still look to him. Genady—he was recon, but he had para training and did most of their doctoring. Then a couple of the older Riders still alive: Tenas and Firo. Morne wouldn't come. Lyn is translating for a work team at the powerhouse. She'll come running if you want her."

Singer's stride lengthened. He broke into a run. He knew too much about prisoners and the asking of questions.

The prisoners had been locked to their cots in a small room off the clinic. Singer could see that the restraints had been used on others before, but that did not cool his anger. He brushed through the group without greeting them and seated himself cross-legged on the table at the head of the room. Saldivar stood at his shoulder, as if on guard.

"I see armed men in this room," Singer announced without looking at them. "A wanderer from the north like me, an ignorant man, might wonder what danger they guard against." He had to say everything twice, once in Delteix and once in Thanha, but that gave him an additional opportunity to watch their reactions.

The Riders shifted uncomfortably, but the others were puzzled.

"We're interrogating prisoners," Truck said.

Singer let Kruger translate that. It was beneath his dignity as an Asharya, but Singer did not want to mouth the arguments against him as well as his own words.

"Ahh, now I see them. Unarmed people in bonds. They are covered with bruises. Could it be that this makes them more dangerous?"

Truck got the point. He turned a dull red and stepped closer to Singer.

"I had friends who spent time in this room," he said. "Some of them died here." He pointed to the nearest prisoner. "This one guarded the punishment cells. They'd be carried in here from the cells after he got through with them."

Singer met his eyes. "Then set him on his feet and kill him," he said softly. The mockery was gone from his voice. "But don't keep him here and study his ways unless you love him so much that you want to become like him."

Singer turned to Kruger. "Forgive me, Grandfather," he said

in Thanha. "I would serve you, but I am sick. A bad smell in this room has made me useless, and I will beg your leave to go where the air is better."

"Unlock," Kruger ordered. Truck raised a hand as if to protest, but he removed the restraints.

"You want to kill him?" Singer asked.

Truck looked at the guard for a long time. The man's face was so cut and swollen that it was hard to tell what he had originally looked like. He tasted like old, crusted blood in Singer's mind. He was cruel. But he was not a coward. He was able to look at Truck without flinching. Singer wished they had followed the old ways and killed those men on the hot field, swept them out of the way. He almost hoped Truck would kill that one before they started asking questions. But Truck dropped his gaze in disgust.

"No. Not now," he said heavily.

"So, no dogs here?" Singer said to the room at large. "No one wants to cut their bellies and eat their guts while they're hot?"

"Singer, that's enough!" Kruger said.

"I hear with respect, my Grandfather." Singer bowed elaborately from the waist.

Silence was thick in the room; it took Kruger a few moments to recover his equilibrium.

"It's great that we're so humanitarian," the para said angrily. "But we need information, and there's no pretty way to get it."

"When you need information, you ask for it, no?" Singer said. "Ask them some questions."

He counted on Kruger's pride to force the Con-el to support him, and he was not wrong.

"Mr. Singer is a negotiations expert, among other things," Kruger said mildly to the Deltans. "Ask your questions."

Reluctantly, the para complied. "There's power being produced here," he said to the prisoners in a low, irritated voice. "We know that damned well, since you've been sending us out to tend the panel farm. And road building. We know about that. Am I right so far?" Their eyes never left his face, but they did not speak.

"Dammit, answer me," the para said.

Singer translated the questions in a low voice so the Riders present would know what was being asked. He saw one of the captured guards glance briefly in his direction. They were not sure who was in charge. Singer took out his boot knife and tested the edge.

"Tell him yes," he said.

The youngest of the prisoners swallowed and said yes.

Singer pulled a scrap of leather out of his pocket and settled down to trim it into thongs.

"Then, recently, you've started bringing in herds of meat animals. We got the scraps after you sent them on. Where to? That's what we want to know. The power. The road. The food. Who gets it? Nupis, sure, but where?"

Having spoken once, the young one found it easier to answer again. "They told us the food would be sent south to Solidari."

"But the road goes north."

"To the sea—they said it would be easier to send it by ship."

"Tell him he's a dirty thief," Tenas said in Thanha. "They stole that food from us and our children."

Singer translated. The prisoner flushed. "Our families are hungry, too," he said angrily.

The stupid-looking guard interrupted him, muttering something in a Deltan lingua Singer did not know. He caught the warning note in it, though.

"What's he saying?" he asked the para.

"He says 'Put your tongue back in your mouth before somebody cuts it off.' " He reached over and slapped the guard across the mouth. "No one asked for your opinion."

He turned to the next prisoner. "You, fatty, let's hear your explanation. Where was that road going to go when we finished building it for you?" The fat man tried to shrink himself, shaking his head nervously.

"To the sea," he ventured. "I don't know! Veck was the head of engineering for that, and you killed him last night."

The para struck him, too. "Don't try to make me believe you're that stupid. A whole camp sent here to build a road? This road that eats up our lives working on it, and you don't even know where it's going?" He cuffed the fat man's head back and forth with his fist till the man's eyes streamed with tears and he crowed for breath. His anger swelled with every blow, and he ended up by driving his fist under the fat man's ribs so hard that the man doubled over, retching.

Singer felt as if his guts were twisting inside him. The hatred in the room vibrated like the warning sound of a buzz snake. Most of it was an echo from Genady and Truck, but when he thought of the bloody rags of Siri's body, their dead still unburied, he felt his own anger rising. It was a sickening feeling, like the hunger of a starving man when he finally got a piece of bread. There was more to it than the desire for revenge; some other force was driving under the surface, but Singer could not stop to find out what it was. He clung to the one fact that the prisoners must not be killed before they could give information.

The guard with the cut face spoke up unexpectedly, breaking the tension of the moment. "Why beat them up? They're telling the truth. The road does go to the sea. The Union wants a port in the north. There's no reason to keep that a secret, I guess. Your spy planes must know it already." His words came out indistinctly because of his swollen lips, but his voice was calm. Singer thought he had not spoken to save his companion pain but only because he was afraid the pain might make him say something. That meant he was probably lying.

Singer had been watching the prisoners carefully as they responded. The young one was terrified, but he was not lying. He did not know anything. The fat one was equally ignorant. The one who seemed stupid was not; he guarded his face carefully. The cruel one's face could not be read, but his voice betrayed him. It was too level, and behind it his breathing was tightly controlled. He was hiding something.

"Haven't you found any maps?" Singer asked Kruger. "They'd tell you where the road goes better than these lying dogs."

"We have a set of plans. They show the route, but they don't answer the question of what, or who, is at the end of the road."

And if these men don't answer, I'll have the utmost difficulty keeping our new allies from beating it out of them. Singer read that in his face. Kruger wanted him to do something before he had to test his authority on his own men. Singer could think of only one thing to do. He would as soon have picked up a snake, but he grasped the cruel one's bruised hand, tightening his grip when the man tried to pull away from him.

I won't be able to do this, he thought. I share nothing with this man.

But that was not true. As he touched the stranger, horrifying memories stirred in him. His heart pounded as if he were the one about to be tortured. He tried to conceal his sickness from the others in the room.

"Check your pulse," he said to the prisoner. He squeezed his fingers around the man's wrist and felt the blood jumping nervously along its narrow road. "Are you a player?" he asked, smiling. "Yes, I think so. You take big chances. You know, a man can keep his face straight, but his heart will give him away. Surprising what good ears can hear."

He quested, fumbling, for a point of contact with the guard's thought. As bait for the truth, only the truth would do.

"They don't understand the things you did," he said, almost whispering. "But I do. I knew a man like you once. Compared to him, you're nothing. He had a lifetime of other people's pain. Pain was riches to him, and he gave it away with both hands. He was a master of torment. You are a child playing with sticks and bones. But I killed him. Do you want to know how I did it?"

He had the prisoner spellbound. The man stared at him, dry-lipped, and saw only the images Singer had salvaged from his memory—resurrected corpses of deeds he had tried to bury. They burned in his mind, but Singer was cold. His own unbearable memories moved closer to him like a cold shadow that moved when he moved and raised its hand to touch his own. But he would not step into that darkness. He would not ask for help from the shadow. Not for this slug, this nobody.

"Ask your questions, Makho," he breathed, still holding the prisoner's eyes. "Don't worry about the answers."

Kruger cleared his throat. He was puzzled, but he would back Singer up. "All right, we've established the direction of the planned road," he said. "Tell us about the destination. Is there another Union settlement there? A garrison?"

The prisoner swallowed hard. "Not—not exactly. No. Not what you're thinking of."

Singer nearly cried out. "Fire!" he exclaimed in Thanha. "Fire in his thoughts. I see the child's dream. A city of burning iron and creatures that run with breath of smoke and fire."

Saldivar translated quietly for the Deltans. The prisoner moaned in fear.

"Please let me go," he begged. "I'll answer you, but get him away from me. He's burning me."

Contact with him was torture to Singer, too. He let go. His fingers had printed new marks on the prisoner's wrists.

"Talk to him but don't trust him," he said. "He'll tell you the truth now, as much as he does to himself. But that's not saying much."

"Tell us, from beginning to end, what you know about the Union presence here," Kruger ordered.

The man gave Singer one look of hatred, then bowed his head, beaten.

"What Erz said is true," he said. Singer quietly translated his words for the Riders. "You killed Veck last night, and you killed Isfan, too. He was the camp commander. I'm only security chief. This is all I know: Before we left Solidari, we were told we'd be working on engineering projects. The settlement needs power. We got up here and found there was a prison camp already here. We took charge of the prisoners and put them to work on the road and the solar farm."

"Why a solar farm here in the middle of nowhere?" Kruger interrupted. "There's plenty of desert closer to the Union Zone."

The man hesitated, and Singer could see his face twitch as his thoughts darted around, looking for a way to lie. At last he gave way to necessity and answered reluctantly. "Turns out the power wasn't for Solidari. It goes out to the coast. This is the optimax area for all the factors they needed."

"And what are those factors?" Kruger prompted.

"Has to be on this side of the mountains, so we get the most sunlight; the survey men say the rain falls on the seaward side. Has to be close to a good road route. Has to be accessible from Solidari but far enough from the Open Zone that the Consorso won't stumble over us on one of their spying missions."

"So you're building a road to the coast. What for?"

The man hesitated again before giving away the final secret. "Why don't you ask your survey pilots. They know! Always flying over us, spying."

"They aren't here right now, and you are," Kruger said.

"There's a city on the coast," the man muttered. "The mountains come down close to the sea. There's iron and coal in the mountains. We send the power and the food up to the coast. I don't know what they're doing there. I only know we're here to supply them."

Tenas would not strike a disarmed man, but he gave the cot a kick that jolted it across the floor and nearly spilled the prisoner off.

"Did you tell him he's a thief and an alley dog? Tell him again!" He addressed the prisoner directly. "The food you sent them came out of the mouths of our children. They were starving in the snow this winter."

The man flinched, though he could not understand Thanha. "We have to have power. You Cons, you have your bloody big petrol field. You have fuel, you have lights. You don't know what it's like between the ████████ forest and the ████████ cold ocean, dragging logs to cook the ████████ fish so you can drag another log tomorrow. And you Cons are sucking our blood along the border. There's hunger in Solidari. We have a right to live." He bit off his words and stared sullenly at the ground.

Tenas spat on the floor. "Nobody asked you to come here. Go home or we'll give you a home. Under the earth, where all the dead animals go."

Singer translated what the prisoner had said, and Tenas spit again.

"He doesn't have a right to live. In his own place, maybe. Not here."

Kruger intervened and returned to the interrogation. "How far does the road extend past this base?"

"There's a dirt track that goes all the way to the coast. That's what they told us, at least. Veck took some people and a truck and drove up there last summer. The built road goes maybe thirty, forty miles. Far enough that we were looking at places to build a second staging camp so we wouldn't have to truck the prisoners back and forth. But then the snow came down heavy, and we had to quit for the winter."

"What have you been doing with the prisoners during the time when they couldn't work on the road?"

Genady, the para, answered for him. "Starving us! They reduced our rations because we couldn't work. They wouldn't run the heaters in our rack. It was easy to see they wanted us dead."

"That's not true! We found other work for them."

"Sure—splitting rocks!"

"Stockpiling material for the road, for when the weather cleared. And hauling wood to provide fuel for their own barracks. That's not against the regulations."

"You sent us out in a blizzard to clear snow from the solar collectors."

"That was necessary! It was an emergency."

Kruger stopped the argument again. "Singer?"

Singer shrugged. "Truth, as he tells it to himself. Not all of the truth."

"You'd better tell it all," Kruger said to the prisoner. "You don't want to annoy these people, and believe me, you don't want to annoy me."

"We never had orders to reduce the prisoners," the man said heavily. "But we had a quota to meet with energy production and the rations we processed and shipped. They said we shouldn't worry too much about maintaining the work force because there'd be more workers in the spring.''

"Expendable," Genady said bitterly. "Isn't that the word? You didn't have to kill us. You just arranged for us to die.''

He raised his voice and spoke across the prisoners to Kruger. "I saw people locked to these beds with running sores from beatings, with feet black from frostbite, dying of fever, dying just from cold and hunger. I begged them to give me medicine and food, even to heat the room!''

The pictures in Genady's mind were cruelly clear; Singer had to make an effort not to see them. He tasted again the bitterness of the healer who had no help to give.

"Time for a break," Kruger said.

They left the prisoners under guard and moved into the next room.

"This isn't a trial," Kruger said when they were out of earshot. "I believe you. But we're here to gather information, not to pass judgment.''

"Someone should pass judgment," Genady said hotly. "They killed my friends. They should be punished.''

"Who is going to do that?" Singer asked. "You?"

As Detrik had, Genady lowered his eyes. "No," he said finally. "I've seen enough killing. I'm sick of it. But someone should. You could find a volunteer without too much trouble.''

"Maybe so. But people aren't tools you pick up and put away. You teach a man to kill helpless people, you have to live with him that way. I'd rather live with a snake in my blanket.''

"What would you propose to do with the prisoners?" Kruger asked Singer.

"We're done with them. Let them go.''

"You mean just turn them loose?" Genady said, incredulous.

"He says he has a right to live," Singer said. "Let him see if the earth grants him that right. Without his fire weapons, without slaves. Let him fight cold and hunger hand-to-hand. If he survives, he has earned his life as far as I'm concerned.''

"They won't earn anything," Genady said. "They'll kill and rob whoever they meet next. They shouldn't be loose on their own.''

Kruger listened without speaking. The small muscles around his eyes and mouth had tightened in the way that told Singer that Makho was making an unpleasant decision. He made a hand gesture he had learned from the Riders. It said "finished.''

"Kill them," he said quietly. "We can't have them behind us."

"Sir, should we form a court or something?" Genady asked.

"No. I take the responsibility. No court. Why play games? We can't have them behind us. That's all."

"I will do it, then," Singer said. *I am the only one, Makho. Any other would be damaged by this order. You cannot afford that. You need their trust. As for me, your responsibility is already mine.*

Kruger's face went even tighter. "Do it," he said.

"I must have permission to be Thanha, my Asharya. I cannot kill a bound man."

The prisoners were unlocked and taken out into the wide-open area. Singer noticed in passing that the bodies had been moved from the bloody ground, the Rider dead laid under a covering.

The Nupis knew what was coming and huddled together in fear that was hard for Singer to bear without retching. If they could have found some courage, it would have been easier for him.

"Give them weapons," he said. The Delh'tani did not move. "Give them weapons!" he repeated in Thanha. Tenas and Kata threw their belt knives and the handguns they had taken as trophies onto the dirt.

The Nupis scrambled for them, and the fear receded for a moment. In that moment Singer struck. He broke the fat man's neck with a kick as the man stooped for a gun, then blocked the stupid one's arm as he tried to point the weapon he had just grasped and cut his throat. The cruel one jumped him, reaching for his knife hand. Singer let him go by, breaking his arm as he passed. Without a pause, his movement a blur, Singer swept up one of the handguns and shot the man in the back as a mark of contempt. The youngest of the prisoners had picked up a knife, but he did not even try to use it. He looked Singer in the face. Then he gave up and shut his eyes. Singer hit him hard and fast. He tasted blood for a moment, and then he was alone, looking down at the bodies and feeling as if something had been torn from him, as well.

Kata reached out and touched his shoulder, but the Delh'tani pulled back and left space around him as he passed. He walked away aimlessly without looking where he was going and found himself in the one place no one else wanted to be, next to the rows of bodies.

Riders did not have the Delh'tani feeling that faces of the dead should be covered, so it was not hard to find Siri. Singer sat on his heels and touched Siri's face. He found he was still holding the bloody knife. His hair was still too short to make any show, but he hacked off what he could and let it fall on the stained blanket that covered Siri's body.

"I cut my hair for you, Grandfather."

He looked up and saw Kruger watching him.

"I didn't know you thought that much of him," Kruger said awkwardly. *He was suicidal. Not fit for command.* Singer heard the unspoken thought.

"He was a hero," Singer said.

"I don't follow you."

"You're thinking he was stupid, they would all have been dead if he'd lived. Think he didn't know that? He fought a losing battle best way he could. He knew it was hopeless, but he tried to eat that bitterness himself and leave them some comfort even if they had to die. He knew he wasn't right for the job, but there was no one to take it off his shoulders.

"Then we came. There cannot be two Asharyas. So Siri went to war one more time. He took a chance. You might have refused. But he knew that only his dying wish would be strong enough to bind his people to a stranger Asharya."

"I'm not their Asharya! I was colonel of the Mobile Force— the Mother heavy, as Truck would say. Nothing more than that, ever. That 'general' shit was just a retirement bribe. This tribal crap—I'm sorry, Singer! But I can't have them calling me 'Grandfather.' It's a lie."

Singer raised his eyebrows. "Oh, yes, and it's a lie when you call me son. Siri knew your heart better than you know yourself. That's the nature of an Asharya. These are your children—your 'boys,' I guess you'd say. He died to give them to you. You have to take them."

"I can't do it. Their ways, their whole culture. It's too different."

"I learned your ways, Makho. Didn't I? You were going to give me a medal once. You can learn, too."

Kruger bowed his head. "When I lost the last of my command—when the Mothers were all dead but you and Saldivar— I swore I'd never command again. Coming up here with you was my own individual decision. I won't be responsible for the lives of others. Never again."

"Tell you a story, Makho. When I was a boy, Hilurin was

Singer for the Rock. Greatest and best Singer in memory, some said. Could take your heart in his hand and spin it like a juggler's ball. He told me I'd be Singer one day, and I said never. Never. I swore it.

"But I needed the music like I needed air to breathe, so I took the music he gave me. But I said I'd never use it. I believed that.

"Then Hilurin went away, and my Grandmother was old and sick, and she needed me. I told myself it was only for a time, I was only playing. But I was her Singer, truly. I knew that. And when your people killed her, in my grief I said I'd never sing again. Never. I swore it.

"But Hilurin told me long ago that was an oath I couldn't keep. He said to me once, 'No one can make you sing, but you have to sing.' He was right. I found another Asharya. I've been his Singer ever since."

"Siri?" Kruger said, startled. Singer raised an eyebrow, and Kruger suddenly understood. "Me? You mean that's what you were doing for me all that time? Bringing me news, keeping me vertical, going the rounds to keep the scouts in shape?"

"Sure. That's part of the job."

Kruger was silent, looking at the past in this new light. Singer kept pressing him.

"Lurya would have said the same to you. No one can make you command, but you have to do it. Have to do what you've got in you. Maybe it'll kill you. So what? Better to die of doing than not doing." He grinned briefly and without happiness. "It's faster, for one thing."

Kruger put off the decision for one more moment. "Talking people into what they don't want—is that just another part of the job?"

Singer ducked his head in denial. "Not often. Mostly it's talking them into what they do want. That's equally hard."

"You think I want this?" Kruger said incredulously.

"What are you now? A fugitive, an exile. Your people threw you away when you got sick. No one had use for you. Take this pallantai and you become a gen'ralh again. Win or lose, what you do will matter. You want it, Makho."

Kruger opened his mouth to deny it, but he met Singer's eyes and gave up. "I'll keep my word to him. I'll do the best I can for them. But you have to help me."

"I'm your Singer."

"What happens next, then?"

"We have to honor them. Bury them. And more than that—
something to make my people and yours run on the same rein."

"How do you plan to do that?"

"I must speak to Morne. But I'm not clean. I have to wash
first. Meet me there."

He headed for the showers to look for Lyn and Palha. Sounds
of laughter and occasional bursts of rowdy singing told him the
party had already started. Inside, the shower room was thickly
fogged with steam. Water and suds rilled across the concrete
floor. The laundry area had been taken over, too, people soaking
in the tubs with their feet dangling over the rim.

Singer shed his clothes and left the bundle with the pile of
others heaped on a dry bench by the door. He was dripping wet
by the time he found Lyn and Janet soaping each other's hair.
Lyn greeted him with playful, slippery kisses till Janet softly
pushed her back to give him her gentle, worried, medikhani
once-over, touching him lightly with her fingertips. The dry,
stony pain in his chest eased a little.

I killed them, Zhanne. They didn't have a chance.

"I know," she said sadly.

"It was in battle," Lyn said. "Same as, anyway. It had to be
done, and they had it coming."

Her eyes narrowed dangerously. She turned and yanked the
lever, spraying them all with ice-cold water. Everyone within
reach screamed. Then she jumped Singer and wrestled him to
the slippery floor, attacking him with the soap. He was slightly
bruised but thoroughly clean by the time she let him up.

"That's enough for the present," she said, sweeping her gaze
over the surrounding crowd. "So far they're too polite to get
right down to it on the floor, but there's going to be an explosion
pretty soon if they keep charging their batteries without plugging
in."

"Pablo has retreated to soak himself in the tub," Janet said.
"I think he's feeling shy."

They found Palha soaking and dozing and climbed in with
him.

"I'm completely warm and completely clean for the first time
in untold ages," Janet said. "I wish I could stay in the water
forever, but I'm starting to shrivel up like a piece of chewy-
fruit."

A burly naked man leaned through the doorway of the wash-
room. His hair was shaggy, and his body showed scars through

the sheen of water on his skin. Until he spoke, there was no way to tell whether he was Rider or Deltan.

"Someone called Singer in here?" he said, peering through the steam. "The old man wants him."

The others started to disentangle themselves so Singer could get out of the water, but he stopped them.

"Please do me the favor to tell the Asharya I'm waiting for him here," he said with a flourish.

The man frowned and then laughed. "Why not? It's your ass," he said, ambling away.

In a few minutes Kruger appeared, skirting the rivulets as neatly as a cat, the remnants of his uniform only slightly damp and his back stiff with displeasure.

"What in hell is going on here?" he demanded.

Singer did get up when Kruger actually entered the room. "Makho, I meant no disrespect." He reached for Kruger, but he was streaming wet, and Kruger stepped back from him involuntarily. Singer continued quietly so the rest of the room could not hear.

"I'm not your soldier anymore, Makho. I'm your Singer. And this is not the battlefield but a celebration. There is—what is your word?—protocol, but it is different. I try to help you learn it." He felt anger from Kruger at what he thought was disrespect. He also felt fear. Kruger had taken on the bizarre command he had been handed, but he was afraid he would lose the authority he needed to fulfill his responsibility to them.

Singer reached for him again, slowly, so as not to startle him. He started to unfasten the buttons of Kruger's jacket. Kruger nearly struck his hand away.

"Stop it, and that's an order, whatever the hell you call yourself. I'm sitting here in the middle of a steam room orgy, and you're making a fair bid to destroy my credibility completely."

"And you diminish my honor in front of my people," Singer said. "It's my job, my privilege, to care for my Asharya, but you won't even let me help you wash, something the youngest and least of the pallantai could do for an honored captain. Your people can't trust you if they never see you among them."

"That's not our way," Kruger said. "The prisoners are some rough chucks. Once they see my bare ass, they'll never take orders from me again."

"But it is our way, and this is our land. If they want to live here, they will respect our way." There was bright metal in Singer's voice. Then he smiled. "And they will respect your bare ass or I will kill them with my bare hands. Our customs are simple and pleasant.''

Kruger hesitated. The anger dissipated, but confusion remained.

"You're the only one here who's still dirty,'' Singer continued. "To be the worst-smelling goat in the pallantai gets you no respect, believe me.''

"What the hell,'' Kruger said finally. He unfastened his own shirt, but he allowed Singer to take it from him and reluctantly let Singer unlace and pull off his boots. Once undressed, he climbed into the tub as quickly as he could with dignity.

"I feel like a ▆▆▆▆idiot,'' he complained.

"That's just what you're not,'' Lyn said. She pushed his head under water to rinse the soap out of his hair.

Kruger coughed and wiped water from his face.

"Look around you, Marcus, and quit shielding your eyes,'' Janet said. "This is mostly friendly relaxation. Singer is correct. The Riders obviously do have protocols.''

"Yes, there are protocols.'' Singer sighed. "I'm breaking them and bending them, both yours and mine. I'm playing with dangerous things, and I need your help. Don't fight against me, Makho. I do the best I can for us.''

"I could be more helpful if I knew what you were trying to do,'' Kruger said. He still sounded stiff, but he was starting to relax. "Ah, God, that feels good,'' he added as Janet dug expert fingers into the muscles at the base of his neck.

"Siri gave you the Riders,'' Singer said. "And now you have a war group of your own people, given into your hand because they have no other leader.''

"I don't know that I actually have any right to assume command,'' Kruger said. "I'm retired. I'm also a deserter, in a sense. And I'd probably be under arrest if we ever returned to the Consorso Zone. Technically, Detrik is the highest-ranking individual. He should take charge, lead them back to civilization, and let properly constituted authority sort it out.''

"You wouldn't be here now if you were willing to submit to those rules,'' Singer said. "You won't send them off into the snow because you know they would die. And in your heart you have already taken on the burden for them. You have to save their lives, or at least spend them honorably, as Siri did for his children. Isn't that so?''

Kruger cleared his throat. "That's not just how I would put it.''

"So now you are Grandfather for two kinds of children, rider of two horses. And I am your Singer, so I must ride those horses with you or die trying."

"If you have an idea how to do that, I'd be most interested," Kruger said dryly.

Singer shrugged, sloshing water over the edge of the tub. "It isn't possible."

"Thanks, I needed to hear that."

"While they remain two, they'll pull in two directions. The two must learn to run like one. Maybe even to become one, but I can't see that far ahead. Tonight I want them just to learn to run on the same rein."

"How?" Janet asked patiently. "You're going in circles."

"I know." Singer was silent for a long time. Then he rose out of the water and shook himself. "Let's go see Morne," he said.

7

The old healer had set up living quarters for the recuperating Riders. Already the room had changed completely from the bare concrete and plastic of its previous existence as a barracks. There was a warm, complex smell of herbs and smoke and other elusive ingredients. Janet had managed to impress on Morne the importance of separating people who were sick, so she had not shoved all the mattresses together to make a common sleeping area. But she had flung blankets and furs over the beds to make them comfortable and homelike. There was a jug of tea keeping warm at the foot of the bed where she sat cross-legged.

Singer entered quietly in deference to the wounded who were sleeping there and sat on the floor by her bed. With a quick

movement of his head he beckoned the others to do the same.
He put his hand on her knee, and she grasped his wrist lightly
in her cool, wrinkled old fingers. The touch was comfort and
peace, like the warmth of the room. There was no need to guard
himself against her and no effort required to make her understand.

What do you want this time, young one?

He saw in her mind a rushing sandstorm from the southern
desert, shot with lightning gleams, with little whirlwinds rabbit-
hopping ahead of it. He rejected that picture with amused dis-
may.

*I'm no stormwind, barasha, to carry everything my own way.
I'm one lonely rider seeking a path through hard country. I come
asking, not commanding.*

"With you it's the same thing," she said aloud ruefully. "I
have sent already for what you need. I wonder if this is right,
however."

She handed him a package wrapped once in rawhide, once in
soft white leather, and once in silk embroidered with all the
hearth signs of the North Hills. Carefully, he loosened the silken
ties on the innermost wrapping. Inside it was packed with small
blocks of green-black stuff that looked as if it might be sticky
to the touch. A breath of sweet, spicy head-turning scent came
out before he pulled the silk over it again.

"There's plenty," he said.

"*Ayei*, plenty for what's left of our people. But you mean to
share this with the outsiders, the strangerfolk, the horse killers
from the other side of the night."

"If they'll take it from us," Singer said. "There is need.
Barasha, think of this. They are like us." She made a denying
gesture, but he insisted. "They have lost their home. They cannot go back. We must show them hospitality, as we would to
any wandering travelers."

"They are not travelers. They are enemies. There's a difference."

"Ah, that's what he said, who now lies cold, killed by what
he wouldn't try to understand."

"Enemies are destroyed by swords, not smiles," she said.
"Your travels have softened your mind and made you merciful."
The last word was spoken with bitter contempt.

"Look closer, barasha. You don't see all my mind," Singer
said. "Do you truly see mercy there?"

She stroked the short, silky hair back from his forehead and peered into his face. Then she dropped her hand. "I see a darkness in you. He-who-is-gone was right about that. But like him, I will walk your path, for I see no other."

"I'll trust this to you till the time comes, then. And I'll ask you to light the fire and speak the words for that one when the singing begins."

She nodded, and he rose to go.

In Kruger's office the people he called his company commanders had already assembled: Thanha elders, leaders of barhedoni, and others who had somehow found themselves in authority.

Kruger cleared his throat. "We have to bury the dead. Singer, I don't know what your customs are."

"On the war road we have to bury our kin where they fell. We'd rather give their bodies back to the earth, but if there are too many, sometimes we have to burn them and bury the ashes. Most important is to do it with some honor and not let the wolves and foxes carry away their flesh."

"This ground is frozen too hard to dig. If it's acceptable to the Riders, I think we'll have to burn all the bodies together."

"Not our enemies," Singer said stonily. "They may not lie beside us. Let the wolves have them."

"Dakko to that," Detrik said. "Colonel, you won't find many here who will lift a hand to dig those bastards a grave."

"We can't have corpses lying around. It's uncivilized. And when it thaws, they'll stink."

"Drive them down the road in a truck," Detrik said. "Dump them."

"Well, that's a possibility. Singer, what ceremony is needed for the Riders?"

"Morne will say the words. Not much is needed. But after that—there should be a gathering. There should be music, food, chah. These people have chewed and swallowed bitter days. This grief will stick in their throats unless you sweeten it. In our own country we would have waited till the fall, till the time of grieving, to feast the living and sing the names of the dead. This time we cannot wait. We may have no home to return to. We need to celebrate while we still can."

"If he's saying we should have a party, I'll drink to that," Detrik said.

"What kind of supplies do we have available?"

Saldivar referred to the list Janet had printed for him. "We have basic supplies for at least two weeks, based on our current personnel. We can stage one blowout, consume the luxury items, and still have marching rations. It appears the Nupis had some alcohol rations.'' He smiled slightly. ''Probably enough to get us all drunk once.''

''All right, then,'' Kruger said. ''Detrik, assemble a party to dispose of the Nupis. Take enough gasoline or other inflammables to reduce the bodies. I don't want to see them strewn around the landscape, regardless of their conduct while alive. Mr. Saldivar, assign responsibility for inventory and get some volunteers to put together food for tonight. You, Singer, ask the Riders to take care of our friends.''

''We should light the fire at dusk. That would be customary. And we'll need another truck to move them to a fit place outside the fence. They must not lie within walls.''

''Do whatever is necessary.''

Detrik and Saldivar went off to their tasks. Singer waited with Kruger till they were alone. Kruger began to pace around, as if he could not speak without moving. Singer noticed the tightening of his face again as he bit down hard on his back teeth.

''You're supposed to advise me.''

Singer waited silently.

''Advise me,'' Kruger's voice grated.

''When my Asharya tells me the problem.''

''Dammit, Singer, you know the problem. I should never have accepted this job.''

Singer realized that Makho could not get the words out. ''Makho, sit down. Sit.'' Kruger sat cross-legged, bolt upright. Singer knelt behind him and put his hands on the Asharya's shoulders. Kruger jerked.

''Advice, not some of your horse taming.''

''Be quiet. This is the best advice I can give you now.''

Kruger's muscles resisted Singer's probing fingers like iron. He stopped trying to rub out the tightness and sat still, his hands resting lightly on Kruger's neck.

''You want me to help you keep a wall between you and my people. I can't do that. They need to feel you among them. You must not stand away from them and show them that you feel a difference between yourself and them. There is a time for bearing the burden and a time for laying it down. Even for the Asharya.''

Kruger shook off Singer's hands irritably.

''An example,'' Singer said. ''You won't touch palms with me where your folk can see you. It shames you.''

Kruger started to protest, but Singer overrode him. "Remember there are two kinds of eyes watching you. Riders will see that you won't touch anybody, and they'll say you're keeping secrets from them. They'll see you don't touch me, and they'll say even his Singer he doesn't trust. How, then, can we trust him?"

"Command requires a reserve. And I require a reserve."

"An Asharya, too, is circled by respect, but Thanha respect is not a wall."

He felt Kruger lean very slightly, very tentatively, against his hands and moved closer so Makho could say to himself that Singer, not he, had initiated the contact. He pulled Kruger gently against his chest. The Asharya resisted for a moment, then let his breath out all at once and relaxed. Singer could hear him criticizing himself for it even while he did it.

"There's no one watching you, Makho. There is supposed to be one place at least where the Asharya can be easy. With his Singer. But you don't trust even me. I wish that Hilurin were here. I'm too young. I'm not the Singer you need."

Kruger made the disgusted noise that he saved for statements too stupid to deny. He reached up and gripped Singer's hand.

"I just can't do it," he said. "It goes against a lifetime."

"Makho," Singer said softly, "I gave you back your life. Now I'm asking you for one day of it."

"And you have the right to it. But—"

"Listen to me. Listen and don't argue. You need your hearth around you. You need them to feel easy with you. I breathe your breath, I know the thoughts of your heart, but you ask me to pretend it isn't so because you can't be easy with it. It's bad for you, Makho. You are hurting yourself, and you want my help. You don't need that kind of help.

"You need this: you need Zhanne and Lyn and Palha, and Ilyun and Morne, and the others. You need Zhanne very much. She is like a light that heals. She sees you completely, and it doesn't hurt. And Lyn—being with her is like walking through fire without being burned."

"This is some kind of a wild party, with drugs, and you're making it sound like my sacred duty to participate."

Singer was angry, but he let the anger go and listened to the words instead, to all the meaning he could get from Makho's mind and his own memories of the Delh'tani ways. He did not like what he learned. Makho had it all wrong, and there seemed to be no way to explain it to him. Singer thought of sharing his own memories, but he knew that would not be right, either. The gathering in had to be new each time, for each new pallantai, not something known secondhand.

"*Gebrith* is not a drug," he said finally. "Not in your meaning of the word. It is not something to buy, something you use to be alone. I have learned from you Delh'tani that even the game of delights can be used to stay alone. You can use other people the way you use your weapons and wire and everything else. You eat drugs, you eat people, like a bad child who finds honey and eats it alone till he makes himself sick.

"Nothing we offer you is like that. Gebrith is not to dull your wits or harden your heart so you can do something bad without noticing. We use it to make things a little easier. Because it's hard to go empty-handed into a new world and not be afraid of what will happen to you."

His grip on Makho's shoulders was fierce, painful, and he forced his hands open.

"I wish Hilurin were here. He could have told you so you would understand. I never saw him smoke gebrith. He didn't need it because he was brave enough to live open-hearted all the time. He gave me what I needed when I didn't know myself, and I loved him." *As I love you.*

He felt Makho tense up again, struggling with a response. The Asharya lowered his head without replying.

"I'll think about it," he said after a minute. "Keep them off my back for a few minutes, will you?"

"Sure. I must speak with the captain, anyway. They'll have to go out among the pallantai today and make the offers—choose who is right for each barhedoni. I will bring the choices to you when I see which way their minds are going. That is custom."

8

When the sun touched the horizon, the Riders and the soldiers stood at attention, backs to the fence, looking out toward the plains, where a pyre had been built for their friends. All had washed and mended their rags as best they could, and the Riders were laden with the ornaments of the dead—a heavy weight for the few who remained. A few had offered chains or arm rings to the strangers, but most of the gifts had been refused in mutual bafflement. The survivors stood together but not mixed, like oil and water in the same jar. The dead were indistinguishable.

The sharp smell of the strangers' machine fuel nagged at Singer. There was something unfitting about anointing dead Riders with that strange liquid. But he reminded himself that the Riders had lived a long time by turning whatever they found to their own use. Hot-burning thornbranches were piled deep and wide beneath the bodies. Riders had hated thorns and had gratefully used them since the first hoofbeat on the northern plains.

Morne spoke the words of parting. The listeners kept total silence, straining to hear her old voice over the sound of the wind. She called a special farewell to Siri, shedding tears for him. One by one the Riders who had been closest to the dead called out their farewells. Their grief was harder to bear than the grief for other deaths. After an ordinary battle they would have said good-bye while they washed and arrayed the bodies. They had not been able to give that care to friends so broken that they had been wrapped in the strange cloth of the enemies and piled together without any parting touch.

Singer waited until they were finished, then repeated their words in Delteix as best he could. He wanted the soldiers to know whom they had lost, even if only in parting. As his voice faded, one of the soldiers stepped out from the group and hoarsely spoke the Alto Fe prayer of parting. One by one others followed him. Those who had no prayers simply spoke the names of the dead and said good-bye. When silence fell again, Singer translated for them, too. The Riders listened respectfully to the alien names set in Thanha.

Morne plunged her torch into the pyre. When the flames first leapt up, they were almost colorless, like a quiver in the surprised air. Swiftly they bloomed out into orange and red like an echo of the setting sun. As the cloak of fire enveloped the bodies, the survivors turned away. The wind carried the smoke away, but the smell of it clung to their throats.

Within the fence other fires had been laid, and the young ones ran to light them. They dropped sweet oil onto the wood and offered it to the pallantai to rub on their hands and faces. It was scented with sage and mint, with summer on the plains. It cut the smell of the smoke, and it was healing to skin chafed raw with cold and hard work. Even some of the stranger soldiers accepted it. Then the young ones brought containers of chah. That was best of all. The containers were passed from hand to hand, lip to lip, from Deltan to Rider without distinction. A unanimous shout of approval went up after the first long swallow. They poured the drink into metal and plastic cups and wooden bowls and drank again. They drank to each other; they drank to the death of their enemies and to their mutual survival.

Singer walked between the fires, feeling their shifting moods like wind flows parting and blending the smoke. Intent on tracing their currents, he did not hear Saldivar till he was very close. Palha had something cradled in his arms, and his dark eyes were lit with pleasure.

"We found something while we were doing inventory," he said, offering Singer the object.

It was a strangerfolk thamla, what they called a *gitarra*. Singer took it into his hands as he would have taken a newborn baby. He touched the strings and let them sing his pleasure for him. Then he held it carefully out of the way while he gave Palha a crushing hug.

"You play first," he offered. "You found it."

Palha had tuned it already. He plucked a few notes, thinking. Then he began to play softly and to sing in the language of his fathers. It was not the same as Delteix, but Singer was able to pick up the meaning. Palha's voice was warm and hoarse, somewhat hesitant. A listener had to lean close.

> White face, full moon
> Black horse, where do you run?
> No rein, no road to guide you—
> Where do you carry your sleeping rider?
>
> Moon weeps, bows her head
> Over the black tower.
> Night's kiss takes the red
> From every flower.
>
> White face by the dark gate
> Run, horse, the hour is late.
> No rein, no road to guide you—
> Where do you carry your sleeping rider?

Singer flinched as if someone had poured cold water over him.

"Stop!" he said. "Why are you singing that song?"

Saldivar looked up from the strings, surprised. "My grandfather used to sing it. It's very old. He told me it was written on Sol-Terra before the migration. When they still had horses there." He touched Singer's hand. "What's wrong, cofra?"

"Nothing. The black horse. Deronh had a black horse . . ." Singer's voice trailed away, and he shook his head violently as if to shake off the memory. "No more about death," he said.

"You play, then. You were always telling me the music was better where you came from. Prove it."

Singer took the gitarra back. Most of the people on that side of the fire had turned to listen. He played the chords for a song everyone had known in the Rock. Voices caught the notes and held the chord; some, at least, of the Riders of the North Hills must have known this tune. It was the kind known as "call-and-carry," where the people carried on the chorus and harmonized on it while one or two singers improvised the verses. It was called "Stallion in the Spring"; it was easy to sing because it was so old and had at least a hundred verses that everyone knew by heart and could embroider on almost without thinking. The tune ramped and galloped like a prancing horse; it pulled the strangers along with it. Singer heard them stumbling over the words, stringing together nonsense in their own language to match the Thanha syllables, and wondered what they would have thought if they had known what they were saying. By the time the song broke up in breathless laughter and another round of chah, he thought they were beginning to get the idea.

"Something in Delteix now," Saldivar murmured at the end.

"You'll have to help me, then."

Palha's rare smile gleamed. "Remember what we sang at the very beginning of the journey? You didn't even have a gitarra then."

Singer laughed out loud. "How could I forget?"

"That one must be as old for us as your stallion song is for your people. I'm willing to bet it's preflight, maybe as old as my grandfather's songs."

When they heard the intro, Lyn and Janet and Kruger pushed their way in closer to help him sing, and when they hit the chorus, most of the camp joined in with a roar: "Why don't we get drunk and screw."

"I hope you know what you're doing," Kruger said in his ear. "These folks are in a volatile condition."

"I'm your Singer, Makho. Roll with it."

Singer, too, hoped he knew what he was doing. He sensed that he had no choice. He rode a wild horse. The only way to avoid being thrown was to urge it forward, always forward. He could feel the power gathering under him.

"Get me some drums, Palha," he said.

Palha knew what he needed; he called up a couple of the Riders and hurried away from the fire. They came back with metal ammunition boxes and some kind of wooden cases, resonant under a stick, and with plastic and metal drums from kitchen stores. The Riders had half a dozen herder's flutes with them. Those who had once been drummers tested the makeshift equipment and grumbled and began to improvise. They played more drinking songs together, the flutes and the drum rhythm lending an eerie resonance that seemed to make more of the song than the plain words allowed.

The music drifted from laughing songs to wild ones. As best he could, Singer played the Medicine Shirt tunes the polvorados liked: "Blood Roses," "Wildfire," "River of Dust." The Deltans were drunk enough to sing without inhibition by then. The Riders listened to the strangers' music and embraced its driving, complex rhythms. They joined in, and as they joined, the music began to change. Singer felt the swing of it changing direction slowly and inexorably as the tail driver felt the swing of the free-running herd ahead of him. He rode it, rode with it. Lyn jumped up and started to dance with the stranger named Truck. Then they were all dancing. Singer's fingers were numb on the strings; he guessed they were bleeding and shaped an image for himself of blood and silver weaving together and threaded that into the song. Saldivar and the Riders were drumming like madmen, as if they wanted to make the earth under their feet shudder and dance like a beating heart.

The stars swung slowly and inexorably above him. Their direction could not be changed. Singer was bitterly sorry that he had no power to move them back to a time when the bones that were scattered had been joined in living dance. Flame and shadow played tricks with the dancers, turning a flash of wild eyes to gold or hollowing a face into the semblance of a skull. Singer called up from his inner eye the dancers no one else could see, and they lived again in burning memory, dancing as the flames danced while the wood had strength to burn. The coals broke and fell together with a sound like a fiery sigh, scattering sparks that vanished.

Again the music changed, but not because the dancers chose the movement. Singer himself embraced and shaped it. He made it an arrow seeking the dark rift in the shining mail, a wave that beat against an unyielding shore. Notes called and cried for their harmonies, seeking and never quite finding. It was a song with an emptiness in it, a wound revealed by every line he wove to cover it. It was a song of need that cried and burned and drove the dancers to seek the fire that would consume them, to rejoice in it fiercely while the night endured. The dancers were fewer now. The shadows moved together until they were indistinguishable. Singer no longer wove the music as a path for their feet. He sang to the silent voices. It was half a song; they never answered him. But the grief in the music closed finally into something finished and whole.

Singer's eyes dazzled. Blinking, he looked up. The smaller stars withdrew into a sky milky with dawnlight. Coals in the fire dimmed to red and black. The power of his music had left him. His fingers were stiff and sore. He had sung the night away. No one was left on the dancing ground. At first he thought he was alone. Then he looked around and saw that his friends were still seated by his knees.

Saldivar stood and took the gitarra gently out of his hands. "It's all right, brother," he said. Singer leaned his head against Palha's chest just to feel the soft, steady beat of his heart.

"What was the last thing you played?" Janet said. "It sounded—I don't know. As if I'd heard it before. Like an echo. Like a song in the mirror."

They were close enough, open enough, that he did not have to speak. They saw again the thin, long-legged girl with her dark hair like a cloud, turning away in the dance. *Risse. The first I had to leave behind. The long grass whispers sorrow over her, somewhere far from here. I never even saw her grave. We had moved on before I was well enough to wake and see.* They saw a spare old man with hair like silver and the grace of a prince. *Hilurin. My teacher. My Singer. My friend. He found me a way to live again when I was dead with Risse. He told me, 'No one can make you sing, but you have to sing.' And it was true. I made a song for them that night. They called it 'Lament for the Flowers,' but it was for her. I turned it inside out tonight. Once I healed them. Tonight I grieved for them. Tonight I have to heal a strange folk, and the only way I can do it is to do what Hilurin did for me: He hurt me, stung me into life. He made me want and need. He made me taste what I had lost.*

"Come on here," Lyn said roughly. She helped him to his feet. "Taste this. You're fading." She handed him a cup with a couple of inches of liquid still in it. Expecting tea, he gulped it and felt it burn its way down, bringing tears to his eyes.

"That's ~~good.~~ *Terrible !!*

Better still was the warmth she touched him with, like a belated lick of fire from her mind to his. *Not burned out yet, Singer!*

The pallantai had all gone. Their hearth mates had chosen them out in the dance.

"They're waiting for you," Janet said.

He could not leave the empty dancing ground before he had finished. His fingers stumbled on the strings, but he found it— the simple heart of the fierce, complicated music he had been playing. He let the notes fall to the ground like a handful of white flowers that left a sweet, dusty scent in the air for a moment after they faded. The music was real. The flowers were only in Singer's mind.

When they were gone, he let Palha take the thamla from him and lead him inside.

Janet and Saldivar slept in each other's arms. Singer had rolled away from them a little, not really sleeping but in the delicious peace of knowing all was well for a few hours, walking like a ghost among their peaceful dreams and tasting their happiness.

He did not need to open his eyes to know who walked softly toward him, barefoot. Singer knew by heart the catalog of things Kruger badly wanted and would not permit himself to consider. The Asharya was breaking his rules for himself as he laid a hand on Singer's hacked-off hair, lightly as a breath of wind.

The words Singer heard were not Delteix but some other language that was as warm and rough as bread in Kruger's mouth. When Singer woke up in the morning, he remembered the sound of them, the Fokish of Kruger's youth and still the language of his heart. He knew that he had not been wrong and that Kruger could become what the Riders needed.

9

He had not yet opened his eyes the next morning when he heard a clear voice calling "He's awake!" Light feet came running. It was the child Roishe. He fended her off as she got ready to leap on him.

"So they found you all safe?" he said.

She nodded, but her smile vanished. "Saw a lot of dead horses," she said, pointing with her chin out toward the mended fence. "And so many brothers and sisters are dead. You gave them to the fire before we even had a chance to look on their faces once more. Your friend the healer wouldn't let us. We've seen plenty of death, barasha—that's what Tenas told her—but she said not like this. Blown to pieces, I guess—like the silangh out there?"

"Yes."

Still gripping his shirt, she leaned back and looked him in the eye. "Singer, will there be anything left of us? Every day someone else is gone. Sometimes I'm afraid I'll wake up and they'll all be gone but me."

"I don't know, sweetheart," he said softly. "Wish I could promise, but Singers cannot lie, and that promise would be close to lying."

He fell silent; her words had called up an image in his mind. He saw the tall Rock standing dark and solitary on the great plain. He wondered what it looked like now. Blown to pieces, he guessed, broken empty, like a robbed nest. The children of the Rock were gone now, all but one.

"That won't happen to you," he said. His hand closed tightly around her stick-thin arm as if he could hold on to her life that way. She looked back at him gravely, not quite understanding but trusting him.

"I came to offer you tea," she said. "I forgot. They're waiting for you."

He shook himself out of his trance and followed her toward the scent of food. The building next to the clinic had a kitchen like the one that had fed the Mobile Force back in the Consorso Zone. Singer did not expect much from the food. All that had ever come from those big metal pots had tasted the same to him. But Zhanne and Morne were sitting on the steps soaking up the sunshine and drinking fragrant tea. Bruised circles lingered under Zhanne's eyes, but she gave him a genuine smile and passed him her cup.

"You found us a good place," she said. "Hot water and artificial light—two of the essentials of civilization."

"Where's Makho?"

"He's been out getting to know the troops." She made a face. "Sounds to me as if we're back in the Forces."

Lyn came out of the kitchen with a plate full of beans and bread and cold meat. She was carrying some kind of round cake between her teeth. She took a bite out of it and gave it to Singer. "I heard that," she said. "That may be his idea, but he'll find out I ain't going back. I flew away."

Singer tasted the cake. It was covered with the glassy-looking sugar the strangers liked to eat. It made the water rush into his mouth, but it was like eating snow. He took a piece of meat off her plate.

"Don't be too sure of what Makho intends," he said. "Remember, he's not the Con-el now. He's Asharya. Makes a difference."

"And you're his Singer." Her gray eyes slitted as if to get a better fix on him. "Does that make a difference?"

He offered her his open hand. She brushed her fingers over the palm, but instead of real contact, she took his hand and bit it gently.

"A slightly different flavor. Maybe just the dirt." So he knew she was joking. Mostly joking—there was a slight warning in the bite. They trusted him now, but they did not want him to change into something they would not be so sure about.

10

They stayed in the camp a few days, long enough to rest, resupply, and mend equipment. Every hour they stayed, they watched the sky, expecting more vitos. Everyone agreed they should leave soon.

They argued about which route to choose. The Riders feared the road and would have preferred to leave the trucks and take the horses back into the hills. But their newfound companions argued that the weapons and supplies they could carry by truck were too precious to be left behind, and Kruger agreed with them. Reluctantly the Rider captains conceded that the snow was deep and treacherous this close to the mountains, that it would be hard to make any speed through the drifts. In the end they decided to take the trucks as far up the road as they could, sending scouts ahead of them to give a warning if anyone else moved on the road.

The Deltans assumed the silangh would be left behind, but on that point they had to yield. Kata, grave in his new responsibility as herdmaster, culled the herd to prepare them for travel. Some of the animals had to be slaughtered, the meat cut in strips and frozen to supplement the provisions they had salvaged from the camp. Kata went through the herd on foot, walking right up to the skittish animals to scratch around their horns and rub their noses, choosing those which would have to die.

"He's young, but he's good," Singer told Kruger as they sat on horseback, watching. "He has a good feeling for the herd. With such a herdmaster you would be rich in cattle, and the kettles on the hearth would be full of meat."

Kruger shrugged. "Farm animals don't interest me," he said.

Singer's horse flexed his neck and sidestepped, showing off his pride, pulling at the bit, challenging his rider and at the same time showing his confidence in the hand that would meet the challenge. Singer stroked the muscles under the rough mane with his free hand, and the horse shook its head as if answering an unspoken word.

The pleasure in that gesture turned over Kruger's memories like a plow cutting through the ground. He remembered how the wet, turned earth had a shine to it like the sheen on a good horse.

I was a farm boy once, before I went to war. Before the war came to me. And now I'm an old man with nothing to show for my life but dead men's ashes.

"God curse all soldiers," he said aloud, and the horse jumped under him at the sudden pressure of his knees. He wheeled it to face Singer. "Damn you, stay out of my head."

Singer lowered his head in the pacifying Thanha way. "I'm truly sorry, Grandfather. Did I say something that caused offense?"

"You don't have to. You don't even have to look at me. I know what you're thinking. You won't let me lie to myself, and sometimes I need to lie to myself."

"You have courage for every wound but this one," Singer said. "You won't endure the pain of remembering what you used to love. I think we are all like that. We cut our homes out of our flesh like arrowheads, to survive, to go on fighting. But if you won't remember, how will you know what you're fighting for? Watch Kata, Con-el. You can learn from him."

He moved off down the hill and into the herd.

Most of the Deltans preferred to climb into the trucks, but some of them were teased into riding by their friends. Now that there were plenty of horses, the Riders played their old games up and down the road, racing and chasing, swinging on and off in midgallop, tossing a waterskin back and forth for miles without dropping it. The prisoners had not played in months or years, and few of them could resist, no matter how often they fell off and had to be swung back aboard by Riders doubled over with laughter. The games helped take the Riders' minds off the fact that they were following a road made by their enemies into enemy land.

Lyn had volunteered to take the vito out ahead of them. "They'll have to send a relief here sometime. Why leave the bird for them? We might want it ourselves one of these days."

She took a load of Riders with her, mocking them out of their hesitation. Singer feared for her, but she mocked him too.

"You make me Thanha and then you want me to be *careful*? Your mind is going, chico. Anyway, I don't plan to get into any trouble with nobody to help me out but these homeboys. I'll find a good landing space, and I'll come back to meet you. I won't go more than a couple of days past the end of the road; all these horses have spoiled me for walking."

She met them on the second day out. "I parked it on a flat riverbank about twenty miles northeast of here. It's high and dry now, but we should try to pick it up before snowmelt time. I don't know how far up the floods come around here.

"Before I set down, I took us up to the top floor and had a look around. There's nothing moving as far as I could tell. I saw some smoke way off toward the coast, and I wanted to check it out, but I was being careful. I would have had to lift over the mountains, and I don't trust the weather here. Can't say what it was—maybe a forest fire, or maybe the chica knows something I don't." She grinned at Roishe, who had ridden up with a spare horse as soon as she saw Lyn coming.

"How is it to fly in the sky?" the child asked as Lyn swung up into the saddle. "How does it feel?" She reached out to touch Lyn's hand. "Please tell me, barasha."

"There's only one thing better, and you're too young for it."

"Will you take me into the sky someday?"

Lyn was about to gallop up to the head of the line but checked herself when she saw that Roishe was serious. "Not this season, little one. There are too many enemies waiting for us there. But when the sky is safe, I'll take you higher than the birds." Over the child's head, Lyn looked at Singer. "Keep us alive till next year and I swear I'll make a pilot out of this baby."

She dug in her heels and whistled to Roishe, and the two of them galloped off together.

Ripples of interest moved through the column of mounted Riders behind them. Those who had been in the sky with Lyn told their story over and over, and the hearers repeated it up and down the line.

"She let me hold its guidestick," one young Rider boasted. "It pitched in the air like a greenbroke colt, and it hummed like a swarm of bees in a cave. She showed me how to move the guide, and the thing obeyed me. It isn't magic. It's a thing made by people for people. It's a thing we could learn. *Ayei*, my words are not enough! You must go there, too. To see from the eagle's height—it's like being on the Heroes' Road and still alive! I'd have to be a Singer to show you."

Singer looked back to mark the speaker so he could talk to him later. The young Rider's eyes were shining as if he had seen something holy.

The advance scouts met them with the news that the road ahead would soon be impassable for the trucks. They unloaded the remaining stores and repacked them on horses. Then Kruger let the drivers pick their own way. They headed downhill, behind a ridge where the trucks would not be easily seen from the road. Halfway down, they hit ice and slid to the bottom.

"You won't get them out of there till spring," one of the drivers said, looking back after he had struggled up to the road on foot.

Kruger shrugged. "If you don't have a road, you don't need trucks. The main thing is to deny them to the NPU if they come to recover their property."

The drivers mounted and rode with the rest of them. The road was still visible, but only as a track, not wide or level enough even for the wagons of the cityfolk. As they came closer to the southern edge of the mountains, snowdrifts piled deeper, spilling over the path.

Kruger pushed them on as fast as he could. They rose before dawn and set up camp quickly as the last lees of sunset faded from the pale hills. Kruger was driven day and night by the fear of NPU reprisal. His ears strained to catch the first hint of vitos coming over the horizon. Singer shared his urgency. The original Riders did not know exactly what their Asharya had to fear, but they understood that he needed haste from them. That understanding spread through Singer and his hearth down to the youngest of the pallantai, and even the children drove themselves without complaint. Because he was a stranger, because women and children were present, Kruger had expected resistance. Day by day he was surprised by their quick response. He felt as if he had picked up an alien weapon and found it balanced and agile in his hand.

11

After days of breaking trail through the snow, they finally rounded the tail of the mountains and began to travel north. The closer he came to his old home, the more restless Singer became. Finally he visited Kruger formally when no others of his hearth were present.

"A little way north of here there's a trail on the mountainside that will take you up the Saddle. Some of the pallantai should know it. The snow will be deep there, but it's only a few more days to travel. Then you'll be in the old grazing lands of the Rock, beyond the mountains. You'll be as safe there as you can be anywhere, I think. You should be able to live from the herds till spring. You'll get most of them over the pass. Be sure to stay off the road. The Somostai built it, and the cityfolk used it. You'd be in danger there."

"That sounds reasonable enough," Kruger said. "But I notice you keep saying 'you.' "

"I'm hoping you'll wait for me, so I wish you a safe place to wait in. I'm going down to the city."

"I don't hear that," Kruger said. "I didn't hear it, and I'm not going to hear it!" It was a Thanha phrase that had sounded strange at first, but suddenly he found it useful.

"You must hear my heart when it speaks, Makho. Zhanne is our kamarh. Her brother is bound in that city. It's not for our honor to leave him there."

"God in heaven, I know that. But if anything happens to you, we'd lose what little chance we've got. For the sake of one man you'd risk all of us.''

Singer took Kruger's hand in the gesture the Deltan still flinched from.

''I was imprisoned in the city of my enemies, and Zhanne set me free. I can never forget that. One man, ten men, a hundred—numbers are important when you reckon with machines. This one man is Zhanne's blood and bone. He cries in her dreams, and I hear him. While he is captive, I am not free.''

The memory he laid against Kruger had an edge like a white-hot knife. For a moment Kruger was restrained hand and foot, drugged but still in agony and in fear that was worse than the physical pain: the terror of being helpless among incomprehensible strangers. Kruger thrust the feeling away from him as if they were sparring with weapons.

''What's all this shit about how I'm the Asharya now? Does that mean anything at all? You're twisting me around like a piece of string.''

Singer let the memory fade and leaned back against Kruger's knees. ''If you forbade me, Makho, I would not go.''

''Fine. That makes it very simple.''

''But you will not forbid me.''

Kruger waited for him to continue the argument. Singer did not say anything. He left Kruger to flounder along on his own.

''We need you here, and you know it. Does the Singer leave at a time of danger?''

''It is not ordinary. Hilurin used to go back to the city every winter to gather knowledge for Grandmother. He went back last spring, knowing that something bad would happen soon, needing the knowledge more than he needed to be with us. Had Grandmother put more faith in him, maybe the Rock would have lived. She was wise, but she couldn't quite believe that anything so strange and terrible as you Delh'tani could be real. As it was, she believed in time to cast me away—one last arrow from the string as horse and archer fall.''

His sorrow moved through the tent like wind, weightless and implacable.

''Let me go, Grandfather, and without your anger dragging at my heels. We can't hide forever. My people never knew what killed them. Maybe I can learn something that will save us, this time. This time the People must live.''

''This isn't the way to find out.''

Singer hid the anger and confusion of his heart in a smooth, calm face, eyes averted so the Asharya would not take offense.

"I have not forgotten the words Cold Eyes spoke before he died. Have you?"

"Cold Eyes?" Kruger looked puzzled, and Singer remembered that the man he had killed had another name among his own people.

"Your Net jefe. The Security commander. Gero." He shivered. Saying that name brought back unreasonable fear. He knew that Gero was dead, yet he could still see those ice-colored eyes staring down at him.

"Sometimes I think I hear his voice. He said, 'If they have broken the treaty—if the Nupis are arming the natives against us—' He was not stupid. The child Roishe dreams that strangers build with iron in the city I saw destroyed. Your enemies and mine have joined together.

"I know why you want to hide, Makho. You think if we move against Delh'tani at all, sooner or later we will have to fight your own people. If you don't turn me loose now to find out what is happening, I think the Somostai and the Union will kill both your people and mine."

Kruger bowed his head then, and Singer knew that he had won.

Persuading the rest of his hearth to let him go was not so easy. Saldivar did not argue about the wisdom of going to the city, but he simply refused to speak about staying behind. He let Singer know by his silence that there would be no discussion.

Janet had already guessed at what he was thinking and was prepared for him. "What would you do if it was your brother? Would you wait here for someone else to find him? No Rider would think of such a thing! If you were a child of ten summers and claimed your right to go, no one would insult you by saying no."

"It's for his sake I ask you, too," Singer said in a low voice. He turned his face away; so much conflict with a kamarh was hard to endure. "Two of us can go faster than three. And Palha and I are used to warfare."

"Oh, and I'm not? Who was it that blew up the airfield at North Fork? Who shot those chucks who ambushed us at my place in Jefferson? Who saved your ass from the PCOM building? Did Lyn and I do that, or was it some army of trained warriors that I didn't see?"

"This is different. Besides, Makho needs you here."

"Marcus is well able to take care of himself. His Thanha's not as good as mine, but it's adequate. He is the Asharya now, without any doubt. He has the loyalty of his captains. There's no medical emergency, and anyway, he's got Morne, who is as competent as I am, and maybe more so under these conditions."

She moved around him till she was in his line of sight again. "I am going. And you will not forbid me."

He made an effort to speak calmly. "The city is dangerous."

She stared at him in disbelief. "You weren't afraid to walk into PCOM armed with a couple of knives and burn the place down. What can be so bad about this little city? It was bombed to rubble, anyway—wasn't it? I'm not afraid."

"Maybe you would be if you had more sense," Saldivar said. He took the edge off his restlessness by flipping his knife into the doorpost over and over again, with barely controlled force.

"Anyway, if I were, it wouldn't matter. I dream Jon every night. I have to get to him."

The urgency of the dream was so strong that Singer reluctantly shared the image. There was the face so disturbingly like Janet's, the shaved head, the haunted eyes, dark as the black robe that clothed Jon. A bitter taste leapt into his mouth: the taste of intense fear barely restrained by desperate pride. He felt the darkness pressing in with tangible weight and seemed to hear a voice within the darkness, whispering things he did not want to know. Jon's nightmares so intimately matched his own that once again he pulled back, roughly breaking away from Janet's offered touch. He knew that he was sweating and that his attempts to straighten his face had failed.

"What's wrong?"

She searched his face, but he held out against her and revealed nothing. If he allowed her to enter the shadows, he would have to confront them himself, and he feared that more than anything.

"The city has taken many things from me. City soldiers killed Risse, the first I ever loved. The blackrobes killed my brother. Now you want me to risk you, too. If I had my way, no one would go with me. Not even Palha. Least of all Palha. The city is dangerous."

"I am coming with you," she said quietly. "The more you talk like this, the more determined I become. The danger is not in the city. The danger is in you."

He turned away from her without speaking and plunged out through the tent flap into the night. It was an unforgivable breach of courtesy for a Rider. It was an insult to her. But he had to get away. Her eyes were too accurate.

"I can't believe you're doing this," Saldivar said. He flipped his knife into the doorpost again with mechanical precision.

"What am I doing that's so terrible? I don't see you offering to stay behind."

He shrugged. "He's tied in knots. You're making it worse."

"Correction: I'm trying to help, and he won't let me."

Saldivar threw the knife again, harder. The point knocked splinters from the post but spun aside and fell to the floor. He swore as he leaned over to retrieve it.

"You know I'm right," she said. "He's doing the same thing to you."

Saldivar tested the point to make sure it was undamaged and put the knife away. He sighed. "Yeah. Sorry. What is it, you think?"

"I can't tell. There's something in the city that seems more dangerous to him than weapons or armed men. But I think it's not what he'll find there but what he'll find in himself if he goes there."

Saldivar made the Thanha hand sign for "great confusion."

"Too right, paliao," she said. "That's another reason why I'm not going to let you two go alone. Sooner or later you will need me."

"Not your kind of mission, Janney."

"Oh, hell. It's like having two brothers right here! You chucks are acting just like Jon! He's five minutes older than me, but he acts as if it's five years. He thinks he's protecting me, but in reality he's only making himself feel important. And ensuring his own safety—because in his heart he's convinced that he's the one who can't get along without me, not the other way around."

Saldivar made the sign for surrender. "I get it, Janney. I know you have to come. I just wish you didn't have to."

Lyn put up token resistance, but Singer could tell that her heart was not in it. She had been happy among the Riders. She rode, danced, hunted, and sparred with weapons as if she had been born to it. She was never without company among the younger pallantai, always in demand. She and Ilyun had become close friends, and Roishe was always with her. She hated and feared the thought of being put back within walls as much as any Rider did. Singer knew that if he gave her a good reason to stay behind, she would reluctantly accept it.

"Zhanne will not listen to reason. If she comes with us, I need you here. I have no other way to speak with Makho. Perhaps one day I can find him from beyond the mountains, but I have never tried it. I know that I can call you if we are in trouble."

She narrowed her eyes for a minute, guessing that he was pushing her into the decision, then shrugged and acquiesced anyway.

Singer broke the news to the pallantai in the morning. They had known that the Asharya was making some important decision. It was better to tell them the result, sweet or bitter, than to leave them wondering.

The Riders watched him wide-eyed. He could feel their anxiety; they had recovered some security since he had come, and by leaving he was threatening that again. To encourage them, he made a fine story of it: a search for a lone brother, a quest into enemy territory, a raid after weapons that could bring them victory. Soon, he was relieved to see, their eyes went to Kruger. They had accepted him as their Asharya. Even without a Singer, they would trust him.

"Once you climb the Saddle," he told Kruger, "you'll be crossing over into Rock country. The land is empty now, mourning them. It will welcome you. When you are settled there, send out messengers to the other Rider groups: Tall Grass People, River People. Your captains can tell you where to find them. Talk with them about an alliance. If the flying people come after us again, we will survive better if we fight together."

While camp was breaking up, Singer took off his newly won ornaments and turned them over to Lyn for safekeeping. Saldivar followed suit.

"I hate this, I really hate it," Lyn said gloomily. "If you let yourselves get killed, don't think I'll avenge you. I'll spit on your graves and call you a trio of stupid meatheads."

"I'm glad you're speaking Delteix, isé," Singer said. "This is a kind of joking the Riders don't really understand."

"Yeah, yeah, I know. Going off to war is a sacred privilege to them. Fuck that." Suddenly she turned and hugged him so tightly that he could hardly breathe. "Sorry," she muttered into his shoulder. "I guess I'm not as much of a Rider as I thought."

"It comes with the gift," Janet said. "Knowing what you have to lose."

"Shut up," Lyn said, embracing her.

Ilyun came over with Roishe by her side. "If you could spare a keepsake for the child," she said shyly.

Roishe's eyes glittered as she accepted the bracelet Singer gave her. "If they hurt you, they'll be sorry," she said. "I'll keep you in my mind always and make you the biggest deathgift there ever was."

Ilyun snapped her fingers quickly to scare off bad luck. "You don't say that while he's right here looking at you! Such words call the crows!"

"I will, though, anyway," Roishe muttered under her breath.

Singer looked after her with admiration as Ilyun hustled her away. "If I'd known her before, I wouldn't have worried so much over that little scratch she had. It would take more than a Delh'tani fire weapon to kill that child!"

When he turned back to his friends, he found Kruger standing there with his hand on Saldivar's shoulder.

"I hope you saved a gift for me," Kruger said. "Because if you didn't, I'll have to pull rank and take one."

"It's not the custom for the Asharya to take ornaments," Singer said. "He has to look ahead for all of us; he can't be burdened with a deathgift for any one of the pallantai."

"Then I'm breaking the custom," Kruger said. "What are you going to do—fire me?" Singer thought he was coughing and then realized that Kruger was cracking a dry, old man's laugh. "Give—all of you. And hurry up; I can't wait here all day while you get sentimental."

There was a murmur of commentary as he walked away, the Riders taking notice of the great honor he had done those three. More hands reached out for a token from the heroes. In the end they ran out of ornaments before the group around them had thinned out. Singer felt good to know that so many hearts would be with them on the journey.

At last the crowd melted away and left them to make their final preparations. Their only weapons were plain belt knives that had been won from the cityfolk and could pass without comment. They changed every remaining scrap of Deltan manufacture for well-worn plain garments. They found plain woven cloaks without any telltale Thanha decoration.

"I'm afraid you'll be cold," Singer apologized. "But in sheepskin and high boots, anyone who saw us would know we were Riders."

They hid some rations in their clothes; Singer did not want to wear packs that would make them look like travelers with a destination in mind. They took a blanket each, rolled under their cloaks, but that was all. It did not take long to finish packing.

They watched the Riders mount up. Then they slogged downhill through the snow while the column pulled out without them. The muffled drumming of hoofbeats on packed snow faded slowly, until they were alone with the vast silence of the hills in winter.

II Serving the Iron Master

1

Singer pushed through knee-deep snow to the crest of a steep ridge and saw the city. Less than a year before he had seen the smoke of the burning city rise in black plumes that towered up past the peaks. All below him should have been darkness and ruins. Instead he saw lights everywhere: not only the flickering orange of camp fires but the harsh white light produced only by otherworldly machines.

He was still staring when Saldivar and Janet caught up with him.

"What is it?" Janet asked wearily.

"The city." He felt like whispering, though it was impossible that anyone down there could hear him. Sullen sunset light bled through rips in the cloud, far out to sea in the west. In the valley below it was already night. Yet beyond a cordon of small white lights the sky glowed red, briefly silhouetting bulky dark shapes.

"Those are perimeter lights like the ones around the camp we attacked," Saldivar said. "But what the hell is *that*?"

"A fire?" Janet suggested.

"Maybe," Singer said. But the light was a pulsing glow with something purposeful about it. A low roar of sound came up to them with the wind. He had expected to find signs of life, but he had never imagined anything so strange, so completely unknown to him.

"The city was dead," he whispered. "I saw it burning. Now something in it lives again. Your enemies have come to the city, even as I feared."

I told you so, said the faint cold whisper in his mind. *Now will you listen to me?*

107

He heard it. He could no longer deny that he was hearing it, but he pushed it away, buried it down deep without answering it. Answering would give it power.

Janet huddled in layers of wool shirts under her ragged cloak. Singer had put on boots as a concession to the weather, but his blanket cloak fluttered open in the wind as he stretched to see farther into the valley.

"How can you do that?" she asked enviously.

He crouched down in the lee of the rocks, wondering how to shelter his companions for the night. Traveling alone, he would have reached the city before dark.

"Partly it's just getting used to it," he said. "The young ones are hardened in their weapon training. I had more. I spent a year with the healers. They taught me the beginnings of what they know about the body. Learning not to be cold was one of the very first things. There are ways—" He shook his head in frustration. "Don't know how to explain."

"Could you teach me?"

"I can't even find the words to tell myself how. I have it in my bones but not in my thoughts. They showed me. They set me to work that was pointless till it suddenly made sense. I'm no teacher. If we had peace, if we had time, I could ask those who are teachers—Morne, the other old ones. Maybe they could tell. But there's no peace, no time."

He began to pack rocks and snow into a windbreak. The other two followed his example and worked in silence for a while. Singer thought of the weeks and months he had spent as a boy, shirtless and barefoot, in a trance of cold and hunger, running till the light faded and his legs folded under him, of hours spent motionless and blindfolded, day after day, matching his breath and movements to the teacher he could not see. Was it possible to teach anyone what he had experienced? He thought Zhanne might learn. She was clever with words, but she saw beyond the words, too, got inside the skin.

He had not allowed them to bring any supplies or equipment with them. Such things gave too many clues to the owners' origins. They had a couple of blankets tied around them under their cloaks. They spread those on the ground and huddled together. They shivered constantly, too cold to sleep. Singer wished he had gathered wood while it was still light. Doing without a fire might be riskier than lighting one; he was afraid they would be frostbitten by dawn.

He had automatically started to warm his own body. Feeling

the others shivering on either side of him, he warmed himself still more, trying to take the chill off them. It was not enough, he realized.

Cautiously he reached out, through the skin huddled against him. Drifting in a stupor of weariness, they put up no resistance. He drew carefully on memories of sunlit beaches and summer noons, as if blowing on embers. Their hearts gradually beat faster as bloodwarmth pushed out to constricted fingers and toes. But that was no good unless he could light the fires that made the body warm. He whispered to them along the intricate nets of the blood rivers and those other nets that sparked like Delh'tani wire. *Get warm.* He felt the tension in their muscles ease as they fell asleep.

He woke up before dawn and let them sleep on while he stretched himself alert and thought about what to do next. The lights in the city below still glowed, as if the people there never slept. While he crouched at the edge, looking down, he heard Janet and Saldivar getting up, shaking out the blankets and getting ready for the road.

He passed them strips of dried meat that had been warmed and softened a bit by being carried close to the skin. They chewed it as they walked and swallowed the juice.

"Leather-flavored chewing gum," Saldivar said. "I'm surprised the Forces haven't discovered this."

The city was still visible below them for a while as they descended. Singer pointed with a stick as if it were a map laid out before them.

"There, somewhat north of the center, stood the master's Great House and its buildings. Dona described it to me. He spoke of storage houses, armories, great halls, and an underground of which even he knew little, beyond the prison rooms where Hadhla was pleased to keep some of those who had displeased him. All that was aboveground is fallen, I think, save perhaps some walls and corners. I saw that with my own eyes. All around the Great House stood lesser buildings—places belonging to the rich and great. That half ring where you see more burned timber and less stone was places belonging to merchants and craftsmen needed by the great. Near the wall, all about, both inside and outside, those were the places they called Lowtown. I wonder if the fire from the sky left anything of that warren untouched."

* * *

Going downhill seemed easier at first but was not. They slid and floundered, never sure if there was a firm surface beneath the snow or not. They were wet and snow-caked to the neck before they came to firmer ground.

After a steep slope of several hundred feet, the path leveled out somewhat and the going was easier. However, once out of the rocks, their position was exposed. Singer hoped that the dun color of their clothes would make them hard to see. He doubted that anyone would bother to keep watch on the mountainside. If they were spotted by chance, he had confidence that they would be able to take defensive measures before assailants from below could clamber up to them.

Soon they reached a point from which they could see the road that ran directly to the city gate. It curved away empty and silent. Still, Singer moved cautiously as he slipped down to investigate. He left Saldivar and Janet out of sight.

"No one on it now," he reported, "but there are many layers of tracks. Great troops of people came this way, many before the snow, some after. I see marks of soft shoes, wooden soles like the ones some farmers wear, feet shod with rags, and some barefoot. There's blood in the snow. Most tracks are men, but some are smaller—could be women or children. There are shod hoof marks of war-horses and boots, some of them walking to the side and some bringing up the rear—their tracks are on top of the others. But there are no boot soles with Delh'tani designs on them, so if any of your people were here, they wore cityfolk clothing."

"Well, what do you conclude from all this?" Janet asked.

"Armed men escorted great troops of people into a city that I thought was dead a year ago. Perhaps they went willingly and the soldiers were for protection. But I doubt it. Why, then? That is what we must learn."

"Are we going to march down that road and knock on the gate?" Saldivar said. He was cold, hungry, and impatient to move on.

"South Road used to run from Iron City down toward the seacoast, past City of Gulls, then through fields and marshes to Rivermouth City. I have followed that road. People of the Rock fought for the master of the Iron City most of the summers I rode with the pallantai. This year he's dust. Road's still there, but you won't find me on it. If I must walk into this trap, I'll find some other way."

Janet cast a longing eye on the smooth road as they crossed it and plunged down the embankment into more snowdrifts on the downhill side. They made their way laboriously down the mountainside, always keeping to ravines and low places where the snow was thickest. The snow made every movement difficult. They began to sweat in spite of the cold, and then, when they stopped to rest, panting and exhausted, the moisture froze in their hair and chilled them to the bone.

Eventually, when they glimpsed the city again, it was above them and to the northeast rather than below them. They had swung in a wide circle around its southern edge, creeping unobserved. Then Singer began to pick a path toward the city, working his way with great caution over the uneven ground. As they came closer, the ground became smoother and flatter. They found themselves walking through cleared areas that seemed to have been plowed fields once. The lumpy furrows had frozen hard and were easy going after ravines and rockfalls covered with snow.

There, at last, they saw people.

At first Singer did not recognize them as such. They crouched close to the ground, scuffling in the snow like animals hunting for food. Then one of them saw the strangers and leapt up. On their feet, they were recognizable as humans—barely. Singer guessed by their size that they were children. They were bundles of rags on stick legs. The largest bundle stepped in front of the others, spreading out thin arms in feeble protection.

"Who are you?" The voice was hoarse and did not carry far, but he thought it was a woman's. "We have *nothing*." She spoke Giristiyah, the language of Singer's city childhood.

"We are strangers, travelers," he answered awkwardly in the same language. The words tasted bad in his mouth, sour as the memory of a long-forgotten nightmare. "We have enough to share."

He held out a handful of dried meat strips. She drew closer and took them with a swift glance at his face to make sure he would not strike her for daring. Swallowing hard, she stowed the food somewhere under her rags. Behind her the children shuffled their blue feet in the snow. One of them began to cry, a thin wail as monotonous as breathing and as little regarded.

"What do you want?" the woman asked.

"News. When I last saw the Iron City, it was burning. Now many people are living here. Why? Where have you come from, and how do you live here in these ruins?"

The woman stepped back, looking around warily. "Run away,

stranger. You look tall and strong. You won't be so for long if the blackrobes find you. They take the men to the mines and the place of burningstone. They don't come back.''

''Take me where you live and tell me about the blackrobes, and I give more food,'' Singer said. ''My friend here is a healer. She will tend your children while we talk. If the blackrobes take us, how does that harm you?''

In her dead eyes he saw a spark of hunger for something more than food. The coming of three strangers had broken an endless chain of wretched days. She craved hope from them, and Singer's words hinted that they might give it. She reached out and tugged at Singer's sleeve.

''Hurry, hurry.''

She pushed the children along in front of her. They followed a narrow pathway trodden in the snow from the edge of the field to what had been the outskirts of the city, until they found themselves under cover in a snow-mounded labyrinth of fallen stones, craters, and half-burned timbers. Singer saw that the rubble held dwellings; he noticed the smell and then the curious eyes peering out at them from rag-curtained doorways or around broken walls. The curious ones seemed to be mostly children and were quickly yanked out of sight again as they passed.

The woman took them through one such doorway into a dug-out shelter. It seemed to have been built by roofing over remnants of stone walls with half-burned timbers and mounding dirt over the result. It stank and it was dark, but it was warmer than outside. Coals smoldered on a corner of the dirt floor. The woman stirred them up and added sticks and pieces of board.

''There's no lack of wood scraps, but you have to scrape in the litter to find them,'' she said.

The children brought out their scavengings and laid them on a plank that served as table and storage shelf. Their forage amounted to an apronful of withered roots.

The woman placed the meat Singer had given her next to the roots. She could hardly take her eyes off it, but the children paid no attention, as if they did not know what it was.

A battered pot sat by the fire, full of half-melted snow. She set it on the fire, and soon it was boiling. Once the smell of cooked meat began to fill the room, the children squatted around the hearth as if they could have fed on the scent alone. The woman gave them each a bowl of broth and a little meat and put the rest in a dish in a nook beyond the children's reach.

Janet produced a small bottle and squeezed a few drops of some liquid into each bowl.

"I told you not to bring things that would mark us as strangers," Singer said.

She shrugged. "Well, I notice you didn't leave your knives behind. This is just a tool of my trade. Nutritional field supplement and antiparasite medication."

Singer refused food but accepted hot water to make tea, which he shared with the woman. The others ate little: With every bite they felt the children's eyes on them, and their hunger seemed to die.

The taste of tea brightened the woman's eyes, and the sight of the children eating softened her face. Singer could see that she was not as old as she had first appeared.

Janet was already squatting on the floor with the children, beginning to woo them into letting her check their swollen bellies and sore-pocked limbs. "Ask her if these are all hers," she said.

"They are mine now," the woman said. "No one else wants them."

"Tell me your name and how you came here," Singer said.

"Selem, Olmalik's woman. We are not from this gods-forsaken place. We lived by the bend in the river, south of the second ford. We paid taxes to the Rivermouth City, but we didn't go there. We minded our farm and troubled no one. Soldiers burned our place in the troubles last summer. At harvest time more soldiers came, with blackrobes ordering them, took what we had left, and drove us like cattle north to this place.

"Took our cattle, too," she added as an afterthought. "Things that flew, like big birds, only they made a noise like giant buzzing insects—they drove the cattle."

"Why? What do they want from you?"

"They separated the men from us right away and took them into the city. The women and children were put to work at first, gleaning what was left in the fields. We plowed and planted winter wheat in some of them, but it was late in the year for that. As long as there was food to gather, we saw the men sometimes. The Somostai would come to collect the food, and they might bring a couple of our men along to carry the load. We heard they were forced to work in the mines and in a place of burningstone full of fires that killed many.

"The blackrobes said they'd give us rations in return for work. At first we ate from what we gathered in the fields. It wasn't much, but maybe better for some than what they would have found on their own. But now there's almost nothing left for gleaning, and they don't come to give us anything. I think they mean to starve us."

"Why don't you run away?"

Selem gave him a disgusted look. "Where can we go? Stranger, do you know how far we walked at summer's end from that bend in the river? How far do you think we'd get, going back in the dead of winter without shoes or food? They have no need to guard us. They know that cold and hunger have walled us in tighter than any fence."

Singer sat and thought for a minute. "If I said I would go and see your men and take a message to them, could you show me how to get there without being caught?"

Selem put her hand over her mouth, and her eyes opened wide. "Why would you do that?"

"My name is Singer. I come from the Riders. My friends here are from the flying people. They're not all bad, and they are not all allies of the blackrobes. The blackrobes have taken the healer's brother prisoner. He is somewhere in the city, and we have come to find him."

He stopped as he saw that she was not listening to his explanation. She was still stuck on his first statement.

"From the Riders?" she said, almost whispering. "You are one of the renegades? But you look like an ordinary person. You speak like one of us."

He caught the images in her mind: bloodied savages sweeping across fields like a hailstorm, creatures who appeared like demons summoned by the warmasters and vanished like ghosts when their destructive work was finished. It shocked him. He knew that cityfolk had a distrust of Riders, but he had never confronted it at such close range. It seemed more than distrust. She feared and hated his kind. He could not understand why.

"You serve the City Masters in their wars," she said passionately, as if she had heard his thought. "How can you be on our side?"

"I rode with the war host, but I never hurt anyone but soldiers, nor knew anyone who did."

"Oh, no! Only destroyed what little we had, trampled our crops, burned our fields, opened the way for the soldiers."

"I knew a woman who came from the farms. Her name with us was Shallas. She came to the Riders for refuge. She didn't hate us. I was born in the city. That's how I know the language.

My father sold me to the Somostai, but the Riders rescued me. If you and your children came to us asking, we'd share what we have with you.''

"Yes, make us horse-riding demons with sharp weapons.''

Singer tried to shrug away her words. They brought back memories of the young pallantai, hardly more than children, forced to fight and die to keep the People alive. Surely it was right; it was the Rider way. But it was painful to remember.

"If you shared our life, you'd take the bitter and the sweet together. Riders hunted down the meat you ate. Is it so heavy in your belly?''

She swallowed the last of her tea gingerly, as if it might have some poison herb in it. "We are between two millstones as it is. If we mix ourselves into renegade affairs, we will surely be crushed.''

"You're being crushed now. You're rotting away here like so much garbage.''

Suddenly he was tired of arguing. If she believed he was a demon, nothing he could do would change her mind. "If you don't want to help us, we don't need you. We'll find our way as best we can. Maybe you don't know how to get into the city, anyway. It would be just like cityfolk to let their loved ones be dragged away without even trying to find out what happened to them.''

That got her attention back. "We know where they are. But if I help you, how do I know you won't make things worse for them? You might do something to bring down the wrath of the Somostai so they would kill us all. Riders take no thought for the fate of any other kind of people. You think more of your horses than of us.''

No one had ever spoken to Singer that way. She was right; he had never wondered about the thoughts of farmers and cityfolk. Riders were not concerned with such things.

"How much food do you have?'' she asked suddenly.

"Enough to keep ourselves for a few days. Not enough to feed all of you.''

"I'm going to speak to my neighbors about this. Their men are in the city, too. I can't make this decision without them. And I can't ask them here and not share with them.''

Singer still did not understand why she fussed over such a small risk compared to the misery she already suffered, but he could not help feeling respect for her. He had always thought that cityfolk were selfish, hoarders of goods who shared with no one. Selem spoke like a Rider and showed wisdom, too, in calling in the strength of her friends for planning. The black-robes had not yet defeated her spirit. It made him curious to meet her man.

Saldivar finally became impatient, listening to them speak in Giristiyah and catching only parts of Singer's reaction to the conversation. "What are you saying?"

Singer explained briefly while Selem boiled another pot of water and sent some of the children to wash and scrape the roots and others to carry messages to her friends.

"She's calling a council, I think."

Soon women and children crowded into the tiny room till there was no space left. They carried their bowls with them. They cast curious glances at the strangers, but there was no talking till they had eaten. Then Selem made a long speech, which Singer translated for Janet and Saldivar.

"I hope she's not promising more than we can do. She's reminding them that running away is hopeless unless they can get their men back, and she is holding out hope that if we get to their men, some way of passing messages may be set up."

A strong discussion followed. Some of the other women felt that the strangers should be stopped, with force if necessary, from interfering. Others suggested bribing them to guide at least a few of the young children to safety. Some thought it would be better to send their children away to the Riders than to see them die. Others thought the Riders were demons in human shape, capable of killing and eating the children of cityfolk. The discussion quieted when Selem reminded them that the Rider in question was sitting within earshot and that he had not expressed an intent to save or eat anybody. In an hour Singer learned more than he had ever known about cityfolk.

"Your proposal is accepted," Selem told him as her guests crowded through her narrow doorway. "Tonight I take you into the city."

Before nightfall word got around that a woman with medicine was in the camp. The mothers with their sick children could not form a line as they would have if Janet had been conducting a field clinic in Deltan territory, but they came furtively, ducking in and out of cover and waiting their turn in the huts that neighbored Selem's place. With a defiant glance at Singer, Janet brought out her armaments: more nutritional drops, Deltan antibiotics and antiparasite medications, antiseptics, and an assortment of small bundles containing herbs that Morne had given her. She demanded a tribute of rags from those who came and boiled them in Selem's spare pot to use as bandages. She had a crew of young ones scavenging more wood to keep hot water ready and a team of slightly older children scrubbing the little ones as fast as the water could be heated. To mothers who drew back in horror at the thought of disrobing and bathing their babies, she gave a fierce look and quelling comments in Delteix, which managed to make her point without translation.

"If anything infectious gets into this place, you'll have an epidemic in no time," she said to Singer. "I forgive them for not discovering antibiotics, but lice are not absolutely necessary, even in a prison camp. I wonder if I could get them to whittle me some combs."

"We're leaving tonight."

"All the more reason to do as much as I can today."

2

Around sunset Selem shooed away Janet's clients. One remained behind, a thin girl whose heavy dark hair hung around her face like a curtain. She hunched her shoulders as she moved, as if protecting or hiding something. Janet beckoned to her to come and be examined, but the girl pulled back. Her smock pulled against her body as she turned, and Janet realized that the girl was pregnant.

"Hey! Come here and let me check you."

The girl understood Janet's intent, if not her words, and stepped back. "Don't need a healer. I'm only here to guide you," she said in Giristiyah.

Selem shrugged. "Leave her alone," she said. "The baby

will die anyway, most likely. Best to let it die before it sees the light.''

''That's not your decision to make,'' Janet said when Singer had translated for her. ''Now, come here, you. I'm not going anywhere with you till you let me do my job. Ask her name, Singer.''

''Hegy,'' the girl said dully, as if the name were just another word.

Janet listened and palpated. ''Ask her if she has any idea how long she's been pregnant.''

''That I know,'' Selem said. ''The flying people wanted girls, so the blackrobes collected some and took them up to the Black City. The man who had Hegy sent her back when her belly swelled. That was maybe three months ago.''

''Healthy but small,'' Janet said. ''She needs more food.''

''Wisdom!'' Selem exclaimed sarcastically.

''Doctor,'' Hegy said in Delteix.

''What?'' Janet exclaimed. ''You speak Delteix?''

''I learn some words from the soldier,'' Hegy said. Her accent twisted the words, but they were understandable. ''He says baby is not his because no flying people can make. That's not truth. Is it?''

''Singer, try to explain to her what a contraceptive implant is. I don't know how. If he was Deltan military, he probably had one—I don't think Nupi policy is any different from ours. If he'd been out in the field long enough, his protection might have worn off, I suppose. So, yes, could be his baby whether he wants to admit it or not. Interesting. If so, that means our people are similar enough to interbreed. I would have assumed that from the physiology, but it would be interesting to have conclusive proof.''

''Do you want to go tonight or not?'' Selem demanded.

''Just a minute. Hegy, this is medicine to keep you as healthy as possible even without enough food. Vitamins. Swallow one every day. Understand?''

Hegy nodded and turned to lead them out. They set off on a twisting path through the rubble. One snow-covered hummock of sticks and rocks looked like another to Singer, but the women from the camp seemed to know their way. They drew slowly nearer to the city wall. Even in its half-ruined condition, it was a powerful barrier. Anyone trying to climb it would be easy to pick off. Singer had already decided that if the city women proposed to guide them up the wall, he would refuse. If he had to go that way, he could certainly do it more efficiently by himself. When they came to the foot of the wall, however, Hegy scurried along it, up and down the rubble heaps. She seemed to be finding her way by a series of sticks planted in the ground, apparently at random. She and Selem consulted several times before choosing their path.

Finally she ducked into a dark, tottering doorway that looked no different from any number of other holes. Inside it was completely dark. They followed her in a line, holding on to each other's clothing. There were several steps down, then a steep drop as if the rest of the stairs had fallen in. Saldivar skinned his knees stumbling over it. Janet fell on top of him and was not hurt.

"Where the hell are we?" Saldivar muttered.

"This was my master's house before the strangers burned the city," Hegy said. Without seeing her face, Singer thought he heard a fugitive pride in her voice. "He was a very rich man. Where there are walls, there's always some that will pay for a hole in them."

They seemed to be in a basement with a dirt floor, littered with rubble and debris. They felt their way across it to an opening. Singer put a hand on Saldivar's shoulder and felt that he was sweating, even in the cold. He knew that Saldivar did not like to be underground. Singer pushed ahead of his friend and examined the wall with his hands.

"It's all right, Palha, if you could see. It's just a doorway. Not like a tunnel. You can walk through upright."

On the other side they had to climb out, with some difficulty, through a tangle of timbers and burned wood. They made a lot of noise, and Singer was eager to seek cover on the far side. They made their way from one set of broken walls to another, through streets that had become troughs filled with rubble. Certain ways had been cleared, but Singer avoided those. If the Somostai had cleared them, the Somostai must be using them, and he had no wish to join them. About half a mile into the city they came to a building that had once possessed a second story. Taking the lead, Selem showed them how to climb the remaining timbers to a place where a corner of floor remained and would support them while they looked down onto a cleared street.

They could see across the city to the plateau of the strange dark shapes, north of the city, halfway between Erech Tolanh and the place where the Somostai lived. The rhythmic red glow Singer had seen before throbbed against the sky from something among those shapes. The dull roar that went with it vibrated through the earth into the stones they were clinging to. The glow looked like fire to Singer, but no one seemed alarmed by it, and he knew no fire that could burn unchecked for days.

They crouched there in the frosty cold of twilight and waited. The cleared street below them led to an open square.

"Beyond the square, that was Hadhla's Great House, I think," Singer said softly. "Do you see the guard fire? Keep watching. There are two soldiers there. You'll see them move."

"What could they be guarding?" Janet asked.

"They guard our men," Selem said when Singer had relayed the question. "They keep them inside somewhere, maybe down in the ground. There's not much left aboveground. Wait. You'll see them."

The next time Singer looked up toward the mountain, he saw red sparks that glowed and dimmed moving down in a wavering line. He guessed they were torches carried by someone on the road.

"Those are the workers coming back from that place of fire," Selem said. "They bring back half of them to sleep and make the others work all night. They must be demons. They never rest."

Singer heard shouts and the clang of iron on stone from across the square. Torches flickered there, as well. Soon a file of men came down the road past them at a trot. Selem leaned close to the edge of the wall, peering eagerly down at them. The prisoners were unchained, but city soldiers armed with long staves and whips paced and herded them as they hurried up the road to the plateau. They moved too fast for Singer to see much about them except that they were clothed in rags and moved wearily, only the fear of the whip keeping them in motion. After they had passed, he saw dark splotches in their trampled path—blood from bare feet in the snow.

"They'll pass the others on the road," Selem whispered. "In this time when there are no prisoners to guard over there, the soldiers go off to take a piss, or sometimes they fall asleep by the fire. It's not a good chance, but it's the best you'll get."

She saw Singer hesitate. "Are you afraid?" she goaded him.

Before he could answer, Hegy took hold of Janet's sleeve and began to talk to her rapidly in her Lowtown Giristiyah.

"Whoa, wait, I don't understand."

"She says it's bad, bad for women if they catch you. She says don't go there, you'll get hurt. She says you are kind and you don't know how bad they will be to you."

The hoarse, pleading sadness in the girl's voice got hold of Singer as he translated. He knew the truth of what she said, but he did not know how to make Janet listen.

"But I have to go. It's my brother in there."

"Do you feel him near?"

Janet hesitated and then shook her head. "No. Not here. But he is *somewhere* nearby. How can I find him if I don't take a chance?"

Singer leaned against her, shoulder to shoulder. Death was a small thing in the face of a hearth brother's need, so he put all fears for himself and plans for his people's future out of his mind.

"Zhanne, if you have to go there, we will go together. I do not believe that even three Riders can win against so many. But if anyone tries to hurt you, we will die gloriously together."

Janet looked confused for the first time. "But if we all die fighting, that won't help Jon."

Singer shrugged. "You will know yourself that you did the best you could. Success is not important, only the courage to try."

He had gone too far that time. She glared at him.

"Bullshit! Stop leaning on me! I see what you're up to."

"Who helps with baby if you go with them?" Hegy said in Delteix. "I have fear for me."

"If she goes back with us, we'll take care of her like gold," Selem said. "She's a great healer. Everybody knows that now."

"Do it, Janney," Saldivar said quietly. "You know they're right."

Janet tugged at her hair, her face screwed up in indecision.

At that moment Singer touched her in silent contact. *We cannot be parted. Not truly. You can speak to us anytime. First news of Jon, we come for you. Promise.*

Slowly she bowed her head, and Singer felt the fight go out of her.

"All right. I give in. You have work that only you can do, and the same for me. I see that. But may the Mother of God help you if you screw up. I will never forgive you."

Singer embraced her, as grateful as if she had given him a reprieve from death. Saldivar took his leave, and they climbed quickly down into the street before she could change her mind. Singer could feel her eyes on them until they disappeared from her view into the shadows. Even after that he felt her presence as a warm color in the back of his mind, some part of her traveling with them.

The breath of the city blew strong in their faces as they scrambled from one hiding place to the next. It smelled of things Singer had not tasted since leaving the Deltan settlements. There was a hot, greasy reek to it that smelled like petroleum to Saldivar and to Singer was only the scent of death-bringing strangers. Beneath the film of oil, the wind carried a tomblike smell of cold ashes. Singer could distinguish another overtone that Saldivar did not notice. The smoke was not just from wood and grass burning, an ordinary fire. It was acrid and dangerous; it told of a fire so hot that it could burn stone and metal, consume the earth itself. Fear burned in Singer like a wind-borne knot of coal lodged somewhere in his heart.

He steadied himself against a pile of debris that had been cleared out of the road. The feel of it against his hand was strange: not rough like rock or splintery like wood but smooth and round like baked clay or Delh'tani pahlastika—or bone. He snatched his hand away as Saldivar gasped "Shit!" Pale reflected light glimmered from a heap of skulls carelessly thrown aside from the more useful cut stone.

Saldivar rubbed his hand against his cloak in vigorous distaste. Singer moved away, but in his heart he knew that no rubbing or washing would take away the taint of death in the city. He was aware of bones beneath his skin, as if the empty sockets of a dead man were looking out through his own living eyes.

"Don't look at them," he said. "These are cityfolk. They belong to the Destroyer. The Destroyer of Flesh will look at you from dead men's eyes. Don't look."

"What are you talking about? Destroyer? What is that?"

Singer did not answer. He drew back from Saldivar's steadying hand. The city and all that it meant were only a year behind him, but it was a part of his past that Saldivar did not share.

They had come to the end of their cover and had no choice but to cross the road. The square ahead of them had been cleared, the salvaged stone rebuilt into low walls at the far end, roofed with sticks and thatch. Glaring white lights hung from poles, illuminating the open area.

"Do your blackrobes savvy electricity?" Saldivar whispered.

"Not last year. There are Delh'tani here."

The spotlights showed Singer the guards as two black blots

of shadow outlined against the wall. One of them rose and strolled off around the corner of a building, his shadow rising and shrinking as he skirted the light. The other stayed put behind the fire, so that it was hard to see whether he was awake. Singer could hear the trampling feet of the returning work group drawing quickly nearer. If they waited any longer, they would be seen by the marching soldiers as they crossed the street. He darted across, hoping the firelight would blind the guard to what happened beyond its circle.

They reached the edge of the square without being seen. Singer considered his next move. He would have liked to kill the seated guard. That would have made him some amends for the feel of bone that would not rub off his hands. But he did not think he could do that quickly without creating alarm. His hand closed on a chunk of stone. He lifted it carefully without shifting the rubble around it to make a noise and slung it high over the guard's head, toward the corner where the other man had gone. It rattled loudly enough in the sharp, cold air. The guard by the fire stood up and looked that way, and Singer took advantage of his inattention to lob another stone. The guard looked all around himself suspiciously, then strode quickly toward the sound, turning his back long enough for Singer and Saldivar to dance lightly over the broken stones and dive into the dark doorway beside the fire. They crouched on the steps within and listened as the guards came back. The soldiers argued uneasily about the source of the noises but shrugged them off in the end as the work of rats or dogs or stray children from the prisoner camp. Singer thought them fools. A Rider would have looked for tracks and found the story, but to city folk a few more tracks in the trampled square meant nothing.

The steps were smooth and broad underfoot. They felt their way forward in the dark at the bottom. The place smelled like a sty, but the air in it moved and seemed fresh. Their footsteps sounded clearly, as if they rang in a big space.

Singer stopped, and Saldivar bumped into his back. Singer's arms were outstretched, and Saldivar felt forward till he touched what Singer was leaning against: a wall. They felt across it till it made a right angle. The stones ahead of them had been joined roughly, the mortar spilling between the cracks. The wall stood between two others, both smooth and carefully fitted, like the floor.

Singer touched Saldivar's palm, his words a mere breath, scarcely audible. "I have been here before, I think. Or somewhere near here. This is a part of the Great House, the master's house. Somewhere in this house I found my brother dying."

His voice sank even lower, and Saldivar remembered the white bones cast away by the road. "I wonder where they laid him. If they found him. Wonder if his body is still here." Singer's hands dug into the wall as if he would try to rip it apart.

Before Saldivar could speak or touch him, the returning prisoners clattered and jostled their way down the stairs, and Singer whipped around to face them. He could see nothing, but he listened to how they filled the room and guessed at their number. Bodies bumped against him, looking for sleeping room. He and Saldivar had apparently taken someone's treasured space by the wall, and they had to do some emphatic shoving and kicking to secure the space for themselves.

By the time all the prisoners had settled down, the room was comfortably warm. Yet Singer lay back to back with Saldivar and felt him shivering. Palha was afraid of the dark. No—of the underground, of confinement beneath the weight of earth and stone. Singer felt his hearth brother's fear seeping into him. Or was it his own fear? He was locked in the dark with dead men who rose from the place where he had buried them and walked as ghosts through his memories.

Zhanne, he called, wondering if she could hear him through the oppressive weight of the fallen city. When he had almost given up, she was there, like a lit candle. The contact strengthened with a reassuring warmth like a spark taking hold in tinder.

You made it all right? he asked. But already he knew that she had. He was close enough to her senses to feel the constrained space of Selem's room around her.

Sorry I didn't catch you right away. I was lancing a boil. Her voice had the dry, sarcastic flavor that usually went with exhaustion. *I think that was the last of them. For tonight, anyway. I've set up a clinic, and tomorrow I'll be training myself some field-grade paras. I just did this with the Riders, and now I'm reinventing the wheel yet again!*

Singer showed her where they were. *Tell Selem I have not tried to find her man yet. I want to know something about him first. I want to look for Jon, if you will help me.*

She withdrew a little. *Just a minute. I'm almost done.*

He quieted his mind and let her memories come to him. He saw a young boy with a shock of dark hair, with small clever hands like Janet's, deftly sketching something on a paper that made her laugh. He saw Janet and her brother with a polvorado shirt, a Medicine Shirt, spread out between them. They had been amicably arguing about its ornamentation. The shirt was so embroidered, patched, and sewn with feathers and mirrors that the camouflage weave beneath hardly showed. Janet sewed on the last ornament: a mirror just above the heart.

Singer remembered that shirt. Jon had left it behind in the desert, blood-drenched, after the raid in which his people thought he had died. The military authorities had returned it to Janet. Months later she had given it to Saldivar, who wore it in the Dust till he, too, was reported missing. Once again it had been returned to Janet, and then she had finally found the message Jon had hidden behind the mirror for her to see. The shirt hung before Singer's eyes, the feel and smell of it stitched with memories.

Singer had never before tried to find a man he did not know in a place that was strange to him. Once he had gone looking for Saldivar through miles of desert, but Palha had already been his friend, the shape and flavor of him woven close to his heart. He did not have the same tie to Jon. He let Janet's dreaming guide him. *He's high up*, she had said. *Like in a tower.*

Singer felt himself drawn up the mountain wall, up the sheer black rock of the Somostai fortress. He struggled against it, his heart quickening with fear, but he was there, in the Black City. He was caught again in someone else's dream as the stranger struggled and his heart beat faster. Again he smelled the maddening scent of blood and the hot, gritty scent of the wind from the Dust. He laid the shirt of his memories over the stranger's twitching shoulders, and the stranger stirred as if to pull the shirt's protection around him.

Medicine Shirt. Bullets lose their power, Singer said.

Like hell, the sleeper murmured. Then the sleeping mind bolted from its dream. *Janney?* the stranger gasped.

Singer struggled to hold on to the contact, but he felt it slipping. He could not keep both Janet and the stranger in his awareness. They were too agitated, both pulling in separate directions. He could feel himself losing Janet, but he was still tangled in her brother's dream.

Kristo! Him again, Jon moaned. *What do you want from me? Damn you, tell me or leave me alone. Who are you?*

There was despair in the voice, behind the bold words. Singer tried again for contact but failed. To the other he remained insubstantial.

Friends, he assured the stranger. But he was shut out from that mind, and the sleeper faded.

Zhanne, I'm sorry. I couldn't hold on to you both. I'll try again. We'll find him.

He could feel her weeping.

It's not your fault, she told him. *He won't open to you. He can't hear because he won't listen. He won't trust anyone. It's always been like this. He doesn't have any friends. He lets me do that for both of us—then he comes around afterward and tells me how the friends I made are not to be trusted. There's a silence in his heart. He sees everything, but through bulletproof glass. Nobody gets in. That's why I had to come with you.*

Singer stayed with her till she was asleep, but he did not want to share her dreams that night. He lay awake for a long time, his thoughts running along dark corridors to the place where the master's son had slept alone without any gift but one: a white horse on a silver chain, clasped in his cold hands.

3

He slept a little before dawn and woke up to find light filtering in through slits high up in the walls. That matched his memory of the lower levels. It struck him as ironic yet fitting that Hadhla's Great House had become a kennel for slaves. "It was never more than that," he said aloud. "Walls can make a prisoner but not a master."

The guards woke them with shouts down the stairway. Singer noted that they did not come down in person. He was disappointed. Their descent would have created interesting opportunities to pick them off while they were outnumbered. As it was, the prisoners had to pass through the narrow door by twos and threes and had no chance to rush the guards on their way out.

Singer and Saldivar shuffled into line with the others to receive dollops of mush from a caldron that simmered fitfully over a fire of sticks and twisted grass. Singer sniffed at the mush. It was starchy, lumpy, white, and nearly tasteless.

"What is it?" Saldivar asked.

"Cattle fodder. It's a kind of root. You can brew chah from it, too. People don't eat it unless they're starving, but it won't hurt you."

The time before Deronh had taken him over the mountains, the time when he had been a very small child living in the back alleys of the Iron City, had sunk beyond recall. Singer had been happy to forget. Suddenly a vivid memory came back to him.

It had been possible for a small boy to squeeze between the pen hurdles when cattle came to market, to hide beneath the mangers and steal raw lumps of the white root. If the boy was seen, he got a painful thrashing from the drovers' staffs. If he came back unseen, he might be caught by bigger boys and get a beating from them after they stole his loot. It had seemed worth the risk. The root did not taste like much—fibrous and faintly sweet—but it was something to have in the mouth, something to fill the belly and stop the hunger cramps.

Singer pushed his bowl into Saldivar's hands. "You eat this. I don't want it."

"You're not getting sick or something?"

"No. I never liked the taste."

Saldivar shrugged and gulped down the rest of the portion. "If you were the master's son," he said when he had finished, "why did you eat cattle feed?"

"Too long a story," Singer said. The fountain in the corner of the square still leaked an icy trickle of water, and he headed for it with long strides. He elbowed other prisoners aside long enough to let Palha fill their water bottle.

"So tell it short," Saldivar said. "I'm in no hurry." Singer could see that he would not stop chewing that bone till he found some marrow, so he tried to satisfy him as briefly as possible.

"The woman who was my mother was not the master's wife. The Somostai arranged for her to get a son off him. But when the time came, she didn't keep her bargain with them. Knowing they could always find her, she left me with someone else and lured them away. I suppose it was someone she trusted; I don't know. By the time I can remember, I was living with an old woman who told me nothing.

"The master's chosen son—my brother, Dona—was sick and like to die. He had coughing sickness as all children do, but he couldn't get better, it seemed. The Somostai told the master they could cure Dona in return for me. Hadhla's persistence finally found me, though the Somostai had failed to do so. One day the soldiers came and took me away from the old woman. They left me on the mountain in the dark, in a place that was sacred to the Somostai god, the Destroyer of Flesh. I thought he would come and eat me. The true plan was for the Somostai to come and get me, but Deronh found me first."

"You never told me that," Saldivar said.

"I don't think about it. Some things are no use to remember. I was born when I took my first breath in the Rock."

Soldiers herded them back into line. A group of blackrobes on horseback had come to divide up the prisoners. Singer let his memories go, like ditching a pack that was too heavy to carry into action. He had to be ready to move in case they tried to separate him from Palha.

The Somostai moved through the line, using their black staffs to prod the captives into groups. They never spoke. The one who came toward Singer seemed to size him up at a glance, lingered a moment longer over Saldivar, then shoved them both in the same direction. Most of the strongest and biggest prisoners were in their group. The sick and scrawny were marched off in another direction.

Singer listened closely to the few words the Somostai exchanged with the guards. "They keep saying 'fon-teri' and 'forno.' These words are not Giristiyah. Are they Delteix?"

"I don't know. Lots of words I don't know."

"Whatever it is, they're taking us there." He knew better than to reach for his hidden knife, but he twitched his shoulders so he could feel the small weight of it shift under his shirt.

They left the city on the north side, on the familiar road, up the shoulder of Old Cloudy. Singer's hackles rose; that was the road where the soldiers had taken him the first time he had left the city behind. A new spur had been added to the road since then. It curved around and up the mountain. It was better than the original road had been: broad and smooth and sloped so carefully that a heavy wagon could travel it without much risk. As they came closer to the mountain, that unearthly glow leapt into the sky again. They heard a hissing roar like a voice from the bowels of the earth. A plume of brown smoke fanned out across the clean morning sky, and the wind off the mountain reeked of burning oil, burningstone, burning metal.

Other sounds became audible beneath the roar; Singer could not identify them. They were like iron-bound wheels rolling rapidly over stony roads, rhythmic metallic thumping and rattling.

"Sounds like a factory," Saldivar said.

"What is a factory?"

Saldivar searched for a way to translate. "A place where metal things are made."

"You mean a smith's hearth?"

Saldivar shook his head but could not think of another way to put it.

Where the rock spur they were climbing joined the bulk of the mountain, there was a broad summit with enough space to build a small fortress. The space had been leveled, and buildings stood there, but they were not fortifications. The first thing Singer noticed was a tower built of metal struts. It held not a gun platform but an arrangement of metal wheels, things that turned and things that moved up and down. While Singer watched, a group of men crowded into a cage at the base of the tower. The cage sank from sight, straight into the earth, it seemed. Singer felt as if the earth were sinking from under his own feet. His eyes were telling him things that made no sense. He took a deep breath and looked again, observing the way the rods and wheels moved.

"There's a hole in the ground. There must be," he muttered. But that did not really help. Why would they pack a wire box with men and bury them in a hole in the ground? Even imagining it made him feel short of air.

"Why?" he asked Saldivar.

"Well, I've never seen one, but I think that's a mine shaft," Saldivar said. "Hesucristo, I hope they don't put us down there."

He was sweating and pale. Along with the fear of darkness underground, Singer got a picture of passages and tunnels in the dark, like the alleys and warrens of the back city but far below the surface.

A blast of heat against his back made him turn around. What he saw made him forget about the mine shaft. A squat black building stood against the mountainside; to Singer it seemed very big, though it was small compared to the largest buildings he had seen in the cities of the Delh'tani. There were no windows. The heat surged out through the open door, a wide door like that on a big barn. With the heat came a fiery glow and a low incessant mutter of sound that caused the ground to vibrate underfoot. The building looked like an eyeless monster head with a flaming mouth that opened to take them in. Singer's hair stood on end. He stretched his palm earthward in a plea for protection. *Earth, we are one. Hide me.* Earth trembled beneath him. There was no hiding place. The prisoners behind him bumped against him, pressing him forward. Behind them came Somostai, prodding with their staffs. They moved on, huddled together like sheep, through the door.

A chaos of noise and heat assailed Singer's senses. His first instinct was to bolt; his second, to throw himself down and cover his head. He stood his ground, trembling. To breathe calmly did not help; the air itself was full of panic messages, singeing and burning, trying to choke him. He felt, saw, heard, and smelled fire in a hundred places all around him. It flowed, it leapt, it swirled. He had never felt such fear in any battle. He closed his eyes against the assault and reached a memory of his old weaponmaster.

"There are two kinds of fear," the weaponmaster had told them. "One is fear of a known threat. This fear is a warrior's tool, protecting him from mistakes and sharpening his mind. The other fear comes of ignorance. This fear is your enemy and must be killed. Look it in the face till it dies. Knowledge kills fear."

With his eyes closed, he was able to assign directions to the noise and the heat. The fire was not all around him; it lurked in specific places. It was contained. When he looked again, the continual flashing and glowing daunted him less. He knew that it would not spring upon him before he could find its source. But he still could not see the purpose behind it.

He realized that Saldivar was tugging at his arm with a grip so fierce that the nails were digging into his skin.

"Come on, or they'll crack your head."

The blackrobes stood close with their sticks poised. The look in their eyes roused a quick flash of anger that eased the fear. They knew he was afraid, and it amused them.

He followed Palha, grateful for his touch. Palha was afraid, too, but he was not panicking. He knew something about this place.

Their group hurried across the shed, walking beside a track made of black metal where men and oxen dragged wheeled carts piled with different kinds of rocks and metal. They passed a huge brick structure the size of several houses pushed together. It had windows of a sort, but they were like eyes of fire beaming forth flames. To Singer it looked like the altars to the Destroyer he had seen in his childhood, but much bigger. Heat reverberated from the great brick walls and lapped around them like a tide.

The Somostai directed them to the far corner of the shed. There was another opening to the outside, and from it a huge pile of blistered grayish lumps spilled across the floor. People bent over the pile with shovels, and the Somostai indicated with gestures that the new arrivals should pick up tools and join in. Their job was to load the dark lumps into one of the wheeled carts. Other men dragged the full cart back along the tracks, toward the brooding fiery presence against the wall. As soon as the full cart was hauled away, another took its place. Somostai stood by to keep the workers moving at a steady pace.

Singer bent to the work. That, at least, was something he could understand, though it was not honorable for a Rider. The stuff they shoveled was heavy, and the motion needed to heave it into the carts set up a warning ache in shoulders and back after a very short time. Palha lowered his shovel briefly to wipe his face. One of the Somostai stepped forward and hit him in the back with the end of the black staff. Singer risked a quick look to note the man's face so he could be sure to kill him before leaving the city. Saldivar picked himself up and started digging again. Singer noticed that since the new workers had arrived, those who had been shoveling had eased off a bit, letting the newcomers take up the slack. He moved closer to the man next to him and jammed the shovel grip into his ribs, as if by accident.

"Do your share or I take it out of your ass in chunks when the beetles aren't looking," he said. Insults and curses in the language of his childhood came easily to mind.

Sweat poured off them, mixing with the black, ashy dust till they were all painted like Singers for the time of grieving. Most of the workers had stripped down to a rag or two. When the next empty cart was a few minutes late, Saldivar started to take off his shirt, but Singer stopped him.

"If they see your scars, they'll know we're not like the others. They'd mark you for a Rider, like me."

An old man with a water jug made his way around the shed every couple of hours. When they paused for a drink, Singer took another look at the fiery altar. He could see that the carts they were filling were dumped into it somewhere.

"What is this stuff?" he asked Saldivar.

Saldivar shook his head. "It stinks like the refinery around here—smells like heavy oil and methane. But fuck if I know what they're burning. Looks like rocks to me."

While he was still watching, another cart approached the wall from the far end of the shed. The men propelling it did not pull it; they pushed it with a long pole and huddled behind a metal plate like a shield. With a scrape of metal on metal, a door opened in the wall, and fire swirled around it. They shoved the cart forward on its track; it tilted, tipping its load into the flames. The fire within flared impossibly brighter, and the voice of the furnace boomed and roared. Some of the workers broke and ran; the others cowered behind their shield till one of the Somostai came running with a whip and they hauled the cart away again. The door closed. Singer's eyes were so dazzled that he saw green clouds everywhere. Before he recovered, their own guard was goading them back to work. But he kept looking back when his eyes were readjusted, until he saw how the door had opened. There was a row of doors, one for each eyehole. Chains ran up toward the ceiling, and a Somostai stood near the place where the chains ended, controlling the counterweights.

In the smoky gloom they could not guess how much time had passed. The man with the water jug had come by three times; Singer thought it must be noon, at least. At intervals, the singeing light flared out from an open door and the roar and boom of the furnace sounded, but panic no longer flared in Singer at the sound. He understood that it was a deliberate part of the mystery—a danger, perhaps, but not an emergency.

Suddenly he heard a new sound, one that seemed out of place, a harsh clanging that went on and on. Everyone looked up; Singer spotted the Somostai door opener on his perch, clashing an iron bar back and forth inside a metal ring.

Down on the ground a man was moving around the corner of the brick wall. Singer guessed it was one of the Somostai, since no one seemed to be giving him orders. He was wrapped in leather, like a smith, but the apron covered his arms and hooded his head. Heavy leather gauntlets covered his hands, and he carried a long metal rod. He turned the corner and disappeared, and Singer saw that the shed extended around the other side of the furnace. On that far side something was happening.

Since the alarm had sounded, no one was working. They had

all put their tools down and stood panting and staring. Even the Somostai stood looking after the man with the pole. Singer laid his shovel down quietly and tested the footing on the pile before him. It slid and rattled, but the furnace roar muffled the sound. He got one firm foothold and scrambled swiftly slantwise up the heap, like a climber over scree. Once on top, he reached back to give Saldivar an arm up. There was barely headroom between the roof and the top of the pile. The air was stifling; fumes and heat collected there from the floor below. They crept along the top of the pile until they could see down into the far side of the shed.

A deep gash of shadow opened below them. It looked like a trench, but they could not see into it as far as the bottom. The man in leather stood on a ridge at the shadow's edge. He crouched, head turned slightly, flinching from the heat that came against him like a solid adversary. He reached out with the rod and struck the furnace wall. Twice and again he struck, and a pinprick of star-white radiance opened in the brick. The man in leather gathered his strength and drove the rod into the opening once more. The edges crumbled, and a torrent of devouring white fire poured forth with a hissing roar that smote the ear as painfully as the brilliance struck the eye. For a moment Singer thought the fire had annihilated its servant. Then he spotted the man again, outlined against the cascading sparks that leapt from the surface of the torrent. He had leapt down the far side of the ridge as the fire poured out and was retreating backward with his face still toward the fire, as if he could not look away. He looked like a black stick figure, insignificant as an insect crawling across a hearthstone.

The liquid fire cascaded down into the trench. By its lightning-bolt glare, Singer could see that a giant caldron had been placed underneath to catch the fire. Singer could not take his eyes off the sight, either. The blackrobes flogged men gaunt as ghosts across the frozen plain and dug cities deep into the rock beneath the city, built furnaces the size of a rich man's house, all to gather that cupful of sunfire. He looked into the heart of the ruined city, into the Somostai secret, but he did not know what it was.

"It's steel," Saldivar whispered into his ear. "Mother of God, they're pouring steel."

"It can't be," Singer said. "Steel doesn't melt. There's no fire on earth that hot."

He had never seen iron smelting, but he knew that iron would melt and run. He had seen bronzesmiths pouring molten metal from their crucibles. Ordinarily the blacksmiths of the People brought their steel in cakes from the Iron City and reheated it for forging. Once, however, he had watched one of the blacksmiths of the Rock heat iron in a furnace. He had wanted a special steel for a very particular sword. The process had been long and awe-inspiring to the boy Singer had been. He remembered it in detail, and he remembered the glowing, spongy lump the smith had beaten on the forge, the scale flaking off under the hammer. The smith had explained to him that iron was strong but could be made to flow, while only forging could change the shape of steel. "The Wind Lord, maybe, melts steel to his will in the furnace of the sun," the smith had said. Singer could still see his face, the red glow of the hearth lighting dreams in his eyes. "But there is no such fire that men's hands can reach. The People are like steel. Wind and fire may forge us, but no man can melt us down or shape us to his will."

"Of course it melts," Saldivar said patiently, as if explaining things to a very small child. "It's been melting for thousands of years. Since the preflight era on Sol-Terra. Steel's in the vitos, the motos. The starships that brought the colony from Delta."

"I never thought," Singer said. He had seen all the metal things the Delh'tani possessed, but he had never asked what metal it was or how they made it. It had seemed too much like magic, not something human beings could do. Stupid, stupid, he berated himself.

"So much . . . ." he wondered. "What's it all for?"

"Don't know. But I don't think it's wheelchairs for old ladies."

The flow had ceased. Shadows repossessed the shed as the glare faded from its blinding peak. Another group of men moved up the ridge, trundling a wooden machine on wheels. They cranked up a windlass and began firing projectiles into the glowing gap.

Saldivar, in his turn, was fascinated and puzzled. "What are they doing?"

"It's a catapult. They're closing up the hole by throwing something in—clay, maybe. I've seen a catapult tear down a wall before. Never saw one build a wall."

The alarm had ceased. The workers returned to their antlike labor. Hastily, Singer and Saldivar scrambled and rolled to the bottom of the heap to rejoin their group. They were too late. The Somostai had seen them. Singer picked up his shovel, crouching obsequiously but getting ready to spring. He spoke to Saldivar, barely moving his lips. "If he touches me one more time, I'm going to kill him." The shovel was good metal, heavy, the edge kept bright by grating on the gray lumps.

Perhaps the Somostai saw something in Singer's face. He did not strike them with his staff. He shook it in their faces and spit out a few contemptuous words, then left them to their work.

"He says," Singer translated, "if we like the fire-that-runs so much, we can work on that side of the furnace tomorrow. Makes it sound like something bad. We'll see."

Singer would have liked to see what they did with the caldron of steel brew. He could not imagine how men or oxen could move so huge and dangerous a thing. Somewhere he heard a throbbing sound, as if Delh'tani machinery were at work. He hoped that on the next day he would have a chance to find out.

The endless process of feeding the furnace began again. The water came around once more, and they drank thirstily. There was not enough to satisfy their need. Thirst and weariness, the hypnotic mutter and hum of the furnace, and the constant rattle of cartwheels dulled their senses. In a few hours' time they had passed from fear that sharpened every perception to a stupor in which they took it all for granted.

The alarm bell sounded again. The Somostai guard looked around but shook his staff at them to indicate that they should keep working. Out on the floor, the Somostai cleared the workers away from the tracks. Singer smelled and felt it before he saw it coming. Scorched air danced ahead of it. An iron cup moved through the air, seemingly by magic, till he saw the hooks that held it to a track in the ceiling. No men propelled the massive object; he heard metal creak and rattle as it moved and guessed there must be an engine he could not see, using the invisible power of the strangerfolk. A red glow rose above the rim of the cup, and bright sparks rose occasionally when it jolted. It stopped at an open door, and Singer saw that a kind of funnel had been moved close to the door. The great hooks moved, tilting the cup, and again the gloom lit up with the glare of molten metal. The furnace roared like a lion being fed.

"Why are they pouring in, when last time they poured out?" Singer asked.

"Don't know. Plenty of things I don't know," Saldivar said shortly. He stabbed his shovel into the pile again.

It is possible to be one of a people that rides between the stars and not to understand any of it, Singer thought as the light faded.

All the Riders can ride; all the pallantai can fight; all who eat resh know where it grows and how to find it. It's possible to wear steel, use steel, and ride on steel and not know where it comes from. But those who know have the staffs of power, and we have the shovels. Palha knows this, and that's why he's angry. He is ashamed to be a slave.

At last a new contingent of prisoners shuffled in. Singer and Saldivar dropped their shovels and straightened painfully. A few more days of that, Singer thought, and we'll be twisted like wet rawhide left in the sun. The new group looked and dressed like all the others, Singer noticed. They, too, were captive cityfolk.

Outside, the cold wind knifed at them. They had forgotten, in the man-made summer inside, that winter still ruled in the outer world. Their sweat-drenched clothes stiffened with frost. The sun had set, and hardly a glimmer lingered in the sky. They were marched back to the underground barracks and given some thin soup and frozen chunks of bread before descending into the dark again.

They were glad to be out of the wind and to have something in their bellies. Pleasure did not exist in that place, but a small easing of discomfort was something to appreciate. As before, they claimed a sleeping place close to the wall. They huddled together, exhausted. Saldivar twitched restlessly. No position seemed to relieve his cramped muscles.

The sewer smell of the big room struck Singer with renewed intensity after he had been away from it. His own smell surrounded him: damp wool and stale sweat. As he dozed, a single thread of something different wove its way through his mind like a waft of air from another place. It had a flavor of wood smoke and horsehide, spice and well-oiled leather. He sat up, startled. The trace vanished.

"Someone's looking for us. Did you feel it?"

"No." Saldivar rolled over sleepily. "I'm no good at this."

"Not true." Singer reached for him. From the feel of Palha's skin, he moved into the unique awareness that went with it. Deftly, he wove himself and Palha together like linking fingers in the dark. He set up harmonies in their blood and breath and the countless smaller rhythms. The ache in Palha's back was a knot in his weaving. He smoothed it out. *That feels good*, Palha said gratefully.

With Palha to anchor him, he stretched out into the darkness around him. Immediately he was caught in the net of a hundred strangers in prison underground. His belly cramped with their hunger; he winced from their raw sores; their tears ran into his mouth. Palha pulled him back. Briefly, he felt the cool, gritty floor beneath him and heard Palha's breath in his ear. *We're looking for Janney, remember?*

He cast again into the night. For a moment he thought he had found her. The contact had a shape and feel that almost matched his memory but were subtly wrong. He moved closer and found himself at the top of a long stairway, entering a lit room. Candles burned there, but their flames looked pale and ghostly in the sharp white glow of strangerfolk lights. Singer's eyes winced shut, but the eyes he saw through in that room gazed steadily at a book on the table and a screen humming beside it. Above the table hung a costly mirror, a rarity in the master's day. To see one's own face was a novelty reserved for the very powerful. Ordinary folk had to be satisfied with their echoes in the faces of others. The man looked up suddenly, aware of Singer's presence, and Singer saw him in the mirror. The man had Janet's face. But his hair was cropped short, and he wore a skull earring. He was Somostai.

No trace of Singer appeared in the mirror. Still the man looked wildly about him and gasped, "Who is it?" Then, as he had the night before, he said, "You again! Who are you?"

Jon fought hard to close Singer out of his awareness, and he was strong; Singer was taken by surprise. His own revulsion against the Somostai dress Jon wore fought against him, too.

We found your shirt, he said. *We're looking for you. Come to us in the place where iron catches fire.*

He did not know the word for the place he meant, so he tried to share his memory of it. Something went wrong. The boiling metal turned into something else, a white-hot starburst that shattered their contact. Jon leapt up from his desk, and Singer found himself back on the cold stone far below.

He found Janet almost immediately, as if she had tripped over him in the dark.

What's the flash? he asked.

That wasn't me, she answered.

A new voice, intense and bright, broke in. With the voice came the roar of the wind from the plains fluttering the tent flaps and the smell of burning thorn.

Palha broke his silence. *Heyo, Lyn!*

Straight, it's me, and about time, too. Show me where you are. I want a fix on you so I can find you fast next time.

Singer took a deep breath and started to spill the day's learning in a torrent of images and half-heard conversations.

Wait, wait. Singer felt her locking in with Janet. Together they slowed him down, then matched speed with him. They handled him like a runaway horse, a feeling that surprised him even while he relived the splendid terror of the furnace. He was not used to being handled. He watched what they were doing. They had grasped his awareness and Saldivar's as a single system and watched the day through his eyes and Palha's, in tandem. It gave him vertigo and surprised him again. Palha had seen things he had not noticed.

Lyn watched and listened without interrupting. When they had come full circle to the underground room, she said, *Wait,* and withdrew from them a little. He caught a taste of the dry, warm complicated flavor that was Kruger.

He tried to hear through Lyn's ears, and she jumped.

Peace! Just let me see what you are seeing.

Makho came into full focus. They were sitting in the Asharya's sleeping place.

"That is steel making," he said. "God in heaven, that's the preflight way. So old it's never been used on Delta—or at least not since the first desperate times of the settlement."

Singer could see the ripple of horror cross Makho's well-disciplined face.

"It's barbaric, putting flesh and blood down on the floor with all that hot metal. You tell them to get their butts out of there before they get dipped and fried. And that's an order."

Even as the Asharya spoke, Singer could see his attention leaping to the information he had been given, playing with the pieces, trying to build a structure that made sense.

"Something missing. The Nupis are at the core of this, but why? Tell him to watch out for them. They are kluge merchants, and this has all the marks of a giant kluge."

Singer saw Makho look sharply at Lyn.

"Singer? Are you listening? Dammit, I can't get used to this." Kruger switched into very passable Thanha. The accent was good, though the idiom was still strange. "This is your old man speaking: I want you back. End of message from Kruger."

They parted gently, as if they were only saying good night. Singer found himself alone with Janet.

You saw Jon. Show me!

The face in the mirror lit her up like a reflected flare. All she saw was her brother's eyes; she hardly noticed his cropped hair and Somostai clothing. *Madre'dio, he's in trouble.*

Suddenly she saw that Singer was staying as far away from the memory as he could. She turned her attention back to him with a motion like turning on her heel. *What? What is this?* He flinched. He refused to show her why he hated the blackrobes, but he felt her turning over things he had said in the past and getting some grasp of it, anyway. She made the connection from Jon's dark clothing to the blackrobes with sticks. He felt her paused sadness like a sigh.

Listen to me. If Jon is wearing a uniform, it's because he's fighting for his life. He hates uniforms more than you can imagine. You're close to him, you must be, if you're getting into his dreams now. You've got to find him. He needs your help, and if anyone can help you figure this out, he can. Jon can take two and two and get more numbers out of it than anyone. Singer! He's not your enemy. Get that straight. No more than I am.

It hurt Singer to be at odds with Zhanne, but he could not accept the young Somostai with her face. Yet he had sworn to rescue Jon. It hurt him, too, to shut her out, but if he opened his heart to her, he risked too much discovery.

4

On the next day the Somostai remembered his promise and moved them from the pile of rocks-for-burning, around the massive furnace to its downhill side. Singer satisfied his curiosity about the fate of the molten steel. The great cup moved down the track and was lifted and poured out by a hook from the roof. It splashed and ran into molds. When the metal had cooled enough that it was no longer liquid, workers dragged the molds downhill to another shed that echoed with the din of hammers.

The Somostai did not trust anyone to direct the pouring of the steel. One of them ran the crane that tilted the cup, controlling it with some Delh'tani magic from above. Others, dressed in leather like the one who punched the taphole, positioned the molds and signaled him from the floor. Singer and Saldivar joined the crew that hauled the glowing ingots away when the pour was over. They worked in heat that blistered their backs and then plunged into the freezing blast of outside air as they rushed the ingots to the next shed. Singer noticed that the older members of the crew coughed constantly. After a few hours he understood why the guard had considered this a punishment. A strong man could live a long time working with a shovel. The relentless alternation of heat and cold could break down even a strong man, and the prisoners were not strong.

When no steel was being poured, their group was marched uphill to drag down more loads of fuel for the furnace. Singer recognized the skill that had gone into planning the place. Everything moved down the mountain in an orderly progression so that the force that pulled things downhill would speed the work along.

"That's the Somostai mind for you," he said to Saldivar. One advantage to their new assignment was that they could speak more freely as they moved from the furnace to the fuel stack. "All this planning to make the machinery convenient, but they use human beings like beasts of burden. Why didn't they borrow a little more Delh'tani magic and move everything by sunpower, not just the big things?"

"Never did forced labor, did you?" Saldivar said hoarsely. He hung on the harness for a minute, trying to get his breath before he threw his weight against the load again. "Power costs. People are cheap. These chucks are dead weight, and this is as good a way to dump them as any."

Singer stopped in his tracks as he tried to assimilate a monstrous idea. "You mean the Nupis and their blackrobe friends *want* them to die?"

"Sure. Didn't you hear what the polvorados we liberated were saying back at the other camp? Working people to death is a good way to get rid of them, 'cause you make a profit on it instead of just executing them. Hey, I grew up in a camp, I know how it works. Where I lived, they didn't kill our bodies, though.

Just killed the hearts out of all those people and waited for the body to follow.''

"War by other means," Singer said.

"You got it."

They leaned into the harness again. Singer pulled till he was sweating, but the words he had spoken followed him as if they were harnessed to him. Whose words were those? They had sprung to mind as if from his own memory, but he did not remember them.

He started to think seriously about finding another way out of the city, with or without Jon. The work was dangerous. He could not afford to expose himself and Saldivar much longer in the mere hope that Janet's brother would show up one day. On one of their trips up the track he saw an iron chisel being used to split large lumps of fuel. He stumbled and fell to his knees, causing the men behind him to trip over him. When he pushed himself upright again, he was holding the chisel under his shirt. He kept his arm pressed to his side till he could pull his belt tighter and make sure the iron tool would not fall out. The hammers in use on the fuel pile were too big to conceal. In the end he decided that boldness was the only choice. He picked up a hammer without trying to hide it and threw it on top of the loaded cart. "Needed inside," he grunted to the only man who gave him a questioning look. It stood among the shovels in the furnace shed for several days, till the Somostai lost his temper near the end of their shift. While the guard thrashed one of the other laborers, Singer slid the hammer under his belt. The long handle fit well along one leg of his trousers. He limped stiff-legged back to the underground barracks with his prize.

"You want to tell me what this is about?" Saldivar asked when they were back in the dark.

"It's about doors. I don't like a place with only one way out."

Saldivar laughed wearily. "I wish I'd thought of that before I came to this world."

Holding the hammer near its head, Singer tapped the chisel experimentally. The iron bit easily into the crumbly mortar in the back wall. By the time the nearest neighbors started to protest the noise, he had already loosened one of the stones.

Each night Singer tried again to contact Janet's brother but could find only traces of his presence. He suspected that the man no longer slept at night. Sooner or later he would have to leave himself vulnerable again, but Singer did not want to wait much longer. He feared for Saldivar. Palha's bones showed, and he endured each day in a dogged silence that worried Singer more than any complaint.

For several days Singer's attention had been divided between concern about Saldivar and thinking about where and how they could move on. He had stopped paying much attention to the Somostai on the floor. He had extracted all the information he could from watching them. On the day after he gained possession of the hammer, however, something different seemed to be happening.

They were getting ready to pour another cup of steel. He could tell by the work pattern around the furnace, by the sound of it, and by the color of the fire that showed through the eyeholes in the furnace doors. More Somostai than usual were clustered around the trough by the taphole. At least one extra was present, though they all wore protective clothing and were therefore impossible to tell apart. They seemed to be arguing with each other. One of them jerked a gloved hand repeatedly toward the ceiling. Singer looked up but could not see anything significant in the girders and metal linkages of tracks and hooks. He edged closer to the group. He could not hear anything they said over the incessant din inside the shed. It seemed they had settled their dispute, whatever it was, because the tapper came forward and they started the pour.

Singer put up his arms to shield his face from the glare. The leaping white fire never lost its fascination, and he stood closer than he had ever been before. The glory ebbed slightly. The cup was full, and the Somostai on the platform above signaled for the power that would tilt the brimming fire into the molds below. The Somostai below had retreated to the relative safety of the dikes next to the trench. Terrifying though it was, Singer wished he could stand where they stood and see what they saw. For the first time, it occurred to him that Somostai might be accessible like any other humans. It seemed impossible that he could find any point of contact with them at such a distance. But if he could touch them, he could see the fire through their eyes. Entirely absorbed in that thought, he moved slowly toward them.

They finished pouring the steel and replugged the taphole. Still they had not noticed that he was not working. They continued to argue among themselves. The great cup of metal came ponderously down its track to refill the furnace. He felt the heat but put it aside as he concentrated on the Somostai. For a moment he encountered the impossible: something familiar in the ungainly forms by the edge of the pit. In the next moment he felt a swift stab of uneasiness that heightened instantly into fear.

The rumble seemed to spread upward through the soles of his feet, a bellowing shock of sound that threw him down and then shook the ground under him. His mouth was open, but he could not hear himself screaming. He had felt this before, when the Rock had been blown to rubble.

The grinding shriek of metal tearing above his head cut through the roar, and he needed no Somostai to tell him that it meant trouble. He looked up and saw the massive cup of fire shudder and jolt. Boiling metal leapt above the rim like a creature in flames, and he remembered bodies he had seen falling in flames from burning vitos. He rose to his hands and feet and crouched to jump and run, but the faint, familiar tug from below held him still. He looked down. He saw a face turned up beneath the leather hood, a white blur in the dazzle of the fire. The other Somostai screamed and ran, too late, as the crane gave way and the white-hot metal lashed out over the lip of the cup like a demon's tongue. The man below looked directly at Singer and did not move. In that moment Singer was caught.

He was in midair before he knew that he was going to leap. He heard Palha's horrified cry and slammed a message back to him: *Stay back!* He felt the impact of his body against the Somostai, clutched the leather armor, and half threw the man with all his strength even as he leapt again. His whole body shrank from the liquid fire that would descend on him before he took another breath. He knew it was too late.

He felt another impact. He and the Somostai crashed together against the rungs of the ladder that led up to the control platform. He clutched convulsively and caught himself with a jolt that twisted his arm nearly out of its socket. He heard the Somostai grunt as the breath was forced out of him, but the man managed to hang on. The rungs of the ladder were hot. Singer looked down and saw that the ladle lay tipped over in the trench, surrounded by metal that had crusted over with glowing red and flakes of black. The other Somostai were nowhere to be seen. Singer dragged himself up the ladder and flopped over onto the platform. Only then, in cold dread, did he think to look for Saldivar. Part of the walkway had fallen down, and the walls had caught fire, but Palha was still safe on the other side of the trench.

Singer realized that he was naked and so was the Somostai. Then he saw the Somostai's face up close.

"You—" he said at the same time that the other man said, "It's you again."

The Somostai grabbed him by both shoulders and stuck a knee into his belly. "And now you're going to tell me who the fuck you are or I'll throw you back in the fucking puddle and watch you fry."

Singer was flat on his back and perfectly safe. He could easily have kicked the Somostai off the platform if he had wanted to, but he had no such wish. The Somostai was Janet's brother.

The other Somostai, who had been watching the whole scene from the platform, bent over them and said something to Jon.

"No, leave him alone," Jon replied in Giristiyah. He seemed to realize where he was and let go of Singer. He looked down into the glowing heat of the trench and shuddered. "He did save my life."

A smell of scorching hung in the air. Even the dirt in the trench was singed. The smoke tasted of metal and of something organic burned to charcoal. Singer felt nauseated. But they were Somostai. If their own fire had eaten them, he should be glad of that.

"Get me some clothes," Jon ordered the Somostai. The man hesitated. "Do it!" He used the peremptory form that implied an order from a superior to a servant. It seemed clear that Janet's brother was not a slave in the city. The other man crawled off along the catwalk, afraid to stand up.

When he had gone, Jon looked Singer in the face again. Singer saw questions crowding his mind, struggling for dominance.

"Now tell me who you are, and quickly." He was still speaking Giristiyah.

"Your sister sent me," Singer said. He used Delteix—not the soldier speech with its thick Spanya accent but the elegant form he had learned from Janet and Kruger. Shock showed on Jon's face.

"She found the message you left in your Medicine Shirt. The authorities picked the shirt up when they found the bodies of your patrol and sent it back with the other personal effects. It took her this long to get here, but she made it. It seems she cares for you."

"Janet is *here*?"

"No. But she is not far away."

"Who are you?" Jon whispered.

Singer grinned. "That depends on who is asking." He shifted

into Giristiyah again. "The brother of my friend? The servant of my enemies? Perhaps you would like to tell me."

Before Jon could answer, the Somostai returned. He brought a black cloak for Jon but nothing for Singer. He was in a hurry, and he was trembling—or maybe the whole structure was shaking.

"Come on," he urged. "Down from here. It could fall any minute."

Jon looked from one to the other as if he could not decide what to do.

The other man began urging him in a torrent of words. It was all Giristiyah but heavily laced with Somostai technical words that Singer did not understand. Some catastrophe had happened, something worse than the fall of the iron cup. More Somostai had gathered on the floor below. They shouted up to Jon.

"Everybody to the"—the word they used was unintelligible to Singer—"it's on fire!"

Singer understood the last part all right. Jon made up his mind and scrambled after the other Somostai, across the catwalk and down another ladder that swung precariously, loose at one end. Singer followed.

At the bottom one of the overseers grabbed hold of him. Primed by excitement and fear, Singer broke his hold and was about to take him apart when he remembered that he still did not know where Saldivar was. Only a fool would start a fight at such a time.

"What do you want with him?" Jon asked. "I need to ask this man some questions."

"Orders are to secure the workers and for all of us to report to the mine storage area immediately."

"Kristo! What is it?"

"I don't know. It's bad. The messenger said something about—"again that word Singer could not understand. "It's like an earthquake or something. The mine shaft is down. We lost the whole team there. Hurry!"

Jon's face changed. The news obviously meant something to him, something that frightened him enough to take priority over everything else, even the possibility of rescue. "All right. But he'd better be there when I come back. Cherish him like your life. And give him some clothes."

Jon took the overseer's own cloak and threw it to Singer.

"Later," he said. He followed the other blackrobes and left Singer to be herded away with the rest of the prisoners.

5

As they walked around the end of the trench to get past the spilled steel, Saldivar came to meet them in long angry leaps, a guard chasing him with his staff upraised. Blows rained on his back, but he kept his place next to Singer.

"Talk to me, Singer." He was speaking Delteix, and Singer realized that it would be useless to urge silence and caution. Palha was jumping out of his skin with anger and fear.

"*Ayei.*" He reached for Palha's wrist to steady him. "It was Zhanne's brother."

"Here?"

"Down on the floor with the steel makers. I jumped before I thought. Then it was too late to think. I was afraid."

"*You* were afraid? Did you see what happened? Steam and smoke—like an explosion. The metal danced. Almost like a gas, not a liquid. Those poor bastards down in the trench—oh, no, you don't want to see that." But Singer grasped his hand and set up the familiar link between them. Saldivar gritted his teeth as the memory leapt to vivid life. "I thought you were down there, but I couldn't see you. I couldn't see you. I thought if you died, I'd feel that."

Singer sent him wordless apology and reassurance.

"Yeah, yeah, fine, but where *were* you? It isn't humanly possible to move that fast."

"I don't know," Singer muttered. He was not sure how he had ended up on the ladder with Jon, and he was afraid to think about it. He changed the subject. "They're locking us up. There's been some big disaster, and all the Somostai have run to fix it. They want us all rounded up till they decide how to use us."

146

"That felt like an explosion to me," Saldivar said. "I thought we were being shelled, but there was only the one hit. What the hell was that?"

They had reached the entrance to their barracks, and the guards shoved them through the door.

"Don't know. I know I'm not waiting here to find out. If it was bad enough to scare the blackrobes, it's nothing I want to get caught in."

Singer rummaged in the dark for his stolen tools. His fist curled lovingly around the hammer handle when he found it. It was not as good as a sword, but it promised the possibility of action. He struck the wall a blow that crumbled another chunk out of the rock.

"About Jon: I think he intends to protect us, but I am not sure he has the power. They will send for us. It will be best not to be here."

He wrapped a bit of rag around the chisel to muffle the ring of metal. He spaced his blows carefully, hoping the guards above would not be able to hear them. The chisel bit satisfyingly into the mortar. In a short time he had jarred loose one of the smaller blocks of stone. He struck it a couple of heavy blows. It grated and slid into the darkness behind the wall. A breath of air came through from the other side.

Their neighbors, somewhere in the dark, were roused by the noise.

"What are you doing?" a hoarse, low voice called.

"Taking apart this wall," Singer answered in Giristiyah. "It's in my way."

Saldivar could not understand him. Straining to catch some meaning from the tone, he noticed how Singer's voice changed with the language. The words in Giristiyah held a note of defiance and danger. The need for force was never far away, as if Singer were speaking always with his fists clenched.

"You'll get us in trouble, get us punished. Who wants to suffer for you, stranger?"

"So go call the guards. No doubt they'll be grateful. Maybe they'll give you a moldy heel of bread for your tale bearing. Maybe, if you keep your mouth shut and let me work, you'll get something better."

The hoarse voice in the dark was warily curious. "What? What's the good of it—more work when the blackrobes have sucked our marrow dry already? There's no way out of this place."

" 'Ignorance says "Show me!" but keeps his eyes tight shut.' " Singer spoke in short bursts as he attacked the wall again. A shower of mortar crumbled beneath his blows. He rocked the stone with his bare hands, heedless of torn palms. Another blow from the hammer knocked the stone from its socket like a rotten tooth. As he paused to check the size of the hole, another shower of fragments rattled down. Had his work somehow disturbed the rest of the building? Above him, stones grated and rumbled. He threw himself down with his arms over his head as a shudder passed through the earth, the ground heaving under them like a ponderous wave of stone. The ominous grinding sound swelled to a humming roar. Somewhere in the front of the room he heard screams, and all around them the cityfolk wailed and cried in terror. When the sound died away, the air was thick with dust. He heard people coughing and moaning.

Singer called out into the darkness, but no one answered him from the confusion. He crawled toward the stairs, shoving bodies out of his way. Some of them were dead, he thought; others were only inert with fear.

There were no stairs. That end of the room had fallen in. There was no doorway anymore. He felt his way across the stone pile. It seemed far too big to shift. Part of the paving from the square above must have caved in, along with the remnants of the walls.

As the prisoners began to understand what had happened, the clamor in the room grew louder and more despairing.

"We can't get out! We can't get out!" someone shrieked. Singer felt his way to the voice and struck the man till he was silent. But the prisoners' terror shrieked at him silently, setting his teeth on edge and making it hard to think.

He crawled back to the wall where he had left Saldivar and found him sweating and shivering, his fingers digging into the mortar at the edge of the hole in the wall. Palha wanted to bolt from the place that in his mind had already become a tomb.

"What happened?"

The question surprised Singer. It was not Palha who spoke but that hoarse voice he had heard before.

"The stairs have fallen down. There is no way out that way."

He repeated it for Saldivar and added, "Either we have been attacked or the Somostai are playing with dangerous toys. Or it was an earthquake. I have never seen one, so I do not know if that is possible. I think maybe they did not stop the fire in time and something else has blown up.''

"What about your way? Can you get us out of here?" the hoarse voice asked.

"Why ask me? Why look to me for help?"

"I have watched you, stranger. You are not one of us. That is clear. I hear you speak strange words to your silent friend. I don't know what you're doing here, but if you know a way out, I want to follow you."

The courage and decision in the voice were like fresh air in the dust. Singer stopped fencing with the invisible speaker and answered him truthfully.

"I don't know. There was a way once. I intend to look for it."

"And what if you go and don't come back? Take us with you now!"

Singer stretched out his arms till he touched the speaker. "Listen to these people! They're untied in the head! They couldn't walk a straight path in daylight! If I find a way out, I'll come back. Meanwhile, find men you know, with some self-control. Quiet these people down if you can. Then we'll see."

He crawled through the hole, and Saldivar tumbled through after him. He reached out to steady Palha and found that his hair was drenched with sweat. In Palha's mind the darkness had weight and pressed down on him relentlessly.

"What the hell are we doing?" Saldivar said. "If you know the way out, why can't we just leave?"

"I promised Selem."

"That's not all, is it? You're trying to start something. You're crazy. Those chucks wouldn't stand up to a pointed stick."

"Understand this, paliao." Singer's voice had gone flat, revealing no more than a hint of the hatred burning within him. "I want to hurt the blackrobes. I will use any tool, no matter how weak or crooked. That hammer you carry—it is no warrior's weapon, but it will serve for something."

Saldivar worked his dry mouth and found enough moisture to spit. "Tools! Those pitiful rejects are handy as a fork in soup."

"Maybe. But the Somostai have made themselves a hostage to their weakness. This work seems dearer to the blackrobes than anything. The man in charge at the place of burning metal was nearly weeping after the accident. Why is it so important to them? I don't know, but I see that they can't do the work without their slaves. Therefore, I will take their slaves away from them.''

"Destabilizing the situation?''

"I guess that's what Makho would call it. Also creating cover for us when we decide to leave. They will owe us.''

He continued into the darkness, moving without hesitation, as if he could see. He could walk upright, his hair only brushing the roof occasionally, and the floor under their feet was smooth and well worked.

"Where are we going?''

"I've been here once only,'' Singer said. His voice was remote.

He trailed one hand along the wall and found smooth, shaped rock with tightly fitted joins. Saldivar followed with one hand on Singer's shoulder and the other hand gripping the hammer. The only sounds were the dusty padding of their feet and the double rhythm of their breaths: Saldivar's harsh and quick, Singer's light and slow as if he were moving in a trance.

After a hundred paces more Singer stumbled when the smooth paving ended abruptly, to be replaced by packed earth. The stones of the wall were still skillfully fitted, but their faces had been left rough. The weight and hurt of vanished time were in their harsh edges. Singer's hand came suddenly to the end of the wall.

He took a step forward into the emptiness and whistled between his teeth, a rising note that echoed eerily around them. Saldivar raised the hammer above his head and found no ceiling.

"We would find stairs beyond this room,'' Singer whispered. "That was the way I came, down from the burning city. The Great House was fallen, and of all its slaves and captains, one only was left behind. I came this way.''

He turned and entered the crossway where the wall opened in an arch. The corridor smelled of dust. The air was staler and stuffier than any they had yet encountered. Saldivar dreaded that closed-in passage, but he dared not stay behind. His breath quickened in the sour air, and his chest heaved as if heavy weights were pressing him down. He thought of the bones buried in the rubble by the city gate. Every step was an effort of will.

"What's in here?'' His throat closed on the words.

"Dead wealth of the cityfolk,'' Singer whispered. "Costly goods, precious things, left behind to rot. I ran this way once, looking for water. I found none.''

"Is that what you're looking for? Treasure?"

Singer laughed. "No—light. And food for the cityfolk. Like dogs: they can't think if they're hungry, and they won't come to you if there's nothing in your hand."

For a minute he sounded more like himself, and Saldivar was reassured.

But Singer did not pause to explore any of the storerooms. He kept moving as if he could not stop. The passage branched and turned; Saldivar tried to memorize the turns but could not be sure he had them right. He knew that Singer's memory was normally infallible, but Singer was not behaving normally. Saldivar's hand clenched convulsively on a fold of the Somostai cloak.

"Where are we going?" he asked again.

The walls cast his voice back at him, muffling and smothering it. Singer stopped again so suddenly that Saldivar tripped and bumped into him. A breath of colder air came through the empty space in the wall.

"Here," Singer whispered. "Lost treasure. The City Master left his greatest treasure here and never knew it. He died here. I couldn't help him. I had to leave him here, in the dark."

In a single horrified moment Saldivar realized why Singer had been going this way. He seized Singer's arms and tried to drag him back, away from that invisible doorway.

"Hesukristo, cofra, you can't bring him back. If his bones are still here, you don't want to see that! He's *dead*, Singer; he's *gone*. He isn't waiting for you anymore."

He talked as fast as he could, knowing that it was hopeless. Singer brushed him aside as if he were no more than another chunk of rubble on the floor and entered the doorway. Saldivar heard Singer's steps moving around slowly and finally stopping. He groped his way back to Singer's side. Singer sank to his knees on the dusty floor.

"*Ai*, Dona! Where have they laid you?" Singer said, his voice choked with tears he tried to hold back. "I have not the right to grieve for him. I made the deathgift for the people of the Rock. The man named Gero ordered their death, and Gero is dead at my hands. But the Somostai killed my brother, and they still live, still rule, still deal out death, and while they live, the air is poison for me."

He struck his fist against the floor. "But Dona never wanted anyone's death. All he asked me for was to find out why, to understand. I've met you Delh'tani and lived among you and flown through the sky in your machines, but I still don't understand what's happening here. I have failed him there, too.

"He said, 'No more killing,' but I've waded in blood to my knees since I left him here. I am a pallantai. I'm no good at understanding. Killing is all I know."

Saldivar grieved for him even in the midst of his own fear. He had seen a glimpse of how Singer's mind set ambushes for him. Singer kept his sanity by living in the present, walled off from memories of darkness. He had opened himself to the past to find his way through the dark and had left himself without protection against the shadows that lived in that past. Saldivar humbled himself and did not even try to keep his voice from shaking.

"Please, brother. It's dark. I know what it's like to be left in the dark with dead men. I'm afraid."

He held in his mind the clearest picture he could make, though it raised a bitter taste in his throat.

I had chicos to right and left of me, dead. Sticky stuff running down over my arm and leg. I couldn't move. There was a quarter of an inch of air, it seemed like, right where my mouth was, and busted concrete block all over my chest that crushed me if I tried for more than a mouthful of air at a time. I couldn't even yell. Just croak like a toad that went under a truck. There was no night and no day to tell how long I'd been there, but I knew it was a long time because they started to smell bad. Oh, madre'dio, it was dark. Singer, please, I need to get out of here.

Singer turned to him with stunned slowness. He ran his hands over Saldivar's face as if he needed to make sure of his friend's identity.

"Palha," he said. "Yes. It's not good for you down here. I'm sorry." He straightened up slowly, pushing aside the past with tremendous effort. "I'll make a light."

He moved away into the darkness. Saldivar clutched in panic and just caught the edge of Singer's cloak as it swirled after him. Singer stopped and waited for him.

"*Ayei*, I didn't know it was as bad as that. We're not lost. Look."

He stood listening, inviting Saldivar to share his perception of the place. From the echo of their breath and steps, from the slight variations of temperature and flavor in the air, from Singer's sense of direction, the room took on a clear shape. It was large; there was plenty of breathing space. Saldivar felt such relief that his fear almost vanished. He gulped the dry, stale air.

It smelled of soured food and desiccated spices, but there was no corpse reek, no horror.

Singer found his way back to the corridor but followed it only a short way before turning into another chamber.

"These are storerooms, I think," he said. "I was crazy when I came this way. I didn't take much notice. But I saw lots of jars and boxes, maybe something we could use."

A moment later Saldivar barked his shins against a container. Singer felt around and found a row of jars sealed with a tacky, malleable substance. He scraped at it with his fingernails until he had a good-sized lump and rolled it around a thread from his belt.

"Give me your flint and steel," he said. "Now we'll find out if this is wax."

He had trouble lighting the wick in the dark with the sparks from the flint. Finally he ripped a piece from Saldivar's ragged tunic and rubbed it in the softened lump. He got the rag alight and used it to light his makeshift wick. The flame flared, dimmed, and steadied, showing them each other's faces in a warm pool of light that dissipated at its edges into rippled shadows.

Singer held it up and examined the jar whose seal he had picked loose. He worked the stopper out and sniffed. A rich, sweet scent arose, but when he tipped the jar, it did not pour. Singer gave the candle to Saldivar and stuck his hand inside the jar. His fingers came up coated with dark, grainy paste.

"Honey!" The word was Thanha; Singer did not know it in Delteix.

"What?"

"Made by little flying, singing things."

"Oh—honey." Saldivar looked at it dubiously. "I thought honey was, you know, like syrup. Runny."

"It turns solid when it sits for a while where it isn't hot. Taste. It's good." Singer could not believe that the Delh'tani, who had so many sweet foods, did not know the taste of honey.

"Isn't it made from bee spit or something? Are you sure this is good to eat?"

"Trust me! You've swallowed worse things."

Saldivar tasted gingerly. Saliva rushed into his mouth, and he was suddenly weak with hunger. His body craved that sweetness. He dipped his hand into the jar and scooped out more.

"It smells like flowers."

"That's what it's made from. Open some more of those, will you, and scrape off the wax. We'll need more lights."

He set the makeshift candle carefully atop a barrel and continued to investigate. He found a large jar that reached waist high; when he knocked off the neck, pale grains cascaded to the floor like sand. He put a palmful in his mouth and chewed.

"Barley meal." He coughed. "*Ayei,* but I'm dry."

"What is this?" Saldivar held up a container that looked like a bloated skin with the feet and head chopped off. "It sloshes."

"Ah—a wineskin if we're lucky."

"It's ugly. They could at least take off the legs so it wouldn't look so dead."

Singer uncorked it and squeezed a stream of pale liquid into his mouth. "A year down here hasn't hurt it any."

He showed Saldivar how to drink from the skin, and dubiously Saldivar tried it. It spilled down his face and chest, but most of the stream went into his mouth. It had a strong golden taste, like honey and fire.

"Kristo! This is wonderful!"

"Don't drink too much of that, or I'll have to carry you back."

Singer had found a tightly woven basket and was using a curved potsherd to scoop meal into it. He knotted up his cloak so he could carry the honey jar in it.

"Take down a couple more of those wineskins. I wish I had some water to mix with this meal, but water comes freely from the sky, so they don't keep it in treasure chambers."

"Where are we taking all this stuff?"

Singer raised his eyebrows. "Back to the cityfolk, of course. Sweet things and strong things to put the taste of life in their mouths."

He checked to see that Saldivar had more candles ready, then picked up the first one and carried it carefully, shielding the flame from drafts.

"One more thing."

He returned to the dark vault they had left. Holding the candle high, he looked slowly around the place. It was empty. There was no sign that anyone had been there. But when he bent lower to the floor under rock dust and rubble, dark stains showed. After so long, it was impossible to tell if they were water stains or blood, and if blood, whose it might be. He rubbed the hard-packed earth and touched his fingers to his lips.

"I don't forget, Dona," he whispered. "My feet are still on the road." He planted the candle firmly on that spot and left it behind, still burning.

6

The way back seemed much shorter with a light. The darkness
that inhabited the passages withdrew like a wild beast, out of
range of the small flame. When they reached the wall that closed
off the underground barracks, Singer climbed back through the
opening with the candle in his hand, leaving Saldivar to bring
the food.

Faces sprang out of nowhere as the light struck them. A soft
gasp of amazement and relief sounded all through the room.
Hungry-eyed men approached them cautiously on hands and
knees, drawn irresistibly to the light, some stretching out blackened and knotted hands toward it.

"I have food," Singer announced. "Who wants to eat with
me?"

He set the jar of honey down next to the candle. People at the
back pushed and shoved; some tried to climb over the others to
see what was there.

"We don't need food. We need a way out."

Singer recognized the hoarse voice that had spoken to him
earlier. The man had a seamed, twisted face half-hidden by a
wild grizzle of beard.

"We can get out anytime." Singer pitched his voice to carry
through the heavy air. He was not worried about being overheard by guards, since tons of rock lay between them. "We can
leave anytime, but there are things to talk about. No reason not
to eat first. The guards cannot reach us now."

The crowd began to push forward, as eager for food as they
had been desperate for light and air.

"Stop it! Are we animals?" The bearded man stretched out

long arms and shoved the others back. "There's plenty for everyone. It's a big jar. Be patient."

He seized the jar with a glance at Singer to make sure it was all right and held it out so everyone in the inner circle could take a palmful. Then he urged them out of the way, hastening some with a kick from his cracked, calloused heel. Singer saw that not all the captives tried to push others out of the way. Some came supporting friends too ill or weak to make their way to the center alone. It twisted his heart to watch them drag themselves.

They ate and passed the jar around until it was so far emptied that they had to reach in to the elbow. Then Singer repossessed it. He struck the top portion of the jar off with a rock; eager hands reached out immediately and seized the shards to clean off the honey that still clung to them.

"I have meal for porridge here," Singer said. "Does anyone have water to share?"

Half a dozen small, hoarded waterskins appeared and were passed up to him, hand to hand. He poured them all into the jar and stirred in enough meal to make a stiff, sweet porridge. Singer held his hand over the mixture and, with the edge of a potsherd, slashed his palm. Blood dripped into the pot, black in the dim light.

"He who eats at my hearth is of my blood, travels the road I travel. Who will eat with me?"

They were silent. They looked at the food with longing but kept their hands from reaching for it.

"Who are you, stranger?" the bearded man asked.

A mutter went around the circle. "He's a renegade," someone in the back finally dared to say out loud. "That's why he's so bold. Renegades bring death and trouble wherever they go. Kill him and take his food. We can find our own way out."

"Be quiet and let him speak," the bearded man said. "Are you a renegade?"

"I am Singer of the Riders. Renegade is a name for runaway slaves, and I was never slave to any man."

"You're here the same as us, aren't you?" someone called angrily.

"I came here of my own free will. I came to bring the Somostai down. Will you help me, or will you be buried when they fall?"

"Help you?" someone cried bitterly. "When was there ever friendship between cityfolk and renegades? We can never be one blood with you, stranger."

"You're very sure," Singer said. "Listen: there was a child born in the Iron City when Hadhla was master. His father gave him no fortune, and his mother gave him no name—or if she did, it was lost with her when she went away. The boy was called Ti'daron, the darkness-born, the bastard. He lived in the shadow of the mountain, and he stole food from the cattle in the slaughter yard to save himself from starving. The Somostai marked his face with a knife, the mark of the Eater, to show that he belonged to the Devourer of Flesh, and he lived in fear that one day the Devourer would come for him.

"One night soldiers came to the place where he slept. The cityfolk, his own kind, watched while the soldiers bound him hand and foot and carried him away. Not one of them stirred a finger to defend him. The soldiers left him on the shoulder of the mountain, in the Place of the Eater, on a night cold enough to freeze a drunkard's piss before it hit the ground. He had been bought and sold to the Somostai."

He paused and looked from face to face. He had called up the phrases and cadence from the memories of that child, like bringing old dusty things long-buried out into the light. Even in the poorest streets there was always someone who told stories, and he knew by their eyes that he had remembered right.

"How will this boy survive, friendless and weaponless? Even if he could break his bonds and flee, where can he run? If he escapes the Devourer's fire, the sting of the bitter cold will stop his breath as easily. And he cannot break his bonds. They are too strong for him. He is trapped like a rabbit caught in a snare with a hawk descending on it.

"This boy has no friends, but he has his eyes and ears. He has no weapon, but he has his voice. He looks around him, and he sees that even the Somostai cannot take away the lights in the sky. The Destroyer cannot reach that high. And he begins to sing, to show the blackrobes he is not afraid. He is afraid—of course he is afraid—but he wants to rob them of their pleasure. He will do that much, even if that is all that he can do.

"A small weapon—a child's eyes, a child's voice. What fool would defy the Somostai with no greater power than that? But it's enough. When the boy listens, he hears the sound of hooves. It is a pallantai of the Riders who hears his voice and snatches him from beneath the claws of the blackrobed bird descending. He runs with the Riders like the wind that cannot be caught in a snare. When the blackrobes come looking, they find nothing. Nothing but the wind that laughs at them."

"Storytelling." The bearded man dismissed his words. "What's the good of that?"

"Best stories are the true ones," Singer said. "I was that boy. Are you cityfolk? So was I. Have you suffered hunger and fear at the hands of the City Masters? So have I. Have you been sold to the Somostai? So was I. There's only one difference between us. I have my freedom."

"Freedom?" a mocking voice called. "What is that?"

"I thought you wanted a way out."

"There is no way out. Where can we go?"

Those words were repeated from a dozen different directions.

"There's always at least one way out," Singer said contemptuously.

"We don't kiss up to death like you renegades. We like to stay alive."

"We can't live on weeds and grass. We don't want to freeze to death."

"Where else can we go? The cities are dead."

The bearded man hushed the clamor of voices. "Of course we want to get out of this place; we don't want to be buried alive. But where else can we go if not back to our masters? The Somostai and the flying people collected all the food for hundreds of miles. Now, in midwinter, where can we go and survive? First they took our food and our livelihood, then they took our flesh and blood. There's nowhere to go unless we could fly over the sea like birds or hide in the hedge like mice."

His clenched fists looked like old tree roots. "We're not fools, stranger—not all of us, anyway—and we're not cowards, though we're not handy with weapons. Even if we could run now—risk starving or freezing—we'd never know what happened to our families. There's nothing we can do to save them."

"I'm telling you what you can do. Kill the blackrobes. Take the city."

The farmer gave Singer a dark look. "Why not fly away? That would be as easy."

"They can die," Singer insisted. "They can be defeated. Even the flying people can be killed. One blow in the right place is all it takes. Their possessions dazzle you. Inside their steel skins, they're soft as rabbits. Join with me, and I'll prove it to you." He held out his hand to the farmer, who looked at it without clasping it, staring at the blood still glistening.

"So easy for you to spill blood, to cut things," the bearded man murmured. "Maybe you were born on the streets of the city, but you're not one of us now."

Singer withdrew his hand. "I became what I had to be to survive," he said harshly.

The farmer shook his head. "Soldiers have trampled back and forth over us for more years than I have hairs in my beard. Do you know what a farmer has to become? A stone. A root. Bend and bow into the earth and hope they'll leave you that. If we raise our hands to them, they won't just kill us. They'll strike down the helpless ones out there, behind the wire. Your way is to strike back. Ours is to cling to the little we have. We still live. We can't gamble that on a mouthful of words from a stranger."

Singer sucked traces of honey from his fingers, disregarding the blood, and watched the farmer. He opened himself to the thousand traces of thought and feeling that Hilurin had taught him to read in a face. The farmer resisted him, mistrusted him, but his eyes almost begged to be convinced. He craved hope as he craved the food set before him. He had refused it but longed for it to be offered again under terms he could accept.

"You have my name. Won't you tell me yours?"

The farmer hesitated as if he feared to give Singer that much power over him. "Where is your renegade magic? Can't you guess?"

"Give me your hand."

The farmer clasped Singer's hand firmly, no longer flinching from the blood on it. Singer wondered if the man truly knew what he was offering. There was no resistance. He was embraced at once by the farmer's loves and fears. He found himself trying to take only what he needed and get out rather than probing for more. The man was Olmalik. Singer knew that from the faces: Selem, a boy and a girl child he had seen in her hut—ordinary faces, yet to the farmer's eyes they shone from within like stars. Singer remembered how Deronh's plain, weather-worn features had shone for him like that, and he struggled against the farmer's memories, refusing to know more. The faces were gone; he stood on a hillside above a plowed field. The gnarled trees around him were laden with an early snow. The bearded man had loved that place. It had been his labor, his refuge. His Rock. Singer struggled again to escape the vision of what had happened next. He closed his eyes, and when he opened them again, the daylight sight had gone and he saw the farmer by candlelight, across their joined hands.

"Olmalik," he said. "Applewood. Your father loved those trees before you were born."

"It's true what they say—you renegades are soul stealers," the farmer breathed.

"I stole nothing, only shared it."

"I would not choose to share those things with a stranger."

"My heart has become a storehouse of lost treasures," Singer said bitterly. "Don't worry, yours are safe with all the rest."

"You are young to know so much about losing everything," the farmer said. "I always thought you Riders were kinless folk, roaming like the wind, uncaring." He seemed to focus on an inward vision, something Singer had shown him without meaning to. He put it aside and looked at Singer again. "I have seen. You do not mean us harm."

"Then will you join with us?"

"I dare not."

Singer made his last throw of the bones. "Olmalik, I guessed at your name before. I was looking for you. Your woman sent a message for you. She still hopes in you."

The farmer's grip tightened painfully. "Selem? You saw her?"

"Yes. She helped us get into the city. She and the children live. Not well, but they live. Take my advice and you can see her again."

He watched the farmer wrestle with himself, watched his defenses break open at last like a tough husk.

"What would you have us do?"

"I will show you the way out. I will show you where to find more food, like this. You know the secret way through the wall? You might not be able to use it. It could be watched. Anyway, you'll have to find your own way back to Lowtown. But once there—if you can't hide from the blackrobes, you're less clever than a rabbit or a rat. Plenty of burrows in that warren."

"But eventually they'll find that we're gone. They'll hunt us all down and kill us. You don't show me how to save our families."

"There's only one way. The Black City must fall."

Olmalik turned away. "Then we're done for."

"No! I have friends—Riders beyond the mountain pass. I have a friend in the Black City. I came here to find him. Once I get him safe, I can bring the Riders down. Hide them among you. Then, if the blackrobes come hunting you, the Riders will protect you."

"Why? Why would you take that risk for us?"

"One hearth," Singer said. "I told you. We'll treat your kin as our own. But then you must help us when the time comes."

"Help you? How?"

"Help pull the blackrobes down. Fight at our side."

Olmalik wavered, appalled by the blasphemous daring of fighting the Somostai.

"No one comes back from the Black City," he said. "No one defies them and lives. Stranger, I will follow you out of this trap, and I will hide like a rat if you can show me where to find crumbs to eat. But I cannot promise, yet, to join with you. When I see with my own eyes that you have gone there and come back, I'll follow you wherever you say."

The others had been watching and listening. Singer watched their eyes gleaming in the candlelight. Most of them would not commit themselves as far as speaking out loud, but he saw them nod, saw their lips move in muttered assent. They huddled closer together.

"We have an agreement, then." He pushed the pot of meal toward them. "Eat with me."

Olmalik patted Singer's shoulder awkwardly. "People here call me Sticks because I've grown so thin. You gave me back my name. I don't believe that anyone can come alive out of the Black City, but for my part, I wish you well."

He took the pot from Singer, scooped out a handful, and passed it on to the men in the shadows. They shared the food from hand to hand, not like starving beggars but like men with a shared purpose. Singer had no illusions that all of them trusted him, but he thought they would follow Olmalik.

While they were eating, he took a chunk of stone and scratched a rough plan on the largest of the potsherds, showing as much of the underground passages as he remembered.

"Keep this; you might want to go back for more food while I'm away. The night is passing. We'd better be on our way."

He let Olmalik pass out candles and organize the group for traveling. Then he guided them to the storerooms to load up as much food as they could carry and still move quickly. The stairs were where he remembered them and in no worse repair than they had been when he had last used them. In a short time they crowded out onto the street and once again breathed the cold night air.

7

The air smelled worse than usual. It was thick with a scorching, sullen reek, as if a great fire had recently been smothered. The stairs had let them out in an area close to the Great House, where they could expect to see many soldiers and blackrobes. Singer split the prisoners into small groups of five or six. He scouted ahead of them and then summoned them group by group.

They had moved slowly but safely through several streets, when Singer heard the sound he had been dreading. Booted and mailed footfalls rang heavily on the pavement. Singer saw the glow of their torches as they approached. The soldiers came around the corner. Singer saw that there were only six of them. They were Somostai, not scholars but tall and strong armed guards. Handing the hammer to Saldivar, he reached for his hidden knife, then realized he had lost that on the floor of the furnace shed. He still had the iron chisel. Swinging it by one end, he gauged the distance and waited. There was still a chance that the guards would pass them by.

But the prisoners were not good at hiding. One of them moved—and was seen. The blackrobes stopped, and their officer, with a wave of his hand, directed them to search the roadside. Singer motioned to the others to be still. He let the Somostai approach until he saw how many men were hidden there and recoiled with an exclamation. The officer ran across the road to see what they had found. Singer threw the chisel like an oversized knife. It spun end over end and struck the officer in the head. He sprawled on the stones without a sound. Before the others could react, Saldivar swung the hammer against the legs of the nearest blackrobe and knocked him over. Saldivar seized

162

the man's torch as it fell and thrust it into the faces of the others, holding them back long enough for Singer to take the fallen man's sword.

With a sword in hand, Singer engaged two of the remaining guards. Saldivar was left facing the others. He fended them off as well as he could, feinting with the torch, catching their blows clumsily on the hammer handle. Singer dodged cuts from his adversaries, trying to tempt them into giving up their advantage by jumping down from the road into the jumble of rocks where he crouched.

"Singer, goddammit, all I've got is this fucking hammer!"

Palha knew nothing about sword skill. Singer had become so used to thinking of him as a brother that he had forgotten that. He could not fight four men and defend Palha, too. He caught the next thrust and momentarily locked hilts with the guard. He kicked the man's knee sideways and set him sprawling among the rocks. Saldivar managed to knock the man on the head with the hammer.

The other three took the lure at last and scrambled into the ruins after Saldivar and Singer, in hot haste to surround and overpower one swordsman and a farmer with a hammer. They ignored the cowering prisoners, discounting them as fighters.

"Put out the torch," Singer said. Saldivar ground it out. The Somostai were left in the circle of their own remaining torch, looking out into darkness.

"They can die," Singer said. "They are already dead men. Remember your children! Remember your dead! Come and prove to yourselves that blackrobes, too, can die!"

The prisoners were still too much afraid to move. Slowly, like men trying to wake up from an overpowering dream, the boldest of them began to circle the fighters in a slowly closing ring. One of the Somostai made the mistake of trying to look over his shoulder. Singer saw the flicker of his eyes and thrust like lightning for his throat. He knew a body blow was no use; all of them wore heavy mail. He failed to hit his target, but the guard parried wildly, and Singer kicked him in the belly hard enough to throw him off balance against the man beside him. Saldivar took advantage of their distraction to swing the hammer in a crushing blow against the torchbearer's arm. The Somostai screamed and dropped the torch. It flickered on the ground. The crowd shifted uncertainly in the darkness. Then one of them shouted something and rushed forward.

Singer lowered his weapon and pushed against the rush of the crowd to get away from the fallen blackrobes. The last of the dying light showed a mass of punching, kicking bodies where the guards had been. Their end was eerily silent. Heavy breathing, grunted curses, and the dull sound of blows would not have carried more than one street away. Their death cries, if any, were muffled by the weight of the crowd.

Singer reached Olmalik, somehow relieved to see that the farmer was standing aside from the slaughter.

"The blackrobes are done for," Singer said against the farmer's ear. "Start pulling them off. Go now! You can't risk staying around after such a disturbance."

"Aren't you coming with us?"

Singer bent over the dead officer, stripping off his clothes and weapons and putting them on himself. "No. I go to the Black City."

He handed Saldivar the clothes of the guard killed with the hammer. Saldivar made a disgusted noise. "There's blood all over this sleeve. Why am I always borrowing clothes from some dead man?"

"Strip the other bodies and make sure to take their weapons," Singer said to Olmalik. "Dump the bodies out of sight, then get out of here."

He was already turning to go when Olmalik clutched at his arm. "Wait! How will I find you again?"

"With Selem you will find my hearth sister. She's a healer. If you need to speak with me, tell her. She can find me. It's more Rider magic, so take good care of her. I'll come back when I've kept the rest of my promise. For now, make them practice with weapons and keep it in their minds that they have killed Somostai and can do so again."

8

Singer and Saldivar jogged down the deserted street, heading toward the road to the plateau, toward the Somostai and not away from them.

"You know we're running straight for trouble," Saldivar said.

"The blackrobes are the ones in trouble. They're like ants in a broken nest. Best place for us is the middle of the swarm. They'll never notice us. Just keep your hood up so no one will see that we don't wear the earring."

"Well, at least I'll die warm and with a full belly," Saldivar said. "If only we could have brought along another one of those wine bags, I'd be a happy man."

For the first time the furnaces were dark and still. A charred smell hung around them. Wisps of smoke still rose from them in places, though it was too dark to see the extent of the damage. All the light and noise came from farther up the road, past the pile of burningstone where the mine shafts bored into the mountainside. White smoke lit by lurid flickers boiled from the opening of one of the shafts. All around it Somostai and city soldiers were furiously at work with shovels and pumps. There was a huge cratered dimple in the earth, and edges of raw rock on the mountainside gleamed in firelight where some force had shattered the mountain itself.

As Singer had guessed, the blackrobes worked on frantically and took no notice of him. His attention was drawn from the crater to a place beyond the lights where dark shapes lay on the ground and there were sounds of moaning. Broken forms on stretchers were loaded into a wagon, and then the wagon rolled away, up the road to the Black City.

"Lean on me and don't say anything," he said to Saldivar. "This is where dead men's clothing will be useful."

They limped along the road, past a line of men hauling water. As they approached the end of the line, the overseer hailed them.

"Where are you going, Captain? Where's the rest of your squad? Report for reassignment."

"I have an injured man," Singer said. He adjusted his posture and language to match the Somostai's expectations.

"What happened?"

"Caught under a collapsing wall. His arm is broken, and he may be hurt inside."

The officer cursed them vigorously. "You fools," he finished. "It's not bad enough to lose the whole team in there, but you have to have stupid accidents? I'd break his other arm for him if I had time. Get him out of here."

"Yes, my master."

Singer dragged Saldivar to the place where the bodies were laid out. Wounded men who were judged well enough to walk were being taken up the road in a convoy behind the wagon. He took possession of one of the horses standing by, slung Saldivar up on its back, and headed up the road with the rest. He glanced around from under the cover of his hood to see what kinds of injuries the others had. They were crushed and burned, some with dangling, mangled limbs that looked as if they would have to be amputated.

Saldivar started to speak but checked himself. Singer felt him reaching for contact, trying to communicate something he thought was important. He saw the awesome fists of fire plunging into the earth, mangling the very rocks and shredding flesh and bone. *Blast wounds,* Saldivar said impatiently. *Those are blast wounds. What have your blackrobes been playing with?*

They were in the middle of the group when they passed through the gate at the end of the road. As Singer had hoped, the emergency had caused so much confusion that no one checked or questioned them. He pulled Saldivar off the horse and ducked into the nearest doorway while the wounded were still being helped through the gate.

Inside, narrow stairs spiraled upward. It was dark again but lit from time to time by torches, the fluttering red light swelling and fading as the stairs curved around. They ran and ran in tight circles, feeling as if they were getting nowhere, always craning their heads upward for a glimpse of a lit door above them.

Singer stopped and pressed Saldivar's shoulder for silence.

They were both breathing hard, but under the echoes of their breath they heard booted feet hammering on the steps above. There was nowhere to hide below. They redoubled their pace, hoping to find some concealment before they closed with the oncoming guard. They saw no doors, no niches of any kind. No hopeful light beckoned from above. They could hear voices as well as footsteps only a few turns away.

The stairs paused in a brief landing, and Saldivar halted at the outline of a door flush with the stone wall. Singer's fingers told him it was too smooth and warm to be metal. There was no latch, no keyhole, no hinge, nothing to show a way of entry. He shifted his sweating hand on the hilt of the hated Somostai sword. It would be easy to pick off the first two or three. After that . . .

Saldivar shouldered him out of the way. "Fresh cuts around the edge of the stone," he said. "This door is new. No card slot. Ah! There's the eye." He reached up to the top of the arch and passed his hand across it. The door slid back into the wall. Blinding white light stabbed out, and Singer jumped.

"Hurry!" Saldivar ordered. "Get in before they see the light." He pushed Singer over the threshold, and the door shot to behind them. They flattened themselves against the wall beside it, hardly daring to breathe, and waited. Heavy steps passed, almost inaudible behind the thickness of the wall.

Singer's eyes stung in the unexpected light, then slowly cleared. There was something he did not like about the quality of that light. It was too bright, too harsh. The color was wrong, a flat bluish-white like nothing on earth. Then he remembered where he had seen such light before—in the Delh'tani "hospital," the place where he had been tied down and stung with metal fangs full of strangerfolk venom. He gasped, and Palha laid two fingers across his mouth. From the urgency of the touch, Singer gathered that Palha had seen someone.

He sank noiselessly into a crouch. When he saw where Saldivar was looking, he stood up again. "No danger from them."

The beds were a kind of cot, like a Somostai imitation of the flat tables the Delh'tani used for their wounded. The people lying there were not Somostai. They were children, women, and old men for the most part. Most of them were unconscious, but those who were still awake sensed his presence and looked up. Singer crossed to the first of the beds—and froze.

Saldivar looked over his shoulder, wondering what had stopped Singer in his tracks. The creature on the bed stirred, and Singer made a faint sound, as if he were the one who was suffering. Saldivar saw the others turn their eyes toward Singer in silent terror.

He put his hand on Singer's arm. "It's the black cloak," Saldivar muttered. "They think you're Somostai."

Singer pushed back his hood. He clenched his fist on the dark robe as if to rip it off, but he did not. "Smells like death in here," he said.

He pulled the sheet from the body on the bed. It was hardly more than a child that lay there, wasted away to a bundle of sticks under parchment-white skin, wasted except for one leg so swollen that it did not seem to belong to the body. It was the swollen leg that stank of decay.

"Don't," Saldivar said. "Not our problem."

He could feel the smell wrapping around Singer like wire, but the fear in their eyes was worse: known through Singer's mind, it burned and froze. It made him sick. For a minute he wanted to move away from Singer and shut him out. Then he was ashamed and held tighter.

Singer knelt by the girl and stretched his hands out to her without quite touching. "Don't be afraid of me," he said. "Don't be afraid. I'll try to help you."

He did not know what to bring her; he had to reach a long way back for a memory that was any good. *Wind blowing, a cold wind that came down from the snowfields on Stormfather, smelling of water. Rain rode the wind's back. A storm was coming.*

Her white lips parted slightly, as if she could feel the cool air. "Oh, that's good," she said. "I'm not afraid of you now. I know you, Uncle Death. I asked the Lady to send you."

"No time for that. I can fix this."

Her body was burning itself up, trying to burn away the poison within. She was like a shape of white ash that would fall to pieces if the wind shook it. The leg was the trouble. It must have been a dirty wound. The swelling meant the blood was not running the way it should; he could clear that, clean away the dead stuff.

But he was stopped in his tracks. Something was wrong. The whole leg seemed dead, like a piece of meat. He could not find anything that connected it to the live child. He had never felt anything like it. He tried to stay calm, not to let his panic wash back over the girl.

It's not me, she said clearly and calmly in his mind. He let himself move closer to her. She seemed to be looking down from high up, as if she were riding with the wind. *Don't touch that. It's ugly. I want to go with you. Take me away.*

I'm not what you think, he cried. *I'm only a man.*

But she clung to him, still trusting him. She was as light as a burning leaf. Her breath was light. There was a long pause, then another breath. Against his will, he had to help her. He let her heart slow down. She was moving away from him, fading on the wind.

Suddenly she gasped again. *There's someone bad with you. One of them. Oh, send him away.* Her body trembled and jerked. He could feel her fear, but he could not reach her this time. She clutched at nothing and died alone.

The faint sound that escaped Singer was as loud as a scream to Saldivar. He had only seen the girl die. He had not understood the rest of it.

"Why did she call you Uncle Death?" he said. "What does that mean?"

"I didn't," Singer said. "I didn't touch her. She was in fear of me, and she left. I was no help at all." He shuddered. "She saw something."

Saldivar tried to comfort him, but Singer turned on him and closed him out. "No. I can't see that. I can't."

"But why did she say that?" Saldivar persisted.

"Barasha Vaharon," Singer said. "Uncle Death. The Riders call him that. It's boasting, I suppose. Others fear him; to us he's a relative. And it takes the fear away. We say that when no one else can help you, you can always count on him. Sometime she must have known a Rider. Excuse me." He turned away and retched violently.

Saldivar held Singer's shoulders and tried not to panic. This is making him sick, he thought. And we can't get out. I don't understand any of this, and he's crazy. Well, I always knew that. Not a reason to bug out now.

9

It was nothing Saldivar said that brought Singer out of it. Singer wiped his mouth and looked up and saw a foot. It was wearing neither a brown Delh'tani boot nor black Somostai leather but a makeshift sandal. Saldivar seized the feet and swept them off the ground as Singer sprang upward to clap one hand over the man's mouth and drag him down. They felled the stranger like a tree; he landed heavily on his back with Singer still covering his mouth and nose.

"If I feel your throat move to call out, you're dead," Singer whispered. "Are you going to take that chance?"

The man on the floor shook his head vigorously, his chest heaving in a vain effort to breathe. Singer moved his hand down from mouth to throat, keeping a close enough grip that he could tighten it to extinction instantly.

The man signed with his hands: *May I speak?*

The gestures were close enough to Thanha hand language that Singer could read them easily.

"Softly," he said. "And to the point. Is there anyone else here or likely to come?"

"No. Not until the Deltanek daymarker on the table changes the number. I can show you if you want."

"What is this place?"

"They call it the special infirmary. It's not like the common infirmary where they send members of the Order. This is where the keep the *speriments*."

Singer didn't know that word. "The what?"

"The people they try things on. Like that girl. She's dead, isn't she? I heard what she called you."

170

Singer's face was expressionless.

"Are you going to kill me?" the man on the floor asked mildly. "You need not, and I'd rather you didn't."

"What was wrong with her?" Singer asked.

"Leg crushed under a cartwheel. They cut it off. They've been practicing that kind of thing since the Deltanek came and they found out it was possible. But that wasn't good enough. They heard that the Deltanek can put parts from one body onto another, even use animal parts in human bodies. The blackrobes are jealous. They want to know everything the sky people know. So they tried sewing on a leg from a man who had died not too long ago. It didn't work. Made them angry."

"You say 'they.' Who are you, then?"

"Me? They call me Bone."

"You're not Somostai?"

"No more than you, Uncle Death, for all your black cloak."

"But you work for them."

"They bought me." For the first time there was bitterness in the man's voice. "No one else had any use for me."

"Why not?"

"Fog-eyed Bone. Can't see beyond the end of his nose." He waved a hand self-mockingly in front of his eyes. "I made myself useful, given the chance. I can see to the end of a pen. I can reckon numbers. So they don't throw me in with the speriments. But still—ugly Bone! Clumsy Bone! No chance of testing him to see if he's worthy to join the Order. He stays a slave. Lucky Bone."

"Lucky!" Singer gestured toward the beds. "You help them torture these people."

"There are two keys to freedom," Bone said. "I have one: not to be afraid of death. The other is not to love anything. I failed there. I love my numbers. I can see beautiful things if I have a quiet place and some paper. My parents sold me for food. I sold myself for a couple of books."

He looked at Singer defiantly. "Make up your mind. Are you going to kill me or not?"

Singer wished he had killed the little man when he had first spotted him. It would have been simpler. He did not want to do it now.

"Depends," he said. He took a closer look at the narrow chest and knobby, jutting shoulders. "What made you this way?"

It was a fair question for a Rider. No one took offense at being asked where he got that scar or how she lost a finger. But Bone grimaced.

"Born that way, maybe. Like my eyes. But I doubt it. Korro heard some chance remark from the Deltanek one day—about a lack of some kind of food and how it made people get sick. He got some babies out of the Lowtown camp and gave some of them Somostai food and some of them even less than they'd been getting. Cattle mush mostly, well cooked. Some of them looked remarkably like me for a while. Their legs got so bandy, they couldn't walk. Then blood started coming out of their mouths, and they died. Lucky babies."

His eyes glittered, and he blinked fiercely to clear them. "What's it to you?" he said savagely. "I can't even see your face. Are you having fun?"

Singer bent closer. "Now can you see me?"

"Yes, I can see you, blue-eyed Death. Why did you come here? Don't you think there's enough death in the Holy City?"

Singer touched Bone's eyelids with the tips of his fingers. The eyes looked the same as any other eyes. He had seen eyes that were cloudy behind their round black windows in old people. Bone's eyes were wide and clear. Singer slipped inside his vision without really intending it. Suddenly he was seeing his own face from only a handbreadth away. The feeling was too disorienting. He looked away quickly. For a minute he could not see anything at all, and then he felt Bone's vision move with him, as if following his request. Bone had been telling the truth. The big room was cloudy and vague, like a high trail in heavy fog. Only the details of dust and debris on the floor, close to his eyes, were clear. Singer tried to focus, but Bone's eyes would not cooperate. It would have been no kindness to clarify the ruin Bone saw around him. Singer could feel fierce pity and remorse tearing at Bone like the claws of some wild thing imprisoned inside him. He could see too well already for the things he was allowed to look at.

Singer looked past that pain, trying to find the beauty Bone had spoken of. It must be something that lay far away from the visible world, Singer thought. How could Bone see numbers? Maybe the Somostai had driven the sense out of him and made him think about things that were not really there. Then he caught a glimpse of something like the sparks he had seen in the Delh'tani patterns of fire. Bone had patterns in his mind. Singer did not know what to compare them to. They were nothing that could ever be seen with the outward eye, but in Bone's mind they were linked to the shapes of real things.

Fascinated, Singer tried to grasp the meaning of those patterns, but this time it was his own mind that failed to see. He did not understand. As he withdrew from the attempt, he became aware that Bone was still pinned to the floor and struggling. The little man's breath wheezed and sobbed through clenched teeth as he tried to throw Singer off. Saldivar reached for his knife, but Singer did not feel any threat. Bone did not want to hurt them, but he wanted desperately to get out of their restraint.

Singer let go of him cautiously, and Bone dragged himself as far as the wall, where he crouched facing them.

"You *are* Somostai," he said. "Korro succeeded at last and sent you here to torment me. But you'll never understand—what a joke. Go ahead, steal my thoughts. Take everything. It won't mean a thing to you. Lucky Bone, lucky to the end." He started to laugh painfully. "I hate you," he said after a few minutes. "I really hate you. Do you want to know why? Because I saw through your eyes for just a moment. Now I know what it's like to see."

Singer spread his hands as he would have to placate an angry warrior. "If you saw with my eyes, then think my thoughts for just a moment. Do I feel like a Somostai to you?"

Bone wrinkled his forehead, eyes inward-looking, reviewing.

"No," he said. "No, you don't." He shivered. "You bring the cold in with you. Snow, ice, cold wind, darkness. And fire in the darkness somewhere. What are those bright things in the dark?" He covered his face with his hands. "Stars! So that's what they look like. I never saw them. When I look up, I can't see anything at all." He sat quietly, calming himself. "You're not Somostai. I don't know what else you can be, but not that."

"What did you mean when you said just now that Korro succeeded at last?"

Bone tried to shrug the question off. "My fear speaking. My only freedom is in my mind. I hear it whispered that one of the master's great dreams is to find the power to see through all concealment into mind and heart. Sometimes I dream he has succeeded."

"Is that possible?"

Bone grimaced. "Korro is shrewd as a demon, but in that way he sees no better than I do—all smoke and fog. Otherwise I'd be dead already. If he knew what this insignificant creature thinks about him, he'd crush me like a bug. What will you do now that you have rummaged my secrets?"

"I would make your eyes work if I knew how," Singer said slowly. "I have a friend who knows about such things. I wish she could see you. She might know what to do. And in return I would ask you to show me more of those patterns in your inner sight. They are like folded music. I see patterns, too, but I don't understand them. You could teach me."

Bone threw back his head and laughed out loud. "Bone met Death in a dark corner. His knees knocked together, and he cried out, 'What do you want of me, Uncle Death?' Death sat down in the dust and picked up a writing stick. 'Teach me, brother Bone,' said he. Lucky, lucky Bone."

He pulled himself to his feet and peered at the Delh'tani box with glowing numbers that sat on the desk. "I have to report the death of that poor child soon, before she gets stiff, pardon me for mentioning it. Else they'll crush me anyway. So tell me quickly what you really want."

"That's what I would do if I could," Singer said. "I have other business now."

He was almost sure he could trust the strange little man. At any rate, he did not think Bone would give him away to the blackrobes.

"My business, in the end, is to bring the Somostai down," he said. "Before I turn my hand to Korro's destruction, I have a friend to find and free. Tell me the way to him, and I'll ask no more of you."

Bone stared at him. "You have a *friend* in the Holy City? I live here, and I don't have any friends."

"He is a stranger here. I think, like you, he was brought here against his will. He's not a tall man—a little shorter than my brother, here; dark eyes, pale skin, very ordinary-looking, but he's not ordinary. He may have been wounded in the head when he came here, and I think Giristiyah is not his mother language. Have you seen anyone like that?"

"You must be joking," Bone said. "No—this is beyond a joke. I see him every day. He used to talk about friends who would come for him someday. But are you really his friend? Should I tell Death where to find him?"

"That joke is wearing thin," Singer said.

"It's no joke. You don't know how fearsome you look from down on the floor. And your friend there—I never did get a look at his face. He says nothing, but he keeps his hand on his knife."

"I'm Thanha," Singer said almost apologetically. "We all look like Death to cityfolk. Your friend might like my looks better than Korro's. Give him the choice."

Bone blew a breath through pursed lips and decided. "Well, you'll get your chance to match yourself against the Master. Korro has made a kind of pet out of him. Chonza, they call him. He's been useful in dealing with the Deltanek. He's not stupid. The Deltanek have brought some beautiful things to do with numbers, and Chonza lets me help with them. He lives in South Tower, on the seaward side, not far from Korro's own rooms."

"How do we get there?"

"Angling for more of my secrets? This one is not beautiful, but it is useful." He hurried them past the rows of beds and through a doorway at the far end of the ward. The cold stench of a jakes hit them before they opened the door.

Bone slid a plank over one of the holes in the stone bench and motioned them to stand on it. "Look up. It's an air shaft. It goes straight up to the roof, but you don't need to go that far. There are two more latrines on upper floors. Be careful as you go through them. You risk catching one of the masters bare-assed, and they would find it hard to forgive that. The first is on the same level with the kitchen storage, but the way to the stores goes past the armory, which is busy and full of spikes as a hive in spring. The second is two turns to the left from the small library. That, too, is buzzing with people. The Deltanek embassy lives there. If you can slip past them and down the wide stairs, you'll come to the tower stair where Chonza lives."

Singer took a dubious look up into the narrow shaft.

"Now you see the disadvantages of being so well made," Bone said. "If you are strong as well as long, I think you can manage. Higher up, the stonework is less careful and the crevices are deeper. You must take your chance; there's no other safe way. If you get as far as Chonza's room, I may see you again."

He hesitated. "Can I give you another piece of advice? Those black robes may have been good for getting in, but you'd be better off without them now. The Somostai know each other, and you'll be caught. You'd be less conspicuous dressed as slaves."

"Good advice, but what am I to do about it?" Singer said.

"Dump those cloaks down the hole. I have some castoffs here, left by folk who won't need them anymore."

Reluctantly, they abandoned their Somostai garments and

weapons and put on the rough, well-worn clothes that Bone found for them.

"Much more suitable. Now, forgive me for not waiting to see you off. I have a corpse to attend to."

He hurried back to his charges, leaving Singer and Saldivar perched atop the jakes. *← latrines*

"You'd best go first," Singer said. "I don't want to fall on you."

He boosted Saldivar into the shaft and pulled himself after. The spaces between the stones allowed no more than a finger-hold, and he could not extend his arms and legs beyond a cramped half bend. His shoulders fit tightly within the width of the shaft and gave him good bracing, but his legs threatened to get jammed. His knees and fingers were scraped raw in minutes. From Saldivar's harsh breathing above him, Singer guessed that he was working equally hard. A foul miasma rose with them, stinging eyes and lungs and nauseating them with its stench.

"If that crooked little man can do this, it shouldn't be too hard for us," Singer said.

"Maybe he's more used to smelling Somostai shit," Saldivar said, coughing. "You'd better pray I keep hold of my breakfast. It's got nowhere to go but down."

After a long time of inching upward in the dark, they saw a dim ray of light coming in through the wall.

"I don't care if there are Somostai in there like flies on horse manure," Saldivar said. "I have to stretch my legs."

He contorted himself through the opening and into another latrine that looked and smelled much like the last. They shook out their cramped muscles and stretched. Without warning, the door opened, and a boy in the dark tunic of the Somostai slaves pushed through with a chamber pot in each hand. They clapped hands to their weapons immediately, but something in the boy's face made them pause. His eyes and mouth stretched wide in terror at the sight of them. Saldivar sprang at him, showing all his teeth in a fierce grimace. The boy dropped the pots and ran. From far down the hall they heard a shriek of terror as he got his breath back. Saldivar helplessly doubled over with laughter. Singer had never seen him laugh so much. Finally he looked up, pointing to Singer with a shaky finger.

"If you could see yourself—" he gasped. "The kid thinks we're demons crawling up out of hell. I don't need to be a mind reader to see that! He's about right, too. Kristo, if I look like you, I'm a filthy mess!"

He made the ferocious face again, and Singer had to laugh, too. Palha's face was seamed and striped with black dust and runnels of sweat. His hands, too, were grimy black and bloody at the knuckles. They looked like claws.

"Back up the chimney with us," Saldivar said. "The kid will be back with the shock squad in half a minute. I feel sorry for his ass when they find out there's no one here."

By the time faint voices rose from below, they had hitched themselves far enough along that they could not be seen. As Bone had said, the cracks between stones were larger there. They could climb easily with hands and feet rather than wriggling along with shoulders and knees. The air was chilly and less fetid. They reached the second opening and crawled out with great relief. Outside the latrine, a trickle of water fell from the rock into a basin. They splashed off the worst of the soot and blood, leaving only a concealing layer of grime.

Singer guessed it was well past midnight. Though they could hear voices from some of the rooms assigned to the embassy, there was no one about in the halls. Guards were posted by certain doors, but they did not challenge a pair of slaves shuffling along. They found the broad shallow stairs Bone had described, descended them, and came to another staircase spiraling down through a tower shaft. Those rooms were clearly private, and they would need a good reason for loitering there.

Singer paused at the top of the stairs. "Second level from the top, did he say? But there must be at least four rooms on every floor. Keep a lookout for a minute. I need to think."

He tried to remember his dream of the man in the tower. The man had been facing a wall, where the mirror hung. At the time Singer's attention had been fixed on the face in the mirror, but there had been other things in the mirror, as well. What had that been behind the man's head? Something soft and folded—a wall hanging? It looked more like a curtain drawn over a window. He oriented the picture in his mind and decided that the window must be in the southern wall of the tower.

Singer felt rather than heard footsteps. They were still far below, but he did not want to be caught and asked his business. He tried to disengage enough from immediate sensory alertness to probe for subtler clues to what was happening behind the closed doors. He caught it: a nervous, highly charged presence, as hard to stay away from as it was hard to keep his tongue away from a cut lip. It was Janet's brother. Singer backed off immediately; he did not want to wake Jon. But he had found the right room.

10

He tried the door. It opened quietly. The room was dark, but he could remember how it had looked in his dream. He could hear the sleeper breathing, the bed where he had expected, against the far wall. He stepped carefully around the table, Saldivar close behind him, and sat down noiselessly in an empty corner near the window.

We'll wait for him to wake, he said silently to Saldivar.

The footsteps he had heard on the stairs continued to approach. They came quietly down the hall—a heavy tread but muffled—and paused outside the door. The latch rattled, and the door opened. Singer did not move. He wanted to know the intruder's motive and intentions first. The man sounded big by the timbre of his breathing and the way he brushed against things in the dark. He moved toward the bed, toward Jon.

Without warning, the big man flung himself across the bed. Singer heard a sharp, choked-off cry from Jon and a curse that turned into a laugh from the big man. Singer jumped onto the intruder's back, dragging him off with an arm around his bull neck. It was not easy, even with the edge of his wrist jammed tight into the big man's throat-apple. To kill such a man was easier than restraining him, but Singer hesitated to kill him without knowing his identity and business. The consequences were unforeseeable. They danced crazily around the room, kicking at each other's legs in the dark.

"Stop it, don't hurt him," Jon called in the strangled voice of one who had had his throat squeezed. Singer did not know whom he meant. It was not easy to hurt the big man. Singer guessed from his thick, enveloping cloak that he was Somostai. Under the cloak he wore some kind of protection—not chain links but the stiff Delh'tani cloth that stopped blades.

The light went on finally. In its blinding white glare, Jon's eyes flashed wide with surprise.

You again, Singer heard him say, though not out loud. Singer reached for contact to beg him to remain silent, not to expose them, but Jon refused. Singer had never felt such barriers. Jon was terrified and furious—Singer knew that much—and he would not permit himself to be touched.

Jon sat on the edge of the bed with his hands on his throat.

"Let him go," he said to Singer.

Singer could not read his intent, but he took the chance and slackened his grip.

As soon as the big Somostai could get his breath, he choked out, "Let go of me, fool." Singer let him go.

"I believe you've just met my bodyguard," Jon said hoarsely.

The intruder also rubbed his throat. A pendant dangled from his neck—a skull face with a ruby the size of a man's thumbnail burning in its open mouth. The chain had cut into his skin in the struggle.

"What rubbish is this? I never assigned you a bodyguard."

"I did this on my own initiative. I was threatened after yesterday's accident. They called me your tale bearer and made it clear that another accident could be arranged just for me. I picked these two out of the work crew because they had both been soldiers. I'm afraid I forgot to warn them of your preference for midnight consultations. It seems they mistook you for an assassin."

"As you hoped, no doubt. Very foolish of you, Chonza. I am the only shield between you and the jealousy of my brothers in the Order. If I were gone, no bodyguard could help you."

To Singer he seemed amused rather than angry, as if Jon had just made an unexpected move in a stimulating game. He beckoned to Singer as if he had not been at Singer's mercy only minutes before.

"Come here, you."

He scrutinized Singer and fingered his scars. Taking Singer by the chin, he turned his face back and forth and looked in his mouth and eyes.

"Unusual," he said. "I may borrow this one some day."

He examined Saldivar less thoroughly.

"Say something," he ordered Singer.

Singer thought fast to find something safe. He remembered how people spoke down in Rivermouth territory from the time he had spent there with the Riders, fighting. "My father was a fisherman, on the rivers of the Morsshe, if it please your lordship." He spoke slowly, matching the accent to his memories as closely as he could.

The Somostai listened carefully. "The accent's right," he said. "And he seems stupid enough. But you'd best instruct these dogs that if they show teeth to their masters again, they'll be grateful for death."

"Master, did you have any business with me?" Jon asked carefully.

The big man grinned. "You know my business with you." The grin vanished. "But that can wait. We have a problem."

"In the interests of brevity, why don't you tell me what you've got that isn't a problem. I've been at the foundry site most of the night. I came back to use my desk and catch some sleep, when you woke me." Jon used the language skillfully for someone who had learned it in captivity. Singer saw Janet in his quickness to catch meanings.

"Yes, yes, I've seen the ruins of the skyfolk machinery. I'm not concerned about that. Our real problem is the temporary failure of my great endeavor. And we've lost the better part of three work gangs. One down the mine, one in assorted accidents, one buried in the collapse of their barracks. To carry on, we have to force the Deltanek to help us find more labor. That's what I want you to keep in mind when you meet with him tomorrow. Don't let him put you off with talk of the shipments of burningstone they need. I don't want my hand to be seen in this at first, nor any mention made of the endeavor. Sound him out, observe him, and report to me."

He turned when he reached the door. "If I were you, I'd have one on watch and one in my bed. It's foolish waste to let them sleep." He left.

"Bastard, bastard," Jon murmured as if they were not in the room. "He tried to choke me. Stupid asshole!"

He was holding himself under such tight control that he was trembling visibly. His rage and humiliation were boiling over the barriers that he had set for himself. Singer reached for him without thinking, but Jon shied violently.

"Don't touch me!"

"That was the Ordermaster, no?" Singer said.

"Yes. Korro himself, and I lied to him for just one reason: that crack you made about my sister when we were up on the scaffold. I'm giving you one minute to explain that. If I don't like the answer, I call Korro back here. Don't think I'll cut you any slack for saving my life. For all I know, you were trying to kill me and screwed up."

He took a quick look at Singer and averted his eyes again. His resemblance to Janet was startling: the same small, agile build, the same deft hands and bright dark eyes, the same guarded look. Yet Singer could see already that their personalities were not alike. Janet had patience almost to a fault. She could wait and watch. Jon was nervous, almost jumpy, quick to leap to conclusions and quick to flash into anger.

"Told you the truth before."

Janet would have read the danger in the softness of Singer's voice, but Jon had yet to learn that. "You said she sent you. That's not good enough. How the hell would you ever have met her?"

"Zhanne—Janet—she's a doctor, no? She saved my life in Jefferson. When we left there together, I promised her I'd try to find her brother. Now I have found you."

"You left Jefferson together? You trying to tell me that you and my sister—" He looked from one to the other. "No, I don't think you know her as well as you say. Shit, she wouldn't even go out to lunch with the doctors, let alone take off through the Dust with a couple of crazed polvorados. So what do you really know about my sister?"

Singer tapped his chest over his heart. "The mirror. She got your shirt back, and she found the message. 'To find me, look in the mirror.' She told me about the game you used to play, the hiding game, and how she could always find you. Because she knew what you were thinking as well as she knew herself."

He had hoped for a crack in Jon's defenses, for the beginning of belief. He was surprised.

"You son of a bitch!" Jon cried. "What have you done to her? She would never have told you that, never. You're with the Net, aren't you? Well, sharks, you swam into the wrong tank this time. The Somostai will eat you alive."

In his grief and horror, he was about to shout for the guards. Terrible pictures forced their way into his mind so vividly that Singer shared them without effort: Janet in the hands of the Net, her secrets torn from her like the guts of an animal that was hunted down and butchered. Singer was too stunned to protest.

Saldivar spoke up unexpectedly. "You're talking to the man who killed Tony Gero," he said in his soft, hoarse voice. "If you quit revving your engines for a minute, he could show you the scars the Net put on him. But Janney, she's fine. Not a mark on her." A slow, reminiscent smile lit his somber face. "You might like to know that poor, helpless little Janney blew up half the airfield at North Fork. That's why she lit out up-country with a couple of—what was it? Crazed polvorados? If you really want to know. For a video rep, chuck, you don't ask many questions."

Jon slowly closed his mouth, and for a moment there was complete silence. "You killed Tony Gero," he said at last.

"It's a long story," Singer said. "Things have changed in the Blue Zone since you were there."

Disbelief and wild greed for news battled for expression on Jon's mobile face. Singer was appalled, thinking how impossible it must be for this man to hide anything. But Jon did not ask for the news.

"Where is she?" he whispered. "Kristo, you didn't bring her here, did you? Nobody could be that stupid."

"How do I know I can tell you that?" Singer asked brutally. "How do I know you are not Somostai? You work for them. You wear the earring. The master comes to your sleeping place at night, and he was not trying to kill you."

Jon's hand went to his ear as if he would tear the earring out. His face twisted with rage.

"Oh, no, not trying to kill me. Just risking it, pushing it to see how far he can go. It's a game he plays. He comes around at night and tries to take me by surprise. I have a knife now, but that doesn't seem to bother him. He just laughs and says 'Next time.' He broke my wrist once, playing his little game. But I thought he was too smart to try anything that would actually kill me. Fucking asshole! He knows he needs me to run his game with the Nupis. He can learn their language, but learning what the words really mean is something else again. He needs me. But he can't resist the gamble. Motherfucker, don't you ever suggest that I could possibly be one of *them*."

Hard as he tried to keep an open mind for Janet's sake, Singer could not look at the shaved head and black robe without revulsion.

"But you work for them," he said.

Jon's hands clenched convulsively. "Yeah, chuck, I work for them. The alternatives were not attractive. I didn't come here for fun, you know. They picked me up in the desert after Nupis smoked the rest of my patrol. They kicked the shit out of me and threw me on a packhorse. I had a head wound that nearly killed me.'' He ran his hand over his head. ''You can still see the dents. I was sick, I still don't know for how long. It seemed like years. It must have been at least a month. Then they kept me in a cell in the dark till I was sure I'd lose my mind. After that, the Somostai started in on me, trying to reduce me to the right frame of mind for a normal slave. I kept shouting, 'I'm a video representative for the Deltan Consorso!' I said it a hundred times a day in every known lingua. It was my prayer beads.''

He laughed painfully. ''I don't know what good I thought that would do me. The funny thing is, it worked in the end. Some bright boy went and told the master they had this weird slave speaking unknown words, and Korro got hot thinking maybe he'd captured a stray Nupi. He wasn't pleased at first to find I was the *other* kind of Deltan, but he took me out of my cell. That was the good news. Then Korro offered to make me a Somostai apprentice. It wasn't the kind of offer you refuse. But I did refuse.''

He looked Singer in the face for the first time. ''They had to give me some freedom to get any work out of me. I smashed a water jug and got a splinter that was sharp enough. The next time Korro came around, I told him I'd kill him if he didn't leave me alone. He said he could have me subdued. I said if he tried that, I'd cut my own throat. I said I'd do my best for them with the Nupis—willingly. It suits my purposes as well as theirs. But if they tried to make me a Somostai, I'd kill myself the first chance I got.''

He turned his palm up and showed Singer ragged lines on his own forearm. Singer had never seen such a thing before. To die fighting hopeless odds was something the Riders understood, but they would never turn their weapons against themselves while an enemy lived within reach.

''I had to start cutting to convince him,'' Jon said. ''Kristo, I didn't know if I was scared I'd bleed to death or more scared I wouldn't. They patched me up, and Korro declared his own kind of truce.''

He slumped back against the wall. ''It's just a game he plays,'' he repeated. ''Nothing interests him unless there are winners and losers. I'm a challenge to him, I guess. To figure out how to break me without benefit of the Somostai rules.

''Damn them to their own cold hell. They don't even have

indoor plumbing, but they sure have mindfucking raised to a fine art.''

He snapped back to alertness. "Even if Jan did send you, you're not here just for me. What's going on?''

He knows when people lie to him, Singer realized. He could see Jon scanning him, alert to every detail of his voice and movements. And when they don't tell the whole truth, he assumes they're lying.

Yet he could not tell Jon about Kruger and the Riders. He did not know if Jon could be trusted not to betray them, even if unintentionally.

"You don't trust me. I can't trust you, either. I don't work for any of you Delh'tani. Only for my own people. And I won't gamble their lives till I'm sure of you. One thing I can tell you: The Somostai killed my brother. I would like to help you, if only to make Korro angry. And then I would like to kill him.''

Jon's eyes flickered. He had not expected that, and he was curious.

"Stay, then,'' he said slowly. "At least till tomorrow. If anyone else comes in here, you can do what you want to them. But don't kill Korro. He's a son of a bitch, but what he says is true. Other factions in the Order would tear me apart in seconds after he died.''

He rolled over and went to sleep. He did not offer to share the bed. Singer stealthily removed one of the blankets to share with Saldivar.

"A cold welcome,'' he said after a few minutes.

Saldivar shrugged. "Little kid in the shitter ran away screaming,'' he said. "We're not a pretty sight. Maybe the brother is just showing good sense.''

"It's dangerous to get caught in Somostai games,'' Singer said. "I don't like staying here long enough to get his trust.''

"Then let's leave.''

"Zhanne would not forgive that.''

"The man's right—you're not in this just for Janney. I didn't get all you said to the labor crew, but I know you were making promises. You didn't tell Makho everything, did you?''

"No. I didn't know everything yet, only guessed. We were far enough from the Delh'tani places to be left alone, I thought. Now I see that isn't true. If we have to fight Nupi vitos and weapons based in the city, we're done for.''

"We did all right with Siri's people against vitos.''

"Once. They can sit here in safety and bleed us and bleed us till there's nothing left."

Saldivar gave up the argument, but he was not convinced.

"Listen, Palha, suppose you had to fight your own kind. Not Nupis but men in green clothes."

"Buck 'em," Saldivar said. "You can't see them when they're up in the sky, anyway. Makes no difference what color they are."

"And on the ground?"

Saldivar shifted uneasily. "If they shot first . . ."

"You'd have to strike the cities if you wanted to get them all. They'd withdraw inside the perimeter."

"No. I don't do that shit."

Singer's questions felt like needles probing for a nerve. *What are you trying to make me say?* Saldivar asked.

"I'm looking for a future, Palha. When I was truly Thanha, I had no use for a future. 'Live worthy, die a good death.' I've had a good death, and now I don't want it anymore. I want my people to live. There's one way to do that: kill all the Delh'tani. That's what I thought I'd do when I first went south."

Saldivar was startled into a snort of laughter.

"Not really possible. You have too many weapons." Singer sounded regretful. "But suppose we got weapons of our own—captured them, as we did at the camp—and tried to throw your people off our world. Maybe I could make the Riders kill un-armed Delh'tani: the medikhani in Zhanne's hospital, all those hungry little kids in the market at North Fork. Maybe. But if I could, they wouldn't be my Grandmother's People anymore. And I am very sure that Kruger would not endure it. Nor would you, my brother. And after I had killed my brother and my Asharya, I would be no Singer anymore, for anyone. So the only sure road is gone."

He felt Saldivar freeze up. He knew those thoughts were the ones Palha tried hard not to have.

"The Somostai have to be thrown out of here so the Nupis will go away. It's our only chance. I can't ask Makho to throw his people away attacking a fortress with air support, nor would he be stupid enough to try it. I have to find him another way, one that might work. We have to capture some time. I need time to find a way. Something is shaping here, and I want to be inside, where we might control it."

"I still think we should run for it," Saldivar insisted. "They have their own troubles here. They'd leave us alone for a long time."

"A long time?"

"Till spring, anyway."

"Now you're thinking like the pallantai," Singer said wearily. "That's not a long time, not really. Not even long enough for the mares to foal. I'm talking about real time—time for children to be born and grow up. Time to get old."

Saldivar snorted again. "Can't really see you old."

"There's not much chance of it while Korro turns the city into a Nupi firebase and feeds the Delh'tani beast with all the steel it can devour. We have a chance to take them by the throat, and we have to risk it. If we turn our backs on the gamble, time won't be on our side. They'll grow stronger while we shiver in the hills. By spring we'd have no chance at all."

Singer twitched his shoulders like a young horse uneasy under the saddle. He felt an invisible weight pressing on him. Each time he tried laboriously to reason his way free of it, he felt it press him harder. I wasn't meant for this, he thought. I can't do it. But he remembered Siri carrying the weight till he died.

"You're not wrong," Saldivar said reluctantly. "It's what Mack would do. But if it'll work—who knows?"

"What do you think?"

Saldivar just shrugged. "Your country, not mine."

Singer felt the sadness in Palha. He knew that Saldivar had simply accepted the fact that they were not going to make it. There was no point making him say it out loud.

They sat in silence through the last watch of the night.

11

They were awakened by the smell of food. Jon was up and eating breakfast.

"I hoped you were just a bad dream," he said, but he shared the food with them. He had eaten the porridge, but there was still a pitcher of sour beer and most of a loaf of hard dark bread. He watched them with disbelief as they gnawed it down to the last crumbs.

"Remind me to notify the kitchen that I'll be needing three rations from now on."

When they had finished, he laid a straight shaving blade on the table. "The Nupi commander is viewing the disaster. When he comes back, I'm scheduled for a meeting with him, and you, as my bodyguard, must attend me. You can't go out in the Holy City without getting your heads shaved."

Singer's automatic reaction was revulsion and disgust. He almost refused. Jon saw his horror. He waved the shaving blade tauntingly and smiled—Janet's brief, one-sided smile.

He scraped their heads bare except for a narrow stripe running over the crest of the skull and ending in a single lock at the back of the neck. Singer winced inwardly from every stroke of the dull blade. A Rider cut his hair in extreme grief. It might be cut for him in extreme disgrace—though Singer had never seen such an event, everyone knew stories that had happened in a far territory or another lifetime. Singer had learned from the Delh'tani to call this a symbolic act, but his body knew nothing of words and felt only the shameful nakedness of his head. The black thing inside him crawled a little farther toward the light.

"My head's a little clearer now," Jon said as he rasped away with the blade. "Run that story by me about how you claim to have met Janet and what you're doing here."

Singer told the story, adjusting the rhythm of the telling and the selection of incidents to suit the reactions that came to him through Jon's hands and the tension in his breathing. He left out, at the end, where Kruger had gone and exactly what Janet was doing. He still did not know how vulnerable Jon might be to Korro's prying.

"So Gero is dead," he finished, "and Nymann, the soldier in charge of all the soldiers."

"The planetary commander."

"Yes. PCOM. That's what Zhanne called him. And that's how she ended up here. With Marcus Kruger, some crazed polvorados, and the people who weren't supposed to exist."

Jon shook his head. "Kristo, I can't believe this," he murmured. "My little sister—"

"Zhanne says you are the same age, no?"

"I'm older than she is."

"She says five minutes and you make it five years."

Jon almost smiled. "You *have* met her. I will concede that."

Distracted, he put the blade down and drummed nervously on the table with his fingers. "If half your story is true, it would change everything. I wonder who's running the colony now. The civilian governor? The civilians have been right out of it since martial law was declared. I can't even remember the chuck's name."

"Vitek Karoly," Saldivar said. "Uncle Vitek, they used to call him."

"Right. He's been a waste of oxygen for years. I doubt he has it in him to do anything. Wonder if the NPU knows we now have no long-range strike capability. That could make a big difference. I'd like your story to be true. It would explain a lot. Explains why they bombed the city last spring."

"Why?" Singer demanded. "I killed Tony Gero because he sent the fire-from-the-sky onto my people. But I still don't know why he did that. Or why he would want to destroy both the Riders and the city. My people worked sometimes for the Iron City or for other cities, fighting for pay. But we knew well that they were our enemies."

"Simple. That's one thing I have figured out since I've been here. The NPU came exploring up the coast and found the cities before the Consorso did. They saw them as a potential resource. Slave labor and extra food—and when they found out that the

Iron City had rudimentary mining technology, that made them really happy. Gero's treaty—the agreement to keep the natives a secret until they could be dealt with—meant less than nothing once the NPU found iron and coal. Well, Gero had long eyes and spotted what they were up to. Probably through a combination of overflights and interior leaks, I'd guess.

"Air strikes against the city and your people were just Gero's little slap on the hand to the NPU. Intended to serve as a warning against treaty breaking without going into NPU-zoned airspace and forcing retaliation. Since the natives never really existed in the first place, the NPU couldn't object to Gero's wiping them out. Clear?"

Singer was so sickened by hate that he could not speak. The strangers had killed his people without even knowing who they were—casually, as one smashed an insect. The message was intended for other strangers. The Riders themselves had been of no importance.

"If it's any consolation to you," Jon continued, "it didn't really work. Gero succeeded in destroying the city. As you see, however, the Somostai were untouched. They were happy to strike a deal with the NPU, gathering the refugees into labor camps and running the mines. The Nupis don't even have to, bargain for what they want, as they did when the City Master was alive. Supposedly they're providing information and food to the Somostai as their part of the deal. That's where I come in.

"See, after the destruction of the city, the Somostai realized for the first time that there was more than one kind of stranger-folk and that the Nupis and us were in conflict. They also realized that our weapons could exterminate them. I don't think they really believed that before. They thought the Nupis were just masters of a bigger and better city somewhere. They were thinking on how to make a profit from the strangers. Since the bombing, they've concentrated on how to stay alive.

"And in that endeavor a tame Deltan is very useful to them. I serve as a liaison between the Nupis and the Somostai. I translate and negotiate. I convey technical information and requirements back and forth. The Nupis think I'm just a Somostai with a talent for languages. They 'taught' me to use a computer, and they're surprised that a native can handle it. Meanwhile, I can pick up all kinds of interesting facts. Some I pass on, and some I don't. I serve two masters and wait for a chance to betray them both."

"We could take you out of here today," Singer said.

There was a long silence behind him.

"No," Jon said quietly. "I want out, but not empty-handed. I have work to finish. If you want an alliance, you'll have to wait till I'm ready. Those are my terms."

Singer could feel the tension in him: Jon did not expect them to agree. Singer had determined one thing—Jon was not a helpless victim. He was playing a game of his own. That might be dangerous, but it gave Singer a better feeling toward him.

"Done," Singer said. "You have hired a bodyguard."

Finding himself unopposed, Jon was at a loss. "Well . . ." he said finally. "If you're going to play bodyguard, you'll need weapons."

He checked under the mattress and next to the table and handed them a couple of knives. "I can give you my table knife and my spare. I can't do without the belt knife."

"Knives are good," Singer said, examining the weapon critically, "but these stink. Good for cutting up bread—maybe." But he tucked the knife away inside his new clothes.

Saldivar belted on the knife that Jon gave him without comment.

Jon swept up the cut hair. "I'll stuff this down the hole next time I visit the latrine." He glanced at a device on the table, a brass column in the middle of a jar of water. "It's still early. I doubt the Nupi is back yet. I need to get some more documents from the library. You can come along. It will be nice not to have to carry things myself anymore."

"What is that thing?" Singer asked. "Why are you looking at it to tell you what to do?"

"It's a clock. Made with water. A certain amount drips in every hour, and you can read the time by the marks on the column. The Somostai heavies all have battery-powered clocks Hazzan had sent in—a few toys for the natives—but I don't rate. I like this better, anyway. It's ingenious and weird."

Singer was not impressed. All kinds of clocks seemed equally bizarre to him. Time passed in sunsets and heartbeats. Even a minute was too big to fit between grooves on a metal rod.

Jon took them back up the stairs they had descended the night before.

"I hope I don't need to remind you not to use any Delteix outside my room—and keep it down even there."

They climbed the shallow steps and passed the area Bone had told them was reserved for the Nupis. Broad halls punctuated by flights of shallow steps took them deeper back into the mountain.

"Past this point you don't go without risking your life," Jon said to Singer under his breath. "I wouldn't go past the library myself without an escort from a real Somostai."

A long table ran down the center of the room they entered. The skylight above it let in a soft, clear light without allowing the sun to shine on the stored books that packed the wall shelves two and three deep. The tables were piled with more books, and wooden crates stacked under the tables and around the walls held yet more. Looking more closely, Singer saw that some of the shelves were really racks holding spools with paper or skin rolled around them.

Saldivar reached for the closest volume, then hesitated.

"It's all right to touch," Jon said. "Nobody's looking."

The book opened just like any other book. Saldivar had not handled many bound books in his life, but he knew what they were. He was very curious to see what the Somostai would think was worth writing down. To his disappointment, he could not read the script.

"It's Giristiyah. Actually it's mostly in an old form that the Somostai use as a semiprivate language, and the newer parts have a higher percentage of special vocabulary for things they've invented that no one else talks about. Even if you could read it, you wouldn't understand it."

Saldivar was offended. He wanted to say, *I can read. I'm not stupid.* He remembered in time that he could not speak Delteix there.

"Those aren't the same letters the Delh'—the Deltanek use," Singer said.

"They're *not* the same as the characters we use. But if I could run some comparisons with historical alphabets, I could probably find out the derivation. The simpler ones have stayed the same—like that one, for instance. Circle means 'o' here, too. That's why I'm pretty sure that the Somostai are right about one thing, at least—they came here from somewhere else. If they were really indigenous, they wouldn't have developed a writing system with so many similarities to ours."

"That's what Janet thought, too," Singer said. "But she figured it out from looking at my blood. Is there writing in the blood?"

"Not exactly, but there are tiny parts that combine together to tell your body things—kinda like words, I guess. You can read them if you have the right equipment." He spoke absently while he gathered a stack of books from the boxes under the table. He rummaged through the scrolls on the shelf, too, and loaded Singer's arms with them.

"That should do it. This place is a mess. The library used to occupy that room across the hall where the Nupis are as well as this one. They cleared out everything and dumped it in here. There's another, bigger library higher up in the city. This one doesn't have any of what we'd call sensitive documents in it, just a lot of records."

Back in Jon's room, they dumped the books on the table that held his small screen.

"I work on this in my spare time," Jon said. "I'm transliterating to Delteix and recording the data in an organized form. It's the only time I've been grateful for keyboard computers. If this were voice-operated, I'd have to write a Giristiyah program before I could use it."

Saldivar had unrolled one of the scrolls and found columns of characters. "What is this? What does this record?"

Jon checked the scroll. "Breeding records for cattle, I think. They have yards of this stuff. They understand that some characteristics are potentially transmissible to the offspring, but they don't know what a gene is, except in a theoretical sense. There was a master in the last generation who specialized in lens making, so they've seen sperm. I've read notes on a dispute between a master who thinks that characteristics are sort of evenly spread throughout the organism, like pigment on skin, and that somehow the sperm are invisibly imbued with it and another who says that there must be little seeds in the sperm for each characteristic, but they haven't found the seeds yet. He was convinced if he could build a better lens, he'd see the seeds. It's fascinating."

He glanced at their faces and laughed. "Sorry. It saved my sanity to have something to think about. I started doing it in the first place to give me a good excuse to have a terminal here, though. I snoop as much as I dare while I'm supposed to be typing arguments about two-headed calves. I wish I had Janney here. I'm just not as good at this as she is."

Something about his words and his laugh sounded forced to Singer, as if Jon were more interested in the Somostai records than he wanted them to know.

Jon tossed the scroll back on the table. Singer picked it up and puzzled over the characters. He had a brief, painful memory of Hilurin's face by firelight as the old Singer patiently taught him to read. He closed his eyes and let the pain pass. When he looked again, certain words leapt out at him. He dropped the scroll as if it had burned his fingers.

What did I tell you? the cold voice that haunted him whispered. *Was I so wrong? You are an experiment. Just like those pitiful nothings below ground.*

"What's the matter?" Jon said.

"The records. You misread. Those are words for people. Not male and female cattle. Men and women. The blackrobes are breeding people."

"What for?"

But he could not tell. The symbols in that column made no sense to him. A cold breath rippled the hairs on the back of his neck, and he heard Bone's anguished whisper: *Korro succeeded at last and sent you here to torment me.*

Jon's face twisted with fear. "Kristo! I try and try to understand what is happening here. Hazzan I get, but Korro is shit too deep for me. So smart and such a fool. Like a laser in the hands of an idiot child. He's so fucking dangerous. You just don't know."

Singer put his face about two inches from Jon's.

"I know," he whispered. "I know these people, and I don't like them. If they get in my way, I will not be the one who fears."

The knife appeared in Singer's hand as if by magic, and Jon was startled.

"Maybe I should be more afraid of you than I am of them," he said, but he seemed reassured. He looked at the clock again. "Time to go see if the Nupi is here."

A room at the top of the stairs looked out to the west. There were fresh marks on the old stones; the windows had recently been enlarged and were fitted with Delh'tani panes of clear notglass. Saldivar nudged Singer; the south wall held a row of video monitors. One of them showed the steps they had just climbed. Some were blank, and some showed places Singer did not recognize. On one screen small figures moved. Singer moved closer to Saldivar and caught his reactions to help judge what was happening. He was not used to video, and it was hard for him to tell just what the little colored shapes meant. He focused through Saldivar's eyes and realized that he was watching a work crew loading metal bars onto ships in a harbor. He stared, fascinated, till voices in the room recalled his attention.

"Chonza! What took you so long? And who are these two?"

The speaker wore the gray NPU uniform. Singer felt Palha's heartbeat jump.

"My bodyguards, Captain Hazzan. I was nearly killed in the accident. Threats have been made."

Saldivar's mustache twitched at Jon's improvised native accent. The Nupi did not realize he was being mocked. Singer also noticed that although Jon was speaking Delteix, he called Hazzan by the usual Giristiyah title for an officer of the guard. It clearly implied subordination to the City Master or, in his absence, the Somostai. It was easy to see that the Nupi had no talent for languages.

"Threats? Who threatened you?"

Singer was surprised to hear real concern in the man's voice and took a second look at him. Hazzan was a round, burly man, his curly hair receding though he was still fairly young. His face puzzled Singer. It was marked with lines of weariness and serious worry, but it was not the face of a fighter. Hazzan was not a killer, yet he was the architect of many deaths.

"Some among the Order do not revere you as the promised skyfathers. They feel that the master defers too much to you, that he does not pursue the supreme right of the Order as he should. As his servant delegated to you, I make a convenient target for their disapproval."

Hazzan frowned, the lines deepening. "Chonza, in the name of mercy—if you seriously think someone is trying to kill you, tell me who it is. I could provide better protection for you than those two."

Jon shrugged. "Best not to speculate or meddle in the master's business. Nobody dies in the city without his permission."

Hazzan rubbed his eyes wearily. "Chonza, why didn't you tell me about this? Why didn't you ask for my advice? I could have warned you about the dangers. We're lucky you didn't blow the top right off the mountain."

"I didn't know," Jon said mildly. "The master tells me when he wants your advice. In this case he didn't tell me anything. Perhaps he feels that I work too closely with you already."

Hazzan poured himself another cup of sour beer. "This stuff is foul," he said. "Listen to me, Chonza, we're all in trouble now. If the heavies in Solidari can't get what they need out of your master one way, they'll try another, you read me? So tell me how bad is it—your so-called earthquake?"

Jon moved around to the other side of the desk. He caused

chunks of text thickly interspersed with numbers to appear on the captain's desk screen, and they discussed technical questions. Singer put the information into his memory as best he could, but it made very little sense to him. Most of the words were unfamiliar, and Saldivar could not help him.

"So that's the damage report. I have a list of materials needed for repair. I can put that up if you want. Most important is a new group of workers. We lost three crews."

Hazzan grimaced. "You gobble people up like chips. Sorry, you don't know what that means. Like snack food. Like nuts? Hell. You waste them! I keep telling you, if you'd treat them better, you'd get better work out of them."

Jon shrugged. "The master says that we cannot afford to treat them well unless you supply us with more food. He doubts you treat your own prisoners better, and he asks if you would like to send them part of your own rations."

Anger showed on the Nupi's face. "You can tell Korro he may end up pulling the ore cars himself. You buggers are supposed to be able to manage personnel and operations yourselves. That's the deal. We set up the plant for you, and you keep it running. You are responsible for the agreed quota, no matter what happens."

"This is understood," Jon said delicately. "I might—just as a might-be—say that there could also be some feeling in the inner city that you have not kept your part of the agreement. That you fail to give us information needed to make the metal you want."

"Korro's trying to put the blame on us?"

Jon shrugged. "You know my master is never to blame for anything."

"Get him in here. I'll explain it to him."

"With respect, Captain, one does not summon the master."

"Summon him."

Jon shrugged again, went to the door, and called a servant.

The Nupi stood with his back to them, watching the picture monitors, till the master arrived. His hands were clasped behind his back, and they could see his fingers working and gripping. He turned on Korro.

"How do you explain this?" he demanded.

Korro spread his hands and started to speak, but the Nupi cut him off.

"Don't bother to concoct a story. I can smell something rotten when I trip over it. You did this. You know, I could have you taken through the air to the home of the sky people to learn for yourself what happens when you lie to us.''

"It would be a great honor for me to see your home," Korro said suavely. "But I'm sure you will not punish me. The sky people are wise and know everything, so they must know that I haven't done anything wrong. It was an earthquake.''

"Bullshit, it was an earthquake," the Nupi said. "I know blast and shock patterns. That was an explosion. Explain why you were monkeying with explosives.''

"I beg your pardon," Korro said. "What is 'monkeying'?''

His voice was grave and courteous, but Singer could tell that he was taunting Hazzan. The master turned toward Jon, as if waiting for a translation. The Nupi actually took a half step toward Korro, his fists clenching, but he stopped himself.

"You know exactly what I mean.''

Korro stood stolid as a rock. "If the captain knows something about explosives, I would be grateful to hear it. As you know, Captain, the Somostai find this subject very interesting. We have long wished you would share your knowledge with us.''

Hazzan kept his voice down with an effort. "All right, all right, call it an earthquake—for the time being. Let's look at the facts. Water has broken into the lower levels of the burningstone mine. It has to be pumped out before we see whether those levels are still workable. The furnace building is a mess. The crane is broken, and the furnace has cooled with the remnants of the last pour inside. It has to be shut down until it can be checked for breaches. We will not make our quotas for shipment.''

"That is indeed regrettable," Korro said. He appeared to be sincere for once. "I can assure you we'll do our best to repair the damage. The laborers we have left will work day and night.''

"That won't be good enough. There's going to be a very serious shortfall, and my superiors won't care whether you call it an earthquake or a tea party.''

"If you would help us find more workers—''

Hazzan cut him off with an impatient slash of his hand. "That's not the first time you've made that suggestion. No. Collecting fugitives for you is not part of the arrangement. We supplied advice and materials to build the installation, and you were to keep it running. That was the deal. You have failed to do your part.''

Korro stepped forward, bringing his heavy, bearded face close to the Nupi. "If we have—and I do not admit that—and if your superiors are as wise as you say, they will surely see that we failed only because you cheated us first.''

"What are you talking about?''

Hazzan was on the defensive, Singer thought, and Korro smelled that as a dog smelled blood.

"We agreed to work for you because you promised to teach us your knowledge. Well, you have taught us—as much as a slave learns to serve his master's need. The mastery of your craft you keep to yourself. Do you teach us to fly your machines or use your weapons? No! You don't trust us. Do you show us how to find and refine the stones and powders you mix in the iron to make the different kinds of steel? No. We're good enough to follow instructions, not good enough to know the reasons behind your orders. We made an alliance with you, but you treat us like servants, not like allies. We are not stupid, Captain Hazzan. We have noticed.''

Hazzan turned his back on them again and poured himself a drink from the jug on his table. "You're not here to accuse me. You're here to plead any excuses you can come up with before I make my report on your inadequate supervision of this project and your irresponsible overreaching in your private experiments.''

His last rebuke was delivered fast and loud, and the words got longer and longer. Korro did not understand it, and Jon had to translate with some difficulty.

Hazzan drained the cup of beer. "I'll send your report to my superiors. Don't expect a favorable response. You'd do best to begin figuring out right now how you plan to fill the quotas with the personnel you've got. That's all.''

Korro stood there for a moment as if he could not believe he had just been dismissed. Then he turned in a swirl of black robes and strode out.

Jon waited to see if the Nupi had any further orders, but Hazzan waved them out, still grasping the cup with his other hand.

"Fucking grayshit,'' Saldivar said as soon as they had reached the haven of Jon's sleeping place.

Jon looked surprised. "Hazzan's not so bad,'' he said. "Not the man I'd have sent to deal with Somostai, but he's civilized, compared to Korro. Sometimes I think about blowing my cover and surrendering to him. Anything to get out of this snake pit.''

"Don't,'' Saldivar said. "You haven't seen Nupi prison camp. I have. 'Civilized' takes more than soap and a wired desk.''

"You've seen one, you've seen them all," Jon said. "You're from the Tregua. That's a Consorso pen. My parents were killed by Consorso security forces on Delta. That's why Janney and I emigrated. We thought maybe things would be different up here. Now I think maybe 'civilized' takes more than we've got. Any of us."

"Last year the master had explosives already," Singer said, "but nothing that could shake the very earth."

"How do you know that?" Jon asked with swift suspicion.

"I was born here. I followed Korro's armies that year. The Somostai had created a fire that would knock little holes in walls. It frightened me then. I had not seen the fire of the Delh'tani then."

He stopped speaking abruptly. He had heard footsteps again. A servant knocked at the door.

"The master sends for you. He's in the small library."

12

"That mirror-that-writes," Korro said without preamble as soon as they entered. "The one you have in your room. Does it talk to Hazzan's? Is there any way you can see through your mirror to Hazzan's and find out what he writes to his friends in his own city?"

"I'm afraid not."

Korro sat drumming his fingers on the table for so long that it appeared he was not just calculating but indulging in indecision.

"Is there something lacking in your writing mirror?" he asked at last.

"Well, that's one way of putting it."

"If you had a better machine, would you be able to find out?"

"Possibly."

Singer heard the guarded excitement in Jon's voice and wished even more that he could understand what Jon was thinking.

"What is 'monkeying'?" Korro asked.

"A monkey is a small animal with a tail. It has a face like a human and hands that grasp almost as well as ours. It imitates what people do, but without understanding."

Korro surged to his feet, rage glowing from his eyes like fire in a sealed furnace. "Come with me."

He took them past the library, higher into the mountain through the corridors Jon had warned them not to enter. Singer looked through one half-open door curtain and saw rows of young people crouched on the floor, chanting all together too rapidly for him to catch the words. He felt their intense concentration like a wave that washed over him as he went by. The one nearest the door held a chunk of rock on his outstretched palm. But Korro strode too swiftly for Singer to see more. A black-clad, shaven young man passed, carrying a box made of wire woven together, which he held well away from his body. Inside, a fat brown rat tried its teeth against the wire and chittered. The young man bowed deeply, averting his eyes as Korro swept by. In a dark, narrow hall the first child Singer had seen since he had come to the city knelt with a bucket and a scrubbing brush. The boy was naked except for a square of cloth knotted at one shoulder and tucked up around his skinny middle to keep dry while he scrubbed. At the sound of their footsteps, he looked up and scuttled out of sight like a mouse bolting for its hole. His face refused to leave Singer's inner sight. Long moments after the boy had disappeared, he realized that the child had had blue eyes. Like Dona's, he thought, and long moments later: Like mine.

It seemed to Singer that they had climbed through time into an older part of the city. The stones were worn smooth wherever hands and feet had touched through the years. Yet the stonework itself looked finer and more polished the higher they went. Normally, craftsmen learned new skills as time passed, but the walls looked as if the Somostai had forgotten things they had once known, and that did not make sense to Singer.

At last they came to a part of the city where the walls were as smooth as if they had been glazed by fire. The chambers were round, connected by ramps instead of stairs, and the walls were inset with panels that resembled the Delh'tani not-glass, unbreakable and translucent. None of the panels shone with light, but they were positioned in a way that seemed to show they were intended to give light.

"These are my own chambers," Korro said. "Few have seen them and kept their eyes and tongues."

"Don't do me any favors," Jon said sourly.

"I have decided. It is necessary that you see this. You choose to bring your bodyguard. What happens to them is your decision."

A long window stretched across one wall, made of clear material too smooth and even to be the same make as the mottled, bubbly glass blown in the city. The view drew all of them. They could see far out to sea, so far that they seemed to be flying toward the western sky.

Korro ignored the view and drew the curtains back from the far wall, revealing another door. Singer saw both Jon and Saldivar look puzzled as they stepped through the doorway and checked to find the cause. He saw a place in the wall that looked like a touch plate—as if the door had once slid shut on its own like the Delh'tani doors. He brushed against the plate as he passed, but nothing happened.

The place within was more like a box than a room, a perfectly cut prism. The air inside was cold and still.

"You are in the treasure house of the Somostai," Korro said. His voice was curiously subdued. "You are the first who is not Somostai to come here since we began to keep records."

"I don't see any treasure."

Singer looked around into the shadows in the corners. He saw no weapons, no ornaments, not even gold coins or the tall jars in which the cityfolk stored precious goods. The wall was not entirely rock, however. Parts of it looked like some other material, wrinkled, soft, and irregular. He stepped closer and touched it. He pulled his hand back quickly; it felt soft, like cold skin or fungus. Then he realized that it was a covering draped over hidden objects. The covering itself was as dark as the rocks, tattered and decayed. He started to lift it aside. He was so interested that he ignored Korro until the Somostai slapped his hand aside.

Korro pushed him against the wall, and it took all his strength not to resist. The Somostai peered into Singer's eyes, and Singer concentrated on not looking back. I have no thoughts, he repeated to himself. I have no fear. I ask no questions. I am what I see: darkness, stone, snow. His heart raced, ready to burst with the loathing of Korro's touch, but he wrestled with himself: slow, slower. I am calm. I feel nothing.

"Don't do that again," Korro said, and dropped him.

Singer breathed again, still careful not to show his relief or his exhaustion, which was as great as he had felt after hand-to-hand fighting.

"Those things are none of your concern," Korro said to Jon. "I brought you here for another reason." He indicated a bench that stood against the wall. "Sit."

Warily, Jon seated himself beside the master.

"We are free of eyes and ears here," Korro said.

Singer felt panic flare in Jon at that statement. The master leaned closer to Jon but made no threatening gestures. "Tell me, Chonza, what did you think when you entered my chambers?"

The question was unexpected. Jon looked blank, as if he did not know what to think. Then a kind of recognition came into his eyes, and he laughed scornfully. "It reminds me of orbital. Viewscreens. Ramps. Like a mountain pretending to be a spaceship."

"Just so."

"What do you mean? What are you talking about?"

"You have surely heard some of the teaching stories. You know we came from the sky, even as you do."

"I know that's what you blackrobes say! I have no evidence whatsoever that it's true."

"They built their first home to remind them," Korro said. "They had been traveling so long, they had forgotten how it was to live under the sky. They still had the machines and the power from the ship, so they built a home within the rock, where they could feel at ease."

His eyes, still glowing with dark fire, dwelt on Jon's face.

"This is all a secret," he said. His voice was not a whisper but a low rumble like a bear speaking. "These are the sacred things of the Somostai that I tell you."

"Why bother?" Jon said. "I don't want to know. It's nothing to me. Keep your secrets. I don't want them."

"It will become clear to you. You refuse to become my apprentice. Yet a time comes when I must have your cooperation. When I have revealed the necessity, you will bow. We have a saying in the Holy City: Need is an iron master."

He appeared to be collecting his thoughts before he continued.

"The skyfathers traveled a long time to this place—longer than they had intended. On their journey they passed through many terrible dangers. They crossed the regions where the Destroyer rules, and he marked many of them for his own with his killing breath. He broke the patterns that make us men in them, and they died in sickness or were born in monster shapes. The powers of their machines wore out so there was not enough food, not enough air. So it fell to the first of the Somostai to choose out those who were not fit and return them to the fire. Only in that way could they reach their destination.

"Even when they found this place and left their ship of death behind, we Somostai were still needed. Still the Destroyer's fire had to be fed, and still there were some unfit for life. Those who went before left us this word: Someday the skyfathers will come again to heal and to reveal all lost knowledge. We must be fit to receive them. Therefore, the Somostai must rule. Do you understand?"

"Not at all. The whole idea makes me sick. You serve a kindly master, I must say." Jon was lying, saying anything that came into his head, because he was appalled and frightened by Korro's words.

"There was a reason for all that happened. The Destroyer is a master of wisdom, not mercy. In the unmaking something new was born. Some of us were not born monsters but only changed. One of those changes allowed memory to pass from one mind to another. Thus we remembered these stories; we preserved some knowledge from before the long journey."

"You don't remember anything. You can't make the lights work. You can't make gunpowder. You don't know anything but a few moldy stories that don't even make sense."

Korro's eyes darkened. "Memory without understanding. Some say it is a curse. They say we should throw it in the fire and forget. Live among our pigs like the farmers."

He put his hand on Jon's shoulder. "In each generation there must be one who can carry this memory. He must take it from the mind of the master before him lest part be lost in the telling from mouth to ear. It is a gift apart from any other skill. Not all who had it have been wise. Not all have been—of a straight mind. How do you say that?"

"They were crazy," Jon muttered. "I can easily believe it."

"Yes. And because of that many things have been lost. Many, many things. In this generation we have not found anyone fit. Some who might have done were lost to the war. Some of the servants of the Order murmur that the skyfathers have come back and so we no longer need the old ways. What do you think, Chonza? Are your people the all-knowing skyfathers?''

Jon did not know what answer would be safe. He shook his head.

"I think not," Korro said grimly. "You have lied to us. You have failed to recognize us. You have concealed from us what you know and don't know. Hazzan fears me now, and so do you. I think you are only lost children of the great night. No different from us."

"What does this have to do with me?" Jon said. He attempted defiance, but his voice sounded thin and strained in the dead air of the small chamber.

"The skyfathers have not returned. Therefore, the knowledge must be passed on—the Somostai must continue. There must be a servant of the Order who can carry the memory of our past."

His grip tightened on Jon's shoulder, and Singer tensed to move in case Jon could not endure it and did something to provoke the master.

"You have the gift, Chonza. I can feel it in you. Sooner or later you will serve me. You will submit. I want you to think about that."

Jon shook his head again. He had trouble speaking, as if his mouth had gone so dry that his lips would not part. "I'll die first. I told you that."

Korro laughed, and his iron fist caressed Jon's shoulder. "I'll tell you a secret, little Deltanek. You will die anyway. But before you die, you will serve me."

He paused and looked around, as if even in the locked room he could not be sure he was not being overheard.

"I will tell you another secret. The Destroyer does not exist. The memories of the skyfathers tell of a black hole that swallows all the light, and from that memory some fools have imagined something with a face that watches us and approves our sacrifices. There is no such being. Only the great night. Fools think we serve the Destroyer. I know better. If he existed, all I do would be done in his despite, building where he breaks down. If he existed, I would be damned to the fire and the cold hell after. He does not exist, and we are still damned, for in the end the great world, the city, and all the stars will be dust in a dark cold room without a door. Serve me, little Deltanek, and live a little longer, for there is no end to the darkness when your candle has blown out.''

The torch flame flickered in Korro's eyes, and Singer shuddered. The master was not mad, no, but *wrong*. His heart was so filled with the voices of the dead that he no longer walked the same earth with living men. *Memory without understanding.* Singer heard it again and felt cold hands fingering over his heart like a blind man picking for dropped coins.

''You Deltanek think yourselves so wise,'' Korro said heavily. ''Hazzan dares to call us animals. We know things that are hidden from him.''

He thrust a small box into Jon's hands. ''Open it.''

Jon pressed the opener with his thumbs, and the gaskets popped open. ''This is the kind of box we use to pack weather-sensitive materials. Where did you get this?'' He looked inside as he spoke and held up a clear, palm-sized disk. ''What is this? Where did it come from?''

''I hoped you could tell me that,'' Korro said.

''Well, it looks like data storage, but they haven't used this kind on Delta in fifty years. We didn't bring any of them with us; they're obsolete. So where the hell did you get this? The Nupis? They aren't this far behind in technology. Nobody on Delta has used these since long before we came up.''

''We found them,'' Korro said cryptically. ''And this.'' He moved aside some boxes that were heavy enough to grate against the floor. Their covering really was made of skin but was not old and tattered. It still gave off a faint scent of new leather. He pulled the covering off one of the boxes in the back.

''This is a computer,'' Jon said. ''It's an old model, too. It's field-sealed—but it looks as if somebody dropped it. The case is cracked.'' He rubbed dust away. ''It has the logo of the Ministry for Research. This is Deltan. It belongs to the Consorso. But it's too old. Where the hell did it come from?''

Singer could almost see Jon's hair standing on end. Something about the machine had upset him greatly.

''I did not bring you here to satisfy your curiosity,'' Korro said. ''Tell me one thing: Can you use this machine to find out what Hazzan is telling his people about us?''

Jon shook his head, visibly rattled. ''Maybe. I don't know. No, I'll be honest with you because I don't want you beating up on me when you find out the truth. This machine is old. You won't tell me how old. So how can I even guess if it's in working condition? It looks as if it's been dropped at least once. Maybe it's hardened enough to withstand dropping. If I had money to bet, I'd bet it was totally smashed."

"If it will really help you, I can tell you that the machine came to us in the year of the rat, six cycles ago."

"Sixty-five years!" Jon exclaimed in Delteix.

"Does that help?"

"Who knows? I'm not an expert. Nobody on Delta would ever try to keep a computer for sixty-five years. There's always a better machine coming along. We just throw out the old ones." He turned to face the Somostai defiantly. "No. There's no way I can use this. They developed a new operating system a couple of years before I embarked. That means something this old can't interface with the NPU computer even if I could somehow break into it. Which I can't. Forget it."

Korro nodded. "You will try," he said. "I'll have the machine brought down to you. It will not be dropped again."

Jon swore in Giristiyah. "I told you I can't do it!"

"I think you'd better try."

Jon bowed his head as if acquiescing. Then, too fast for Korro to stop him, he crossed to the other wall and pulled the covering away with one decisive yank. The piece he held in his hand crumbled into small flakes. A box fell to the floor and opened, spilling a heap of small objects to skitter around their feet.

Singer looked but was disappointed. The objects beneath the covering were basically rectangular, but their outer surfaces were corroded and blotched and their outlines were blurred. He could not imagine why they should be shrouded in reverent secrecy.

Korro struck Jon a backhanded blow in the face that resounded in the confined space and spun Jon to the floor. "I told you not to do that."

Jon pulled himself upright, pressing a hand to his bleeding mouth. "You want me to give you what I know, you have to show me what you've got. Truth for truth."

He crouched and picked up a handful of the pieces he had spilled. "What are these? Since you're telling secrets."

They were cubes, clear and faintly bluish, almost like the pieces of ice Singer had seen in Delh'tani drinking cups. Within them lines of faint rainbow shifted, as if their clarity held a concealed structure.

"Treasures of the skyfathers," Korro said at last. "We no longer know what they are. We don't remember. If I give them to you—can you tell?"

"Don't know. But—" Jon paused to spit out a mouthful of

blood. "If these are data storage, too, they may hold the memories. Then you could have it whole again. You could know."

Korro decided abruptly, as he did everything. "Keep them, then. And try. Put them in the box with the others and follow me."

Jon looked bewildered. Where could he follow?

"Captain Hazzan has an appointment, though he does not know it." Korro pulled down a handle, and a metal ladder descended from the ceiling. He climbed it and, at the top, turned a metal wheel. With a slow grinding sound, the roof slid back into itself, letting in a gust of icy cold and a powdering of snow. He stepped out into daylight; the others followed.

They staggered under the force of the wind. Bitterly cold, it scoured them with gritty snow so that they could not see where they were till they turned their backs to it.

They had come to the roof of the world, Singer thought, or as close to it as they were likely to get without wings. Between gusts of snow he could see the sheer peak of Old Cloudy. They must be standing on the last shoulder before the final sharp ascent. Holding one rapidly numbing hand before his face, he turned into the wind again and saw that the ground on the seaward side ended in a cliff's edge. Clouds foamed below the edge, hiding the shore and the sea beneath them. The place where they stood was strangely flat and unnaturally even. He scuffed the drifted crystals aside with his bare foot. No doubt about it; the stone he was standing on had been cut level, as clearly as the passage they had climbed through. The flat place was ringed with a rough circle of stones so tumbled and weathered that it was impossible to say what purpose they had served—but they had once been shaped and placed deliberately.

As he stared, the wind dragged aside the veil of snow for a moment, and for all his warrior's wariness, Singer nearly cried out. He could not possibly have prepared himself for what he saw: a shape taller and broader than any man, an inhuman face with a fanged, open mouth. For a moment Singer was frozen in childhood terror. His hand flashed to his face to hide the long scar the Somostai had marked him with, the mark of the Eater. The scar was gone. Saldivar stumbled to his side, almost breaking silence in his concern, and Singer came back to the present just in time to prevent him.

Korro laughed, though even his bull voice was muted by the wind. He clouted Jon on the shoulder.

"Are you afraid, little Deltanek?" he roared. "Did you see

the Devourer? Do Deltanek know fear? Can they see the spirits of the dead? There are many, many of them in this place, whirled around by the wind, because their bones have been burned in the Destroyer's fire and they can never rest.''

Singer rubbed his frosted face till the skin stung. *The mark is gone,* he said fiercely and silently to Palha. *No one, not Somostai, not anyone, can buy and sell me. Their Eater is a thing of metal and stone, a dead thing that never lived.*

He was afraid all the same, not of any spirits in the wind but of things once dead and buried that seemed to move coldly in his heart when he stood there where the devourer of hearts ruled.

As the wind came and went, Singer saw more dark forms gathering in the circle of fallen rocks. For a moment his guts seemed to turn to ice. Long ago he had been bound and left in a circle of rocks to wait for the Eater. Deronh had found him first. But it seemed that in the end his road had led him back to the Place of the Eater. He gasped in the wind, and the cold air was a friend to him. The wind from the snowfields did not belong to the Eater. It scoured this place with restless anger.

The dark shapes were not ghosts or demons but Somostai. More and more of them gathered in the circle, coming from entrances he had not seen.

Up from behind them came more steps, angry and stumbling, not steady and soft like those of the blackrobes.

"They told me you'd sent for me. What's the meaning of this?" Hazzan demanded.

Four guards escorted him: not city soldiers but tall, strong, shaven-headed blackrobes who kept their eyes on him like four ravens looking at a corpse. Singer thought Hazzan looked scared.

"I invite you to this ceremony to show we admit a mistake and want to correct it. It is an honor for you, to show our good faith. There is nothing to fear. Are we not allies?"

Such mocking reassurance stiffened the Nupi's pride. Singer could see him swallowing his fear.

"What is this place?" Hazzan asked.

"This is where we deal with mistakes."

Somewhere, someone began beating drums, not in any discernible rhythm but in a low, erratic rumble that made the stones they stood on vibrate.

"Bring him out!" Korro roared.

Two blackrobes stepped out, carrying a twisted figure between them. It was hard to make sense of the outline, backlit by the glow of the fire. It was a man, but his legs wobbled out of his control like a drunkard's. His arms were doubled behind his back as if he had been bound. The Somostai had run a pole through the crook of his elbows, and with that they held him up and dragged him along.

Hazzan's protests went unheard as the Ordermaster strode away from them toward the fire. He began a ritual, exchanging responses with those who held the prisoner. All the while, the wind blew and the drums hummed like an engine. The Ordermaster had his back to them, and Singer could not hear what he said, but snatches of the reply came down the wind to him. They spoke the archaic and stilted language the Somostai used on formal occasions, and Singer could not understand some of the words.

"The subject has been examined . . . emergency regulations . . . not viable . . ."

The subject understood. He had heard this ritual before. As they proceeded, Singer felt the man's terror like a snake winding itself around his throat. Even across such a distance it befouled him and made him sick. More terrifying still, he could feel Korro's presence getting stronger, towering up like a fire feeding on what it consumed. The Eater was a lie, but Korro was real. The victim begged for mercy, but he was gagged, so only Singer heard him.

The Somostai pushed the man to his knees and pulled his head up by the beard. Singer was too far away to see the blade, but he saw the quick stroke of the guard's hand. The terror guttered out in a choking rush of blood.

When the victim stopped kicking, they lifted his body by the arms again and threw it into the pit. Dark smoke rolled slowly across the pale mountainside. The guard picked up a container from the ground and splashed the contents against the feet of the statue. The liquid steamed and showed black against the snow.

Singer heard the Nupi behind him vomiting. His own mouth was bone-dry and tasted of bile. He bent and scooped a handful of snow into his mouth and let the cold trickle down his throat, numbing him to the smells of fresh blood and singeing flesh.

Saldivar stood by him like a rock, unmoved. He let his hand brush Singer's wrist under the edge of his cloak. *Lay it on me if you need to.* But Singer moved away from him, fear surging up again. Singer felt as if he were clinging to the edge of a pit. If he reached for Palha, they might both go over the brink. He could not share the half-formed images that writhed in his heart like shapes in smoke. Sharing them might give them strength. He could only lock all his thoughts in iron cold and wait, hoping the fear would pass.

The blackrobes filed out, brushing past them like shadows. Singer marked with his eye the place on the far side of the circle where a few of them seemed to vanish. He could not see a door, but he memorized the place to investigate later if he could. Having something, anything, to take his full attention gave him some relief.

Korro swept up to them, eyes glittering, face flushed as if he had drunk the blood himself.

"What in ~~fucking~~ *hell* was that?" Hazzan choked.

"That was the man responsible for the safe management of the foundry," Korro said. "You said that your people took errors seriously. So do we."

"You didn't have to *kill* him." The Nupi made a massive effort to pull himself together. "Look, I don't want anything to do with your religious affairs. This is a practical question. You don't get results by killing your best experts for one mistake."

Korro smiled. "For all of us there comes a time when we can serve the Destroyer best in another form. That time had come for him. Captain, I suggest you go indoors. You look pale. The cold afflicts you."

A pair of Somostai eased Hazzan down the steps, and Korro followed.

Singer looked around. The circle seemed deserted except for a handful of blackrobed figures tending the fire pit.

"Come," he said softly to Jon and Palha. "We're leaving by another way."

Hoods up and head bowed, walking in file like good servants minding their own business, they circled around to the far side of the fire pit, to the edge of the plateau. The mountainside seemed to fall away into white emptiness. Clouds and wind-whipped snow hid the sea that lay somewhere far below. Singer paused at the edge. He had seen the blackrobes come to this point and disappear. There must be a way down. The wind erased tracks swiftly, but Singer tested the drifts with his feet and felt out a path that had been trodden firm and was still visible once he found it.

As he stepped over the edge, he heard Jon gasp. He looked up, grinning.

"It's all right. There's a way down."

13

He led them from ledge to ledge, following a narrow trail that zigzagged down the sheer mountainside. Sometimes the ledge was no wider than the ball of his foot. Where there was no ledge to follow, steps had been cut out of the rock, and the slope was hollowed out above so that the climber could lean into the mountain. Metal pegs had been hammered into the rock at intervals to serve as handholds. They were slick with ice, and rust bled into the rock around them. Singer could have danced down the path blindfolded on a clear day in summer.

They came to a ledge a little wider than the others but cracked almost in half. The crack ran up through the rocks above and widened into a hole big enough for a man to climb through. The snow on the ledge had melted and remelted. Warmer air rose from the mouth of the crack. Singer edged closer to taste the air and found that it carried warm, sour scents—organic smells, not the cold taste of water and rock.

Singer gestured for the others to back up so he could return to the downward climb.

"I thought we were looking for a way in," Jon called into the howl of the wind. He did not move out of the way.

"For you, yes. Go on back and wait for me. I want to go all the way down!"

"What the hell for?"

"I need a safe way for my friends to enter the lower city. This might be it. But I'm not taking you with me. It's too dangerous."

"You still don't trust me, do you?" Jon shouted into his ear. "Well, I'm coming with you, anyway. Take me where Jan is. It's the only way I can believe you."

"You don't have to see her," Singer said patiently. "Any time you want to, you can talk to her through me."

"What—you've got a radio or something?"

"No." *You know! You could hear me now if you'd let yourself,* Singer told him silently.

Jon's control was weakening. After what the master had shown him, he wanted any kind of help, but he would not allow himself to reach for it. "Stop it!" Jon pushed at Singer hard enough to sway him dangerously. "No more mind games! I want to see her now—or I'll blow your cover and you can go ▒▒▒ yourselves."

Singer wanted to kick him off the mountain and wait for him to bounce. At that moment he felt that he hated all Delh'tani. They had no sense of the fitness of time or place. They argued, argued. They had no trust and no manners. Nevertheless, if Jon insisted, there was nothing Singer could do. His mind flashed ahead to the difficulties of taking Jon down this unknown trail, trying to find a way across the snow, to enter the city again unobserved. It would mean giving up his half-formed plan to destroy the Somostai. But without Jon's cooperation they could not stay in the Black City.

"Behind you," Saldivar said.

Singer heard a muffled exclamation of surprise behind him. Turning his head, he saw a dark shape catching up with them, nearly within reach of Jon, who was in the rear. Singer cursed his own carelessness. The Delh'tani should not have been last. He should have been protected between two warriors.

Saldivar was just ahead of them, already on the downward path, and could do nothing. Singer was trapped in the mouth of the opening by Jon's body. If he tried to move quickly, he would knock Jon off his perch. He felt Jon sway as the Somostai grasped Jon's shoulder and demanded to know his business. Even then, if Jon had yielded and moved carefully out of the way, he could have given Singer a chance to act. Instead, the Deltan shoved the Somostai away and, in the struggle, slid from the ledge with a single sharp cry. Saldivar tried to catch him but failed.

Singer reached up till his fingers found one of the metal pegs. Leaning out perilously from the path, he came face-to-face with the Somostai and kicked out twice. The first kick loosened the blackrobe's grip on his own handhold. The second swept him off the path. They heard a thud and a rattle of stones as he hurtled down and disappeared.

Saldivar had not made a sound, but he was panicking within. "We've lost him, we've lost him," he panted.

"No. He is here," Singer said. Jon's presence clung to the mountainside; Singer had not felt him die.

"Yo, here!" The hoarse cry seemed to rise from directly beneath their feet. "██████████, I can't see a fucking thing. Help!" he added as an afterthought.

Singer sank to his knees, then stretched himself out full-length and reached down as far as he could. "Can you see my hand?"

"No! I've got my face jammed into the wall. If I look around, I'm going to come off."

"Can you reach another hold and get up?"

"Sorry, I'm not a climber. Can't tell one crack from another. Can't see anything but ██████ white, anyway." His voice shook, and he gasped between words. It was taking all his effort just to hang on. Singer had located him: He was just below the ledge, where the rock bulged slightly. His fingers gripped the upper side of the bulge, his face and chest pressed against the curve, and his legs hung over emptiness. Singer felt how his cramped fingers were growing numb; when they had lost all feeling, he would slide from the mountain like snow in spring.

Singer stopped shouting into the wind.

There is no more time to think about it, he said. *You have to let go one way or the other. Which do you want?*

Jon heard him speak softly and distinctly, as if Singer had suddenly appeared next to him and whispered in his ear. For a minute he thought that Singer had somehow climbed down to him. Then he realized that he was hearing directly from mind to mind. Even at that point Jon's pride would not let him say "Help" again, but Singer felt his ferocious opposition yield like a fist unclenching. Singer moved with delicate precision. He could not afford to startle the Delh'tani or distract his attention from his fingertip hold on life.

He found his way to the responses that would pour most of Jon's remaining warmth toward his cramped hands. *See how easy it is?* he urged Jon's shivering body. *Get warm!* But he knew there was little reserve on Jon's wiry frame. The warmth would not last long.

He took a moment to absorb the full shock of Jon's position. He was surprised that the Delh'tani had been able to hang on so long. At last he dared a look through Jon's eyes. At first he saw nothing but a shifting shroud of white. *Look up,* he suggested. *Slowly. Nothing to fear. Think we are horizontal.*

Easy for you to say, Jon breathed, but he turned his cheek slowly against the rough stone and gave Singer another six inches of view.

There, in line with your elbow and up.

Jon's eyes could not distinguish the hold from the rest of the cliff. Singer tried again, defining and emphasizing the roughness of the tiny projection.

That miserable blister?

It's as good as the one you're on now. Don't grab. Slide up to it. Easy.

Jon's other shoulder shuddered as he put his weight on it. He hooked his fingers over the new hold just in time and clung to the cliff, gasping.

Deep breath. Deep and slow. Easy, easy. All right? Now slide your other hand straight up; use your fingers. You'll have to feel it—there!

Enough feeling had returned that Jon located the hairline fissure he could not see and jammed his fingers into it.

Now you have a good grip, Singer approved. *Get your knee up.*

Jon levered upward with his elbows and pushed one knee against a sharp place. The rock bit into his skin, but he hardly felt the sting. He was breathing in deep gasps. Singer knew his arms would not hold out much longer, though he tried to conceal that knowledge from Jon.

I want you to get your other knee up, then pull straight up and push your hand right up past the hold and grab me. My hand will be right there.

Jon gasped once more and then surged straight up, using the last of his strength in one desperate push. For Singer, it felt strange guiding Jon's hand while he stretched his own downward as far as he could reach. His hand smacked against Jon's wrist, and he clenched his fist and pulled. He had no leverage and could not roll away from the edge. His side pressed against the wall. Jon scrambled with his feet and kept moving up till Saldivar got a hand under his armpit and jerked him back onto the ledge.

Jon lay flat on the path, trembling from head to foot. "Thanks," he said when he could control his chattering teeth.

Singer helped him sit up and wrapped him in his cloak. "When you think you can, go on back to that opening we saw and get inside. Find the way back to your sleeping place, if you can, and wait for me."

Singer assumed the question was settled. Jon looked up at him.

"Just tell me one thing," he said. *How did Tony Gero die?*

All Jon's senses were wide awake, and the power of that contact was like one of the Delh'tani guns that fired a burning light.

Before he could save himself, Singer's mind returned to the place that was always waiting for him. He saw the man's cold eyes staring down at him, enjoying his pain, and felt the bands cutting into the skin of his wrists. In a moment Cold Eyes would come close enough to touch, and then—then he would know something that would destroy him.

No! He was still holding Jon's wrist, pulling him upright. His grip on the Deltan closed with crushing force. He had to free himself from Jon's relentless probing. He drove for Jon's weakest point. He knew how to trigger the core memory; Janet had shown him. Jon's knowledge avalanched around him in splintered brightness till suddenly it went dark.

Jon was trapped, crushed, in a moving swell of bodies that lifted his feet from the ground and tore his mother's hand away from him. His ears were shattered by the terrifying sound of adults screaming. Suddenly the pressure was released, and he was hurled to the ground. Heavy bodies fell on top of him, and he struggled for air that was raw with the smell of blood. He was alone, screaming silently for an answer from the only voice he would ever trust again.

The link between them snapped abruptly.

"Kristo," Jon whispered.

"Does that satisfy you?" Singer said savagely. "What Korro is looking for, what Zhanne tried to find—it exists. Gero died of remembering. That can happen. Don't try that with me ever again."

Jon bowed his head, still rubbing his numbed wrist. "Does Janet know what she's running around with?"

When he's frightened, he tries to strike back, Singer thought. Do not harm him—he is Janet's brother.

"You're a charged weapon," Jon said. "And I think you're in worse trouble than I am."

Singer did not trust himself to speak to Jon again. "Please see him back safely," he said to Saldivar. "I have to make sure of this path."

"I don't like this," Saldivar said.

"I'll be back soon." Singer was fifty feet down the path before Saldivar could say anything more.

He traveled faster without the others, without having to worry about them. The wind dropped as he came down through the clouds, and he was able to see farther ahead. The path leveled out, dipping through a jumble of talus and then rising to run along a ridge at the bottom of the cliff. As he loped along it, he heard a faint, pounding roar and wondered if it could be machines again. It did not come from within the mountain. He looked around for the source of the sound. Just then the late sun broke through the clouds in the west and showed him the sea, dark as steel, still breaking in great surges that shone like snow. That was the rhythm he heard. He forgot his danger and his haste for a moment. He had seen the sea only once before, and that time Dona had been at his side. The sea still beat against the rocks, but Dona was gone. Singer shook himself and turned back to the path.

A few yards farther on the path turned abruptly east and went over the ridge, down toward the narrow coastal plain. Singer wondered why. The Somostai must have some business in hand between the mountain and the sea. He remembered that Jon had talked about crops and cattle breeding. Perhaps they had their own byres and fields, hidden from the rest of the city.

He followed the ridge away from the trodden path. He had to go more slowly, picking his way through tumbled rock and drifts of snow that gave way under his feet, tipping him into hidden gullies. The ridge began to rise again, and he saw that it rejoined the mountain on its southern flank. Clinging to its highest edge, he saw what he had been hoping for: the blackened stones of the Great House, marking the center of the ruined city. He was too far away to see the improvised shelters of Lowtown between himself and the Great House, but thin trails of smoke showed where the refugees had camped. It would be hard work to break a path through the snow to the city's edge, but he thought it would be possible. It was not for him that day, however. The sun was already low over the sea, and the climb back up would be slower and more tiring than the way down.

14

Saldivar and Jon had returned without incident to Jon's room in the tower. Huddled in his cloak, Saldivar kept a lookout by the window as the sun set and the sky darkened. Jon had curled, shivering, on his bed and fallen into an exhausted sleep. When a sliver of moon had risen far enough to send an arrow of light through the window, Jon suddenly sat up.

"He's all right so far," he said.

"How do you know that?"

"I just saw it."

"Dreamed it, you mean."

"I know damn well when I'm seeing the truth and when I'm not. Call it dreaming if you like. I thought you'd want to know."

"I want to know for myself. I don't have it, though. Like being born with no sense of direction. When they're here, I'm with them. When they're gone—" Saldivar shrugged. "Just as well. Knowing something bad was happening but not being there—no." He fell silent. In spite of what he had said, his thoughts were far away, seeking along the path for Singer in the dark.

Jon cleared his throat. "I wish your chico had left my head the hell alone, but he didn't. Now your damn worrying is bleeding through, loud enough to keep me awake. He has a big problem, all right, but it's not your doing. He's trying to protect you, I think."

Saldivar laughed without pleasure. "I know that. It's the mistake he always makes. Nothing I can do."

"It's something he did," Jon continued, as if puzzling it out for himself. "He's ashamed of it. And he's also scared to death.

He made a choice to stay alive, but there's a price attached to it that he doesn't want to pay.''

"How do you read all that?'' Saldivar said stiffly.

"I could read him because he was reading me. And our cases are much the same. I know you don't think too highly of me. I'm selling myself off to the Somostai piece by piece to buy a little more time. You don't approve of that, do you? You think I should die like a man. Riders don't bargain. All that good shit. I'll tell you something. You don't die like a man in here. You die, that's all. You fall down the black hole, and you're all gone. I would definitely prefer to put that off if I can. And your Singer is just the same. There was something he loved too much to let it go, and now he's suffering the consequences.''

Saldivar did not say anything.

"Well, that was stupid,'' Jon said. "Now you're not only worried, you're also pissed off. Doesn't matter if I get any sleep, anyway, I suppose. Look, I'm sorry. Would you come over here for a minute? I can't see you.''

Saldivar hesitated, but he crossed the room. Jon reached out in the dark and got hold of his hand.

"I don't actually know how to do this,'' he muttered. "But this is why—''

The pictures poured into Saldivar's mind like jewels spilling into his hands, the colors impossibly bright, the detail impossibly sharp. Even the Somostai on their windswept, blood-stained peak had a hurtful kind of beauty. Wounds, scars, a twilight-colored flower seen for an instant by someone hanging head-down over a packsaddle, the flower crushed out of sight by shod hooves the next instant: images reflected and refracted, illuminating or eclipsing each other in a pattern that spread in all directions till it came to rest in a final symmetry. Blue, green, cloud white, and white repeated in dazzling light: it was the world seen in Jon's eyes—one glimpse, never forgotten, as he was loaded into the shuttle. Saldivar could not deny the truth of those patterns. They were the same thing he heard in Singer's voice: love that ached and burned for a truth that could never be entirely told, for a beauty that scars could only make more dear, for a world always waiting on the edge of sight or hearing, always ready to be born again.

"God, stop,'' he said painfully, and the next minute wanted to cry, "Give it back, let me see it again.''

Jon let go, accepting defeat. "Sorry. Didn't mean to offend you.''

"Not what I meant." The words seemed to tear Saldivar's throat, but he made an effort to speak. "I get it. It's not that I don't want to talk to you. I can't. Can't say what I—what I really mean. It just. Doesn't." He made a strangled effort to clear his throat. "Makes it hard to be around people like you who talk all the time. I can't. Singer's different. He knows me."

"I see that." Jon sighed. "That's where I envy you. You can trust someone. I know I'm a bullshit artist. I say a lot of things. But not what is really important, any more than you do. What you saw—that's what there is to me, if there is anything. If I die here, it will be as if I'd never been born. Nobody else is going to come along and do my job for me. See, that's why I didn't tell Korro to go piss on his boots. I wanted to *see* what was going to happen next."

He kicked the covers off and flicked on the light. "That's why I started going on patrol with those poor fuckers in the first place. I wanted to make some flix that would force people to ~~stop and~~ *see* where they ~~really~~ were and what ~~they really~~ they were doing. Most people get through life by never taking a good look at anything. That way they never have to know. Talk about 'casualties' while their eyes wander off into the yonder.

"The first day I was here, I didn't have an assignment. I sat around the reception center watching Janney work. She had work to do the minute she arrived. There was a guy they had worked over and shoved in the corner to wait for a bed—his arteries were ripped up so bad, they couldn't stick them back together, and my modest sister was swearing like a sailor because they couldn't get her a graft in time. Anyway, I sat there and watched the blood run down all those little tiny wrinkles in the skin of his hand until it quit dripping. Then I started drawing his hand. I sat there all day till it was night just to draw one ~~single~~ hand on one useless C3 volunteer—the kind they were stacking up like garbage bags and bulldozing under. One hand, and I hadn't seen it all by any means. Here—this is what I was looking for. You want to take a look at these?"

The path was drifted inches deep and very slippery. Singer was tired. When he came to the cleft in the cliff, he thought he could face even the darkness under the earth more easily than he could face that grinning figure with blood-soaked feet that waited in the Somostai holy place. He climbed through the opening.

There were no torches in the tunnel, but enough light to guide his steps filtered in from somewhere ahead. He turned a corner and was half blinded by the bluish-white glow of Delh'tani ceiling lights.

That must have meant the place was important. The Nupis were miserly with their gifts of power and equipment.

The big room had a vaulted, irregular roof and seemed to be another reworked cavern, not part of the fortress that had been built with stones and mortar. The sound of running water echoed through the cave from pipes that came from the walls and gushed into a series of stone troughs. Singer felt heat coming from somewhere—ovens or boiling pots, though he could not see them. Half a dozen blackrobes worked at tables made of some unnaturally smooth Delh'tani material. Some had vessels made of the Delh'tani glass that was clear like water, and some turned and chopped masses of dark stuff. The air tingled with layers of scents: sour, spicy, moldy, acid-sharp.

He pulled his hood up and walked straight on. A couple of the workers glanced up, but no one stopped to question him. At the end of the cavern he came to another set of stairs that wound upward and passed through the roof into a man-made hallway lit with smoky torches. He was able to find his way to levels that he knew and finally back to the corner tower and Jon's sleeping place.

15

When Singer stumbled into the room, he found the other two awake. They had turned out the Delh'tani light, but the Somostai candles flickered low in their holders. Jon's ink and brushes stood on the table again, along with the pitcher and two cups. Saldivar was sitting with his feet up, looking at a handful of drawings, and his face had relaxed into the easy, humorous expression he wore with his squad in the Forces, with Lyn and Jan and people he trusted. He smiled at Singer, though some of his ease departed, for he knew that Jon and Singer had not yet made peace.

He waved a page at Singer. "Look at this, cofra. That's telling it straight, no?"

The sketch showed two polvorados scrambling through the heart of a thornbush. Singer could almost feel the thorns.

"See the face on that one? That's Marquez. We were in the same landing shuttle. He could move faster than any fat man I've ever seen. He lost his gun in the bush once—thorns hooked it right off his shoulder. He was moving too fast to notice. Afterward, he wanted to go back for it, but once he cooled off, he couldn't get back in. Couldn't figure out how he got through the bush in the first place. It was solid thorns.

"Jono here says he knew Marquez up north. He smoked it last winter. Too bad."

He carefully laid the picture back on the table and picked up another one. "Can I keep this?"

"Sure—it's not that good." Jon looked pleased anyway.

Saldivar showed it to Singer. "Janney when she was little. So serious! It's a good thing I didn't know her then. I was a punk—she wouldn't have liked me." He folded the portrait very carefully and tucked it into the front of his shirt.

It was clear to Singer that Jon and Saldivar had been making friends in his absence. He was not sure whose idea it had been, but it seemed to have worked.

"Tell me where the kitchen is," he said. "I need food."

He found his way without much trouble and brought back an armload, giving the kitchen slaves a fierce look in lieu of an explanation.

Saldivar ate hungrily, but Jon tried a mouthful or two and gave up.

"I brought soup," Singer said. "No chewing."

Jon shook his head. "Don't bother. I'll eat later."

His eye and the side of his face had swelled and turned black where Korro had struck him. It was painful enough to stop him from eating, but Singer guessed it would take only a few minutes to ease the swelling and persuade the cuts on the inside of his mouth to heal. The scrapes and bruises he had received in the fall were more serious. Jon's pain nagged at Singer.

"Why did you provoke him?" Singer asked.

Jon started to smile and winced. "If he had known how badly I wanted that computer, he would have had second thoughts about giving it to me. He's figuring all the time, almost like a computer himself. The one time he doesn't think is when he gets mad. Get him to hit me and he forgets what he's doing for a minute or two. Someday he'll catch on to this trick and really kick the shit out of me, but I'm doing all right so far."

He smiled again, ignoring the pain. "Besides, I really wanted to know what was under there. I didn't think I'd get another chance. It was a pretty good bet he wouldn't kill me, since he had just ordered me to do a piece of work for him. He loses his temper, but he doesn't lose his mind."

Saldivar cleaned his bowl with a piece of bread and filled it again. "What did you want the computer for?" he asked. "You said it was no good."

"It's no good for what he wants. Maybe Janney could find a way to break into Hazzan's computer; I sure can't. But it's worth a lot to me for other reasons."

He grimaced in frustration; Singer could feel the things he wanted to say jamming up as he tried to get the words through his cut lips.

"Two things I wanted when I headed north with that patrol last year: one, to find secret POW camps and prove Nymann and PCOM were liars. No luck there. The Somostai caught me before I got anywhere. But the other thing's even bigger: Where did the first colony go? Nobody knows, but that's what we're all fighting over, supposedly. I thought, Maybe they're lying about that, too. This computer: If not from the first colony, where the hell else? If I can get into these records, I could be the first to know what really happened. Maybe the war is for nothing! Maybe the Nupis had nothing to do with the disappearance of the first shipload. Worth a fat lip, no?"

"I hope it's worth more than that to you," Singer said. "You know that Korro signed a death order for us when he took us in there. He cannot show us his secrets and let us live. Eventually he will kill you."

Jon shrugged. "I knew that already. He talks to me sometimes because it's too dangerous to talk to anyone in the organization. I'm his trash bag. When he's done—" He made a crushing motion with his hands. "Disposable. But it's worth it. I want to see what really happened."

He reached for the wine jug and tried to pour a drink into the

undamaged side of his mouth. The strong wine ran into his cuts
in spite of careful maneuvering. Drops spilled out over his shirt.

"Damn, that smarts."

"Janney wouldn't let you drink at a time like this," Saldivar
said in his quiet, deadpan way. "I can hear her now. 'Alcohol
is not good for you when you're already in shock.' "

"Yeah, well, she's not here."

"Let me have a look at those cuts," Singer coaxed. "I'm not
Zhanne, but I can help."

Jon waved him away. "I've had worse. Hands off."

"You took my hand today. You might give me yours in friendship."

Jon looked ashamed for a minute, but then he was on guard
again. "You want to snoop around inside my head 'cause you
still don't trust me. Well, ~~screw~~ that." *Nute to*

Singer realized that Jon was more than a little drunk. Saldivar
was getting angry, but Singer felt a rueful pity for Jon, wearing
himself out like a green horse fighting hobbles.

"You have it backward. I need you to trust me, and I don't
know any other way to show you."

"Need me? What for?"

"Zhanne and Palha and me, and Lyn and Makho, we're one
thing now. She needs you."

Jon concentrated on getting more wine into his mouth. "Hey,
chuck, you may be a liar, but you have a great imagination. Jan
and you two is crazy enough, but Kruger? You expect me to
believe she's made friends with Mack the Knife?"

"What do you think?" Singer asked very quietly. "You can
tell when people lie to you. Do you think I'm lying?"

The danger in his voice caught Jon's attention, and Jon looked.
"No," he said, and lowered his eyes. "I guess you're not lying."

Singer held his hands out, palms up, and waited. After a
minute Jon clasped hands with him.

Jon's hands felt like Zhanne's: wiry, deft, small—hardly bigger than hers—and alive with nervous energy, as if sparks should
have been visible up and down his arms. Singer could feel the
tension in him. Jon was ready to leap back at the smallest hint
of a push from Singer.

Carefully, as if with his fingertips, he felt for the configuration
of thoughts and feelings that was uniquely Jon. Briefly he connected with direct and tightly focused power. Then the contact

vanished. Jon's fear walled him in like a cold fog, a diffuse but unyielding barrier.

Singer found Jon's pulse with his fingers and relaxed, matching himself to Jon's rhythm, leaving himself unguarded. He imagined the game he was playing: He stood with eyes shut, perfectly still, in the middle of the grazing ground, a chunk of grain and honey on his outstretched palm. He heard the wild young horse circle him with spooky, uneven hoofbeats, felt the rush of hot breath on his neck as the colt curvetted past him. At last flexible, exploring lips snatched the bait. The colt galloped off in triumph, thinking he had gotten away with something, but there was a scent and feel in his wild head that had not been there before. He would come back.

Singer felt Jon daring to approach, to make glancing contact. Jon saw the picture; he was offended, intrigued, caught. Singer did not try to push past the surface. Holding Jon's attention with the memory, he worked quickly while Jon was not looking. He felt the rush of heat to the damaged flesh, the temporary throb of pain that eased as the inflammation subsided.

Jon felt it, too, and jerked his hands away from Singer's to feel his face. A rainbow bruise still colored his cheek and circled his eye; Singer had not quite finished.

"No," Jon said, and his voice trembled. "Get away from me. I prefer the pain I've already got. I'm used to that."

"You can talk to Zhanne," Singer said.

"No," Jon said again. He backed up till he bumped into the wall and leaned his head against it. Both eyes looked bruised.

"No. The whole world cannot see inside my ████ head. That is too ██████much. Anyway, I don't believe you. I don't believe you."

Singer did not press him. He closed his eyes and relaxed, thinking back to the first time he had seen Jon's sister.

She came to me with a light, like a child with a candle, in the darkest night. Believe me, I do know your sister.

Singer went looking for Janet then, beyond the walls that surrounded him, beyond the towering weight of the mountain, out into the storm winds that screamed down from the pass—no. He put away those images. That was the wrong way to think of it. She was not in a far place. She was there, near him, close as a handclasp. From heart to heart was no distance.

Singer? She was awake; she had been taking another dose of Morne's medicinal tea to a sick woman. He showed her Jon and felt the shock that stopped her with the cup still in her hand.

Jon!

He won't hear you, isé. I tried.

That's crazy. He hears. He's like a radio telescope when he turns it on. Total accuracy.

He's afraid to let me in. Even to find you. He talked to Palha, but he won't talk to me. Why is that? What am I doing wrong?

He felt her frustration. She would have liked to hurl the cup against the wall.

It's not what you're doing. It's just you. Pablo's all right with Jon because Pablo doesn't have the power you have. He sees that power, and it scares him, and that makes him mad, so he just shuts you down. It's his stubborn *pride. If I were these, I'd* make *him listen!* The intensity of her feeling grew until it was like a shout inside his head.

Another voice interrupted her. *Janet?*

Jon had given up the fight. As Singer had hoped, Janet's brother had been listening. Singer was washed in their reunion as if he had tumbled into a spring stream. Greetings, endearments, and fragments of memory overleapt each other like pebbles in a stream, voices eddying around each other. He tried to put some distance between himself and the two of them, but Janet reached for him and gave him what felt like a kiss: warm contact, brief but full-length. Palha came into focus beside him, happy and slightly embarrassed, and Singer knew that he had received the same.

You all look bad, Janet said. *When are you leaving there?*

Not soon, isé. There is a chance here to take the city and throw the Somostai out. We're staying here with Jon to gather knowledge. I'm going to ask Makho to send pallantai down to Olmalik. Help me find Lyn, and then you can talk to Jon as much as you want.

With Janet to reinforce him, it was only a moment before he felt/heard the murmur and rush of voices that was the camp. He brushed against a feeling and then recognized it. Lyn always smelled like foreign spices and honey no matter how much she sweated.

Bullshit. I reek of manure and old socks. She seemed pleased but not surprised. She took their contact for granted, as always. *Looking for Mack? He's "in conference," as they say in civilization. He sent out messengers right after you left us, and now some of them have come back with reps from the Tall Grass and River People to discuss a joint foray against your Somostai. He says this is a hell of a time for his Singer to run out on him, and where are you now that he needs you. Just kidding.*

He's doing great even without you. Morne knows all these chucks like the back of her hand, and she briefs him on protocol. You should see him schmoozing with the pallantai with two kilos of gold around his neck. It's an outrage to his Fokish soul, but I think he's beginning to like it.

Singer laughed. *Thanha know steel when they see it, decked with gold or not. They'll listen to him.*

Dakko. They're listening. They're hurting, and they want blood. They want something to eat, too. I think they're ready to fight.

Singer could hear her talking to someone in the background while she kept a tight grip on him, as if holding his hand while she issued orders. Singer looked through her eyes with longing at the sheltered interior of the tent, the worn felt walls still brave with embroideries under the smoke, and breathed through her lungs the smells of burning thorn, resh cooking, horses and sheepskin. In spite of their battles and marches, the camp smelled better than Siri's camp in the foothills. There was enough to eat and enough fuel to keep the tent warm and dry. Sickness and wounds were being healed. He wanted to do as Palha urged him, to run for home and let the future take care of itself.

Through her eyes he saw Kruger push the tent flap aside, and he felt her grasp the Asharya's hand.

My Con-el, I will make this swift if you will hear me. We were right: The Nupis have made an alliance with the Somostai. They are making steel and other things I don't understand—mining some black stone that burns and then cooking it till it stinks very badly and turns to slime. I don't know all the other things they do, but they have Nupi weapons and advisers here. They can land and fuel vitos. Our people will be in danger anywhere in the north. They can hunt us down. And I think it's possible that with metal and fuel from the Somostai mines, they can destroy your Consorso.

He felt another presence, new but not entirely unfamiliar, intelligent, cheerfully pessimistic, unsurprisable.

Genady, Lyn supplied. *Marcus has found him useful. A steady man.*

If you did as much damage to the airfield as you show, he could be right, Genady interrupted. *The Consorso position always rested on the refinery and on a marginal superiority in the air. If the Nupis solve their fuel problem and feel themselves safe from long-range air strikes, they can hit the refinery and strangle us.*

We can distract and trouble them here, Singer continued. *I think the slaves will rise with us if we can show them some hope. But they cannot strike the Nupis without weapons. Our best chance is to infiltrate pallantai with fire weapons, then bring together the uprising from within and your attack from outside. You must send clever fighters, those who can improvise and who will have the patience to teach cityfolk and the wit to see how.*

I have sent messengers to the wintering grounds of the other Rider groups, Kruger said. *We have contacts coming back now. I'm trying to coordinate a strike force. I don't like sending people into what may be a trap when I'm not sure yet if I'll have backup for them.*

Singer could see Makho through Lyn's eyes, standing arrow-straight, not showing the worry in his heart. A good Asharya, Singer thought. A joy to the heart it would have been to ride among his chosen hearth if only we could have fought this war in the open.

We're all in a trap here. Makho, he said as if in Kruger's ear. *Our only chance is to strike before it closes.*

Kruger nodded to himself, then thought Singer could not see him, then wondered if he could. *I'll ask for volunteers. You'd better have a damn good route worked out for them.*

I hear you, my Asharya. I have a good route. I have Zhanne's brother, and Zhanne is safe for now.

Kruger's thoughts were already running ahead into the future. *Speak to me again tomorrow, when I've had time to work out the details. And come to me earlier in the evening. I'm an old man, and I need my sleep.*

Singer felt him recede out of contact.

"I need to apologize," Jon said. "What I did back there on the mountain—I jumped you when you weren't looking. That was wrong. I won't try it again."

His reserve had not vanished, but his face had more life and warmth in it than Singer had seen.

"Jan's right; you look terrible. Why don't both of you get some rest? Jan and I have some work to do on the computer. Take the bed for a change."

16

The master was not present when Hazzan called them early the next morning. The Nupi slumped over his desk, showing none of the arrogance he had displayed earlier. The pitcher was already half-empty.

"Sit down," he said to Jon. "And send your meat outside."

"Excuse me?"

"Them." Hazzan indicated Singer and Saldivar.

"They stay. I'm staking my own life on them. You may as well risk yours."

"Tell me, Chonza—" He paused, as if trying to find a safe way to put his question. "How serious is your master? Does he really believe in all that stuff up on the mountain, or was that staged to shake me up?"

"He was happy to shake you up," Jon said. "But that does not mean that he himself disbelieves in the power of the Destroyer."

"The Destroyer? That statue? Korro's too smart to worship a piece of wood. There must be something else going on here."

Jon gave him a contemptuous look. "Forgive me, Captain, but you reveal yourself as a stranger. That is only a picture of the Destroyer, suitable for the eyes of ordinary men. The Somostai know that the Destroyer himself is invisible. He devours light itself, so how could he be seen? He is a darkness at the center of the universe. No one escapes him, but he spares us to serve him for a time."

"Good God!" Hazzan peered at Jon. "Is that what you think, Chonza?"

"I would not presume to express an opinion about the fate of

227

the universe, my Captain, but one thing I do know: There is a darkness in the master that will happily swallow you if you stand too close."

Hazzan groaned. "I thought you people were on the road to civilization! I thought the Somostai were there to promote knowledge. This is barbarity. Chonza, I'm an engineer, in the name of mercy. Do you know what that is? I build things, make tools. I'm not a murderer. I have no grand schemes. I'm just an ordinary man."

"You should have looked more carefully before you tried to make a tool of the master," Jon said. "There are weapons that are dangerous for the one who wields them, as well."

Singer heard someone coming, but before he could alert Jon, Korro had already swept into the room.

"I heard my name, Chonza," he said jovially. "Your words are well spoken, as always. Captain, a very good morning to you. I trust you spent a pleasant night."

Hazzan straightened himself in his chair, assuming the air of command again. "In fact, I have spent the night seeking a solution to our mutual problem."

"Excellent!" Korro said. "I, too, have been seeking an answer. I believe I have found one. I have ordered that the workers from the burningstone mine should be transferred to the foundry until it is repaired and working again. After all, we don't need the burningstone if we are not making steel. We'll have to skip sending one or two shiploads of burningstone to your people in the south, but surely that is no great matter to the wise and powerful flying folk."

Hazzan sprang to his feet and leaned over the desk toward Korro, emphasizing his point with a clenched hand. "You had no authority to give that order! You are to carry out *my* orders, do you understand? The burningstone shipments *must* continue. Any interruption will have the most serious consequences possible for you and everyone in the city."

Singer expected Korro to respond with an outburst of his own, but he read only satisfaction in the set of the master's shoulders. Korro nodded as if confirming a point that pleased him.

"Captain, please do not upset yourself. I meant no harm. I can only plead ignorance yet again. You do not show me—what is it you call it?—the 'big picture.' So I make regrettable mistakes in the small tasks you allot to me." The scorn behind his words was impossible to miss, even for a foreigner.

"Just make sure that boat gets loaded," Hazzan said.

"It shall be as you wish."

"And I have a better idea for solving the labor problem," Hazzan said. "You will organize work groups of all the Somostai who can be spared from other duties. They will work in shifts to repair and restart the furnaces and foundry. Their superior knowledge and skill will be invaluable. I believe they will be able to complete repairs much faster than the slave workers. Don't you agree?"

Korro swelled with rage, but he growled something that might have been taken for assent and left the room.

"You will need a bodyguard more than I," Jon said.

"Do you think I'm afraid of him?" Hazzan said. He laughed shortly. "On the contrary. I don't want anything to happen to him. I'm only afraid of what he'll do to my plans if he keeps screwing around. He doesn't know what he's messing with." He tapped his desk, calling up files and comparing them. "I want you to give me as complete a duty roster as you can for all the Somostai. I want to make sure Korro isn't shitting me. I didn't give that order just to yank his chain. Making the black-robes work is the only way we can fill those quotas fast enough. I can't let him hold out on me."

"I don't have that information," Jon said. "It may not be written down. I don't know. Wait a minute—there is someone who has a rough list in his head. Order Bone sent here. I'll get what I can from him."

Bone arrived quickly, closed his eyes, and began droning a list of names and duties for Jon to type into Hazzan's desk. Hazzan paid little attention as Jon worked. He paced the room and flicked through his monitors, checking on the progress of work. The dock monitor showed workers idling about, the anchored ship empty. Suddenly, a messenger arrived and the scene changed. Workers sprang into action. They opened the hatches and began shoveling the black lumps into the sling and working the crane that dumped the sling's contents into the hold. Hazzan grunted with satisfaction.

While Hazzan's back was turned, Jon printed out two copies of the rough schedule Bone had given him. By the time Hazzan turned around, Jon was tucking one copy into his belt pouch. He handed the other to the Nupi.

"I'm keeping a backup for my own reference, with your permission."

"Sure, fine," Hazzan said without looking. He ran through the list, marking certain names that he recognized. "If Korro doesn't put these people to work, I want to know about it. The only ones to be excused are those I've circled. Tell the master from me that if he wants to spare any others, he'll have to clear them with me first.''

Jon looked dubious.

"Don't make the mistake of thinking the master is as powerful as he believes," Hazzan said. "If you're wondering whom to serve, I can tell you that you will serve yourself, the other Somostai, and probably the master himself by doing what I ask.''

"I will keep that in mind."

Once safe in his room, Jon unfolded the copy. Between two pages of the list, he had printed the short-form record of the last three days' transmissions from Hazzan's station.

"See? Easy!" He puzzled out the words. "This isn't really code. They're using standard forms. Any video rep could read this. Well, the gist of it is that Hazzan's superiors are very much disturbed by the foundry accident. They're questioning Hazzan's ability to control the situation. And he seems to be concealing information from them. He hasn't told them the Somostai were at fault. He hasn't told them the master is trying to manufacture explosives. He hasn't told them about the sacrifice yesterday. He's trying to present what happened as purely accidental. Interesting. It seems that Hazzan is playing his own game here. For some reason he does not want Nupi headquarters at Solidari to step in. He's probably convinced he can run this himself and doesn't want their interference. Anyway, they demand that the coal shipments continue unhindered, or else, and they've given him one month by their reckoning to get the steel shipments back on schedule. Not much time.''

"It's time enough to call the Riders down," Singer said.

"I'm wondering what will happen if the Somostai don't comply. Maybe you didn't notice that Korro was playing games with the Nupi. He deliberately threatened the coal shipment to find out how important that was to Hazzan. He got what he wanted—Hazzan's reaction showed that the coal is indispensable to the Nupis. Korro will make some use of that, but I don't know what.''

Hazzan sent for them again in the afternoon.

"I'm going down to the harbor personally. I want to see for myself that Korro is cooperating. I'll need you for communications.''

Horses were ordered for them, and they rode down through the ruined plateau and southwest toward the harbor. When the road leveled out and the wind smelled of salt, Singer was tempted to let his horse go. With a clear road before him and a good horse under him, it was almost impossible, an act against nature, to let the chains of forethought drag him back.

Saldivar rode close to him. "Take it easy," he said under cover of the hoofbeats. "If you and that horse start dancing, the whole world will know where you come from."

Singer had seen a harbor before, but the sight of men in wooden structures floating on the unstable surface of the water still seemed strange to him. Saldivar had grown up on the barren ground of the Tregua, the desert left behind when the jungle had been torn down. He had never seen the sea. Jon had traveled far on Delta, a world of many coasts, but the wooden ships he saw rocking clumsily at anchor, stuck all over with masts and yards and festooned with ropes, were completely outside his understanding.

One sight was familiar: bent backs under heavy loads, hurrying as well as they could under the hard looks and the blows of blackrobed overseers and their armed servants.

"How close to finished is the loading?" Hazzan asked the blackrobe in charge.

"Close enough. They'll sail with the tide tomorrow, about midmorning it should be. We'll load all night if necessary."

Every sackful or barrow load of the black burningstone had to be carried by hand down the long wharf to the place where the big ship was anchored. The men toiling to load the ship looked like an endless procession of ants. He almost said something before remembering that he must not speak before his supposed master.

"I'd like to take a look for myself," Hazzan said aloud to the Somostai.

The blackrobe shrugged. "Please yourself."

They turned their horses over to a guard and walked out the long, narrow wharf. They had to go single file and take pains to avoid bumping the overburdened workers who staggered along beside them. Singer's heart swelled with anger at the sight of them. He would have liked to banish them from his thoughts like so many pack animals, but he felt their hard-drawn breath brush his arms as he passed them, and every breath seemed to whisper "I am a man like you." Even pack animals got better treatment among the Riders. It had been so much easier to live when only Thanha were human.

He wanted to kick the guards off the rough planks into the restless, dirty black water and restrained himself with difficulty. Since he could not strike them, his anger turned toward the wretched slaves themselves. He wanted to seize them and shake them till they dropped their burdens and demand of them, "How could you let this be done to you?" But at that, he remembered that he was weighed down by a burden as heavy and dark as theirs, and their rasping breath changed its tune and questioned him: *What is this weight you carry? Whose slave are you?*

They went up the ramp to the ship's side but did not go on board. The hatches stood open, and the ship lay low in the water. Inside the hold the dark heaps of coal had risen almost to the loading marks. Men with shovels worked in the hold to level the cargo as each load rattled down. In the stern the hold seemed to have been topped off already. Men worked to draw ropes tightly over heavy canvas covers stretched over the coal heaps.

Stacks of coarsely woven blankets were piled along the deck, ready for some kind of use. As they watched, workers tossed the blankets down after the coal, and the shovel wielders spread them over the leveled and finished sections of the cargo before stretching the canvas over them.

"What's that for?" Hazzan asked.

The overseer shrugged. "Something about keeping the damp out—I don't know. Orders. Very particular orders, it was. The blankets came down by cart from the city. I was told that any old rags wouldn't do. Something new they're trying, I suppose. Not my business."

A thin man they had passed on their way caught up to them at last. Bent nearly double under his sack of coal, he hardly had the strength to swing it down from his back and dump it. He faltered in the act and sank to his knees in a paroxysm of coughing as the last of the coal spilled across the dock.

The Somostai sent him sprawling with the butt of his stick. The man tried to crawl out of the way, still coughing. Finally he was able to get back to his feet and take a few uncertain steps, but he fell again before he reached the shore.

"Excuse me," the Somostai said. "It's a cursed nuisance."

He hurried to the fallen body and poked it vigorously. The man did not move. The Somostai turned him over with the stick. Singer could tell by the way the head flopped that it was useless to interfere. The Somostai ordered the next two workers in the line to set down their loads and push the body off the dock. It bobbed away with the other debris.

"It's the coughing sickness," the Somostai explained when he returned. "This crew is rotten with it. Usually they can at least get themselves back to shore before they drop dead."

"Coughing sickness?" Hazzan asked. "What is that?"

The Somostai seemed surprised that he did not know. "Just as you see," he said. "Most folk in the city have it as children. Sometimes they die of it, but if the first time doesn't kill you, you seldom catch it twice. It seems to grow strong when people are hungry and weak. If you have it for the first time as a grown man, it can kill you. I suppose poverty is the reason so many of this crew are going down with it. I've never seen so many at one time. It is a little strange, but then, these workers come from all over. Maybe the sickness is different in different parts of the land.

"I only wish it had not happened with my workers. I heard an interesting project proposed to the master once. If we could find some way of giving it to all babies, then those who were going to die of it could be gotten out of the way at once. Not a bad idea."

Hazzan frowned. "That's not my concern. What I want to know is how long it will take for this cargo to arrive in the flying people's city."

"Well, that depends on the weather at this time of year. I suppose that's why they're in such a cursed hurry to get loaded. A week should do it. If it takes more than ten days, we'll all be in trouble."

"Why so?"

The Somostai looked surprised. "Why, surely, Captain Hazzan, you would know better than I. All I know is that the master gave clear orders for the utmost speed. If you had heard him, there would be no doubt in your mind."

17

They returned with Hazzan to the Black City and were just taking their boots off when Korro arrived.

"Where in cold hell have you been?" he asked Jon.

"I went with Captain Hazzan to the harbor, master."

"Did you learn anything about the explosion this morning as you came through the city?"

"No, master. The captain went straight to the harbor."

Korro threw his gloves on the table and glowered at Jon. "You fool. You could have made yourself useful. Instead you indulge yourself in idle curiosity. There's nothing for you or Hazzan at the harbor. That explosion was important."

"I didn't see any damage—nothing to compare with the last time."

Korro waved his hand impatiently. "No, no, no. It had nothing to do with the last time. That one was a disaster. This was nothing, or so I hear. Someone captured one of the Deltanek, killed him, and blew up those fire eggs they carry on their belts. It might have been an accident. The city guard was jumpy, however. Quite properly so."

"Forgive my impertinence, master, but if it was nothing, why are you making something of it?"

"Your impertinence is less reprehensible than your stupidity. Someone killed him. Who is living in my city who dares to kill a Deltanek? Who is *able* to kill a Deltanek? What they did with his weapons afterward is irrelevant. Independent action is a greater danger than any amount of strangerfolk weaponry. You would do well to remember that."

"I understand you perfectly," Jon murmured.

"Do you, indeed?"

The master put his heavy hand on Jon's shoulder and pulled him closer to scrutinize his face. "You took a very big risk when you left the city without my permission. You know that, don't you? Perhaps one risk too many."

He fingered Jon's cheek and jaw, tightening his grip till Jon winced. "It seems I didn't hit you as hard as I thought. That may have been a mistake. Still, you came back instead of trying to get away. That speaks well for you."

Singer breathed easier. It seemed that Korro had talked himself out of his suspicions. Suddenly the master shoved Jon against the wall so hard that Singer could hear the crack of his head meeting stone.

"Why did you come back?" Korro shouted. "What game are you playing?"

"Where else could I go?" Jon choked out. "Hide on a ship that's making straight for Nupi country? I know what Hazzan's masters would do with me."

Korro began to laugh and let go of him. "It's for your own benefit that I want you close to me. It has been suggested to me more than once that I'm harboring a snake in my breast and would do better to crush your head before you sting me."

Jon sat down, rubbing his head. "I already knew that," he said. "Why do you think I looked for bodyguards?"

Korro leaned over him confidentially. "I think I know who caused that explosion."

Singer mentally reviewed his weapons and mapped out the best combination of attack and escape to use as he waited for the master to name his suspect.

"We finally had workers to spare, to break into the underground barracks that collapsed. There was no one inside. Somehow those men escaped."

"How did they do that?" Jon interrupted. "You have always told me that is impossible."

Korro looked annoyed. "I certainly won't explain it to you. Someone who knew the Great House before it fell had to have helped them. Obviously some member of my Order has so far forgotten himself as to use slaves as tools. That was a mistake. They'll get little use from those farmers' sons—however tall they may be."

He gave Singer a look. Singer relaxed all his muscles instantly, trying to look stupid, but he was not sure he had fooled Korro.

"I tell you this because I want you to know where your advantage lies. It is not I who want you dead—not at present. I want your eyes. You make a good observer because my enemies think you don't know what you're seeing. I know better. You make a good tool for me. Answer to my hand and I will keep you well. Disappoint me and I'll give you to the Devourer. Now you understand."

"Yes," Jon said.

"Now to another problem. Have you been able to find out what Hazzan is saying to his masters?"

Jon looked sullen. "Not with that equipment. It's quite impossible. I told you that."

"But there is a way."

"Sure. Just let me use Hazzan's equipment and I'll know everything he knows. But I doubt you'll find him willing to cooperate."

Korro scratched his beard. "The captain's goodwill may not be as important as it once was. I'll let you know. Meanwhile, keep working with your machines. Only the Devourer's mouth is inescapable. All else can be adjusted."

When he had gone, Jon heaved a huge sigh and reached for the beer jug. "I thought we'd smoked it for a minute there."

As Singer started to speak, Jon held up his hand for silence. "I am, as the master so kindly observes, not blind. If you know any more about his escaped prisoners, it's best you don't tell me." He gulped the rest of his beer. "Spending time with Korro is enough to make a believer out of anyone. Talk of the Destroyer! Kristo, it sometimes feels as if he'll suck my soul out and swallow it whole. Concealing anything from him is like hanging on to hot iron. The need to let go is intense."

Singer could feel the sharp ache in Jon's head. He would have liked to ease it, but he knew that Jon would see any approach just then as another assault on his privacy. He climbed the steps to the empty storage room at the top of the tower to be alone, calm himself, and look for Kruger. He shared all that he had seen with the Asharya and made arrangements for the first group of Riders to cross the pass and be smuggled into the city. There was some comfort in being Kruger's eyes and ears again, as he had been so many times before.

Some comfort—but it was not enough. The words he had heard in his mind tortured him. The Delh'tani had thought he was an experiment. Bone, too, had spoken of such things. He rose, slipped out of the room, and made his way down through the levels to the infirmary. As he had hoped, he found Bone sleeping there. He pulled the little slave out into the hall. He could not bear to reenter that room.

"When you first saw me, you said that Korro had succeeded. What did you mean? Tell me. I have to know."

Bone sighed. Singer almost thought he saw pity in Bone's clouded eyes.

"You've heard the master's speech about the Destroyer and how he changed the patterns in us. Well, in every generation some are born with a gift or curse caused by those little changes. It manifests itself in different ways—unfailing memory, uncanny luck with dice, a way of knowing others' thoughts and hearts or of bending their thoughts to one's own. Sometimes as a great gift for music or a talent for war—both because the artist knows with subtle clarity how the others will react.

"But it's unpredictable and incomplete. For a very long time the Somostai have dreamed of causing those things to breed true and thus making human tools to use in creating rule and power for themselves. They matched men and women with certain qualities, hoping the children would also carry those things.

"The results have been unreliable. Hadhla was one of their best successes, as I read the records. Yet his understanding was partial, and that creates unstable men—always peering into others' hearts, fearful of being deceived, raging at any sign of opposition. So they moved on from him. They bred him to another strain, hoping to combine the best of both. They had great hopes for the result—an heir to the city, trained by them to be completely Somostai, who could see men's hearts and bend them to his will. And then they lost the boy. That loss was one of the worst defeats Korro has ever suffered. He still regrets it bitterly and has caused many to suffer for their part in it."

A muffled sound escaped Singer, and Bone swung his fogged gaze in Singer's direction.

"You don't like that, do you? Well, think on this. Korro knows that among the Riders another strain has been growing—a wild strain, one he cannot control. Hadhla would have liked to put an end to the Riders once he no longer needed you for his wars. Korro wanted to preserve you, hoping someday to tame you and use you.

"You Riders have perfectly performed an experiment Korro can only imagine. Listen: You take people from anywhere, anyone who wants to come. Then they are tested in training and warfare. Those who are brave and strong live, yes. But also those who are quick to see and perceive, those who best judge an enemy and who work best with friends. They are the ones who live to have children, and their children again are tested. You have collected the seeds of those changes from all over the land, as children collect resh beans.''

''How do you know all this?'' Singer asked.

Bone shrugged. ''I hear the masters talk. This matter of a successor is much on Korro's mind, and none here have been found fit. But about the Riders—that I figured out for myself. If I could see to find my way, I would have joined them long ago. I am glad you asked me about this, because I want to warn you. You hold a prize Korro has long desired for himself. That is not a safe position. Be careful. Do not let him guess what guest he is harboring.''

Singer slept badly that night. He had dreams: first, a group of children playing—no, fighting. Gradually he realized that though they were bare-handed, they were not playing the training games of Thanha children. They wore Delh'tani clothing. They kicked and bit with total dedication. Gradually their attention focused on one or two of the weakest, then only one. Singer felt feet that seemed to be his own slamming against fragile ribs, his own hands thudding on flesh in blows he recognized as trained and lethal. The children had chosen the weakest among them to destroy. Singer felt the body he dreamed gasping and trembling, eyes swollen nearly shut with bruises, but in spite of the effort he was stone cold inside. The cold voice said, *It isn't me,* and he felt a relief that sickened. *It isn't me, it isn't me,* Singer cried, struggling, but he could not break free of the dream.

Something even worse waited for him farther down. He struggled again and nearly woke but sank back into sleep again. The dream had changed. He saw Hilurin for the first time since the breaking of the Rock. He had never dreamed Hilurin. Sweet joy replaced the fear.

Help me, Lurya. Tell me what's happening.

Hilurin only looked at him with eyes full of secrets and pain. The old Singer raised a hand to his mouth, and Singer saw that his wrists were chained. Hilurin opened his lips, but there was no sound. The Singer was mute. That anguish stabbed Singer awake.

He broke his custom and drank Jon's beer till he could feel its effect. Lurya was dead. Dead and still in chains. Something dead is hunting me, Singer thought, as the Somostai are ridden by dead voices they no longer understand. He thought of Hilurin with longing and grief. And anger. Yes, he was angry at Hilurin, and the anger rubbed salt into his grief.

"You didn't tell me, Lurya," he said softly. "You told me I was Hadhla's son, but you didn't tell me why. I did not mind so much that the Thanha made me a weapon. They were my people, and I loved them. But to be bred by blackrobes for their own reasons, to be a thing of theirs—that's worse than being owned. It is an insult I can never wipe out, for it is written in my blood."

He huddled by the window, waiting for the dawn. He did not want to sleep anymore that night.

18

Three days later he crouched for shelter behind rocks on the eastern edge of the plateau where the Place of the Eater had been built. A narrow trail, seldom used and roughly maintained, fell down the steep slope to the high saddle that led to Thanha country. Perhaps the Somostai had once kept watch there, but Singer could see why they had long ceased to do so. Horses could manage the pass, but slowly and with difficulty. There was no danger of sudden invasion by a war host. On the eastern side there was no easy entrance to the Somostai fortress. The mountain spurned all hands raised against it, while the Somostai set their gaze toward the south, where they expected danger.

He was alone. His absence might be made plausible, but if Korro found Jon and Saldivar also missing, he would certainly be alarmed. He had been in contact with Janet and had arranged through her for Olmalik to create a diversion within the city to cover their arrival.

At last he located the Riders as faint flecks of movement on the trail far below him. They were well camouflaged and moving cautiously. By moonrise the Riders had reached the rim. There were half a dozen Thanha and as many Delh'tani, each carrying fire weapons and one with a bow and several spare quivers. They also carried some medical supplies Janet had requested, concentrated Delh'tani rations, and ammunition. Singer saw a face he recognized, one that did not seem to belong in that company.

"What did you bring *him* for?" he asked.

"I was not brought, I volunteered," Genady said before anyone could speak up on his behalf.

"I sent for the pallantai," Singer said. "You are not a warrior."

"Excuse me? I am not a warrior? Would you like to explain how I got into this fix?"

"You are—" Singer looked for the word. "A scientist."

"A fancy word for curiosity with an organizing principle. I'm a Rider, right? And half my hearth is here. Where else would I be?"

He had hit on an argument that Singer could not contradict. Singer shrugged and hurried through the rest of the greetings. He meant for them to cross the plateau while it was still dark, before the moon rose high. He sent them across the open space by twos and threes, with himself and their group leader watching for any sign of Somostai. Genady was in the last group; he paused in the middle of the circle and looked around.

"What is this?" he called to Singer, who was concealed in the shadows where the moonlight could not reach.

Singer broke out of hiding to hurry Genady out of his dangerous exposure. "It's the Place of the Eater! Get out of it!"

"No, you idiot, I don't mean that stupid statue. I mean this place. It was built for a purpose."

"That's what I said. Come on!" Singer actually grabbed Genady's arm. It was a thing one would not do to a Rider, but the Delh'tani's stupidity was beyond comprehension. Genady permitted himself to be hustled, but he craned his neck to look back.

When they crouched at the top of the long trail down, Genady kept hold of Singer's arm.

"This is important," he insisted. "That ring up there. I don't care what your blackrobes have turned it into; it was built as an observatory. There aren't any instruments, but the foundations are there. I've visited every ground-based observatory on Delta, and I know the sites. It's perfect. I've got to go back up there and get a close look at it.''

Singer would have pulled on his own hair if his head had not been shaved. Always it was this way with the Delh'tani. Clear, obvious priorities, such as good cover and prudent haste for the well-being of the brothers, got muddled while their minds strayed to irrelevant speculations. You must not think of them as Delh'tani, he rebuked himself. They are your brothers now, and you must give their observations the same courtesy you would give to any brother.

At the same time Genady stopped speaking in frustration. Singer got a quick flash of himself as Genady suddenly saw him: wild, unreasonable, stone deaf to words of tremendous importance.

"Look," the Deltan said. He laid it out like a diagram in his mind, and all at once Singer *saw*. A circular tower, capped with a dome, rose above the unnatural flat stones of the plateau. As if by some Delh'tani magic, the dome split and a cylinder showed in the widening aperture. At first Singer thought it was a big gun, but it pointed upward toward the night sky. Genady showed him that it was like the seeing tubes the soldiers carried to make far things look near. This tube, however, could pull in the stars themselves, close enough to be examined.

Caught by the vision, Singer stretched out his hand as if he could catch a star and hold it in his palm like a jewel. So that was Genady's passion. No wonder he found it hard to leave the place where such things had once been possible.

Genady let the images fade. He still had a hard time maintaining such contact for long.

"Not quite like that," he muttered. "It's not so glorious in practice. But to find the record of their observations—what a treasure that would be. It could tell you where the Somostai came from. Who the skyfathers were.''

"Now I understand," Singer said, shaken. The Delh'tani could exasperate him beyond endurance with their childish lack of concentration. Equally, they could astonish him by a devotion to knowledge so deep that they forgot even the danger to their own skins. "I understand. But this is a raiding party, not a scientific investigation. It will have to wait. Believe me, you do not want to interview any Somostai tonight.''

Reluctantly, Genady followed the others over the edge and down. Singer stayed behind for a minute to blot out any revealing footprints. Then he caught up with the others.

The moonlight was still a danger if anyone was watching, but it was an advantage, too. They found their way down without accidents, though a number of the Delh'tani slipped once or twice and had to be steadied by their brothers. Passing the point where Singer had looked out from the ridge, they descended to the snow-covered slope below the outskirts of the ruined city. *Tell Olmalik to do it soon, isé,* he said to Janet. *We're crossing the snow now.* He moved slowly, waiting for the promised diversion.

Olmalik's people came through with a bang. Somewhere in the central city an explosion echoed off walls like a thunderclap. The flash lit the snow with red for an instant, then died in a column of black smoke that glowed at its center. Even from a distance Singer could hear startled outcries in the city.

"This is our chance," he said to the others. "Time to move. And if you have to kill someone, try to do it quietly."

At the foot of the ridge they floundered into waist-deep snow. Their struggles to make haste would have been ludicrous if the need had been less urgent. They broke through the last drifts and ran up the slope toward the edge of the city. Sweat froze in their hair. Their breathing sounded as loud to Singer as a whole herd of cattle, but they reached the edge of the city without being seen.

In a few minutes they were all inside and safely under cover in the dugout shelter that Singer had seen before. It had been extended and improved.

Olmalik stepped forward into the light to greet them. Hunger and worry had further gnarled his face; it took a moment to recognize his expression as a smile. He took Singer's hand and touched the others as Singer told him their names. Singer had to translate the rest of the conversation twice: into Thanha for the Riders who did not understand Giristiyah and into Delteix for the Deltans whose Thanha was shaky.

"I sent for my people, as I promised," Singer said. "Will you receive them as allies?"

"Gladly, if they are willing to share this life. This is the safest place we have. We built an escape route that we hope is well hidden. It runs underground part of the way to the fence. The blackrobes have been here twice, tearing the place apart to look for us. Some of the women said we should be given up rather than costing any more lives, but we had enough relatives in the camp to shout them down. There's no more of that kind of talk since we circulated rumors of our plan to rise against the Somostai. No one believes we can win, but it gives them something to look forward to. They won't live through the winter with things as they are.''

"Do the blackrobes still feed the women?''

"Barely.'' Olmalik's mouth set grimly on that word. "This is hunger time. Only those who came here in the last levies of the fall are able to work with us. The others stay in their huts. To keep warmth and breath in their bodies takes all their strength. Until last full moon the blackrobes forced the women and children out into the fields to pick up wood and scavenge roots from the frozen ground. Now there is almost nothing left for gleaning. I think the blackrobes intend to starve them.''

"I knew you'd need food, but we couldn't bring enough to help,'' Singer said. "You'll have to make do with what you got from the storerooms. My people packed in only what they could carry over the mountains on their backs, and most of that weight had to be weapons. Each of them is armed with fire weapons from the flying people. I have not brought such weapons for you. You have no time to learn their use. They'll be more help to you in the hands of the Riders outside the walls. We have brought edged weapons and arrows, as many as we could carry, and warrior knowledge that will do you more good than anything. You must search these ruins for any scraps of metal you can find. They'll do for arrowheads and for other purposes my friends will explain to you.''

Olmalik nodded. "We thought of that already,'' he said with pride. "We have been making arrows and whatever else can be contrived without a smithy.''

He narrowed his eyes and leaned close to Singer. "We've done more than that. How do you think we drew off the guards? One night in our scavenging we found a soldier of the stranger-folk walking in the Somostai part of the city. We set upon him and stripped him of his life and his strange weapons. The sorrow of it was that two men and a boy died learning to use those weapons. But we did learn it! That big bang was set off in your honor by a child I sent into the city. A child! If they treat us like rats, they will learn that rats have teeth.''

Darkness scoured away the bright fullness of the moon. Singer took a second group of Riders down the cliff path and then a third.

"There will be one more group after this, and that will be the last," Singer said to Olmalik at the end of the trail. "It would be leaning on luck to bring any more people by this road."

"Good," Olmalik said. "I can't hide and keep more than that, anyway. We have weapons enough to take the guard posts nearest the wall and hold our ground against reinforcements from up the mountain—if your promised war host is not too long in arriving."

"They are gathering on the far side of the pass. They'll be ready to ride in a few days. I'll let you know through Zhanne. Where is she?"

"She sent word that she was too busy to come to this meeting."

Singer found Janet in the shack she had set up like a medical tent. The patients lay in cramped rows, some on cots made of boards but most of them on the ground. There were not enough blankets to go around. Janet stood at the end of the tent, holding out her hands to be rinsed by a child with a jug of water. When she saw Singer, she turned to him and leaned her head against his chest, but she held her hands up out of the way so they would stay clean.

"What's going on here that's so important?" he asked.

"Take a good look at it. This is our future. They're starving all over this camp. I don't even bother to bring in the malnutrition cases. There's nothing I can do for them. They have to have food, and I don't have any. Not just hungry, Singer. Starving to *death*. The little kids are the worst. They have this look of endless woe, as if life itself had betrayed them.

"Then there's frostbite. Fingers and toes turning black. Sores. Dysentery. Madre'dio, it was bad enough to see your Riders in the shape they were in. This is ten times worse. We don't have till spring. These people will all be dead by then.

"Do you know what I've been thinking? Wondering what it was like in the Consorso Zone this winter. I saw only chronic malnutrition before we left and lots of preventable deaths from infectious diseases. But I give them a year or two, and the civilians will be dying off like these poor bastards. Sooner or later the refinery will go, and that will be the end. New Hope! What a joke."

She buried her head in Singer's cloak and clung to him. He felt her touch in his heart.

I see death everywhere. Our foothold on this world is not secure enough to keep the war alive and ourselves, too. It's like something dead that keeps eating, anyway. Your Somostai and our PCOM are going to feed us all down the hatch. It has to be stopped.

He thought she was crying, but she looked up at him dry-eyed, and he realized it was only a cough that shook her thin body.

"Hell, no," she said. "I don't cry on the job." But her lip trembled. *You've been hiding out from me ever since Siri died. Morne was right. There is a darkness in you, like the shadow of a storm, and you won't let me see past it.*

He could feel her gentle vision searching him even while she spoke.

"No!" He held her tighter, trying to soften his refusal. "If you could see what I see—it would be real. Now it's not, quite. Like a song is not quite real before it's sung. I won't take you there, paliao. Not till I know there's a way out."

"Is there a way out?" she asked sadly.

"There is always a way." But the words came from his lips only, not his heart, and she knew it.

"Oh, hell," she said, letting him go. "Now I'll have to scrub all over again. Debriding gangrenous ulcers because I don't want to cut this woman's leg off if I don't have to. Want to stick around? You can be my barf tech. That's the one who holds the bag for the surgeon to upchuck in when necessary."

She smothered another fit of coughing. "All that isn't what I meant to say," she observed. "You distract me. Coughing. That's the point. We're having an outbreak of respiratory infection. If you don't move fast, I predict you're going to lose a significant part of your pallantai. They'll be too sick to fight. A word to the wise."

"If it's coughing sickness, there's nothing to fear for the pallantai. They've all had it already. Anyway, it's probably just one of the lesser sicknesses that makes you cough. Nothing to worry about."

But he kept remembering the dead slave on the dock. The Delh'tani seemed to have medicines and machines to cure everything. Surely a sickness of children and poor people could not harm them. Yet he looked at Janet and was afraid.

"Are you all right?" he asked.

"Sure, it's just a cold. Don't worry. My self-diagnosis is infallible." *I don't want you to worry about me. This is where I belong. It's my job. Just don't let us be wasted.*

She kissed him good-bye in the Thanha fashion: a kiss on

each cheek and a kiss on the lips. *Kestri, andri, paliao. My heart, my soul, my right hand and my left.*

"Now get the hell out of here."

Why had she not pressed him for his secret? That was unlike her, he thought. He said to himself that it was because she was tired, or perhaps she respected his wish and trusted him. In his heart he knew the only possible reason: She had a secret of her own. Because he did not want that knowledge, he buried it deep with the other unwanted secrets. But the fear would not go away.

19

The last group brought hardly any food. Their personal equipment was limited to belt packs. Ten were Deltans, only two were from the Riders, and all twelve were big men, big enough to carry the heavy captured weapons that could stop a vito with one blow or fire hundreds of bits of metal in the space of a breath or two. Though their leader greeted Singer with a handclasp instead of a kiss, he wore an embroidered camisa and gold wolf's heads dangled from his ears.

"Kruger says they're ready to ride," he said as a greeting. "He has Riders from the Tall Grass and the River People with him, waiting for your word."

The moon was hardly high enough in the sky to light their climb. Singer knew the road like the back of his hand, but the soldiers were bigger and clumsier than the other groups, and the heavy weapons were awkward. He did not lose any of the people, but one of the fast-talking guns slithered away when the soldier carrying it fell and barely saved himself.

Singer had found a new route around the snowfield, one that

seemed well enough concealed that a planned diversion would not be needed. He preferred not to alarm the guards again.

Olmalik smacked his hands together in satisfaction when Singer introduced him to the group. "I like this," he said. "Cunning and stealth are good, but big men with big weapons are even better."

"If you are prepared to put them to use, my Asharya is ready to ride. I need to arrange the signal with Zhanne."

"Your healer is with the sick, as usual," Olmalik said. A shadow crossed his face, and Singer knew that Zhanne was not as well as she had wanted him to think.

In her makeshift medical tent Janet was sitting down with her head in her hands. That in itself was a bad sign. As Singer came in she straightened up instantly and turned to meet him. The movement triggered an attack of coughing. At first she tried to suppress it with a hand to her mouth, but she ended up bent over the table, gasping. She tried to speak and started to cough again.

Singer caught her by the shoulders and picked her up. There were no empty beds. He tried to lay her down, but she pulled herself into a sitting position to gasp for air again. He propped her against the wall with his cloak under her head.

"Don't be mad," she whispered. "I couldn't help it."

Singer wanted Morne badly. He was too shaken to trust himself as a healer. "What is it?" he asked her, though he knew already. He had heard that rasping in the lungs before: the slave on the dock.

She gathered her remaining strength to give him a diagnosis. "I don't even know that. It causes acute inflammation in the lungs, and I think it must be putting out toxins that weaken the whole system, because I feel like shit in six colors. I have no treatment. So it's just a race. Me or them, who can outlast. Like us and the Deltans, no?" She laughed and started coughing again. "That hurts," she observed.

She covered her mouth again. "Stay away from me. You cannot get sick."

"I won't. Dona had this. He nearly died of it. I had it when I was a baby. He said you don't get it twice, not unless you're very unlucky."

He pushed the damp hair back from her face. Her skin was hot. He let his fingertips rest lightly on her chest. He could see the pulse in her throat beating far too fast, almost flickering. Her skin was always pale, but now even her lips had lost all color and her closed eyes were bruise-colored as if she had been beaten. He moved in deeper, and the sickness caught at his breath like fear. Her lungs rattled and clogged, strangling on their own defenses as they tried to capture and expel the enemy. Where was the enemy? He searched, forgetting his surroundings in his concentration. It was everywhere and yet elusive, so small, so fast, and growing constantly. He was losing himself, losing his own body. He found himself standing beside her again, gasping. He had forgotten to breathe.

"I don't know what to do," he said. He thought heat might kill those tiny enemies, but Zhanne's fever was already dangerously high. Her body was running at the edge of its ability; he was afraid to interfere and disturb the balance that was keeping her barely alive.

Teach me something, he begged her. But her attention was not focused on the place where he was. She was waiting somewhere else while her body fought its battle.

Suddenly she touched him again. *Get Jon. I want—no, he wants—he's trying* . . . She faded out again.

Jon was there, sharp and vivid enough to touch, though he almost jumped out of contact in his urgent fear. *Singer! You've got to get back here right away, it's—dio! What's wrong with Janney?*

Singer let him see.

Kristo! She looks just like Hazzan!

Jon substituted the image of the Nupi captain, blue-pale, head lolling as the Somostai dragged him out of his control room. Hazzan struggled feebly, made eye contact for a moment, and tried to say something that was lost as he coughed up bloody sputum.

He tried to tell me something.

Jon was in the Nupi's room, watching the monitors. No one was working anywhere but the mines, where a team of emaciated workers dragged a cartload of something that was not coal with frantic haste, under the lash of the blackrobes. Singer saw the scroll of paper Jon held in his hand but could not make any sense of the symbols on it.

Korro sent me here. Said I could use the equipment all I wanted to now—he was pleased as fucking hell. This message was on, had been repeating God knows how long while Hazzan lay on the floor hacking his guts out. They plead for contact—three dozen, four dozen times. Then they tell him they're putting the alternative measures into operation—effective three hours before dawn. Singer, they'll be here before the sun comes up. If they're sending vitos. If they want to take the city. If they wanted just to destroy it, we'd be dead already. The hi-fighters could be here from Solidari in an hour. What are we going to do now? The Nupis don't know Thanha from blackrobes. We're all microbes to them.

He turned abruptly from Singer to Janet, calling to her, trying to wake her. Singer knelt on the floor. He guessed at what had happened. Hazzan had had a vision of the city working as a unit under his orders, producing the goods so desperately needed in Solidari. That plan had fallen apart when Korro had realized that he was not getting the knowledge he expected from the flying people. The accident had finished off any chance for negotiation. Hazzan's NPU commanders, in their alarm, had lost patience with their native allies and were coming to take control of the situation.

Jon, he called.

Reluctantly, Jon abandoned his efforts to wake Janet.

She's dying, isn't she? he asked, and his thoughts were heavy and saturated with dark grief, like pigment bleeding down a wall. *Isn't there anything you can do? No magic?* The irony of those last two words tore savagely at Singer and was meant to.

I don't know how. I don't know enough about what her body is doing. Maybe she could teach me, but not now. Wounds and bruises, yes, but not this. I will tell Olmalik to move her to a safe place till the fight that's coming is over.

No! Jon clung as if he were physically there beside her, almost crying in frustration because he was not.

She's no closer to dying than you are, Singer told him brutally. *We'll all take the road together if we can't be lucky, strong, and clever. You've got to fight for her chance to live and let her do the same. Your sister is Thanha now. She understands that choice. I need your help* now.

Jon straightened up slowly. His field of vision broadened enough to let Singer see Palha standing next to him.

You should have taken me with you, Saldivar said quietly.

Just what do you expect me to do? Jon asked simultaneously.

Zhanne was my link to Olmalik. Now I've lost that, and there's nothing you can do about it. But I also needed her to keep in touch with Makho.

You can do that yourself, Jon said.

I can't be sure of that. I'll be busy here. If something takes my attention, or if I get killed, we will need backup. We don't have it unless you will help.

Scornful rejection from Jon. *Bull. Just because I do it with Janet doesn't mean I'm about to squeeze into Marcus Kruger's bullet head with him.*

Singer leaned into Saldivar's solid strength. *Don't let him bug out.*

He cast for the keen, bright presence that was Lyn. He found the confusion of voices, wishes, and perceptions that made up the war host. He skipped from the surface of one mind to the next and heard stamping hooves, felt the wind, smelled sweet oil on hair braided for war. Lyn was not there.

Unexpectedly, like a child slipping a hand into his in the dark, another mind slipped into contact.

Hello. Where are you? She was bright and unafraid like Lyn but very young. He caught a glimpse of saddle trappings seen from low down. The child must be holding someone's horse.

It's me, of course, she said impatiently. *Roishe.*

He sent her the thought of Lyn and immediately got back a picture of a vito, wound about with delicious fear and longing excitement. *Grandfather sent her to bring the flying thing. She wouldn't let me come. They won't let me come with the pallantai, either. I'm angry. Singer! You tell them. They'd listen to you!*

They may have to take you, he said grimly, and had to override her delight. *Get Grandfather for me.*

Seeing Makho through her eyes, he found it easy to speak to him. Makho grasped the situation in a few quick and mostly wordless sketches. He was appalled, but Singer could see him immediately turning the situation over in his mind, canceling his preconceptions and calculating new outcomes.

So I still need you to ride with all speed, Singer finished, *but don't come down to the city till you check out our position. If we've already lost, don't lose the rest of the pallantai in a death charge against Nupi air.*

Don't teach your Grandfather to kill Nupis, the old man said dryly. *Just give me the facts. I can deal with them.*

Zhanne is sick, and you've sent Lyn on ahead. I can't be sure of reaching you without them. You'll have to take the child along. Let her ride behind you. That way you won't take too many risks.

Makho was scandalized by the idea but reluctantly agreed.

This is your other contact. Jon?

Jon took hold as if he were snapping a physical link into place. Singer felt nothing but amazement in Jon's mind. *So, I still think*

*it's impossible, but I'm performing a willing suspension of dis-
belief for the duration.*

A pleasure to meet you, Mr. Logan, Kruger said formally.
Even under these unusual circumstances.

Singer let them fade to the back of his mind. The last thing
he heard was Roishe uttering a shriek of triumph as the Asharya
told her she could ride with him.

I'll be back as soon as I can, he said to Saldivar privately
while the others were busy. *Stay with Jon. Don't let anything
happen to him.*

Palha questioned whether Jon could hold them all together.

*No fear. Can't you feel it? He's solid. Better than Zhanne in
a way, because he knows how to lock people out. He'll concentrate—no matter what happens to those around him. Zhanne is
not good at that.*

Singer became aware that someone was looking at him. He
could tell by the cramped feeling in his legs that he had been
crouching motionless for some time. The observer was another
child, impossible to distinguish as male or female by its skinny,
raggedly clothed body. Singer thought from the sense of him
that he was a boy. The child was ready to run away at the first
sudden move. He could not believe that a man in dark clothing,
with a shaved head, meant him no harm.

"I'm not Somostai," Singer said. "I look like it, but I'm
not."

The child bit his lip and fidgeted, trying to decide if he could
believe that. His need to know won over his fear.

"Is the lady all right?" he asked anxiously. So much fear and
misery flavored the words that Singer longed to comfort him,
but he could not.

"She's very sick," he said gently. "But don't give up hope.
There's still a chance for her to get well. I'm going to tell Olmalik to move her to a safe place. Can you stay with her on the
way?"

The boy nodded vigorously, happy to be given something to
do.

"Please bring me some water and a clean rag if there is one."
He showed the boy how to wet Janet's lips. "Keep dripping
water like this. Can you do that for her?"

The child nodded, taking the rag into his thin, dirty hand.
Clearly he would have done anything for her, and that somehow
made it easier for Singer to walk away from her.

He braced himself for the interview with Olmalik. He knew

it would not be easy. When he walked into the bunker, all the farmer's captains were waiting for him, and with them, Genady and the rest of the Delh'tani and Thanha reinforcements.

"The time has come," he said, and felt them all breathe in together like runners stepping up to the mark.

"I have sent for the Thanha pallantai. But the fight will not go as we hoped it would. There is news from my brothers in the Black City. The flying people are coming back. They are displeased with the Somostai and want to kill them, take the city for their own."

"Then let them have it," one of the gaunt workers cried. "It will be a pleasure to watch the blackrobes fry in the fire from the sky."

Many voices approved his words, but they quieted down when they saw that Singer had more to say.

"The flying folk don't know black robes from white or one man from another. To them we are all vermin. They'll kill the Somostai, all right, but they won't stop there. They will kill us all without ever seeing our faces. They'll push the ruins in over our bodies and never give our buried children one thought."

The workers stared at him, horrified.

Olmalik, seeing that Singer was trying to alarm them, refused to show fear. "So what do you propose to do about it?" he asked.

Singer took a deep breath. "We're going to have to help the Somostai."

Olmalik's control broke. "Help the Somostai?" he cried. "Help the Somostai? Are you crazy?"

Singer crossed the circle at one bound to stand next to him, avoiding, by one crucial inch of space between them, the killing insult of touching him in anger.

"Maybe I am crazy," he breathed. "Maybe I have gone crazy by crouching under the fire-from-the-sky one time too many, not fighting back while it hammered the world to stinking ashes. Maybe I have gone crazy from living like a rat and eating death for breakfast. But it will be springtime in hell before I get crazy enough to stick my hand in the fire to make sure the Somostai burn their fingers."

He backed off and glared around the circle, his chest heaving. "I want to see the Somostai burn as much as you do. I want them to learn what it is to fear, to be driven and slaughtered. Any good I do them is bitter in my mouth, but their destruction will be no good to me if I don't live to see it."

He turned on Olmalik. "We struck palms for a bargain, remember? I kept my word! Now keep yours and win your freedom or prove to the Riders that all lowlanders are cowards."

Genady stepped forward, an unlikely ally. "He's right, you know. Translate for me, Singer. Tell him that all of us have seen what the flying people can do. If we can deal with them, the Somostai will be a piece of cake."

Singer translated his words and then the words of Riders from Siri's folk who told what had been done to them. Olmalik's head sank lower and lower, and at last he shook it in frustration like a baited bull.

"We will fight," he said heavily. "Not because we care for glory in the Riders' eyes. We fight to live. But after that—we finish the blackrobes."

"Set up your positions as you planned," Singer said before they could argue again. "But don't move until I send word. Don't show yourselves to the guards till Korro agrees to a truce."

As he left, he met a small group of women carrying makeshift stretchers, transferring some of the sick from the tent to a more protected place. One of the stretchers bore Janet. He touched her hand as he passed, but she was still unconscious.

He turned and ran with the fighters through the twisted paths left among the rubble, leaping timbers and heaps of stone, sliding in and out of snow-covered craters. It eased his fear to run, to push himself to the limit after so many days of confinement.

20

Jon looked up and saw the Ordermaster on the other side of the desk. He glanced left and right, thinking for a moment that Singer and Kruger were in the same room with him. Singer was far off already, but Kruger said very clearly, *Who the hell is that?*

Jon flinched, expecting Korro to hear. He felt the Ordermaster's curiosity dragging at him like a barbed hook. To explain the fear on his face, he held up the printout, now crumpled in his hand.

"Hazzan warned you not to meddle in his affairs. You've really done it this time."

Korro snatched the paper but could not read it. "What does it say?"

For the first time Jon sensed fear in the master. Vital information he could not grasp without help from one who hated him: that was a cause for fear that even Korro could feel. Jon laughed out loud.

"You may never know. Why should I tell you? And if I do tell you, how will you know that I'm telling you the truth?"

The master's hand closed around Jon's throat. "I can have you killed and worse than killed."

"Then I would become even less reliable than I am now."

Korro ground his teeth but took his hand away. "Your death is certain. I advise you to postpone it as long as you can."

"Don't bother trying to scare me. You've been superseded. Hazzan's masters in his own city have lost confidence in him and have decided to come here and take control into their own hands. By force, naturally—they would see no reason to discuss it with you. You're less than an animal to them—some kind of bug, perhaps."

"When?"

"They've already started. They'll be here before dawn."

Instead of pacing the room as he customarily did when thinking, Korro sank into a chair. Fear did not show on his face, but Jon could smell it, sharp and sour. Korro had seen the bombing that had ruined the Iron City.

"Can it be prevented?"

Jon shrugged. "You may be sure Hazzan's masters could do the same to you as mine did. If they send the high-flying ships with the city-killing thunderfists, nothing can prevent them. It isn't likely, though. They badly want the mines and the foundry for themselves. If they strike the Holy City from the air, they risk destroying all that. I think they'll come in the small machines—the vitos—and drop armed men as well as fire-from-the-sky."

"They cheated me. The Destroyer's curse is on them. There

must be a way to defeat them.'' Gathering strength from his rage, Korro sprang to his feet and roamed about the room.

"There may be a way."

"Name it!" Korro roared.

Jon hesitated. It seemed like madness to tell Korro anything, but he could hear Singer urging him to hurry, and he could hear the hoofbeats of Kruger's troops—or was that the rhythmic beat of vitos flying?

"Maybe you've noticed that my other bodyguard isn't here."

He got the desk between himself and Korro. The Ordermaster's eyes betrayed him. He had not, in truth, noticed, and that oversight was enough to frighten him into a dangerous rage.

"It seems he wasn't a farmer's son, after all. He was Thanha— another thing you never told me about, master. Interesting people, don't you think? He has been smuggling some of his friends into the lower city with captured weapons. Fire weapons from the flying people. They meant to use them on the Somostai. Give them their freedom and they'll fight Hazzan's people instead. He's waiting for you by the iron furnaces to hear your answer.''

Korro made no move to attack him. He was too greatly astonished. "A renegade in the Holy City! And he dares to summon the Ordermaster! Chonza, I hope you will live to answer all my questions.''

The master called a troop of guards to attend them, and kept a good hold on Jon till they were ready to mount and ride down the road. He squeezed Jon's shoulder in a friendly-looking gesture that sent pain lancing up Jon's neck.

They clattered into the open space before the foundry building and pulled up. Torches flared all around the space. Their light gleamed from sweating horsehide and links of mail revealed by flaring cloaks but illuminated little beyond the tight knot of horses and men.

"Come out, renegade!" Korro bawled.

An arrow from nowhere hummed across Korro's saddlebow and plunged into the packed earth, making his horse dance nervously. While their eyes were on the arrow or elsewhere, seeking its source, Singer materialized in his customary way, leaving no trace of where he might have come from.

"I know that you wear a coat of protection made by the sky-folk,'' Singer said. His voice was conversational, but it carried clearly to every corner of the yard. "My friends, however, will be pleased to shoot you through the eyes if any of your men move too suddenly. Or the throat. Or pin your legs to the horse's sides and then fell the horse. Though I would hate to do that. The horse did not choose you as a master.''

"You've made your point," Korro said. He raised his voice to all the Somostai in the yard. "No moves against the renegade.''

"My friends will fight for their own lives against all enemies,'' Singer said. "This morning that meant you blackrobes. But the flying folk are a worse threat—tonight. Give us what we want without a fight and we won't have to kill you for it. Simple as that.''

Korro laughed in his face. "What have you got that you dare bargain with me? Make it short or I'll have you swept out of my way and then clean up your skulking friends.''

Singer called an order in Giristiyah, then repeated the cry in Delteix. "Light it up!''

From two different points in the darkness flares hissed up into the sky and burst, showering an angry red and lurid white glare on the upturned faces. Even Korro's guard flinched then, and some of the less well-trained soldiers cowered or threw themselves on the ground. Saldivar listened nervously for the sound of approaching vitos and hoped the glare would fade before it made a target of them.

"That's what I've got, blackrobe. Weapons to knock the flying people out of the sky. Friends who know how to use them. We could use them on you if you'd rather.''

The flares died, and the Somostai were blind for a few minutes.

"What do you want?" Korro cried into the darkness.

"My friends say they're free men and will be treated so. You swear a truce of battle with them to deal with them in good faith while they fight beside you. After that, work for wages if they choose and fair payment for the work already done. You took them from their homes unwilling. You owe them what they need to get back.

"As for the Riders, we want nothing of you if we can't have your blood. But we swore our own truce with these men, and we'll fight for them.''

Korro's hesitation was barely perceptible. "Agreed.''

"Swear it!''

"I swear," Korro said slowly, "by the Master of the Somostai, by the Devourer of Flesh, the one to whom all must come in the end. I give up my claim on these men and swear not to strike them down in battle. Will that do, renegade?"

"It will do for the time being," Singer said. "Now, come down off that horse and we'll talk."

It was a strange conversation, more like a wrestling match than a tactical conference. Each grasped and feinted, trying to gain the maximum benefit while revealing a minimum of information.

I don't feel him lying, Jon said to Singer. *But be careful. He isn't telling you everything. He has a reserve plan.*

I'm not telling him everything, either, Singer assured him. *Makho, for instance. He will be a surprise. I came to bring the blackrobes down. I haven't forgotten that.*

He felt Jon's relief.

When they had reached agreement on the orders to be issued, Korro turned to ride back with his guard. Jon followed, and Saldivar wheeled his horse to go with him. Jon stopped him with a hand on his rein.

"Don't think to lounge in the Black City when fighting men are needed here," he said in loud Giristiyah. *Stay here. I don't need you.*

He felt Saldivar start to look around at Singer and jerked on the rein again.

Don't. Korro already suspects you're with the Riders. Don't let him know for sure. He made sure that Singer, too, heard that message.

You're going back there alone? Singer asked. What he really said was wordless: *The Black City, accurate in detail, but saturated with darkness, imbued with menace, a prison for the heart; then Jon alone, bearing all the light in the picture inside himself. That Jon wore the Medicine Shirt his sister had embroidered and a headcloth like those of the pallantai.*

Jon was surprised again by the supple power behind Singer's communications. A simple question could be embedded in an intricate fabric of understanding; a simple message could be a gift of strength. He pushed aside Singer's intention even while he was warmed by it.

No big deal. From Hazzan's room I can monitor all over the city. That could help. And I'll be safer there than anywhere.

Till after, then. Embedded in those words was the warning that safety, if any, would last only till the threat from the Nupis was ended and the promise that Singer would come back for him before then. Jon hung on to the network in his mind as he rode behind Korro.

Saldivar went to help the blackrobes who were working feverishly around the foundations of the factory and foundry sheds, placing packets as if they were some kind of charges. He slit one open to look inside and found a black powder unlike any explosive he had ever worked with. He placed a pinch on a rock and, with some difficulty, struck a spark to it with his flint and steel. It exploded with a sharp crack, blowing off a pungent smoke that smelled very much like the smoke from other devices.

"Son of a bitch," he muttered to himself. One of the blackrobes grabbed him by the shoulder from behind and expostulated with him in Giristiyah. When Saldivar shrugged and shook his head, the Somostai made it clear to him with vigorous gestures that he was doing something dangerous and forbidden. The Somostai took the package away from him and put him to work with the others. He found it hard to get used to working shoulder to shoulder with the blackrobes. As far as he could tell, however, their methods were sound. The charges were not well shaped, but they were well placed if the Somostai planned to blow up the foundry and to mine selected areas around the furnaces and mine entrances. They had no detonators and seemed to be depending on cord fuses. They also spent a lot of time placing and aiming devices that looked to him like big wooden slingshots. More packages were piled next to these, along with fire tubs and lighting sticks. Saldivar did not think much of their chances.

At last they had finished their preparations and taken their positions, and there was nothing left to do but wait. Singer could feel the dawn coming, though it did not show. Little currents moved uneasily in the air. The steady wind pattern of winter was starting to break up. He remembered what the Somostai at the harbor had said: This was storm season. He thought he felt the storm turning itself around on the mountain like a wild animal stirring in its sleep, but he could not tell for sure whether it would wake. The unease in the air might be only the anticipation of a fight gnawing at every ragged man in the ruins.

Beyond the mountains, dawnlight would be streaming in from the east, under the shield of clouds. He remembered the ride to the pass as it had been: the horses' hooves cutting patterns into the heavy frost that sparkled in the new light, the air so fresh and cold that it danced in the Riders' lungs. He wanted to find Roishe and see it all through her eyes. But it was not fair to use her innocent sight, taking the risk of darkening her vision with his own fears. He contacted Jon instead.

He felt something pressed against one of Jon's ears. The Deltan was listening intently, and Singer remembered, from his other life as one of Makho's soldiers, the little voices that spoke in one's ear, from one machine to another. Aware of him, Jon showed him what he was looking at on the monitors. Shadows were dark and quiet everywhere, except in the harbor picture. Small dark dots, hardly to be seen, showed against the sky far out over the ocean. Jon did something at the desk, and the contrast of the picture changed. The dots stood out as glowing patches. Some of them ran together so they were hard to count, but Jon thought there were about a dozen.

Vitos, I think. Not fast enough for anything else. They'll be here in a quarter of an hour, best guess. What's up?

Find Makho and ask him his position, Singer requested. *Tell him what you just said.*

Jon locked onto Kruger fast enough to surprise Singer. Roishe was there, too, hanging on behind the Asharya's saddle. Two hours of walk and trot, with the prospect of much more to come, had made Kruger somewhat testy.

Watch what you say in front of the child, he said. Beneath the words was a warm recognition of Singer's presence that made Jon feel very much alone.

The guests will be joining us in a quarter of an hour.

Damn it. Kruger inadvertently struck his heels into the horse and was distracted while he got his mount back under control. Roishe laughed and drummed her heels against the horse's flanks.

"Quiet!" Kruger snapped in Thanha, and she was immediately still.

Korro accepted our proposal of alliance, Jon told him unemotionally.

So even if we prevail against the Nupis, Singer said, *you may have to act against the Somostai when you get here. I won't strike the blow that breaks the agreement, but it will be broken. My Con-el, if you have a chance, kill him for me.*

Kill him yourself, Kruger said. *I don't do your job for you.*

You'll do as you see fit, my Asharya. Only beware of Korro. He is a snake. Be careful. And hurry here, old man. I want to see you. ''I want'' was the strong form, hardly ever used because it was not polite.

If you know a way to hurry this animal, I wish you'd tell me.

No time to give you riding lessons, Makho. We're going to be busy here in a few minutes.

Till after, then, paliao.

Do you hear them? Jon asked at the same time.

Singer listened. No doubt about it—he could hear the far-off vibration that would soon become a roar. In the moments he had left he reached out for Janet. She was unconscious, sunk deep in fever dreams. Her body glowed with heat, and her dreams were fire. Singer touched her briefly with the cold of the dawn wind but quickly withdrew. He did not even know enough to risk reducing her fever. For all he knew, it was the only thing that was keeping her alive.

Live, Zhanne, he begged her. *Just live.*

He felt Saldivar's hand on his shoulder.

''She said we had to win,'' he said aloud, ''because if we didn't, none of us would ever sleep again. Too many bad dreams.''

''Come on back, brother,'' Saldivar said. ''It's here.''

21

Singer heard it: The vitos were coming, very close now. In a moment their running lights seemed to jump into view as they swept in low from the water, and his heart took off running with a mighty leap like a scared horse, as it always did when he heard the sound of engines in the sky.

Kruger had said they would come in from the sea, hoping for surprise. But the surprise was that they did not all head directly in toward the plateau where the foundries were waiting to be plucked. One group jinked south and swooped over the defenseless shanties spread out in a ragged skirt around the base of the plateau. They laid down fire neatly, almost contemptuously, as birds leave their droppings when they quit the perch.

A low, unbelieving cry rose from the workers as they saw their shelters burst into flame and thought of the helpless ones they had left behind. A few of them broke cover and looked as if they would run back, though there was nothing they could do.

Zhanne! Singer could not tell the fire of her dreams from real fire, and she had no awareness of her surroundings to tell him where she was. He could feel the pain like iron claws ripping her lungs and gripping her spine, but it was not the killing agony of fire. He had known that fire, and he did not find it near her. The air strike had missed her for the present.

Saldivar shook him urgently. "Stay with me!"

Singer had a brief flash of Jon on the floor in Hazzan's room, a yell of terror torn from him by the sound of shells striking the roof of the Holy City.

I'm fine, Jon said unemotionally even while he continued to cry out. *Under fire outside I can handle. Barely. Inside, I scream. Doesn't matter—they're all doing it. Vitos on the roof; I didn't expect them to come after the Somostai straight out, but I think they're landing troops up there. A troop of guards just went by, armed to the teeth. I hear a lot of yelling in the passages. Watch yourself! I've got them on screen. The vitos are coming down.*

Then he was up and scrambling. *I'm following the master. Has something up his sleeve. Watch yourself,*

The main body of vitos, three flights of three each, swooped low over the plateau, flying flat-out and sweeping the area with rapid gunfire as they went by.

"Hold your fire, hold your fire!" Singer shouted. Some of the men who had not taken adequate cover had been wounded or killed in the first pass. The casualties encouraged the others to keep down. They had so few of the Delh'tani weapons that they could not afford to fire at once and lose the element of surprise.

The second group of vitos lifted off from the roof and dropped past the cliff to start a second run. Suddenly their engines were drowned by an earsplitting roar that seemed to come from the mountain itself. Clouds of white smoke, lit with sparks and flame, hid the flying machines for a moment, and when they burst out of the cloud, two of them listed badly. One veered erratically, tried to pull up, and struck the mountainside in a ball of fragments and fire. The other roared off downhill, barely keeping above the ground, and set down on the road below the city.

The others pulled away from the cliff, regrouped, and went back in, flying very fast.

Cannon! Jon said, nearly dancing with agitation and triumph. *Kristo! The* ~~son~~-*son of a bitch was making cannon and never* ~~me~~ *told me. And all this time Hazzan was hassling me about missing hundredweights of iron.* ~~damn.~~

Through Jon's eyes Singer saw a long narrow niche newly built into the fortress wall, crowded to chaos with half a dozen teams of sweating Somostai, choking with fumes and heat. The "cannon" looked like long thick tubes of metal on tracks. They were hot and fuming through holes at their ends. He gathered swiftly from Jon that they were like the shoulder-held tubes that fired on vitos. They used some powerful, compact source of fire to blow projectiles from the tube's end and smash whatever got in their way.

Must have been very close range, because they don't have the muzzle velocity to knock down a vito otherwise, and of course they can't be aimed with any precision, and they're hard to adjust—Korro must have been thinking of a conventional attack by way of the road. Jon was talking very fast.

Get out of it! Singer told him urgently.

The returning vitos blew out the fortress wall. The rockets penetrated the rock itself before exploding, and Singer had a brief, horrifying glimpse of the carnage among the cannon before the wall caved in and put an end to it. One final shot exploded in midair among the vitos, spraying a rain of vicious metal shrapnel, and brought down a third vito.

Good trick, but it only works once, Jon said shakily. He was hugging his arm to his side, and Singer could feel blood trickling down his face from cuts inflicted by rock splinters.

Singer grabbed his own head as the vitos roared close overhead. On the second run they laid down antipersonnel mines. Some of them exploded on contact with the ground; others went off a couple of feet before landing, saturating the area with tiny flying knives that would flay anything they touched. Cover that was good enough for bullets was not good enough for these, and there were death sounds all around. Singer ground his teeth at losing those men before they had had a chance to strike a blow, but coldly he knew that it was good. Those who survived were angry and desperate, ready to fight, and they would fight with respect for the terrible power of the enemy's weapons.

A third time the vitos swept over. Half of them hovered overhead, while the others settled to earth and started to disgorge soldiers. Apparently they believed there would be no resistance.

"Wait!" Singer said to Saldivar. He did not know how much longer the others would be able to hold their fire. He was leaning on his luck, and it could break at any moment.

"What for?" Saldivar said fiercely.

"For all the soldiers to be out and the second landing group to be on the ground. Maximum exposure."

The empty vitos pulled out and hovered in turn while the next group neared the ground. Singer felt the tension humming in the frightened men around him. They would not hold much longer.

"Now!"

Saldivar got to his knees and heaved the firing tube up on his shoulder, gulped a breath, and put a rocket straight into the right engine of the nearest vito on the ground. The ship blew up with its full complement of soldiers still on board.

That was the signal for the others to start firing. One of Korro's big wooden slingshots, hidden in the door of the foundry, cast a package that burst into flame and burned brightly at the soldiers' feet. Lit up, they made a clear target for flights of arrows that sang down on them from archers perched on the cold blast furnaces and the flat roofs of the shop buildings.

The Rider Delh'tani with their stolen weapons hit and destroyed the other two vitos on the ground before they could lift off. The flight that had been hovering above went into evasive action and escaped. They fired flares to light up the ground and swooped back over the plateau to lash the defenders with rapid fire. Glowing bullets, flares, and smoke made the scene flicker as if lit by lightning. Running forms flashed out of the smoke in a moment of brightness and disappeared into the surrounding dark. It looked like one of Jon's blood-bright images ripped into a hundred shreds and tossed in the air to reassemble itself.

A couple of vitos concentrated on knocking down the snipers on the roofs and furnaces with sprays of high-velocity bullets that rattled resoundingly against metal, pocking precious equipment full of holes to get at the vulnerable flesh behind it. One by one the snipers tumbled from their perches or hung limp in the metal framework.

The Rider Delh'tani had used up most of their rockets and

failed to bring down any more vitos. Three vitos still dodged back and forth above the battle, and three more came flying in formation uphill from the crackling ruin of the lower city. They had dropped off the soldiers they carried to comb through the area after the bombs had blown it open. Those troops worked their way uphill through the shantytown but had not yet reached the plateau.

Korro's wooden slingshots cast more packages into the center of the square, where the Nupis still clumped together—packages of wood or metal that burst when they hit the ground or sometimes burst overhead while still in the air, hurling forth their contents of metal and fire. They took a toll among the enemy, but they were inaccurate, and the defenders had to pull back or risk being blown to pieces by a stray shot. The farmers and cityfolk were afraid to charge the enemy weapons. Singer had to admit that they might have been right, but the resulting stalemate kept the two forces separated too well.

"They're going to come back," he said to Saldivar. "We've got to close with the ground troops before they can drop any more things on us. Take it—I'm going up."

He ran, crouching, long legs bent to make himself as small as possible, around slag heaps and piles of trash toward the black bulk of the blast furnaces on the other side of the square. Saldivar followed, protesting till he ran out of breath but gathering up all the Riders they came across.

"Charge them," Singer ordered, "and I'll break off halfway there and head for the towers."

Leaving Palha was the one thing he did not want to do, but he had a cold, sick memory/premonition of the gunships coming back, dropping shells or something worse. He grabbed a Delh'tani who was crouched in place with one of the few remaining rockets.

"They're going to come in again. This time don't wait for them to pass. Hit the first one, on the way in."

He raised a yell, and the Riders charged across the broken ground, firing as they ran. They exchanged heavy casualties. Singer heard his brothers falling around him. He had to leave Saldivar there and scramble for the towers while the Nupis were distracted. A final shot from the Somostai catapult landed among the Nupis and scattered them as the Riders closed with them. Then Riders and Delh'tani struggled hand to hand, using clubs, knives, and anything else they could get hold of.

Singer climbed the tubes and brackets that coiled around the blast furnace, taking the skin off his hands in his haste and not heeding it. The fast-talking gun dangled from his back, a heavy weight, and he had to take care it did not catch on anything as he scrambled upward. Wind whipped around his face; there was a storm coming for sure. He glanced down once and saw that some of the slave workers had followed the Riders into the charge. Others still cowered in their hiding places, paralyzed by the noise and the flame and the screams of the dying. They simply did not understand how to fight, and no amount of encouragement would change that.

They're sheep, the cold voice in him whispered. He did not know what sheep were, but the memory came: fat white herd animals, not like tough, horned silangh. *They need a master. They beg for one, then bleat while he protects them. Why should you work for them unless there's a profit?*

Singer shut down the voice with a violent effort. He had other things to think about. He had reached the top and sprawled out onto the platform where the little cars tipped things into the top of the tower. He gulped air while red and black spots swelled in his vision, but he had made it before the vitos had arrived. He rolled on his back and trained the gun up toward their bellies.

You'll be damn lucky to pull down one of those with that pissy little gun, the voice said. *Those fuckers have armor.*

He tried to stop the voice, but it tantalized him with half-glimpsed memories. There might be something useful in there if only he could reach it. But there was no time. The first ship was nearly on him, flying over so close that he could almost reach up and pluck one of the smooth gray fire eggs off its belly. He opened up with the gun and saw sparks fly from the metal as the ship passed over. The din deafened him, but nothing happened. The vito stooped down toward the landing zone; he heard a *whuff, whoof,* like a bull snorting, and felt an uprush of hot air. Red-orange glare lit up the square like daylight.

He did not have time to look behind him, but he knew what had happened. The fire was big enough to suck away the air he needed so badly. The whole south edge of the plateau must be burning—everything south of the precious foundry. He felt himself losing consciousness and struggled to keep a grip on knowledge.

Your friends are barbecue, the voice said, pleased and confidential. *Small loss.* It did not care, really, which side was winning. It enjoyed the losses so much more. It offered what he needed so badly: intelligence, understanding, a plan to make sense of his confusion. *The troops coming up the road can still get here, and if the Nupis hang on at the landing zone till then— filleted like fish, sweetheart.*

"All right, then, tell me," Singer said to the voice. "Tell me what I need to know."

He let go of the long struggle to deny those memories access to his waking mind and let the alien, ugly knowledge roll over him like an avalanche. It splintered categories as boulders splintered flimsy wooden walls; it tossed up things he thought he knew, as if in derision, and whirled them off in flames. He screamed in pain and recognition as the second flight of vitos passed over him. He really saw them for the first time. He grasped what they were and the meaning of the bits and pieces that until then had made no more sense to him than the beads on a fancy blanket. Twin swellings near the tail of the thing came into sharp focus.

Auxiliary fuel tanks, the voice said. *They couldn't get here from Solidari and back without them, but it was a bad idea to hit the landing zone with them.*

Singer began firing again reflexively while the plans and memories still flashed through his mind with the inevitability of steel linkages and gears. Droplets rained down on him; half his mind screamed in fear, and the other half was calmly satisfied. *Do it again!* The second vito came by to his right, still close enough to fire on. The third was blocked from view by the other two. The gun, too, had changed into something strange in his hands. He understood all about it now, not just how it was made but why and how it did the things it did. To the Singer of the past it had seemed a weapon of fantastic power, but suddenly he recognized it as pathetically small to bring down a ship from the sky. Still, he would try, as a boy aimed his small arrow at the most vulnerable point of some mighty prey.

The first gunship did not fail immediately. It drifted downward as the rip his bullets had torn in the tank grew wider and the fuel poured out instead of reaching the engine. Suddenly the engine quit, and the vito plunged to earth in eerie silence. As it struck, the leaking fuel from the second vito finally reached some spark and flamed up. Two simultaneous fireballs, one on the ground and one in the air, swelled and thundered together. Singer pressed himself flat to the tiny platform. For a moment he thought the vito would come down on him and engulf him, but it tumbled past him and crashed in a long smear of thick black smoke.

The third vito of the flight eluded the crash by miraculous flying and screamed past less than fifty feet from the ground to complete its mission: firing a rocket into the dark arch of the mine shaft, where the catapult was hidden. The muffled explosion tore a gaping rent in the mountain itself. The rocks settled inward or leapt out from the cliff, and clouds of smoke and dust shot out of the mine mouth as it crumbled shut. Pulling past that low had given some reckless pallantai one last shot, however. The ground shuddered again as the vito came apart in a flaming hail of fragments and the larger chunks smashed into the cliff.

Singer, his defenses in ruins, heard them all die: pilots, Somostai, children and sick people sheltering within the mine. There was a split second of terror as they saw it coming, and then the wall of fire or rock that tore them loose from their lives in an agony that was brief but seemed to last forever. He had been there before, when the Rock had died. He lay with his face to the metal and screamed, and the voice in his head smiled and showed him more pictures.

And there were three more vitos coming.

Other voices ripped and tore at him, demanding their share of him. He could hear Jon far off demanding, *What the hell is going on there? Somebody answer me!* Closer to him, just over his head, he could hear the voice of the wind. Clouds gathered and turned, spun faster by the heat that rose from the burning. He was dizzy with it, as if he would spin from his perch and fall.

He made a great effort and turned his head to look at the vitos. They shimmered and glowed through the curtain of vibrating heated air that hung over the fire in the south. As they parted the curtain of smoke, the voice in his head tempted him.

You don't need a gun, anyway. Think about what you did to me. Why don't you just ask them nicely to go die?

"I won't do it," he whispered with his lips against the taste of rust.

You could if you wanted to, the voice said. *Hell, look at what you've already done. Why stop now?*

"I can't."

Bullshit; you could if you tried.

"I won't try."

But he was already trying, reaching out for the pilots. He knew now just where they sat and the look of things around them. That helped. It was hard to tell them from anyone else.

They were young and terrified and full of killing rage against the things that forced them to know that fear.

Go home, he pleaded. *Go away. Something is going to happen.*

What the fuck? Say again!

He lost his grip on them and had to cling to the platform. He was so dizzy, and something quivered in the very air around him. The lead vito glowed strangely with something more than the firelight.

Singer gave it up. *Wind Horse, come down to me,* he prayed. *Come with your lightning hooves and your bright eyes and carry me away from here.*

All his hair stood on end, and the air pricked him like barbed wire. He had a sensation of some giant beast brooding over him, seeking a place to strike. He rolled on his back and looked up, saw the vitos still coming, and the power stooped out of the storm. There was a crack that left him deaf, and a whiplash of violent white light that seemed to explode inside his head, and a scorching, dangerous scent that scornfully trampled the ordinary smell of burning underfoot. He thought the vito had fired on him. When his senses cleared, he felt the lead vito going down and saw the bright lash of the lightning strike like a snake again and again. It struck the vito, and it struck to the right and left of the tower, but it did not strike him.

The voice seemed to be laughing. *Oh, yes, you'll do it if you're pushed. Small changes but damned effective ones. And why shouldn't you protect yourself? Why not give the bastards what they deserve?*

Suddenly there were three vitos again. He thought his eyes must be wrong till he heard the joyful, unmistakable yell.

Here comes the shock squad! Lyn screamed as her stolen vito dropped out of the clouds like an arrow, nearly vertical, swept over the remaining vitos while they were still dazzled, it seemed only inches above them, and put missiles up their tails like a boy plugging rabbits. The cloud of fragments swept past Singer's head again, and when he dared open his eyes, he saw Lyn burst out of the fire cloud and pounce on the Nupi troops that had reached the road. Her gunners were no half-trained Riders but professionals from the prison camp. The Nupis disintegrated as if they had been made of snow. The snow was black and red.

When Palha touched him, Singer kicked out before he thought, and if he had not been so weak, he would have pushed the Delh'tani off the tower.

"Stop it, you butthead, it's me." Saldivar spoke in anger because he was scared, but under that was a quick rush of joy because the movement proved that Singer was alive. "Are you all right?"

"No," Singer said, forming the words carefully with a tongue that felt stiff and unnatural. "No. I am not all right."

"You hit?"

Singer could only shake his head.

"Come on, let's get down from here."

Singer's hands were slick with sweat, and he had lost his grace. He slipped and grabbed and had to pause many times to regain his balance, with Saldivar coaxing him along. When they finally reached firm ground, Saldivar pushed him down behind a derailed ore cart. The cart shielded them from the blast of heat that still radiated from the fire the vitos had dropped. None of the workers who had hung back under cover had survived it.

The Nupis retreated step by step toward the shelter of the foundry building. Under the direction of a couple of Somostai, the defenders shaped the fight so that the Nupis thought they were gaining ground rather than losing it. A handful of Nupis finally broke through and gained the doorway, then covered the others with fire from their weapons till they were all inside and firing again. The workers broke and ran. The Nupis shouted defiantly from inside, thinking they had gained at least a breathing space, perhaps the victory.

Then the Somostai lit their fuses. The explosion that followed was small compared to the ear-bursting blasts they had already endured, but it blew the furnace shed to burning rubble.

22

An eerie quiet settled over the plateau. The wind moaned, the fires muttered and crackled, and thunder grumbled high up in the clouds. Fat drops of rain splattered down, oily with smoke, too few to put out the fires. The sounds of battle and the cry of the fighters had ceased.

Many of the dead were burned fragments in the ruins of machines and buildings. The rest lay heaped where they had fallen, Nupi gray and Consorso green, Rider and Somostai, farmer and cityfolk, gripped together in death. The sound of weeping came from a small knot of survivors crouched helpless by the stone-choked mouth of the mine. One of them clawed at the rock with his hands and sobbed.

"My wife, my wife! I sent her there to be safe. She could not walk for the hunger sores on her legs. I saw them carry her in. *Ai, ai!*"

Olmalik came up, walking slowly and stiffly because of the strips of rag knotted around his thigh. He was blood-streaked from head to foot but had only that one injury. He caught the man's bloody hands and held them back from their battering.

"Come," he said gently. "All we can do for the dead is bury them. These are buried already. No more harm can come to them. We need your help with the living."

The man stared at Olmalik as if he could not understand his words, but he let himself be led away.

"Victory," Olmalik said to Singer.

Singer only nodded, accepting the bitterness in the word. "Selem? Your children?"

"I don't know." Olmalik looked toward the burned shanties

and closed his eyes against the sight. "I didn't know they could do that. So fast. Like firing a hayrick. All of us just mice inside."

Singer nodded again, his eyes dark as burned coals.

"Your friend?" Olmalik asked.

"I don't know," Singer said in turn. "I didn't feel her die. But—" He shrugged. "There were so many."

Olmalik waited, but Singer said nothing more.

"We'll join you in a minute," Saldivar said.

"Is he hurt?" The farmer was immediately worried.

"I don't know. Give me a little time. Please."

Olmalik drew his huddle of survivors away.

Saldivar crouched down at Singer's side. "Hey, cofra, we did it. We beat them." He laid his arm over Singer's shoulder. There were no marks on Singer, but something was wrong.

"Useless," Singer said, still staring dead-eyed off into the smoke. "Those were vitos. It took everything we had to beat a couple of flights of vitos. When they understand what happened, they'll send the hi-fighters and flatten the mountain. And even if we could beat them again and again . . ." He clenched his fist on a fold of Saldivar's shirt. "Why didn't you tell me? Why didn't Makho tell me?"

"Tell you what?"

"There are more of you coming. More Delh'tani. They're on the way even now. More soldiers. More fire weapons. I have seen a fire that could eat the world."

It took a minute for Saldivar to understand him. "The colony ship, you mean? I don't know. It won't be here for years. Maybe never. I don't think about it. I guess Mack wouldn't, either. That's planning—for the desk buggers in command. Kristo, why think about it now?"

"Today was for nothing," Singer said, shaking him in his impatience. "That ship. No colony. It's full of soldiers. They're bringing new weapons with them. The one that breaks the invisible. Aah, I can't think of the word, but I see it. If we killed all the Delh'tani, still there'd be more."

"How do you know all that, about the ship?"

Singer let go of him, pushed him away. "Cold Eyes told me," he said remotely.

"Cold Eyes? Gero's dead."

Saldivar waited for an explanation, but Singer did not give him one.

"What happened to you, cofra?" Palha asked. His voice was

quiet, but his eyes were panicking. "Did you get hit in the head? What's wrong?"

Singer could see his fear. Palha was less than an arm's length away, but Singer did not dare to reach out and touch him again.

Saldivar had an idea and caught it like the last branch on the way down. "I want to find Janney. Can you walk?"

"She might not—be here anymore. I don't know." But Singer got to his feet and started downhill, lurching and catching himself again but refusing Saldivar's offered arm. Saldivar finally realized when he had seen Singer this way before: in the caves where Dona had died. He felt a small easing of his fear to have some kind of possible reason for it. Then it had been memories that had overwhelmed Singer and tainted his present reality with old horrors. Perhaps something of the kind was happening again.

As they reached the road, picking their way through Nupi corpses, craters, and ice slicks where the snow had melted and refrozen, they passed the downed vito, the only one that had made a soft landing. It was surrounded by angry slave workers. Most of the crew was still inside, dead or unconscious, but the pilot had unbelted and sprawled half-out the door. The workers hung back at first in superstitious fear of the stranger fallen from the sky. When they saw that he was bloody and groaning, they lost their awe. He was too dazed to shoot at them. By the time Singer and Saldivar came up to them, they had pulled him away from his machine and were manhandling him, gradually growing bolder as they saw that he could not fight back.

Singer could not keep a straight face anymore. His lip curled back in a snarl as a bitter, burning taste rushed into his mouth. He was among them in three quick strides, before they saw him coming.

"Stop it," he said.

The man who had the pilot by the hair let him drop to the ground. The pilot was bleeding from the nose and ears. The other workers began kicking him, and he could not curl up to protect himself. He only moved his arms ineffectually.

The worker had weapons and did not see the danger in Singer. He pulled a short sword out of his belt and waved it under Singer's nose. "I don't take orders anymore. Be off."

"He dropped fire on our people," one of the others said, emphasizing his point with another kick.

"And you ran away," Singer said, showing his teeth. "This is a good time to be brave, now there's no danger."

Throughout the battle Singer had not touched his Somostai

sword, and he did not reach for it in that moment. He blocked the worker's clumsy sword thrust with a hand strike that sent the sword spinning, then struck him in the face and kicked his feet out from under him.

"Olmalik wants you down there." He jerked his head toward the ruins. "Move. This one is mine."

Saldivar understood some of the words, having picked up a little Giristiyah by then. He pulled out his own sword. He could not use it any better than the disarmed slave, but the threat backed up Singer's words. The workers moved away downhill.

Singer squatted down by the pilot and ran his hands over the man's face and chest. "Are you hurt?"

The pilot groaned and clasped his belly where he had been kicked. He doubled up in a spasm of coughing, grimacing with the pain in his ribs but unable to stop. Singer felt his forehead again. It was burning hot, though he had been lying in the snow. He lifted the pilot's head while the man gasped and crowed for breath.

"You're sick," Singer said, holding the pilot's eyes.

"They're all bloody sick," the man wheezed in temporary clarity. "Everybody who's not flat on his back got sent on this mission." He started to laugh and began to cough again. When he finished, his lips were blue, and he looked frightened.

"I was flying second seat. Old Junkman went stiff—I thought he was hit, but he just passed out. I had to take it down. I think they're dead. Are you a medic?"

His eyes rolled, and he stopped talking. Singer put him down gently and absently, as if he were thinking of something else. He sat in the snow staring at him. Saldivar finally shook his shoulder to get his attention.

"What now?" Saldivar gestured to the pilot.

"Oh. Help me put him back in the—in his machine thing. Vito. Maybe he won't freeze to death. I don't suppose the city-folk will help him now."

He straightened up slowly when they had loaded the pilot back into his seat. He met Saldivar's eyes, but without touching him. "You go and find Zhanne for me, if you can, and stay with her. I have a job to do."

"What are you talking about?"

Singer listened, frowning; he was talking to Jon, but Saldivar caught only fleeting bits of the conversation because Singer was not sharing it with him as he always did. Singer was keeping him out.

"Zhanne is going to die unless I go back to the Black City,"
Singer said finally. "I understand now why she is sick."

"What do you mean?" Saldivar reached automatically for
contact, and Singer pushed his hand away. To a Rider it was the
equivalent of a blow. Sick at heart, Saldivar tried to catch him
by force, but Singer evaded him, holding up his hands in a silent
plea.

"Please, paliao, listen to me. Remember the man on the dock?
The one they threw into the water? He was coughing like this.
Like Zhanne. Like my brother. He remembered having the
coughing sickness when he was a child. Before the Somostai
decided he should live and be Hadhla's heir. Everyone gets this
sickness, but they don't all die. Only the Delh'tani—they aren't
used to it. They get much sicker. Somehow the Somostai have
learned to make people get sick. I didn't think of it before. I
didn't know there was warfare with the invisible things—" He
switched into Delteix, stumbling over the pronunciation.
"—bakh'terro-losshikal war. Now I know. But if Korro started
it, he knows how to stop it. He must know! He would not start
a fire he couldn't put out—would he?"

He sat down on the vito's crumpled landing gear and put his
head in his hands. "Ayei, Taurhalisos! Maybe he would. The
Somostai were right. There is a black hole behind the starlight.
Cold Eyes told me that."

"Why do you keep talking about Cold Eyes? Gero is dead."

Singer shook his head. "Palha, I have done a terrible thing,"
he said painfully. "He is not dead. I have brought him here, to
our hearth."

"That isn't possible." Even as he spoke, Saldivar realized
that he no longer knew what was possible with Singer.

"I used the Singer's gift to kill him. I knew it was wrong, but
it seemed like the only way. I thought I would pay by dying there
with him. You and the others wouldn't let me die. I carry his
life and death around with me instead. I thought I could keep
him dead, but I'm losing. He's eating me up. I can't, I won't
share that with you."

Singer had jammed his fist against his teeth. His hand was
bleeding. At least Saldivar thought it was bleeding. When he
took Singer's hand in his own, the skin was whole.

"I knew the Rock was gone," Singer cried. "But I wanted
to go home. I thought I could save something for them, for the
ones who were left. I was wrong. They're going to die, anyway.
I should have let them go their own way."

He sounded as he had when Gero had been racking him; worse, Saldivar thought. He had never broken then, but he was breaking now.

"My face is in the dirt," Singer said. "I'm a fighter who can't fight anymore. I see their whole lives in their eyes in the moment when I take it all away. Maybe it was not wrong once, but it's wrong now. I can't do this anymore. But if I walk away, I'm betraying everyone who trusted me.

"I bend people even when I don't intend it. Zhanne followed me here, and now she's dying. I took you away from your own kind and made you like myself—someone who can never go home. What kind of love is that? I have one thing left to do: walk into the Destroyer's mouth. Let me go, Palha."

"Shut up," Saldivar ordered. "Let me talk." His throat closed up the next minute. "Shit, ~~_____,~~" he choked. He had no words for what he wanted to say, and if Singer refused to share his mind as he always had done before, he would be trapped in his silence again. There was a heart language where the words had life in them and did not stick in his throat like bones, but it was Singer's language.

"What kind of talk is this?" Saldivar burst out. "What is this talk about leaving?" Without Singer, he could still speak Thanha. He had all the words he needed, and he was surprised to find that even at such a time, so wrung with grief and pity for Singer, he could feel happy.

"Listen, *andriao*, I don't think much of this Uncle Death stuff. Death is no friend of mine. It's shitful and it hurts, but it's coming to get me no matter where I am. It doesn't matter. The only thing that matters is for me to be with you to the end."

Singer was shaking his head, but his fist was clenched around Saldivar's hand. "It's all burning," he said. "I wanted to know that I'd be leaving you safely out of it."

Saldivar laughed, a sound of genuine pleasure that pierced the smoky haze that seemed to surround Singer. "I settled all this stuff with myself when we first came to the city. I'm not outliving you. Once I got that straight, I quit worrying."

"But—"

"Shut up," Saldivar said, lapsing briefly into Delteix. "Look, isé, I never had anything to lose. You're the one and only thing I fought for, all my life, and won. If I die fighting, I still win. All I have to do is not give up. I don't need to live easy, and I don't need to live a long time. I don't need to know what you're doing if you can't tell me. I need you, and I need a place to stand. And that's all."

Singer felt strength flowing to him, warm and steady. "Palha, you *must not* come with me," he said in agony.

Saldivar laughed again, his dark eyes glowing as if he had been invited to a party. "You still don't get it, do you? Well, I do. In Delteix I'm still dumb as a rock. Just another piece of obsolete equipment. I'm Thanha now. Thanha gave me back the words and made me the Singer's brother. You think Korro scares me bad enough to make me give that up? You know me better than that.

"Isé, it suits me to give you your own way most of the time, but you don't give the orders once you're dead. If you want to keep calling the tune, there's only one way. Stay alive. Now let's go twist Korro's crank."

He pulled Singer to his feet and steadied him as they climbed. At the rate they were going, they might reach the summit in the middle of the night. Singer was not living in the ordinary kind of time.

Saldivar whistled for Riders whenever he saw one on their way up the mountain. The first one he caught was Genady, looking pale and sick but unhurt and in command of himself.

"Where's Lyn?" Saldivar asked him. "It would save us a walk if she would bring her bird in here."

"I think she's leapfrogging the Rider vanguard into the city. Mack is in hot haste. Where are we going?"

Saldivar's explanation was interrupted by shouts and the sound of clashing weapons from the road.

"Shit, what now?" Genady said in disgust.

A well-organized, well-armed group of Somostai had stopped a band of survivors heading down the road to join Olmalik. The Somostai, with their black staves and spears, expertly handled, pushed the workers into a huddle where their short swords and knives were useless.

"What are you doing?" Singer called across the gap to their captain.

"Reclaiming these prisoners."

"The master swore a truce!"

"Battle truce. Battle's over."

"Let them go. You can still be spared."

The captain lost interest and went back to his business. "The master gives the orders here," he threw back over his shoulder.

The Somostai struck down those who continued to fight, impaled them and left them writhing, and herded the rest back up the road, toward the prisons of the Holy City.

Singer drew his sword for the first time, in such rage that he did not think of waiting for the others to follow. He was barely conscious of Saldivar behind him, running to keep up, with nothing in his hand but what seemed to him a clumsy bar of metal. Singer ran in under the blackrobes' spears and cut down two of them before they knew he was there. It had become absurdly easy for him to counter their attack. He could read what they would do in the flick of an eye or the twitch of a finger, almost by the way they breathed, long before the stroke reached him. It was as simple as slaughtering sheep. Once he had started, he drove on blindly, goaded to fury by the wet, red knowledge he had tasted, desperate to finish it and stop the brutal messages that stabbed deeper than any blade.

He stumbled because there was no longer anything in front of him. He turned, catching his balance again with a wrench, and saw no one but his friends, staring at him. The blackrobes lay sprawled in a crooked line, black crow tracks on white. Two of the workers still wallowed in the snow. Their cries sounded distantly in his ears, inhuman as ravens crying. He did not need their voices to tell him what they felt; it twisted his guts and made him stagger as he crossed the snow to them.

Both were disemboweled, bellies ripped open by the spears that still pinned them in place. Memories that were not his mocked him with pictures of places where even this could be healed, clean white places in some other world, far from the dirty, smoking midden where he knelt in the bloody slush. Here he found no healing for them, only the ugliness of hidden things ripped open and irrevocably spilled. Their suffering was an obscenity that drenched him like a gout of blood. Make it stop, he thought. He had no defenses left at all.

He had flung himself down beside them in the snow. When he came to himself, they were quiet. He reached out with sticky fingers and closed their eyes because he did not like the way they looked past him without seeing. He got up, found his sword, and stuck it back into his belt. It was a clumsy piece of Somostai workmanship, without the least hint of grace or keenness. He wished that he could at least have had his own weapon.

Only then did he notice the others watching him: fascinated, disgusted, cringing. They quickly looked away as he came toward them. From one of the workers he heard something different under the disgust, a touch of pity. Like a dog that gets the taste of sheep's blood and goes crazy, the man was thinking. It'll run through the herd ripping their throats out. You have to kill it, no matter how good a dog it was before. Singer looked him in the eye, and the man lowered his gaze like the others, but Singer could still hear him thinking. *Thank you for my life, renegade, but still it isn't right to turn a human being into a slaughtering machine. He'd be better off dead, poor boy.*

"No more of this, no more," Singer said to Saldivar. He was not sure whether he had spoken aloud. "It gets worse every time." *A self-limiting reaction,* the voice in his head said sardonically, and he had a brief moment of regret for all the new words he would not be able to use. "I'm losing myself." He swayed on his feet.

"Is he all right?" Genady asked.

"No. He isn't," Saldivar said. He looked around the sky for Lyn and did not see her. *Where are you, tiger, when I need you? Singer can't call you, and I don't know how.*

He turned to Genady. "Find us a few Riders to cover our ass. We're going up the mountain, and I won't go there completely bare. You, there, send down to Olmalik and tell him that the master has broken the truce and we're going to take him out."

"Tell him—" Singer forced out harsh, choked sounds. "Tell him to defend himself but not to follow us. Don't break what's left of them against the black wall. Tell him to wait for Makho. He'll know what to do. Tell him—" He forgot what he wanted to say. "Tell him good luck."

He heard a familiar humming in the air, and though he knew it was not likely to be more enemies, he could no longer stand before it. He threw himself into the ditch at the side of the road, hugging his head.

Saldivar jumped after him, bewildered till he looked up and saw the vito coming. *What ~~the fuck~~ is going on?*

It was Lyn. She slewed around and landed in the middle of the road.

"It's all right, it's Lyn," Saldivar shouted in Singer's ear. They ran to the vito and boarded before the wash died.

"Take us up," Saldivar said. "Did you hear me calling you?"

"No, Jon sent for me. He said he'd lost Singer and the master had broken the truce. He sounded frantic. He told me to go find you. I dropped off a load of Makho's boys back there in the square. Where are we going?"

"To kill Korro, I think."

"Outstanding! I saw some little bone children back there.

Nothing but live skeletons with eyes. I can hardly wait to meet the smoking asshole who invented this place. I'm going to nail his head to the wall and blow his kneecaps off.''

Singer put a hand on her arm to interrupt her. "You must not kill the master. He's the only one who knows how to heal Zhanne. I think he knows. I think I can make him tell me. If he doesn't, if I can't—you can kill him, but it won't help.''

Lyn was silent while she fought the treacherous wind currents still swirling around the mountain. The storm clouds still hung low, hiding the peak. Smoke of every shade from white to black rose like columns to fan out against that ceiling of cloud.

"Hesukristo, that's an almighty big fire," she muttered. "There—on the plateau. Is that my landing zone? Looks like a tabletop covered with cockroaches.''

She wrestled the vito down, bringing it in close to the mountain and swinging it around to clear a spot with her downdraft. The big fire leapt and spread in tattered streamers in the draft. The blackrobes scattered sideways like beetles, scrambling over each other to escape the descending vito.

"You wait here," Singer said. "Save yourself if you have to, but don't get out of the machine.''

He left them without looking at them again.

23

He had lost his orientation. Only the immediate present was real. Other places existed as vivid images of a certain point in time, but there was no relation among them. He knew Gero's office as well as the black rock of the mountain, but he did not know how far off it was or in which direction. Lyn was real as long as she stayed put, but the thought of her leaving the plateau caused vertigo. There might be nothing beyond the flaring light of the Devourer's fire.

As he jumped out of the vito, he felt the mixed currents of fire-heated air and wind off the snow rush over him. The massive fire glowed white-hot in the bottom of the pit and reflected from the dead-flat eyes of the image above it. The stones before the Eater were already dark with blood that had melted pits into the snow where it had splashed. The air carried raw, maddening smells: fresh blood, charred flesh, searing heat and smoke. Welding them all together was the dominant stink of terror. Fear steamed up from all the Somostai as a hot horse steamed in the wet, but that fear intensified over the half circle where pale naked skin showed among the black cloaks, the area where more prisoners were herded tightly together.

On the other side of the pit Korro stood with a respectful space maintained around him by a hollow square of armed Somostai.

Singer. Jon was not crying out to him for help, though he stood next to the master, under guard. His voice was heavy with despair. *Name of God, you meathead, why did you come up here? It's just what he wants. I didn't call you, I didn't. Did I?*

"Welcome," Korro said.

I lost you back there. I saw the vitos go down on the monitor. But what happened to you—I thought you might be dead. I was still getting something—Kristo, it was getting *horrible—and I—and I—"* Shame hid behind the hurried message. *I had to pull back. I lost you. I couldn't find Janet, either. You shouldn't have come here. Somebody has to get to Jan, and the master seems to have plans for me.*

Singer kept moving toward Korro without breaking stride.

"I am glad you have come of your own free will to see who is still the master here," Korro said. His voice was resonant, confident. He had them all in his fist. He could shape their attention to his own ends.

"What are you doing with these people?" Singer demanded. "You swore an oath to give them a truce and freedom."

Korro laughed. "I swore an oath to serve my master. I said I would not oppose you in battle. The battle is over. Now is the time for repaying the Devourer for the lives he put in our hands. The people you see here have no further use. It is time for their unmaking. Those others below can work till they have served their purpose. That is the Destroyer's bargain. Always a price."

"Do you think it's over?" Singer said. He sounded as if he

would weep. "You live because they made too many mistakes. They're not stupid—they'll learn. You need allies."

"I think not," Korro said. "The Devourer has given me the knowledge to destroy the skyfolk. They will fall from the sky like flies when summer ends."

"You fool," Singer cried. "If you wiped every one of them off the earth, there'd be more. Hundred of thousands more, with weapons that can burn this whole mountain to a cinder and shrivel and blast you with plagues out of hell. Your Eater breaks his own tools. He has put you into the hands of people who serve him far better than you ever could. Make peace while you still can."

The blackrobes stirred and looked toward their master, stirring up the fear scent as they did so. Korro could see their uncertainty. They feared the skyfolk. The battle had not been the easy victory he had made them expect. They waited for his answer.

"How do you know they're not the skyfathers you were waiting for?" Singer pressed his advantage. "Maybe the Eater has cursed you for opposing those he sent to be your masters."

Korro's anger grew along with his fear at every challenge from Singer.

"They have been tested and found wanting," he shouted for the blackrobes' ears as much as for Singer's. "They did not give us knowledge, as the skyfathers will do when they return. They cheated us. They get sick and die from a disease of children. So be it! Let them die!"

Singer dropped all threat from his voice and bent his head, pleading, creeping closer to the master all the time, as if he would kneel to him.

"At least give us medicine for the Delh'tani friends who fought beside us," he begged.

Korro threw back his head and roared with laughter. "Listen to this! The renegade is begging for mercy! Is that why you came here, renegade? To beg on behalf of your skyfolk friends? Mercy is not a Somostai virtue. Your friends will die, and you with them. All of you will be a gift to the Eater."

He whirled and snapped an order to the tall guards on either side of Jon. "This one, for instance. He will never be a good Somostai. He has lied to me at every turn. Into the fire with him. Let the Destroyer purify him."

The guards held Jon at the edge of the pit. He gave Singer one look and then shut his eyes. Singer could smell singeing wool where Jon's cloak dragged on the heated stone. He could hear Jon repeating *I will not beg. I will not beg,* while fear seared his throat like a hot iron.

But the guards waited for a sign from Korro.

"Strange, I was told that renegades never beg," Korro said. Cutting the foul taste of fear, Singer could taste the pleasure the master was feeling, and he was sick and faint with it. He struggled another few steps closer. "No closer without safe-conduct," the master said. "I know renegade treachery. Another step and your friend goes. I was also told that renegades never bargain. Are you an exception? Would you like to bargain for your friend?"

Don't deal, Jon said desperately. *Don't!*

"Your terms," Singer said.

"Kneel, now, and allow my servants to bind you. Then I will let your friend go."

Singer could see for himself that the master had no intention of honoring the bargain. Nonetheless he sank to one knee.

I'm risking your life, and I'm sorry, he said to Jon. *Lyn won't let them kill you, I don't think. But this is how it must be.*

"I foretell the future for you, blackrobe," he cried as the guards approached him. "There is no future for you. You'll never see another dawn. Look for another master, you fools. Korro is going to die."

He felt the Somostai soldier's hand on his shoulder and heard Lyn's guns at the same moment. He realized too late that she might have taken his words as a command. Fortunately, her attention was all on Jon. She shot the guards who held him, driving them backward with the force of the impact. They dropped Jon on the brink of the pit. He scrabbled back from it, his clothes smoldering, his knees too shaky to let him leap to his feet.

Go to Lyn. Go!

Singer upended the guard who had laid hands on him and leapt on Korro like a wild animal. He had no thought for defending himself, but he automatically got a grip on Korro's neck as he closed with him. He could throw the master and probably break his back, but he did not intend to do so. He only wanted to keep the master from killing him outright. He felt the master's knife against his ribs as they grappled. Korro nearly stabbed him in his rage at being robbed of his prey, but Singer could feel the master restraining himself. The Somostai ran toward them.

"Touch me and I break his neck," Singer said. "My friends will shoot anyone who draws a bow."

Singer had gained the position he wanted: close to the master, with his own body protecting Korro to make sure he would live long enough to answer Singer's questions.

He could feel Korro's wet, grinning teeth and hot breath next to his ear.

"I am not afraid of your knife, renegade, wherever you're hiding it. I can spill your blood long before my life runs out. If I fail, my servants will do it for me. So what have you gained?"

Korro's bravado was more than confidence in his guards. The master had the physical courage of a bear or a bull. Singer yielded to him very slightly, just enough to make him feel secure. He stopped trying to resist Korro's gloating malevolence. It was easy to let the master come closer. Korro craved his frustration, his hatred and grief, and Singer let him feel it. He endured Korro's intrusion till the master was so close that he could speak with no more effort than a whisper in his ear. Then he had him.

I gain this, he said silently.

Singer felt Korro's defenses tremble with the shock and knew in that moment that he had been right about the master. Whatever gift or curse Singer bore shadowed Korro, too. He had guarded himself with wall within wall, sheer and thick as the walls of the black fortress, but within those walls he was awake and listening.

Singer tried to take advantage of that moment off balance, but he did not know the master's mind well enough to strike effectively. He had never before tried deliberately to control, and he fumbled. He felt Korro's hand move convulsively with the knife and stopped it, discovering as he did so that blocking a movement was far easier than forcing its initiation. As Korro recovered his equilibrium, Singer caught a brief glimpse of the knowledge he wanted. He had hoped that it would come to Korro's mind unbidden when the question was asked, but Korro was too well defended. Singer knew that the thing he wanted existed. He had seen a place for it in Korro's memory, but he still did not know where to lay hands on it. He felt a thin trickle of blood running down his ribs, warm at the source, then cooling, sticky. He knew that Korro felt it, too, and that it pleased him, and Singer was sickened by that intimacy but could not let him go.

You! the master said in one long breath of astonishment, and Singer saw glimpses, against the master's will, of half-hidden images: a bright-haired child's face suspended in the moment of astonishment before tears came, the blood spilling from his slashed cheek.

You're Hadhla's son. (Back from the dead?) Singer heard him thinking before he suppressed that moment of weakness, of superstitious fear. *The scar is gone. I'd have known you else—how?*

Korro reined in his mind, concentrated. *You should have been one of us. What waste.*

Singer could feel Korro's thoughts cascading, tumbling, looking for some means he could use, even now, to bend Singer to his will.

No need for planning when there's no more future, blackrobe, Singer told him. *All your plans have brought you to this moment, and they end here.*

The cold ghost of Tony Gero breathed through his words, frosting them with venomous malice.

Even in death there are choices. Ah, Master of the Black City, you know that better than I. Answer my question and ask for Thanha mercy. It's better than what you will get if you deny me.

He did not have to summon memories to threaten Korro. Just one of the throng that screamed and struggled for his attention, clawing to escape through the cracks in his heart, could frighten even the master.

Korro pressed closer with a strange kind of pleasure in the horrors he saw. *Can you truly kill from within, like this?*

Singer answered neither yes nor no but let the master tremble on the brink of the dark abyss of Gero's death. Korro shuddered again with the intensity of recognition. The knowledge that was destroying Singer was no surprise to the Somostai.

You have become one of us. Yes, and more than a servant of the Destroyer—you could have been a master. Kill me now, take the knowledge from me, and you'll be a master. All those of the Order who are standing here will obey you. I wonder if you have the strength.

Singer realized that he could not break Korro's defenses. Every effort to do so brought him closer to his own breaking point, to the moment when he would lose himself in Gero's memories and be unable to find his way out. He would die ruined and forsworn—no Sky Road for him—and leave behind nothing but a mouthful of sand for those who had trusted him.

Unexpectedly, Korro called out to the guard again. "Get the old man—Hadhla's pet. Bring him to the fire."

Look around, Korro said with a laugh that was even uglier in the silent speech. *If I'd known you earlier, we could have had some pleasant entertainment.*

Singer forced Korro to turn slightly so he could see over the master's shoulder, though he knew what he would see.

The old man was dressed in prison rags and bound. Something had happened to his face, his whole left side. His mouth drooped a little sideways; his left foot limped as he was dragged to the edge of the fire. Hot air, quivering over the pit, distorted his face, but Singer would have known him anywhere. Even so bound, he carried himself like a prince. It was Hilurin.

Singer had not thought that he could bear more pain and live. He found he was wrong.

"It would be a waste simply to pitch him in. Perhaps you would bargain again, renegade. Not for his life. That I cannot give you. I vowed to kill him long ago. But as you say, there are choices even in death. You may prefer him to die in one piece. With both eyes, say. Bow to me and we'll talk about it."

"Shut your mouth, or I kill you now," Singer choked.

"Please don't trouble yourself, dear boy," Hilurin said in his most absurd accent, the one he reserved for the city. "If they try any such foolish thing, I assure you I will simply withdraw from the game. It will be no great inconvenience, considering the appalling condition in which I find myself."

No, oh, no, not you, please, Hilurin. I thought you dead once and endured it. To lose you again is more than anyone could bear.

There was no way to prevent it. He knew well that Korro was lying, just as he had lied about Jon. Lyn might shoot the guards again, but it would not help. Hilurin was bound and could not run. There were too many others. Someone would push him over the edge. If Singer killed the master, the Somostai would kill Hilurin before he could stop them. There was only one way to avoid watching Hilurin die.

It took only an instant for the argument to play itself out in his mind and only that instant for Korro to feel his momentary distraction and take advantage of it. He had almost forgotten the knife till he felt the split-second flare of Korro's will to strike. It was not too late to prevent it, but in that instant he heard Jon's voice in memory: *The one time he doesn't think is when he gets mad. Get him to hit me and he forgets what he's doing for a minute or two.* Always one last move—sometimes the move was not to move at all. He let go his guard. Korro's knife grated against his ribs, and the master himself, so long pressing to take possession of Singer's mind, suddenly found no resistance at all.

The master was falling, falling, through a blazing tumult of images. The world suddenly expanded around him in a limitless sphere of chaos, leaving him hanging weightless in the center of a vast explosion. In that moment the master lost what he valued more than his life: control. He was not the master anymore.

Singer fell with him, still gripping him, refusing to let him escape. He plundered Korro's mind for the one thing he needed as he had once pillaged the storerooms beneath the Great House to find a drink for Dona, dying at the master's hand. It seemed to take a year, an age, but it lasted only from Korro's grip tightening on his knife hilt to the moment when the pain reached Singer's riven body and he fell to his knees. His vision tattered toward darkness as if the wind had whipped a black cloak over his face.

Jon, leaning out of the vito, unable to bear safety without sight, saw him fall. He tore Saldivar's gun from his grasp and fired. He could have hit Singer even at that range; he knew he was no marksman. A dead, stone-cold certainty held him steady and told him he would not. He saw Korro's hands jerk out and his head fly back. The master's blood splattered Singer as he fell. But it was Singer who screamed.

The Somostai surged forward toward Singer, but Lyn held them back with a spray of bullets that sent up bursts of snow at their feet. The armed Riders waiting in the vito leapt out, freed to act at last. They leveled their weapons at the remaining black-robes, nearly trembling with eagerness. Perhaps the blackrobes could have overwhelmed them with numbers, but no one was willing to be the first. A wild, raucous yell rose from the center where the prisoners had waited their turn. They did not know what was happening, but they understood that Korro was dead. Hands from behind caught hold of Hilurin and dragged him back from the edge. The guards struggled to keep hold of him. The prisoners swarmed over them with fists and teeth, with rocks and the split sticks used to pinion them. The other Somostai were warned away by more gunfire. The disturbance died quickly to a grim thudding of blows on unresisting flesh, then to silence.

Saldivar hurled himself toward Singer, wrenching his gun back out of Jon's hands with such force that Jon went sprawling. He rolled over, picked himself up, and ran after Saldivar.

"He told you not to shoot Korro," Saldivar snarled fiercely.

"But the master was killing him," Jon panted.

Saldivar plunged on, unheeding.

"God, what have you done?" he heard Saldivar cry. He did not know who the question was for.

Singer's eyes were half-open, and he was still, barely breathing, but his skin was cold and blood welled from the wound between his ribs. Saldivar crouched beside him, speaking to him in rapid Thanha that Jon could not understand. Jon thought Saldivar did not know that he was crying. After tearing off the front of Singer's shirt to get at the wound, he made a pad of the cloth and pressed it over the wound, trying to stop the bleeding. It was not working. Blood had already soaked through the cloth and reddened his fingers. Singer's lips were blue-white.

"My heart, my heart, you've got to stop bleeding. Can you hear me?"

Lyn came running to them; she had turned over the vito to someone else when she saw that Singer was not going to get up. She bent over his body with Saldivar and touched him gently but got no response.

"Kristo, if only Janney were here," she said hopelessly.

"Can't we get him in the vito and take him somewhere?" Saldivar said.

"There's not another medic for hundreds of miles," she said. "Trying to move him could kill him."

"Can't you do anything?" he asked. He was nearly as white as Singer.

"I can't find him," she whispered. "It's like—like he's already gone away somewhere."

"I saw him get better from a hit worse than this," Saldivar said. "I don't understand."

He heard a step behind him and ignored it till someone bent down beside him and touched his shoulder.

"Forgive me," the voice said in Thanha, "but I am a very old friend."

The man's left arm trailed, and the twist to his mouth made his speech a little indistinct, but some hidden music in the voice reminded Saldivar of Singer.

Lyn saw the white hair and rain-gray eyes, the fine, long fingers. "You're Hilurin," she exclaimed.

"Yes," the old man said courteously. His mind was on other

things. He took Singer's face in his hands, touching his neck to make sure of a heartbeat. He had the same listening expression they had seen so often on Singer.

"Ah, Singer, didn't I say you'd break my heart one day?" he said.

"What's the matter with him?" Saldivar demanded. He hoped again, painfully. The old man acted as if he knew what was happening, as if something could still be done to help.

"You're his kamarh," Hilurin said. "Then, please . . ."

You—stranger in Somostai clothing—you shot the master when Singer was without defense against him. Singer was killed twice, once when Korro stabbed him and once when Korro died. He cannot find his way back alone.

Saldivar had the feeling that Hilurin was trying to choose words quickly, to give him some idea of a reality that would take too long to share.

Singing is warfare—to take on grief and pain and turn it to music, kill death, loot and spoil it, and use that power to make the dead heart sing again. To sing those sorrows we have to know them. But he has the power no one has ever had, the power to go too far. To know a thing so entirely is to become that thing. He has become the enemy he killed and the death the enemy died: not just the evil suffered but the evil done and delighted in. He has true knowledge, true memory. He cannot forget. And he won't come back. He loves you, and he's afraid of what he can become.

Lyn shot them a quick picture of a door slamming, a question. *If he won't let us in, what are we gonna do? Blood runs fast.*

You are his hearth now, but I knew him a long time ago. Stay with me.

24

Singer screamed once, the death cry the master did not have time for. Then his precarious grip on awareness was torn loose by the master's last memories spilling over him like blood. He was falling again from one remembered torment to another, the same eyes always watching him—clear ones, empty and cold as ice, or dark ones that burned like coals—never able to rest long enough to remember where he was.

He gave up and let himself sink into the drowning surge of alien memories. His last desperate effort was to fall as fast as he could, like a spent arrow, all the way, all the way down, past the memories and the words, to the bedrock at the bottom of the world, the wordless cold and dark.

This is where I, too, belong. This is where I came from. This is the place you can never truly escape. Cold hell no road leads out of.

He heard a sound of crying, a wordless keen like despair made audible, an endless grief that no one would hear. Even here he could not escape from his companions. They were both here, both alone. They could not hear him. They had never been able to hear him. But he would hear them crying forever.

There was a boy who sang in the dark. He got out.

You can never get out. This is the only real thing. The rest of it was dreams and lies, and in the end you know you've never been anywhere but here. You always knew that, didn't you? That's why you were so afraid of us that you had to kill. You took any weapon in your fear. You used the Singer's gift as a weapon. And look where you ended up. It's perfect!

The cold whisper could not laugh in that place, but there was an endless mockery that cut as deeply as the endless weeping.

You need me, sweetheart. Admit it. You need me to live. Without me you can't learn fast enough. You can't change fast enough.

The voice changed, became caressing, insinuating. *Admit it. It's more than need alone. You want me.*

He felt the force of what was offered pressing him again like the wind from a furnace: knowledge torn hot and smoking from a racked world, black, sooty knowledge under the tongue of demon fires.

He writhed in denial but could neither escape nor speak. No, he thought. Not like that.

You think there's another way of knowing? The voice laughed at him. It seemed to possess him from the inside.

There is no other way. You run away from me because you know it's true. No? You don't want to believe that? Then prove I'm wrong. Ah, but you'd have to live to do that, wouldn't you? You can't live without me, and you won't choose to live with me.

Cold, delighted mockery stabbed him again. In that other place he was bleeding to death.

Face them with the one thing they can't take, and they fall apart in your hands. Too bad you don't like the recon I brought you. I didn't invent any of it. That's your world, sweetheart. What are you going to do about it? Nothing, I guess. Well, that's all right with me. Let the bitch burn.

Burn. The memory squeezed him in a glowing iron fist.

It hurts, he thought.

He felt as if someone were stooped over him in the dark, watching.

That's the only way. Hurt them. Hurt them till they give you what you want. Tear it out of them and throw the rest away. And if they don't have anything you want, hurt them because you can. The more you hurt them, the less you feel it. You can make it all go away.

Something was wrong in the voice, some change, some displacement. He heard the sound of crying again, obscuring the words, making them false. He listened with all his fading strength.

I don't hear that!

The voice was high and ragged, getting younger and less certain the more he listened. He made an effort that seemed to cost him everything, the last torn bits he had left, and reached not for the way out but toward the sound of crying.

He touched something not with hands but with a silent shock of recognition. There was a moment of confusion: Was that the same boy, the one who had been singing? No. The self-picture Singer had from his mind was dark-haired, pale-skinned—and "funny eyes"; Singer could hear multiple voices in the boy's mind, saying that. "The kid has spooky eyes." The boy had thought they meant ghost eyes. Eyes that were dead? A bad thing to say to a young one.

Eyes: He was crying, without tears, but Singer could feel the shaking within. He would stop soon. Crying did no good.

Singer wanted to take him up and carry him away. Someone had carried the boy away long ago. But as he reached to embrace him, the boy grew taller and the memories came quickly into Singer's reach.

His mouth went dry—or was he only feeling what had been true for a long time, the deathly thirst of his bleeding body?

The bad dreams that had haunted him had all been true. The boy Anton Gero had been used without mercy. He, too, had been made a weapon.

They did that to you?

The memories fell like blows that split undefended flesh. They could not be comprehended, only suffered, but Singer reached again.

Get away from me! the dead voice shrieked, and the boy stood over him, tall, dangerous, staring down with a strange look of hatred, terror, and recognition.

He has all the weapons. Why is he afraid of me?

Singer's hand found a solid physical memory at last. There was a lock around his wrist, hurting as if it had scraped his skin to the bone, but his own fingers had closed on the stranger's wrist and held him fast.

Get away from me!

Singer remembered. That was the last thing Cold Eyes had said as Singer had forced on him the killing weight of a thousand deaths relived.

The glowing iron fist of shame closed around him as the dead man's memory showed him what he had done. He had betrayed his gift—to bring down a demon, he thought. He saw it differently through other eyes. He had killed a gut-shot, thrashing creature, still vicious but as pitiful in its way as the writhing slaves in the bloody snow outside. And with that creature he had killed a naked child. He had killed the boy who had waited in the dark all his life for someone like himself and had seen him only at the end, when the rescuer had come too late and pushed him into the fire.

He knew, with grief instead of the relief he had thought he would feel, that Cold Eyes was truly dead and could not hear him or answer him. It was forever too late to go back for that child, as it would always be too late for the boy named Singer to find his way home.

Still he reached for them. It hurt like scraping through broken glass or crawling through fire. It hurt as much as being alive again. He could not quite touch them. He could hear them crying in the dead man's voice.

He had come to the place where they had all learned pain. It had been the dead man's only possession—his talent, his revenge, his bedfellow, his only pleasure. The dead one had learned to worship the darkness that opened like a sore in the heart of the world. The bitterness of all the wrong that had followed twisted Singer's mouth like poison, like a bitter chewed-over cud that could never be swallowed. He had given them plenty of pain. He strained to reach them and could not.

"Brothers," he gasped. For a moment he touched them. There was a sound that was not crying. The word had weight and shape in his mind and hummed, almost too low for hearing, with rough discordant vibrations: something to work with.

He remembered that he had a name.

Singer. It woke more echoes.

There had been a boy who sang in the dark, who sang against fear.

There had been music and light.

He heard the fragile broken music of the child's voice coming back. With it came the other memories, like scalding drops of metal, one for every note.

"It's too hard," he gasped. But he could hear them listening in the dark. He started to bind the memories into the song, holding them into the shape he needed, and the music gathered in his mind.

It was not enough.

Get away from me.

Memory flashed on Singer like lightning: The crazy man—himself—eyes burning like arc lights, legs in bloody rags, seized his/Anton's wrist in a grip of glowing iron, and he was burning, burning, burning. In the heart of the fire Singer reached out, not with hands, and stretched himself into the skin of the man he had killed.

He was stripped down like a sword blank in the fiery forge. It felt like dying, but a fierce rightness followed as the whole structure flowed and re-formed itself at last into another kind of order. The fire faded, the dead voices ceased, the weeping was still.

Rest, Anh'ton. The dying is over.

There was only one sound, beating faint and far off like hoofbeats coming for him, hoofbeats of Deronh's white horse coming through the shadows, hoofbeats of the Wind Horse with his lightning eyes.

The hoofbeats changed back to the sound of his own heart beating—too fast and faint; he slowed and deepened it. He had bound the child's song into the music, a narrow filament stronger than steel, delicate as flute music. The music demanded more, called for patterns he had never tried: thunder of drums in separate timing to define limits for discordant phrases, discords playing off each other where they crossed. It would be a strange piece of work, he thought—more rhythm than melody, harsh themes, rough music. Yet it needed something dominant to unite it all, something with strong harmonies but not too sweet. Swiftly he shaped and anchored the basic structure. He needed the strangerfolk music; nothing Thanha had ever been so complicated.

He had strung and woven the strangers' lives and deaths, their unearthly knowledge and the memories of their flesh along the crossing lines of the music. He had built a net that shone and sang and was strong enough to carry them all. His riven flesh had knit itself together with the music. When it was ready, he stretched out and found his body waiting at the right place in the song.

25

Ugh, it's cold.

"He's got to stop bleeding!" Palha sounded despairing.

Singer sat up, and the soaked cloth dropped to the ground. It took more effort than he had expected. He did not try to stand. He rolled over onto his hands and knees and dragged himself across the few feet of snow that lay between himself and the dying master.

Korro's face was shattered; his body was rigid, breath snoring slowly. Singer touched him with a single swift, embracing offer of peace, comfort. There was very little consciousness left in that body. Singer probed for it carefully.

In a last flicker of strength Korro recognized him and feebly slapped at him: rejection, wish to hurt, regret, and fury at the weakness that made it impossible.

I knew your mother, renegade, he said clearly and triumphantly. Then he lapsed into confusion as his body failed.

Singer found Palha at his elbow, helping him to his feet, and clung to him. Warmth and sweetness flooded him almost too strongly, as if Palha had shoved a chunk of honeycomb into his mouth.

I came back, brother. The Eater couldn't chew me. I'm all right.

He clung till he had his equilibrium back, then stood clear and raised his arms to the blackrobes. "Look for another service," he said. "The skyfolk have come, and the Order is ended."

Get a good look at yourself, Palha said. Half laughing, half crying, he shared his sight. Singer was grimed with soot as if

294

he had been painted black and was wet from chest to knee with his own blood and the master's. His eyes were an uncanny blue against that background.

No wonder they're scared, Palha said.

Not scared enough. Singer focused on the statue of the Eater, still towering above the pit full of coals.

Get it out of my sight, he told Lyn. She laid down lines of bullets on both sides of it to move the onlookers back, then fired one of her last shells. The image shattered and collapsed in a column of smoke that cleared slowly to reveal a jagged stump where the statue had been.

Singer felt them wavering. Most were terrified, but a solid core of fighters still asked themselves if it might be better to resist to the last than to wait for the victors to deal out their fate. Singer sorted through the strands of resistance and surrender, then picked his way through the crowd to the man whose will to fight seemed strongest. Onlookers shrank from him, opening a path that he could walk without looking.

He put his hand on the man's face as he had seen the master do with Jon. He felt the Somostai flinch from his bloody fingers and knew that he had won already, but he spoke for the effect on the rest of the crowd.

"You are thinking that it might be better to fight." He let the words echo in the man's mind. "What will you win that way? The Somostai will never rule again. And what if you could raise the master from the belly of the Eater or put another in his place? Would you really choose to do that?"

He read the "no" in the slight stiffening of the man's shoulders, the movement of his eyes.

"Out there, on your shield hand, the sea," he said softly. "On your sword hand the great plains where the Riders live, and far to the south the homes of the strangerfolk from beyond the sky. All those places you've never seen. Why spill your blood on this rock? You could walk away from it."

"You'd never let us go," the Somostai said. It sounded like a defiant certainty, but it was a desperate question.

"It's possible," Singer whispered. "So many things are possible."

The sea danced in the Somostai's head, dark yet shining, deep, immovable, but always moving; dancing on its surface was the ship that carried him away.

Singer drew his hand slowly away from the man's face and left him standing, dazed with possibilities, his hands hanging open and loose at his sides, his weapons forgotten. By ones and twos, then in a wave that broke without brightness, the blackrobes knelt and put their heads to the ground in submission.

Hoofbeats on the road—the mounted reinforcements had arrived at last, Olmalik at their head, his big body jolting stiffly astride a lathered horse. They had been toiling at top speed up the mountainside ever since Lyn's vito had taken off.

They slid from their horses, reaching for weapons as they hit the ground. The Deltans did not know where they were or what to expect; they waited for orders. Olmalik's farmers and cityfolk had blood on their minds; Singer could feel their hearts leap at the sight of surrendered Somostai, ripe for slaughter.

"No more killing," Singer said to Olmalik. "Korro's dead. They've surrendered."

Olmalik's men had spent an hour kicking their horses up the road, with plenty of time to work themselves into a red heat of fear and vengeance. They advanced on Singer in spite of their leader's restraining command.

"We don't take orders from you. The blackrobes' blood is ours."

The first, boldest, and least intelligent man rushed toward the Somostai with drawn sword. He had not collected himself to oppose Singer; he took it for granted that an unarmed man would get out of his way. Singer walked into his path, turning slightly so that the uplifted sword slid past him harmlessly while his knee caught the farmer's leg and threw him off balance. As the farmer fell, Singer caught his sword arm at the wrist. The man's weight twisted the arm as he went down, and the sword dropped from his grasp. Singer picked it up and threw it. The blade turned hilt over tip, scything through the air, and clattered on the stones far down the trail.

"You want blood, do you?" Singer grasped the twisted arm again casually but in such a way that the furiously struggling farmer gasped and held still. As Singer held him, he gasped again, soundlessly, and his face went from cold-roughened red to dead white.

"You want to pick up your babies and have that on your hands? Want to wake up on spring nights next to your wife and see those faces? If you won't take my orders, take my advice. Don't."

The man sat in the snow and sobbed. The rough heat of his anger, nursed like a horn of coals inside his shirt, had been snuffed out suddenly, and he was cold and sick with shock.

"You've won," Singer said to Olmalik. "You can afford mercy. They deserve death, but let them find their own. Don't take it on yourselves. Revenge is wolf bait. Fat tasty meat going down, a bellyful of knives after you swallow."

"What are we to do with them?" Olmalik asked. "We can't let them go. We'd never sleep easy with such men around. Put them into their own dungeons?"

Singer shuddered. "No! No more prisoners." He tried to think. It was difficult. The rush of battle blood had long since been exhausted. The cold was creeping into his bones. "Put them under guard in the cellars where they kept us till tomorrow. My Asharya will be here then. We'll talk."

Olmalik set his men to searching, disarming, and binding the Somostai. They went about the task roughly, with many blows and curses, but they had lost the edge of the rage that made it possible to kill the surrendered.

"What about this carrion?" one of them called, prodding Korro's body with his toe. "Shall I throw him in the fire?"

Singer tried to call out an order to him and found himself too weak. Saldivar was at his side again, urging him to sit down and rest but giving him support to walk when Singer insisted.

"No fire," Singer said. "Over the cliff. Let the seabirds and the foxes have him. So we'll cheat the Eater in the end."

Jon stood on the other side of the body, his face closed tight with anger. "I say burn him. Burn them all. I saw you try to help him, and I don't get it. Why?"

"For what he was," Singer said wearily.

"He was a son of a bitch!"

"He was somebody's son. A child, once."

"Oh, sure, to understand all is to forgive all, right?"

Singer shrugged. "I don't know what that means. His people were hungry. They sold him for a mouthful of chah. The Somostai used him like a rag."

"And what about it? Do I look like I'm crying? He made himself a monster. He had the choice."

"Yes. There is always a choice. Always, even at the end. So I would have given him that choice one more time. For our sake, Jon, paliao. For what we were and what we lost. You are angry, brother, and with reason. I'm too tired to be angry now. I only feel the waste of it. Forgiveness is not a Thanha virtue. But we don't like waste."

"Waste! You want to talk about waste—he's killed my sister.

Janney is dying somewhere, and you take time to worry about these scum rats.''

''The Somostai have medicine. I learned where they keep it.''

''But—how? He died without telling you anything.''

Singer put his hand to his head wearily. ''Didn't you know? I'm sorry. I thought you heard. Sometimes your defenses are too good. He told me, yes. He told me everything. I don't think he had much choice about that.''

He reached out for Jon. ''Come here. I'll show you. I don't understand it well enough for words.''

Jon came reluctantly, not ready to let go of his anger. He allowed Singer to touch him at arm's length, but at the first touch he dropped all resistance and leaned into Singer's arms, shaking.

All right. It will be all right. Singer had no strength to do more than hold him, but the mere fact of contact seemed to help.

So tell me. No time to waste. Jon straightened and braced himself again as Singer showed him the place he had seen, full of strange smells and skyfolk equipment, that Korro's memories recognized as a place for making medicines and also sicknesses. He showed the locked doors and the sealed jars inside and indicated which ones held the materials they needed. Jon also absorbed the technicalities of the experiments and how they had been carried out but stored them for future reference.

''Where's Bone?'' Singer looked around for the little slave, suddenly afraid that he had not survived the battle.

''I'm here.'' Bone ducked around and under the backs and elbows of bigger men to get to Singer's side, so quickly that it seemed he must have been watching for the opportunity.

''Bone heard Death say he would change his occupation,'' the slave said. ''If there's to be no more killing, what shall we do for a living? Command me, blue-eyed Death, and I'll be your friend. I know where all the bones are buried.''

''You worked in the infirmary. You must know the place where medicines are made.''

''Yes. I have seen it.''

''Go with Jon—Chonza—and help him find the green stuff in glass jars, the medicine Korro made to stop the coughing sickness. Take a handful of well-armed men with you in case there are more than bones yet within.''

''The key is around his neck,'' Bone said. He opened Korro's shirt and drew out a chain with half a dozen keys. The master's skull pendant fell out with them. Bone snatched his hand back from the staring skull face as if the silver were white-hot. He seized the chain of keys and hurried after Jon: first to the vito, where Jon picked up volunteers to accompany them, then to the descent into the fortress.

When Bone had gone, Singer bent and snapped the chain. He dropped the skull and ground it underfoot till it lost its shape and the stone popped free. He picked up the stone. It lay in his palm like a burning ember or a great drop of blood.

"I accept deathgift for this man, too," he said aloud. "I vow a gift in his honor: a world where he would never have existed."

He swayed again as he straightened up. Someone caught him—not Palha but another. At the first touch of skin on skin he was immersed in that familiar, long-missed presence.

"Well sung, namesake. Today I hold your cloak for you. You are the Singer for all of us." Hilurin's marred voice held nothing but victory and joy, and he spoke to Singer's soul, not holding him away beyond a fence of words as he had always done. Singer saw his own face through Hilurin's eyes, striped with red and black.

"Painted for the singing," he said. The same memory came to both of them at once: the first time Singer had held Hilurin's cloak for him, followed him and cared for him through the great singing. Afterward they had gone to the riverbank with all the pallantai to wash away sorrow and be clean for the celebration.

"Thunder River, so cold and clean," he murmured. "I wish we could be there now. But a new name won't do for us now, Lurya, even if our people were here to give it. We need a new world."

He was drifting away from consciousness. Hilurin had wrapped him in something warm, and it felt wonderful. He did not want to pass out. He was afraid that Hilurin would turn out not to be real. But he could not help it. He pushed up through thick layers of sleep to search for Saldivar and Lyn.

He saw them together, waiting for Makho. The vito stayed, stayed as if anchored to earth, keeping a wall of tangible fear before the blackrobes, till Makho came and it sped away, carrying Jon with a blue-green hand-blown jar that held healing for Zhanne.

Palha anchored and confirmed the picture. *We'll stay. Don't worry.*

Palha was shaking him. *You still with us? Jon says Mack is on the way. They're in the lower city now . . .*

Singer felt him reorient, stop translating into words, and simply show what Jon had seen: the advance guard of the pallantai coming up through the Black City, running a search and destroy, meeting Jon and coming with him back to the plateau.

We'll go down as soon as Mack comes. Take you with us. You won't miss a thing. Now give it up, cofra.

Palha laughing at him—it must be all right. He fell asleep standing up; he did not even feel them catch him as he fell.

III Riding the Wind Horse

1

By morning the wind had died down and the clouds had cleared away, letting the sun slant through. Singer slept, crumpled carelessly against Saldivar's shoulder, the depth of his peace showing how great his need had been. Always before, he had fallen asleep sprawled out like that but had ended up curled protectively with his arms around his head, as if to ward off the next blow. It seemed that he felt safe only where he had laid down all his defenses. Saldivar watched the sun move slowly over Singer's face and hair and thought he understood the Riders at last. Cities and land were no use to them, and gold was only an ornament. The perfect killing skills that terrorized outsiders seemed to them a fragile and faulty defense for their only real treasure: each other.

Before Singer opened his eyes, Saldivar felt the golden, supple many-layered thing that meant Singer was touching his mind. It had no name and did not resemble anything else that he could use as shorthand. It was stronger and clearer than it had ever been before, and as he wasted a few moments to savor it, he realized that it had been there all along.

I have been/am/will be always here/there, Singer said. It was more like music than anything else, Saldivar thought: a chord of light and sound, each single element clear and distinct but joining into an identity that lived on its own as well as in its parts. Ah, but that did not describe it, either.

"Bullshit," he said, and smiled. It was Singer-in-mind, that was all, as the hand on his arm was Singer-in-skin.

Singer opened his eyes at that and raised his eyebrows.

" 'Bullshit'? Is that how you greet me on the far side of blood

303

and fire? Fine words you teach me, man of the sky people. 'Bullshit.' 'Shut up.' ''

He sat up suddenly and scanned Saldivar's face. "Where's Zhanne?''

"I was with her most of the night. She lived through the shelling because they never moved her. There was a kid with her who insisted on staying in Olmalik's command bunker. The firebombs missed them.

"We gave her Korro's medicine first. I couldn't tell. Couldn't see if she was getting better or not. She looked—'' He swallowed hard. "She looked like death with a hangover.''

Singer saw her through Saldivar. She was corpse-colored— blue around the mouth and eyes, yellowish everywhere else. She seemed to have shrunk to a bundle of sticks in days. Tearing spasms of coughing shook her chest and made her head flop around without bringing her to consciousness. Her hand in Palha's felt hot and paper-dry, like a lizard's claw on a rock. Jon held her other hand, and his face, in the shadows of the tent, was almost as pale and drawn as hers. Lyn sat on the floor by the foot of her pallet and fidgeted or got up to pace the tent, to bring more cold forehead cloths, more snow for Janet's lips, or to plague Morne with asking if Jan should have another dose of the Somostai brew. Hours passed, with a muted accompaniment of moaning and crying from the wounded in the background. A change seemed to creep over Janet, something elusive, as the night seemed to be changing though it was still dark. She coughed less; her breathing was harder to hear. Palha did not know if that was good. He had not dared say anything to Jon, though when their eyes met, they both recognized the change. It might have meant that she was weakening, sinking.

"Morne came by to check just before dawn. She leaned her ear on Janney's chest. Then she huffed at us and said we should go to sleep and stop 'stirring up the air,' is what she said. 'She's going to be fine, but she won't get well faster for your pushing.' Jon and Lyn said they'd sleep on the floor and wait.''

He looked slightly shamefaced. "After she said Jan would be all right, this was the only place I wanted to be. Took awhile to find you. They left you alone. That wasn't right.''

Singer hooked an arm around Saldivar's neck and shook him affectionately. "You get more Thanha every day. I think they had better things to do than worry for my honor and assign people to watch me snore.''

He looked around for clothes in vain. The makeshift tent

where he had been sleeping, made from a strip of something that might have been sailcloth, held down by piled stones, was empty except for himself, Palha, and a couple of blankets. He rubbed at his bare chest, and flakes of unidentified sticky stuff fell off.

"They could have washed me. This is disgusting."

He stuck out his hand for a knife, and Palha gave him one of his own. He picked up a blanket and hacked slits in it for his head and arms, wrapped it around himself, and tied it with a strip cut from the hem. He balanced the knife in his hand for a minute, then gave it back.

"Don't you want this?" Saldivar asked. "I don't know what happened to that sword you had, but it's not here. You'll need something."

Singer shook his head. "I'll need something, but not these. Music is not a weapon. I got that all wrong. It's not a weapon, but it's all I have. I can't keep the music and keep on killing people. So . . ."

Saldivar put the knife away. "I guess I won't have much use for this, either."

Singer gave him a worried look. "You might have to, Palha. I can't say if killing is wrong for other people. Works pretty well sometimes. I only know I can't do it anymore."

"I'm not 'other people,' " Saldivar said. "I'm your kamarh. One heart. Right? What's no good for you is no good for me, either."

Outside the tent, Singer scrubbed his face and hands with a handful of snow. The snow was heavy and damp. The storm had brought in milder weather. He looked around to get his bearings. "Where are we, and where is everybody else?"

Down below, to the south, lay the burnt-matchstick remnants of the firebombed shantytown. When he turned around, he was surprised to see the walls of the Great House rising up close behind him.

"We moved the wounded and the kids and the sick people— well, I guess that adds up to just about everyone that was left— we moved them up into the city. What's left of the walls makes better shelter than any of that shit left down there where they were living. I guess I should have told them to put you inside. But I don't like it inside walls anymore, either."

"Where's Makho?"

"He showed up right after you passed out, just like Jon said he would. He was sorry he'd missed all the fighting. He's probably been up all night with Olmalik and the other captains, getting the place organized. He set up medical teams, search teams for Lowtown and also to clean out the Black City, and supply teams to comb through the storerooms and set up rations. Bone went out with those folks. Genady, too. Said he wanted to get a list of interesting things the Somostai had before the place was looted.

"Your old man—Hilurin—he went with the group sent down to let all the prisoners out. Don't know where he is now."

"With the healers, probably," Singer said. "He used to do that at home. I'd like to see him before we find Zhanne."

Saldivar took him through the snow-piled courtyard to the place where the wounded lay.

"This was probably the guardhouse," Singer said, looking around. "Low-built, with a lot of timbers. It kept part of its roof, but the feast hall caved in."

"The Somostai garrison had been living here, I think. It was convenient—they left a lot of beds and jugs and things behind."

The Riders had set up a zigzag doorway to keep out drafts. As soon as Singer came through it, he saw Hilurin. The old man was talking with Morne while he washed his hands. He took Singer by the shoulders and gave him a long, close look. Then he smiled.

"Your face is still dirty. You have black around the eyes." He picked up the cloth he had been using and washed Singer's face. "Eh, what's this? Since when has the young Singer been shaving? Things have changed since last I saw you."

"I thought you were dead," Singer said. "All this time I thought you were dead, and you were in the city with me. I dreamed of you night after night. You came to me wearing chains. And I never guessed."

Hilurin's eyes darkened, and he looked away briefly. "Korro put me in prison when I refused to acknowledge him as the Master of the City. I seriously considered becoming dead in some expeditious fashion. However, I wanted to see you again."

"How did you know I wasn't dead?"

"I saw Dona dead."

Saldivar saw him, too, for the first time. He knew that memory had gnawed at Singer for a long time, but Singer had never allowed him to see.

"I saw his wounds," Hilurin continued in a low voice. "He had a hard death. But someone had closed his eyes and folded his hands on his chest. His face was quiet. As if someone had been with him at the end. And when they—disposed of his body, something fell from his hands. Someone had left ornaments with him. As if that someone were one of the Free People. Korro picked up the thing that fell, and I had only one look at it. It was enough. Enough to keep me alive.''

He fumbled in his shirt with his good hand and pulled out one of the leather pouches in which Thanha kept everything from smoking herbs to uncut gemstones. He turned it over and shook it. A thin silver chain slithered out. The pendant was a white horse carved in ivory.

Singer's fist closed over the carving. He sank to his knees on the floor and started to cry. Hilurin went stiffly down on one knee beside him and cried, too. They wept passionately and extravagantly, crying, "*Ai*, Dona, *ai*!'' and ended up rolling on the ground with their arms around each other, sobbing.

Saldivar felt like an idiot at first, silently watching them carry on like that. He was embarrassed for Singer and himself, but after a moment he saw that no one else in the room was looking stiffly away. They glanced over and clicked their tongues sympathetically, then went on about their business if they were busy. Those who had no urgent work and some of the wounded came over. Some of them shed tears for their own sorrows; some of them sat quietly together, their faces full of memories. None of them wore the impervious self-possession Saldivar had become used to in Singer. Everything they felt was laid open at that moment. He realized that although Singer loved him, he had been treated as an outsider in many ways. Singer was doing the right thing for this time and place; Saldivar was the one who looked strange.

He sat down on the floor with the others, and a teenage boy with his head swathed in bandages and one arm in a sling leaned against his shoulder, crying silently. Saldivar could not grieve for Dona, since he had not known him, but for Singer's sake he remembered all that he could about Dona, and for Singer's sake he was grieving. Dona had died hard, but he had died like a prince, and Saldivar almost envied him the tears Singer shed.

A memory came to him from a time long past: bare feet flying in the gritty road that was the camp's main street, blood pooling in the dust beneath them. He had not seen his cousin's face after the boy had been shot for stealing; they had not let him get close enough. His last look had been those feet, torn where the dogs had savaged Beni when they caught him. A few of the smuggled food packets Beni had died for lay scattered in the dust around him, and Saldivar remembered that his mouth had watered even though his stomach was hollow and sick with grief for Beni. After that he had lost the others one by one, his cousins and friends, till he was left alone, starving and sick for them all, a long, long way from home.

It was not his way to weep as the Thanha wept, but he buried his face in his hands and mourned in silence for all the dead. Hot, painful tears ran through his fingers like blood. Alone, alone, his grief cried to him, but then he felt the murmur all around him, like words of consolation spoken just below the level of hearing. The Riders were with him. He understood what Singer had meant by feeling-for-the-People. It had come to him. As fast as the tears flowed out of him for what he had lost, the Riders gave back to him. They whispered to him that wounds could heal and grief could pass. *Resh is for hunger, and the brothers are for sorrow.* So they sang it.

Singer sat up finally and leaned against Saldivar's knees, drying tears with the back of his wrist like a child.

"Can I keep this?" Singer asked.

"It's yours," Hilurin said. "Bone found it with other small things of value in Korro's own chest. I knew he would keep it. I waited a long time to give it back to you." He put the chain over Singer's head.

Singer took a deep breath. "I want to see Zhanne now."

Singer entered with careful, silent steps. Janet seemed asleep, but she opened her eyes and looked around instantly when they came in.

"When are you going to learn that you can't sneak up on me anymore?" she whispered.

"I wanted to surprise you with a gift, but I don't have it in my hand. You have to close your eyes and see it."

He touched Saldivar's hand to let him see it, too: stems wound with small scalloped leaves, holding flower buds that had hardly begun to open, more green than white. They held a faint, dusty sweetness. In Singer's memory the stems had been braided into a green circlet studded with flowers. He slipped the flowers around Janet's neck.

"I can see it," Janet said. "I don't want to open my eyes. It's been so long since I saw flowers."

"Not a deathgift. A rememberer." He checked her mind for words. "Souvenir. No. Memorial. It is for Risse. The first I loved in the way of kamarh, with all my heart. When I saw her die, the sun turned black for me. She should never have gone with the pallantai. Her strength was for healing, not killing. But we were the Riders. Fighting was our life. She had to go. I was afraid for you, so afraid I had done that to you.

"These flowers were hers. She wanted to find out what they were good for, but she didn't live to do it."

She was still too weak to reach up and embrace him, but he felt the embrace, anyway. He sat on the floor so she could touch his face.

"I wanted to tell you," he went on. "Risse was right. Dona was right. You were right. I have been wrong for a long time, but now I understand. I have to find a different road. I need a road to a place where Risse would have lived and Cold Eyes and the master would not. So you have to get well very fast, isé, because I will need you."

She smiled. "There's something else in your thoughts, too, no?"

He jerked his chin up in the brief arrogant yes of the Riders. "There is another reason I want your people to live. One that is just for me. I don't understand what I am, why I can do these things, what it is that I do. If your people live, maybe someday they will tell me. If they die, if they end up stuck here, orphans, then I will never be more than something left behind. Like those things of the skyfathers the Somostai kept without understanding. I will be left over. A strange thing, a useless thing that does not fit in the world. Dona told me I had to find out why. That was his last gift to me. He made me ask that question. And now I can't stop asking it. I need to know why. I want to stop your people from dying, because every one of them that dies takes something out of the world that I might need to know."

Janet lay back and closed her eyes, smiling. He could feel the light of her perception washing through him like the full moon rising over the plains, edging every blade of grass in silver or, like rainwater, gathering in the lowest places, finding its way through every obstacle in the end. To be visible again was an exquisite pleasure.

"You never did like living within walls," she said. "You feel good, too. You and Pablo feel like a big river now. Lots of power, all the currents gathered in and heading in the same direction. Before, you were like a storm—reefs and undertow everywhere and the chop going different directions. Even Jon has untied some of his kinks. No more incoming from your bad dreams. I'm just going to float downstream for a while."

She fell asleep smiling.

Lyn and Jon had gone out to get food and returned to find her sleeping.

"Here, eat this shit," Jon said, handing Singer the bowl of soup he had brought for Janet. "It's supposed to be medicinal, and you're the one who lost all the blood. Or do you replace that by magic?" His tone was belligerent, and Singer gave him a questioning look.

"He's pissed because you didn't tell him all your secrets," Lyn explained, ripping off a hunk of bread with her strong white teeth and chewing it as she spoke. "Me, too. Only I'm so glad to see you on your feet and in your right mind that I don't give a flying fuck. Come here and let me feel your breath before I really get mad."

She kissed him thoroughly while at the same time she ran her hands down his ribs and tasted his senses to make sure he was really feeling all right.

"You can have all my secrets now."

"That's outstanding," she said, grinning at him wickedly. "When do we start?"

"Start what?" Marcus ducked through the curtain between wards.

"*Ayei*, Makho!" Singer turned to greet him and got the full-dress Thanha welcome: a kiss on both cheeks, a kiss on the mouth, and a bear hug that made him wince as he was crushed against the Asharya's gold ornaments. Kruger eased up but did not let him go.

"Heaven and earth, boy, the sight of you gives me joy." Singer understood him perfectly but thought his voice sounded a little odd until he realized that Makho was speaking Fokish, his mother language.

"What have you done to your hair?" Kruger's eyes were wet, and he returned to Delteix in self-defense. "Looks like you were shaved with a rusty chisel."

"True enough," Singer said, grinning at Jon. That reminded him suddenly of how dirty he was, clothed in nothing but a smelly blanket. He disentangled himself from Makho. "I regret greeting my Asharya like something out of a pigsty. I have not had time to array myself in honor of this victory."

Kruger laughed so hard that it looked as if he were having a heart attack. Singer saw that Makho had learned to do many things he had avoided in his old life.

"Jon has been telling me what you did on the mountain,"

Kruger said, sobering up. "I want to hear it from you. All of it."

At that moment Morne strode toward them with the step of a much younger woman.

"This is not a visit to your hearth sister, this is a council of war," she said. "The sister is sleeping while you carry on over her tired body, keeping others awake. My hearth is a place for healing, not for captains to wrangle. You are disturbing the atmosphere. Get out!"

Kruger put his hand on his heart and bowed elegantly. "My heart and my sweetness, only your expressed wish would move me from the delight of your presence."

"Dio, the Mother heavy makes a joke," Lyn said.

"My tent is around the corner," Kruger said. "We can go there. Morne, barasha, please send to me when Janet wakes."

2

Singer felt immediately at home when he saw the Asharya's sleeping place. The Riders had set it up in the angle of a couple of ruined walls, clearing the rubble out of the way so the floor was level. The tent commanded a view of the road and stood in a place where all could find it and get access to the Asharya. It was modest, even severe within, befitting the Grandfather of the People when his children were suffering, but coals burned in the center and the kettle was kept hot so the Asharya could offer tea. There was room inside for the Asharya's private council corner but also for a couple of young messengers, some older captains to guard and attend the Asharya, and a few of his hearth to care for him. It even smelled right: sweet herbs and smoke, leather and resh beans.

"It pleases you?" Makho asked.

"This is a good place. Like home."

"You sound surprised. Don't be—that would be offensive to your Asharya. If I do something, I do it right, no?"

Olmalik was already seated by the fire with Genady, Bone, and the Asharyas from the People that had joined with Makho to take the Iron City, with one or two of their senior captains. A short, strong woman named Rak'andav led the River People. The Asharya for the Tall Grass was named Tiluva, the name of a small bird, and that went strangely with his bony, heavy-browed face. Both of them were younger than Kruger, and their captains were younger still. It had been a hard year on the plains.

As soon as they were seated and had exchanged greetings, Olmalik spoke.

"Before we talk about the next campaign, I want to settle the blackrobe question. My people are not pleased to guard and feed them. Their presence makes bitter hearts. I think if they stay here much longer, something will go wrong and there will be killing. If my people smell blood again, it will be slaughtering time. I don't want to see that. Moreover, food is scarce. My woman brings me plenty of news about the hunger in our camp. Men with starving children don't want to feed prisoners. Please devise some way to get them out of our sight."

The discussion took a long time because everything had to be translated by Singer and Hilurin from Giristiyah to Thanha and back again, with occasional forays into Delteix for Kruger and Jon. Once they understood Olmalik's speech, the Riders from the other groups shifted uneasily.

"Riders take no prisoners," Rak'andav said.

"They don't slaughter the unarmed, either," Lyn said, leaning toward her to emphasize the point. "We had no choice but to accept their submission or kill them with skyfolk fire weapons. It wasn't a fair fight. I was there. It would have been my job to mow them down. I hate the sons of bitches, but I don't want that job. Got any volunteers?"

"Give them weapons and let the pallantai kill them in fair fight," Rak'andav suggested. "That would get rid of them."

Tiluva shook his shaggy head. "Be serious, Raka. We're all tired. No one wants to play games with the blackrobes."

"It would not be a fair fight even if you gave them weapons," Bone said. "Most of your prisoners never learned to fight. They didn't know Korro was leading them into a war. Many of them never became masters. They were permanent apprentices. You have men there who tended animals and kept breeding charts, wrote records in the library, distilled plant essences, or supervised the kitchens. They are not captured warriors. If you treat them as such, you're fooling yourself.''

"They're all Somostai, so they're all guilty," Rak'andav said, jabbing the ground with a stick of firewood. "They all profited from the dead, whether they knew about it or not."

"War is one thing, murder is something else," Kruger said. "Do we want our first act in victory to make murderers of us?"

"It is not murder," Rak'andav said, raising her voice and making herself taller where she sat. "It is justice."

"Then what about us?" Singer said quietly. " 'We are the Riders. Fighting is our life.' Yes, I know we never harmed the helpless. All we did was to take money from the City Master for fighting his wars. We went up against the soldiers of his enemies so he could use his own troops to subdue the farmers and cityfolk. We made Hadhla master of three cities. Without us he would have been dead long ago. The cityfolk call us wolves and renegades. They would be well pleased to see us crushed by the hammer of the skyfolk if things had gone differently. Think about that when you speak of justice."

"Talk!" she said, making the hand gesture that said "Throw it away."

"Hear this, then," Jon leaned out of the shadows where he had been sitting, partly hidden, behind Hilurin's shoulder. "I have cause to hate the blackrobes as much as any of you, and more than some. Hilurin and I were prisoners in the Black City for a year. I'd like to kill the bastards, but I just can't see it. Can you? If you think you can do it, be my guest. Pick up the gun."

Rak'andav slowly lowered her head as Singer translated Jon's speech. "No. I'm not eager for that honor. One or two of them, yes. Five or six, even. But all of them, no." She shook off the unpleasant vision angrily. "But what else can we do? This is a hard time. Too hard to waste kindness on prisoners."

"I have been thinking of something that might serve," Singer said. He waited courteously for Kruger's approval.

"Go ahead."

"Mark them. Mark them and turn them loose. Then it's up to them and those who meet them."

"Let them go?" Rak'andav was scandalized. "You're crazy. Anyway, where could they go? They'd have nothing to do but turn bandit."

"Offer them the same bargain they gave the farmers. They

can work for us for their food. Not forever; there have been slaves enough in the city. In the spring, when the crops are planted, they can go where they will. Then you can treat them according to whatever laws you follow in your country—punish them if they commit more crimes without covering ourselves in their blood.''

"I would accept that choice," Kruger said.

"I believe my people will accept that if the blackrobes turn out to be useful," Olmalik said. "There will be no mercy if they cause trouble."

Rak'andav thought about it, biting her lip. Singer could see she had not been Asharya long. She had the restless impatience of the pallantai and had not learned to keep her deliberations guarded.

"That's wise," Bone said. "There is a treasure house of knowledge buried in the Black City. Make the blackrobes raise it from its tomb. Even the skyfolk can learn something."

"I agree," she said abruptly. "We've wasted enough time talking about it. We'll do it your way. There's always time to kill them later. But I don't trust them."

Tiluva also agreed. "But how will we mark them? And who will do it?"

"Let Rak'andav find some among her people who will do it," Kruger said. "She will not be tempted to show too much mercy."

Kruger was slowly and subtly establishing himself as the leader, helped along by Singer and Hilurin always at his side. The other captains accepted his suggestion, and Rak'andav found herself assigned the unpleasant responsibility.

"Now we have something more important to decide," Kruger said, beckoning a messenger to bring the tea and pouring for the captains with his own hand. "We can't stay here long. It isn't safe. The skyfolk on the south coast may come to punish us at any moment. They have flying machines more powerful than any we have seen yet. I will not give you false encouragement, *barosani*. Yesterday we had a very small chance. We took it and won. If they come against us again, we will have no chance at all. None."

" 'None' is a rash word. How do you know till we try it?" Rak'andav asked.

"Courage becomes the pallantai," Kruger said. "Walking into the fire is not courage, however. Remember that I have commanded a war host among these strangers. No one knows better what kind of weapons they have. If they had known how strong we are, we would be dead already. We live only because they despised us and thought to take our lives cheaply.''

Rak'andav was fidgeting again before he had finished his speech. ''What then? Are you saying we should run away?''

Olmalik looked alarmed. ''My people are sick, they're wounded. We have—'' He choked off the word, remembering. ''We *had* many women and children. We don't want to lose more than our grievous loss already. We are starving. We are far from our homes. How will we live till spring if you don't help us? Maybe the Riders can run away when they like, but we can't. Safe or not, we have to stay here or die.''

''I don't suggest running away,'' Kruger said. ''The reverse, indeed. We must move south as fast as we can and hope to strike them before they know we are upon them. Those who cannot go with the war host must shelter here as best they can. I want a task group to examine the grounded vitos and see if they can be made to fly again. I want another group to search the city and find out whether the Somostai kept any reserves of fuel for their allies. You, Jon, must investigate Hazzan's files for maps and strategic information. Our chance of surprising them is small but better than waiting here for them to choose the time and weapons.''

This talk was more to the Riders' taste, and they signed approval and encouragement before he had finished speaking. Singer, however, put a hand on Kruger's arm, restraining, pleading.

''My Grandfather, hear me, please. I learned something from Korro before he died. He found a way to send the coughing sickness south. From the bodies of sick people come seeds of more sickness. That is well known to the sky people, but they did not know that Korro had discovered it. He packed the cargo of coal and steel in blankets that were stiff with infection. I do not think the skyfolk suspected it. I think they are sick to death at this moment, as Zhanne was. Perhaps they are too sick to use their wisdom to find a cure. Without the medicine we gave Zhanne, they will die.''

''I can confirm that, Marcus,'' Jon said. ''The last messages Hazzan received were emergency calls.''

Kruger's eyes gleamed. ''Excellent. We may have a chance, after all.'' In his mind was the hope, remote but still possible, that they might overrun the Nupi base completely, acquire their weapons and resources, and treat with the Consorso government as equals.

Singer spoke rapidly, letting his fear show openly. "Makho, forgive me, but that is the trap we must not fall into. What do you think your people would do when they saw us occupying the position of their enemies, offering them a threat? Do you think they'd welcome you home with open arms? I think not. They wanted no part of you when you worked for them, when you gave them your submission. Now you have become a renegade. They'd do their best to kill you."

"That might not be so easy with us sitting in the Nupi headquarters. If I had access to that airfield . . ." Kruger fell silent.

"He's right, Marcus," Genady said. "You wouldn't. Nor would most of the others. If we defeat the Nupis, we'll become a replacement enemy, but without the will to fire on our own people. We have to avoid that position."

A spark of anger glowed in Kruger. "This is the position in which I find myself," he said carefully. Singer looked down, knowing that Makho was too high-hearted to blame another for putting him in that position. Still, the blame was Singer's.

"I have to play it as well as I can," Kruger continued. "If we get surrender from the NPU and then offer peace to the Consorso, they may take it."

"Do you think the Net will let them?" Jon asked. "Peace means that Net secrets will find their way into the open. There would be big trouble for the Net, the military, and the governor when the POWs come back and tell their tales and the native inhabitants, who supposedly don't exist, walk into North Fork."

"It's a risk. But there is no alternative."

"Something else I learned, not from Korro," Singer said. "Sometime soon another ship comes from your far home. This ship is full of soldiers, expecting a war. They bring weapons that can pull down the sky. I don't understand them, but I have seen them. What happens when the Nupi ship comes and finds that you have destroyed their brothers?"

"I don't know what happens then," Kruger said. "I have to get to next week first and worry about next year or five years from now after that."

"I'll tell you what happens!" Singer cried. "I saw it happening. Tony Gero used to have bad dreams about it, and what causes bad dreams to a man who is a maker of nightmares is bad indeed for the rest of us. Two ships full of soldiers come, and they tear this world apart. If we want to live, it's not enough for one side to win and the other to lose. We have to be one people when the big ships come. All of us. Any other way means we'll all die in the end, and this will all mean nothing. The Rock, the Mothers, the defeat of the Black City—all of it nothing but a little spark of brushfire in a burning world." His grip on Kruger's wrist was as painful as the intensity of his voice.

"Get a hold of yourself," Kruger muttered in Delteix.

Suddenly he was looking down from a very great height at a circular darkness edged with a pale, glowing line. Shapes were outlined on the darkness by nets of white light. In the blackness where the nets did not reach, orange and yellow sparks burned. Kruger thought he should recognize the picture, but he did not. The outlined shapes were familiar, nagging at him.

"It's Delta from orbit!" he exclaimed. "Those are the coast cities and the burn-off on the isthmus."

The picture changed. One node of the net of lights was eaten away by an irregular, glowing sore, surrounded by more sparks that flowed together till they joined and enlarged the smoldering area.

Haven. Recon photos from the satellite monitors after the bombing.

"God in heaven." The picture blinked out as Kruger recoiled from it violently and Singer let him go. "You never saw that. How could you?"

"Not with these eyes."

Kruger stared at Singer as if he could penetrate through his skin into the secrets within. "You really do have everything Gero knew."

"Yes. Can't always understand it or get to it when I want, but it's there. That picture burns in my mind."

Kruger felt a need to sit down, but he was already sitting. He gulped hot tea. "They wouldn't be such fools as to send those weapons with the colony ships."

Singer shrugged. "Gero thought yes. Look what a handful of your little bombs did to the Rock," he added bitterly.

"Mr. Singer, you're the worst kind of scout," Kruger said. "Commanders like people who come back with more precise confirmations of what they already knew. We don't like people who blow us off the range with information we never even knew existed. You won't be thanked for this kind of work."

Singer relaxed just a little. "I do this kind of work only for you, Con-el."

"Well, what in heaven's name do you suggest? I assume you don't consider unifying the planet by force as a viable option?"

"I thought about that," Singer said seriously. "I don't think we can do it."

"I agree with you there. But what's the alternative?"

"The unexpected," Singer said. "Take the Nupis medicine. Help them cure their sickness. Then talk to the survivors—not surrender talk. Just peace. They say that Riders don't bargain. But I've seen sugar tame more horses than the whip."

"There's just one problem with that humanitarian proposal," Kruger said dryly. "In their state of panic, they'll fire on us before we get close enough to offer our assistance."

"That's why the pallantai is not going," Singer said.

The Riders had not been able to follow the whole conversation, but they were all ears once the discussion returned to matters they could understand. Half a dozen voices threatened to interrupt.

Hilurin held up his hands for silence.

"I need a map," Singer said, frowning in frustration.

"I could print one for you off Hazzan's equipment," Jon offered.

"I need one now."

He looked around till he found one of the skins Kruger was sitting on, a large well-tanned hide with the hair scraped off. He pulled it from under the Asharya and flipped it over. The underside was white and fairly smooth.

"Do you have brushes and ink in the tent?"

Singer spread the hide in front of Jon and handed him the brush. "Can you paint this?"

Singer laid out the map in his mind and waited for Jon to take it, if he would. Jon responded as hungrily as if he had just been handed a chocolate bar.

"Kristo, it's beautiful," he said reverently, painting contours with deft precision and at top speed. Symbols and conventions that Singer had not recognized came clear as Jon looked at them. The Riders pressed closer to see the map taking shape.

Beautiful—if you knew how long I wanted a map. A flash of pure envy. *What else have you got? You have maps of everything! Photos, file numbers . . .*

Jon's naked hunger startled Singer. His first reaction was to defend himself, but keeping information from Jon was an act of cruelty and was just what Jon expected. Singer held still and let him look. *It's all yours.*

Jon stopped dead. He wanted to turn Singer's memory inside out immediately. His fingers tightened on the brush and left a blot. He spit on his shirt and sopped up the spot, then kept painting.

"This is done small to cover a lot of territory," Singer said. "On the east and southeast edge, you skyfolk brothers may recognize it. In the north, my brothers from the plains and the city can see the mountains and the pass into Rider country. On the west, you see it goes south down the coast, past the southern cities, and here, south of the mountains and east of city farmland, is more territory the NPU claims. The circles Jon is marking show the Nupi city—here—and out in the empty lands more Nupi outposts. There, closest to us, is the one we took last month. The circles with a cross through them are Consorso outposts."

Kruger frowned. "That can't be. I never heard of them."

"Many things you never heard of, Makho. Now, pay attention. This is the reason for showing you the map. These Consorso outposts—here and here—hold Nupi prisoners, just as those Nupi outposts over there hold more brothers like the ones we turned loose. That is what I want you to do, Makho. Take the pallantai and ride to those Nupi camps. Wait there for word from me. It may happen that you can take your brothers out without a fight. That will give you a bigger war host and maybe another bargaining counter with your people in the colony."

"Word from you? Where are you going to be?"

"As soon as Zhanne is well enough, a few of us—as many as Lyn can take in one of the vitos—will light at the edge of Nupi territory and walk in. We'll take medicine with us. We'll go softly till we find someone we can talk to, and we'll heal as many as we can. I don't think they'll fire on us. Then we'll talk."

Kruger sat back and rubbed one hand over his eyes. "That's the damnedest plan I ever heard."

"Negotiation, Makho. Isn't that what you call it?"

3

They flew south at night, skimming the wave tops, following the line of the coast. Lyn flew so low that they could smell the salt and sometimes catch a spray of cold drops from a wave crest breaking high. The speed of their flight frightened Hazzan; he clenched his hands on the edge of the seat and swallowed hard. Singer dropped into Lyn's mind, felt her confidence, and did not worry. He loved the onrushing wind, the feeling of running unchecked between the sea and the sky.

"Riding on the sand would be even better," he said to Janet.

She looked up long enough to smile but kept her attention on the rack of sealed jars on the floor between the seats. "There must be a lab in Solidari. I hope there are some technicians left alive, because I'm not qualified to do this kind of analysis."

Lyn had put Hazzan in the copilot's seat for the flight into Solidari so he could answer when the airfield challenged them. "If you have coastal defenses, Hazzan," she said, "this would be a good time to tell me about them."

Hazzan gulped and did not say anything. Since he had recovered from the sickness, he had been silent and pale. He accepted food without looking at the giver and ate without apparent pleasure. He spoke as little as possible. Singer had seen Hazzan flinch when he looked at the ruins of Erech Tolanh, but he did not know if the Nupi felt shame because of what he had done or because he had not succeeded.

"What do you think, Singer? Do you think he's lying?" Lyn asked.

"I think he's airsick."

"Well, I don't want to fly right into Solidari harbor. I think I'll cut inland before the moon gets any lower."

The vito wheeled gloriously and swooped over the beach and up, past the coastal rocks and into the night sky till Lyn leveled out so abruptly that their stomachs lurched. Singer laughed out loud. He felt Lyn talking to him through the swing and thrust of the forces she was using. He understood how it worked, and for the first time he was completely unafraid in the strangerfolk machine.

A thick carpet of trees swept under them, soft black, darker than the sea, without any glimmer of foam. Lyn cut back the power, and they slowed till they seemed to drift almost silently above the dark branches.

"Oh, we're not all that silent," Lyn said grimly. "Nobody who's ever heard vitos coming, on the ground, mistakes the sound for anything else."

"It's too dark," Hazzan said, a fearful edge in his voice. "We should have seen lights by now. We should have been challenged."

"Nice of you to let me know," Lyn said.

Hazzan called the airfield repeatedly, asking for clearance, but heard nothing.

"Where's the hospital?" Janet asked.

"I don't know," Lyn said. "Would it be marked?"

"Not anymore. In the last round of the bombing, marked buildings took direct hits. I was working in North Fork when the hospital there went down."

"The Union forces didn't begin that action," Hazzan said sullenly. "We responded to Consorso aggression."

"That song plays both ways," Janet said. "What does it matter when fire and chunks of concrete are raining on the beds and you can only get one more man out before the whole place goes up, and they're all screaming for help and none of them can walk? I don't know who started it. I only wish they had all been with me then."

Hazzan shut his mouth and stared at the floor.

"I'm wasting fuel," Lyn said. "Where's the fucking hospital, Hazzan?"

"I don't know. I can't see anything. Turn on your light."

"Why don't I just land and invite them to shoot me?"

"I can't tell you where to land if I don't know where I am. Fly around in circles all night if that's what you want."

Lyn turned on the searchlight. They were still over trees, but there was a gap to the east that turned out to be a road. In a few minutes she came to cleared land and followed the road through it till buildings appeared. Occasionally they passed unmoving vehicles on the road. Once they passed the carcass of a vito that had crashed and burned. Remnants of smoke still trailed from it, turning opalescent in the beam from the light.

At intervals there were irregularly shaped piles of drab-colored stuff. Lyn swooped down to roof level.

Saldivar took a look through his lenses. "Bodies," he said. "Died on the street, or maybe they hauled them out of the houses but couldn't bury them."

"Where is everybody?" Hazzan asked, fear in his voice. "Where are the emergency trucks? The search teams? Why are the lights out all over the city?"

"Do you see anyone alive down there?" Janet asked quietly.

Lyn drifted along the street, listening to outside audio. It was eerily quiet.

Janet moved over by Saldivar and found the building by the emergency vehicles parked behind it. They set down in the parking lot and went in through the emergency door. The floor was filthy, and there was no one staffing the reception desk. Somewhere a phone sounded, unanswered, and when it finally stopped, another one sounded farther away. They picked their way forward, toward the treatment area, through rows of people laid out on the floor. Some of them, next to the walls in orderly arrangements, lay on pallets. As the rows spread out from the walls toward the exit, the sick lay on blankets or spread-out coats, tablecloths, ponchos, pieces of plastic, and finally the bare floor.

The big doors swished open, and a para came through, carrying a jug of water and a tube. He wore civilian clothes, but a holstered handgun showed under his hospital coat. He was too tired to look surprised.

"What do you want?" he asked, kneeling by the first patient and beginning the job of trying to give her water.

"I want to see your chief medical officer," Hazzan said.

"She's busy. Look, if you're not a doctor and you're not dying, get out of here."

"I'm a doctor," Janet said. "And a couple of my friends here are paras of a sort. They know enough to help out."

"No shit?" He spared them a quick look. "Then get busy. We can use you. Get another jug and help me get water into these people. They'll snuff it from dehydration before the disease gets them."

"I need you to take me to your jefe right away," Janet insisted.

"Don't bug her. The paras inside can tell you what to do."

"I've got something better than just a few extra hands. Pay attention. This is important. Most of us have had the disease and lived. Captain Hazzan and I had it only days ago. We recovered."

That got his attention. "Where were you? Here in Solidari?"

"No. Up north."

"That's restricted information," Hazzan said at the same time.

"Never mind about all that," Janet said. "Just take us to the medical officer. I can tell you she'll be pissed off if you don't."

The para left his jug on the floor. "Hope you're not making this up. She'll kill you."

The treatment area was warmer than the lobby and even more crowded. The air was thick with the bad smell of sickness and the sound of coughing and moaning. The para took them to the chief medical officer, a stocky woman, brown-skinned like Hazzan. She pushed her cap up on her forehead with one wrist, keeping her hands away from her face. The cap's tight edge had cut a deep pink crease in her skin.

"What?" she said to the para, as if patience and endurance could not spare more than one syllable.

"Nasri, these people say they had the plague recently, up north someplace, and they recovered."

"Shit," the doctor said. She stuck out her gloved hands as if to seize Janet, then let them drop to her sides.

"We've come to give blood," Janet said. "Thought you might want a look at our antibodies."

"Godmywitness," Nasri said. Then she shoved the para with her elbow. "Get their ▮▮▮▮▮▮ blood, Gil. What are you waiting for?"

"Not him," Janet said, detaining Singer. "He has unusual blood. I don't want to go into it right now, but he would confuse the problem."

"Record everything," Nasri said to Gil. "Every little detail. Print copies and backup."

The look she gave Janet was flat with exhaustion, but Janet detected a trace of pity in it.

"Too late," the doctor said. "Even if you're not shitting me. The best he can do is take samples and store them. We can't spare the time to hunt for the bug, and none of us who are left on our feet are qualified for the lab work, anyway. Still worthwhile, though, for anyone who lives through this. Our observations may give them a head start on developing a vaccine. Best we can do.

"You're a doctor? You can start anywhere. We're doing life support, and that's about all. We've tried our antibiotics, but they don't work. You have any bright ideas, check with me."

"I have one right here," Janet said. "I have a sample of something I think is an antibacterial agent that works on this stuff. It's what they gave me and Hazzan. It seems to be a native plant derivative, but that's all I know about it. Do you want me to take it to the lab?"

Nasri pounded the heel of her hand against her head. "I'm dying and I'm imagining you, right? This is a stress hallucination. God, I don't have a lab. They're all dying. Shit. ██████ it, if you're a ██████ miracle, why the hell couldn't you have come yesterday?"

Janet struggled out of her pack and pulled one of the precious handmade jars out of it. She forced it into Nasri's hands.

"Take me to the best lab tech you have left. I'll fix him. Then the next. When we have a team, they can start working on this."

Nasri clutched the jar, and gradually her face cleared as if strength were flowing back into her through the cloudy glass. "Over here," she said. "What do I do with this?"

"I've been giving it orally because I didn't have any other delivery system. When these people are on their feet, they could try purifying it and using it intravenously, but we don't have time to try it right now. Listen, there's a case of these jars out in your parking lot, in a salvaged vito. Send someone out there to get them before anything happens to them. But save some for analysis. That's all I have."

She went to work on the lab techs. It was wonderful to have good equipment again, she thought. Then she saw just how dirty and inadequate this place would have looked to her before the journey with Singer. Mile by mile she had not noticed her viewpoint changing, but it had changed. All the while her fingers and her eyes and ears kept busy.

"Show my chicos your most essential people," she said to Nasri. "We'll start with them." She hated doing that; it was all wrong to put the doctors first in line, but it was logical. As she worked, she kept a light link to Singer so he could take knowledge from her if he needed it and so she could see what he was doing and learn from it.

Singer kept moving. To give medicine to everyone in the hospital seemed an unending task, and when it was done, it was time to start again. He let Saldivar feed them water and medicine while he lingered by those who caught his attention for some reason and by those who seemed closest to death. He touched them to lend them strength, balancing and encouraging their bodies' effort to throw off the invaders. He listened to Janet as she worked and learned more with every patient, till he could sense and identify the invisible invaders when he met them in the sick and could speed the body's own fighters to the rescue.

The sick people made a constant background in his mind, a low dissonant mutter of oppressive dreams, an unrelenting ache. They dragged at him like an undertow. Above that drone of pain he distinguished personalities that were awake and conscious. He tasted Nasri and trusted her: like Janet, she was a warrior soul, and healing was her only love. He did not need to watch her; she would do no harm. He checked the paras and the handful of other doctors still working in other rooms. He felt no threat from any of them, only fear, grief, weariness, and the dogged determination to continue. He called them all brother as he touched them and hoped they could hear.

The windows brightened into full day. The next time Singer looked, it was dark outside. He checked Janet surreptitiously. She had been out of bed for only a few days.

I heard that, Singer. Don't bug me. The lab techs are coming around.

The doctors and paras had not stopped to sleep or eat, but when the word went around that a few of the patients seemed to be rallying, they all gathered to see. One of the techs opened his eyes, and Nasri bent down to give him more water.

"How do you feel?"

"Like shit," he croaked. "What are you all looking at?" He coughed long and hard and spit out blood-flecked sputum.

"God, that hurts," he said weakly, but the next minute he struggled to sit up. "I can breathe better this way."

"Now that you're awake, we can give you something for the chest pain," Nasri said. "Gil, make sure he keeps drinking. Feed him tea with sugar and get him some protein broth if you can find any.

"Listen to me, Nito: You're the first of all these chucks to get up again after going down with this. Nobody else has made it.

You're a guinea pig for the new medicine, and I tried it on you first because I want you in the lab finding out what it is as soon as you can hold your head up. You don't have to walk; I'll get you a wheelchair. Just get your brain and your hands working again.''

"Dakko."

Gil stuck rolled blankets under the tech's shoulders to keep him semiupright, and he leaned back to rest again.

"It's working, it's working!" Nasri threw her arms around Janet. All the doctors hugged each other, pounded each other, and waltzed around each other, staggering with exhaustion.

"Hot damn and heavy damn, it's working." Nasri allowed herself the luxury of two noisy sobs. Then she blew her nose ferociously and went back to work.

Singer was focused on the sick again with renewed determination, and he did not hear people coming to the door till he heard Nasri cry out.

"I don't know who you are, but you can get the hell out of my hospital!" she shouted. She stood in front of Janet, stretching out her arms as if she could shield them all.

A squad of armed soldiers flanked the door, weapons ready. A man stepped out from behind them. The man was not tall, but he had an effect on the others that made him seem bigger. His hair was smooth and black, but his sallow face was aged, marked with a web of wrinkles. He wore a tidy, complete uniform, the first Singer had seen, and it was decorated with metallic insignia. Something stirred in Singer's mind, and he recognized the man.

Gero had known him; it was Luis-Win, executive chairman of the New Peoples' Union. He ruled the Nupis, his power hemmed in by the structure that had given it to him. He was capable and agile but had a streak of violence in him that made him ruthless when he had been too much thwarted. Gero had fostered that ruthlessness by his offer of a treaty that would strike aside the frustrating presence of indigenous life. Singer sent Saldivar a quick, desperate command. *Get Hazzan out of here. If the chairman recognizes him, we've snuffed it.*

Nasri recognized the man, too, but still defied him. "Chairman or not," she said, "tell those chucks to put down the guns or you are going to wish you had never been born. Tomorrow or the next day you're going to start coughing, and where are you going to go then? I won't have armed men in my hospital."

Luis-Win gestured to the soldiers to put up their weapons.

Only then did Singer realize that he had missed the most important fact: The chairman carried a blanket-wrapped bundle in his arms. The blanket fell back as he moved, revealing a child's face.

"I've brought you another patient," he said. "I want a private room for him, the best care."

"There are no private beds, Chairman. Not for anyone. There's no special care. We do the best we can for all of them."

"This is my grandson," Luis-Win said. His face threatened to twist out of control.

"Give him to my assistant," Nasri said implacably. "They'll do what they can. This sickness has no respect for connections."

Singer wondered why she had spoken so harshly.

The chairman bent over in a spasm of coughing, clutching the child desperately in trembling arms.

"So your quarantine didn't work," Nasri said. "I warned you that it would not. You took supplies and personnel we could have used to save lives and barricaded yourselves behind a wall of guns. I told you guns can't fight the plague. Now tell me why I should help you when you wouldn't help us."

"Please—the child," Luis-Win said. The word came to his lips with such difficulty that Singer thought this might be the first and last time Luis-Win had ever said please.

"Let me take care of this," Singer said to the doctor.

He took the chairman to a small consulting room that had no one in it because it was out of the way and full of spare equipment that was no use for this emergency. Among the other furniture crowded into it was a bed and a chair.

Singer closed the door behind him. The way the child's arm had flopped out of the protective blanket when Luis-Win coughed had already told him that it was too late. He folded the blanket back from the boy's white face and felt for a pulse. The skin was cold in spite of the blanket.

"He's dead."

"Then revive him! Why do you think I brought him to the hospital?"

"It's too late," Singer said gently. "He's been gone a long time already. Nothing I can do."

"This is my grandson," Luis-Win said, as if that could make a difference. "I told my son when he died that I'd make sure the boy was taken care of."

Luis-Win laid his burden down on the table. Singer saw how

reluctantly his arms loosened their hold. It was hard for him to part from that beloved weight, never to take it up again. Singer ached with the blind pain in the Nupi leader. One week earlier, one day, Luis-Win would have been an enemy to be hated, but that pain was spreading through him like a crack in stone. He was no longer invulnerable.

He raised his head and cried out in anguish. "The greenshits did this to us! The Consorso! I'll see them dead and buried, I'll pull down the sky on them!"

"It was not the Consorso," Singer said.

Luis-Win noticed Singer for the first time, suspicion flaring in his eyes. "Who, then?" His hand moved toward a hidden weapon.

Singer listened for the knowledge from Gero's memories.

"You gave the order yourself, Mr. Chairman, though maybe you have forgotten. It was under something called Research 9.4, I think. You told Captain Hazzan, the man you put in charge of supply operations in the north, to have the Somostai list for you the native diseases that might prove effective against Deltans. For use against your enemies."

Deep in Gero's memory, Singer found Delteix easier to think and pronounce. It was strange to hear his own voice speaking so coldly and cleanly of the Delh'tani's dirty secrets.

"You rescinded that order because Hazzan told you Somostai manpower was urgently needed for more important projects. You put it on hold. But it was an idea that held great power for the Somostai. Korro did not forget. He kept working on it."

Luis-Win had forgotten to protect himself. His hand sank, trembling.

"Kill him," he whispered. "Kill them all."

"Korro is dead already. He knew he was a broken tool you would throw away. He was not stupid. He was accustomed to being feared and respected—as you are. When he knew that you would throw him away, he wanted revenge, even as you wish not to die without leaving a memory behind. He left you this sickness as his curse. My friends and I killed him. I have avenged your son's son for you before he died. Will you thank me?"

Luis-Win could hardly hold himself upright. Singer tasted the bad taste in his mouth, the heat that dried his lips.

"Who are you? What do you want here?" Luis-Win whispered.

"I am one of the hidden people. One of those you made the agreement to destroy. You killed our children, too.

"I want the same as you. I want my people to live. There's only one way for us: The war has to stop. Both sides have to accept our existence, stop using us as counters in their game. I want you to call North Fork. I want you to negotiate a truce."

"I will not beg." Luis-Win spit out the words. "I ask nothing from the greenshits. If they had not driven us into this condition, we would never have had to deal with the natives. Without the Consorso this would not have happened. We will not die quietly and get out of their way. They will be punished, enough to remember it till the next ship comes. And then our people will finish the job. We'll have peace then, when this world is wiped clean."

Singer saw it again, clearer, stronger: the fire that could eat worlds. Luis-Win was willing to die if he knew his enemies would burn afterward.

Singer spun around with his back to the Nupi to master his anger; when he turned again, he was not angry. He reached out and touched Luis-Win for the first time.

"That won't help," he said wearily. "I used to think like you. I've had my bellyful of revenge now. You won't be here to see it. No one will praise you. You'll be bones in a heap, under the ruins of your city, and the child's bones will be scattered there, too, with no name on them. Foxes will tear and eat that flesh that was so dear to you. Is that what you want?"

"I want to go back," Luis-Win cried, and bit his lip in rage. He had not meant to show any weakness.

"Sit down, Mr. Chairman. You are tired." Singer helped him to the only chair and sat himself on the floor beside him. "I want to show you something," he said.

The chairman's mounting fever thinned the wall between his inner and outer vision and made it easier for Singer to touch his mind.

"It is dark outside," Singer said softly. "It is dark on the road. There is no way back. I see a way for you, ahead. It is a hard way, but in the end there's a city where your people live and are happy, where the dead sleep and are not forgotten. There is time there, time for other children to be born, time to grieve, time to remember."

"He's dead," Luis-Win said. The child came so strongly into his mind that tears were torn from Singer's eyes. He saw how good the boy had been—as good as any child that died in the blackened snow at Erech Tolanh. "What's the good?"

"Maybe they have another life somewhere, and if that is so,

will he come to you as he used to do, or will he turn from the blood on your hands even there? Revenge is not a gift to offer someone you loved. Even if there is no other life, they live in us. We have to keep our hearts clean for them so the memory can stay. Too many cruel things, too many ugly things, and they leave us.''

He was talking to himself as much as to the Nupi. In such close proximity to Luis-Win, he could feel how far the sickness had burned into the chairman, like a fire eating away the structure of a building while the outer shell still stood. It might already be too late. Luis-Win was no longer capable of rational decision.

''Mr. Chairman, please come with me. You need help.''

Luis-Win waved him away, the gesture of one accustomed to command. ''Leave me with him. I'll come when I'm ready. Leave me.''

His hand dropped to his lap. He was drifting into the heavy sleep of sick men. None of his dreams touched on the failing city. He wandered, searching for the dead boy, following after him.

Singer rose, and Luis-Win did not stir. Singer stood looking down on him for a moment, then left the room and closed the door softly after him. He went to look for Hazzan.

Saldivar had taken Hazzan into the back hall, away from the chairman and the NPU troops. They had squeezed uncomfortably into a doorway to stay out of the way of the medical staff. The floor of the hall was carpeted with sick people.

''I don't think he will make it,'' Singer said to Hazzan.

''Who?'' But Hazzan knew who he was talking about.

''The chairman. He is an old man. He does not have the strength for these changes.''

Despair showed in Hazzan's face. ''Without him we're lost. He's been our leader for twenty years. I know the other senior officers. They're used to standing in his shadow. There's no one who can make these decisions. You've got to save him!''

Singer kept his face very straight. He did not want Hazzan to see what he saw: the old man left alone to journey farther and farther out of reach.

''Since we came to Solidari, have you seen anyone who outranks you and is still walking?''

Hazzan's eyes held the look of a rabbit that saw the fox, but too late. ''What are you getting at?''

''Answer the question.''

''No, but there could be someone. Luis-Win had taken most

of the senior men and their families into quarantine, hoping they'd remain safe from contagion. It looks as if most of them have been flushed out, but there could be someone still alive who hasn't come in to the hospital yet.''

"You are a man who respects numbers and the futures they cast. How likely is that?''

"Not very.''

"Someone has to be in charge here.''

"It's not up to me to decide.''

"You see what's happening. No rescue teams, no one taking stock of food and fuel, no one assigning jobs so the most important work gets done. The hospital is the only thing in Solidari that works.''

"You don't understand,'' Hazzan said. He sounded as if he were pleading against a death sentence. "I am afraid to touch it. I don't trust my own judgment. What we did in the Iron City—''

He stood in the doorway and pressed against the jamb to stop the trembling of his hands. "I'm not a politician. I wanted to build something. Look what I made! A death machine. How can I ever trust myself again?''

"No one here has clean hands, if it comes to that,'' Singer said gently. "But we're still alive and we have work to do. Planning, fixing, building—you can do all those things. Solidari will need rebuilding when this is over.''

Hazzan sat down in the doorway and put his head in his hands. "When it's over? Will it ever be over?''

Singer touched him and knew it would be best not to press him then.

"I need to talk to Makho,'' he said to Saldivar. "Come outside.''

4

They breathed deeply in the relief of cold air and clean darkness. They walked out to the center of the smooth pavement to get as much space between themselves and the walls of buildings as they could and hunkered down in the moonshadow of the vito. Singer looked for stars, but in the lowlands, so near the coast, clouds covered the sky.

Turning back to earth, he tasted the bitter foam of Saldivar's wish for some Delh'tani beer. He smiled, and it felt strange, as if his face had not done that in a long time.

Chah, he corrected Palha. *Cold, clear, biting, eye-stinging chah.*

"I want to mellow out, not freeze-dry my brain," Palha said. "I'm not much good as backup for you here," he added. "I've been thinking about this. I don't know anything about peace. Nothing about healing. Talking to people."

Singer felt him wishing again for a beer, for a smoke, and moved closer.

"You help," he said. He leaned into the ease and strength of Palha's presence and let him feel how good it was: like walking off the hard road onto green turf; like a fresh wind, plenty of air; like a patch of sunlight on a cold day; like a mouthful of warm bread to a hungry man. Singer rested there for a minute, then moved on, seeking Kruger. It was getting easier. He managed to find the Asharya without having to wake up Roishe.

Makho had been asleep. At first he tried to incorporate Singer into his dream and go on sleeping, but Singer insisted, and he woke up.

I can't get used to this, he grumbled. Then he woke up enough to be alarmed. *What's the matter?*

His mouth tasted bad, his eyelids were stuck together, and his joints ached. Singer thought, from within Makho's dreams, that it did not feel good to be old.

I hope you didn't wake me up just to commiserate with my extreme age and decrepitude, Kruger said. There was a bite in his voice, and Singer saw, out of the corner of his eye, the young Kruger disappearing into the deep green tangle of his dreams, young and wild as the beasts that haunted them. He wanted to follow, but the dream vanished like water through sand and left him with an almost physical shock.

~~**Somebody**~~, *boy, you have the strangest manners,* Kruger said, but shared sadness gentled his voice, as if he knew already what Singer had come to tell him. *What is it, then?*

Singer took the burden of the night and unpacked it, spilling out the worst before Kruger and hearing him groan as he saw and felt and smelled it.

He saved the hardest thing for the last: the dead boy and the struggle with Luis-Win.

Luis-Win. Good God.

Kruger was still in the dark. It was easier for him to talk to Singer when he was not confronted by the fact of his absence. Singer felt him salute in the dark.

I could not change his mind, Makho. I think he's dying.

He felt another touch in the dark, an unmistakable greeting—Hilurin.

Killing a man is easy compared to changing his mind, Hilurin said.

Singer ached with confusion. *I thought I was tired of war, Lurya. This peace is worse. My enemies have faces. They enter into my heart as I contend against them. Now I know what you endured all those years—living in Korro's house, singing for his princes. But I do not know how you endured it.*

Hilurin's touch was as warm as a hand on the shoulder. *I told you long ago that one gets scars in this game as in any other. This is not peace. This is war by other means. If we succeed, perhaps, some day, we will see peace. Perhaps. Peace—that would be a new thing.*

Singer felt the longing in those two old warriors, the wish for peace as a condition they could only imagine, having never in their lives experienced it. He thought that for himself life with the Riders had been all the peace he needed. Their summer wars

had been an acceptable part of life, hardship that made survival
all the sweeter. He knew that since he had been a boy. For those
who understood the situation, for those who accepted the responsibility, there was never any peace.

Where are you now? he asked.

In the dark, they answered in unison, and snorted with laughter, even as Kruger began to send him a detailed view of the
day's journey, cross-checked by Hilurin. Singer recognized the
terrain only from the map. He had never seen the place.

*Keep moving toward the closest camp but take care. You must
give me time to get to the Blue Zone. I still have hope that I can
make arrangements here for you to take the prisoners without a
fight.*

He embraced them both and returned to the smell of oil on
pavement, to Palha and the lights of the hospital waiting. The
pull of all that needed doing inside dragged at him like a strong
current. He yielded to it and felt the need draw answering
strength from him.

I lived in the shadow of the old ones' strength all my life, he
thought. Now I have the power to make them a gift—buy peace
with the lives of my enemies.

Standing over his last patient, he stretched and came back to
full awareness of himself for the first time in hours.

Dr. Nasri touched his shoulder. "Rest," she urged. "You
and your friends can take a couple of hours to sleep. We can
carry it from here."

There was something else he needed more. He looked around
vaguely and did not find it. He held the image lovingly in mind
and waited till he felt one of the sleepers rise to it like a fish
rising to bait. Somewhere there was a storage room where busy
medikhani had dumped the baggage people had brought with
them when they had trekked to the hospital. He slipped out into
the corridor and began opening doors. It could not be far away,
for the medikhani had no time or patience to carry bundles more
than a few steps.

The right door was blocked open by a well-worn backpack
and a pair of muddy boots. A heap of cast-aside possessions
spilled over the floor of the small room: threadbare jackets,
plastic bottles half-full of water, baby slings—whatever sick and
frightened people had snatched up to help them to their destination. Singer rummaged.

"What are you looking for?" Palha asked, then answered his

own question by following Singer's line of thought. It forced a
smile from him. "You're nuts—but that looks like a case in the
corner under the red bag."

He dragged out the stained green plastic box and opened it.
Singer lifted out and lovingly examined the guitar inside. It was
handmade from wood and strung with steel and gut, not one of
the battery-powered electronics. The range and versatility were
less, but it warmed in his hands like a thamla as he tuned it.

Janet, Lyn, Genady, and half the other medikhani from the
hospital had stretched out in the corridor just off the big room,
with coats and ponchos to keep them off the cold floor. There
was no bedding to spare, but they were too tired to care. Singer
found a place in the corner and slipped into the music as the
others slipped into sleep. He was too tired to create a lament
for all he had seen that day. He took what came to him out of
their dreams, worn and piecemeal, and played it back to them
alive and fresh. He slipped the sorrow from their hearts as he
would have eased some treasure from the clenched hand of a
sleeping child. Nasri had ordered the doors propped open to let
in the cool night air, and he sang its freshness into the music.
He rode the gentle wind back and back till it seemed he was
with his *beshani* again, listening as a girl whose bones were
ashes now sang him to sleep on his first night in the Rock. In
their dreams they shared one sleeping place, one hearth, and the
dream had become part of them like all their other memories.
They would never entirely forget. They would find elusive music
on their minds long after they awoke.

> Every day a new sun
> In the sky
> New light
> In the new child's eye
> In the hearth,
> New flame
> New day, new name
> New bread,
> Warm and sweet
> New grass
> The new colts eat
> New dance, new game
> Wind tells a new name
> You will wake in a new skin
> A new song will begin

Fold away the old
When the old is done
Every day a new sun.

The sleepers breathed easy, their fever ebbing. Singer felt the
dawn coming, and his hands rested quietly on the strings. The
last verse he sang, in a whisper, held the names of the lost
children, all those he remembered. They would sleep in the
minds of all who were there that night, like grass seeds blown
far from the plains. They might be silent in the dark, or they
might spring up again unforeseen. He had scattered them. It
was the best he could do.

He caught Zhanne looking at him.

"What's the matter?" she asked.

"I felt him die as I was singing. Luis-Win. Maybe I could
have kept him alive. Changed his mind. Maybe."

"You can't start thinking like that," she said sadly. "I do it
all the time. Maybe I should have treated that one first. Maybe
if I'd gone to surgery sooner. Maybe if I hadn't tried the surgery
at all. Start thinking those things and you get paralysis. You
make the decision and go on."

5

He slept till midmorning, until he was awakened by a change
in the sounds around him. He heard a murmur of voices. The
first batch of patients they had dosed were feeling well enough
to sit up and ask what had happened. The hospital was more
crowded than ever, for Lyn and one or two other pilots who
were well enough had been flying out into the city and its surroundings, collecting more desperately sick people. The con-

valescents were not yet well enough to be left on their own. Some of them had been moved out into houses and offices near the hospital, with paras to look after them, but many of them still remained in the emergency ward. Fueled by hope, the doctors drove on, working harder than ever.

Singer asked for Hazzan and found that he had cleared out an office for himself and was hard at work, planning and organizing the tasks that were being done.

"So you were right about Luis-Win," he said.

"You're thinking I had something to do with that," Singer said. "Why don't you ask me? I didn't. I could have tried harder to help him get well, but in truth I don't think he wanted to. He taught Korro how to kill his grandson. That made him sad."

"Name of God, you're cold."

Singer shrugged. He did not say "I don't care what you think of me," but Hazzan reddened, anyway.

"All right, you saved my life," Hazzan said. "Why me and not him? I'm not your tool. I won't be remembered as the man who sold us out."

Singer was tired of standing in front of the desk. He sat down cross-legged on top of it. "The Consorso bombed my home. They killed everyone I knew. Why should I sell you out for their benefit? I don't like either of you."

"Then what do you want?"

"I want to save what little I have left, not throw the rest of it down the same hole. Look around you! Can't you understand that? Talk to them. It's all I'm asking you."

"How the hell can I talk to them? What am I going to say? The minute they know or guess our situation, they'll send an army of occupation to crush us. I have been working on this all morning. Right now we don't have the resources to mount any kind of defense. We can destroy them totally from orbit, and then their orbiter will do the same to us. If I let them have even a sniff of the predicament I'm in, that is the choice I'll end up with: bend over for the tire tracks or initiate the destruction of every Deltan on Nuvospera."

"And if you won't negotiate? What kind of world will be left for them—the ones who survive this sickness? They'll be dying of cold and hunger soon, like the farmers in the Iron City. You need help from the Blue Zone or you'll be eating roots and bark like the wild animals."

Hazzan lowered his head into his hands and groaned. "Do

you have an option to offer me, or did you come here to torture me?''

"I learned something from the Somostai," Singer said. "Knowledge is the sharpest sword. You have knowledge they want. You can give them Korro's records in return for their help.''

"I don't have Korro's records.''

"Jon and Zhanne brought a sample along for you to use in bargaining. The rest are in a safe place in Erech Tolanh. Bone can tell you where. Only Zhanne says she wants first option on working with the data when you make the agreement.''

Hazzan stared at him.

"I will tell you something else. The Consorso needs peace as badly as you do. Their chief of security is dead, as you may have heard. General Nymann and most of his staff died at the same time. Their military high command is now in the hands of a colonel—someone like you. Their airfield is seriously damaged, and many of their military aircraft destroyed. They need a truce, though they won't ask for it. Offer them something they want and I think they will deal.''

Hazzan wavered but finally shook his head. "No. They won't be content with information. They'll want guarantees. I will not concede anything touching our sovereignty.''

"You can make a gesture of good faith that won't cost you anything.''

"How?''

"Kruger has gone to find the camps where lost Consorso soldiers are being held prisoner. Give the order for those men to be turned over to him without a fight. Release of prisoners would show good intentions.''

"I don't know how to contact such a place. I do not even know that they exist.''

"Ah, but I do. Give me and Zhanne a little time with your magic mirror and I can show you every secret in Solidari.''

"Assuming that is true and they really exist, what would Kruger do with the prisoners?''

"Take them down to North Fork and let their own people care for them. You can't feed them, anyway. If you let them die in prison, the Blue Zone will never forgive you. Turn them loose— it puts an extra burden on Consorso resources and makes you look good. And it wins you my goodwill. When I go to North Fork to see the civilian governor, I will have a good feeling for you that he will surely see.''

Hazzan shook his head again slowly. "I thought I heard Korro say that Riders don't deal. No. I won't beg. I won't go to them first. But you get the governor to call me, and I'll talk to him. I will do that much."

"Done. And one more thing I need: transportation to somewhere near the Blue Zone. We don't have time to walk."

Singer gathered his team together as he waited for Hazzan to arrange a flight. Janet consented reluctantly to leave, since the immediate emergency was over.

"There are other medikhani here," Singer said to her. "I need you with me, to carry news of the epidemic to the ones in the Blue Zone, so they will put pressure on the government to stop fighting and look for a cure."

Janet screwed up her face in distaste till she looked like one of the children they had recently been dosing with green medicine.

"Petersen," she said. "My old chief of medicine. That's who you'd be dealing with. Surely you remember him. He's the one who had you tubed, tied, and sedated in Jefferson. He's the one who bared his backside for the Net and turned you over to them for interrogation. You were my patient, Hospitals are for healing people. He let them torture you. You want me to ask him for help now? You must be joking."

Singer touched her gently. "I honor your anger. It saved my life. But he tried to save my life, too, in his own way. It's true the Net pushed him, and he bent. Still, I owe him something, and we need his help now. Push him the other way. See what happens."

Janet butted her head against his chest as if against a wall. "Back when you were totally unreasonable, I could at least argue with you. All right, I'll try it your way."

Jon burst into the room, followed by Genady. "I heard you were leaving for the Blue Zone. I'm going with you. Listen: I can help. I know some people."

Once Singer would not have known what Jon was talking about, but with his new memories, he understood. "You mean you have contacts with the antis," he said.

Jon looked startled, but hurried on. "If you want to put it that way. I didn't say anything earlier. I didn't know how far to trust you—or Marcus. I'm not used to thinking of a military officer as a friend. I had to be careful, dakko?"

Singer waited patiently.

"Anyway, there are people in communications. We had a plan for taking control of the system—if we'd ever had any good news to flash. And some of those friends have more contacts, people they wouldn't introduce me to because they said I was too exposed. They'd pass your news on for you, maybe to people who could help more."

Faces rose involuntarily in Jon's mind, and Singer checked them against the Gero-memories. He was interested to see that several of them had been considered completely reliable. "You'll have to get rid of Jaramillo," he said without thinking. "He was working for us."

Jon looked at him and turned a shade paler. *Us?*

Singer shrugged. "It's confusing sometimes. I don't want it, but I'm going to use it. Don't worry. I know what I'm doing. One thing I need from this mind is a way to reach the civilian governor. If it's true, as Jon says, that he is now in charge, then he would be the only man with authority to do what I need: end the rule of the soldiers and begin to talk peace. Gero did not trust him. Gero always suspected him of being secretly in touch with those people who opposed martial law and wanted to limit the power of the Net—antis, like those friends of Jon. Still, the governor never acted openly to oppose the military commanders. I must see him before I can know. I have his codes. I know how to contact him. I don't know if he will speak to me."

"That's where Genya can help," Jon said, trying to push Genady forward. "He knows Vitek."

Genady looked embarrassed. "There aren't many Slavas in the colony. We all know each other. 'Tight as ticks,' I think, is what they say about us. We're all more or less related to each other. Calling Governor Karoly 'Uncle Vitek' started with us, I think. He and my father had been friends at school, and when my parents were killed, he took an interest. He'd send me money on my birthday and have breakfast with me occasionally, to see how I was doing."

"What did you think of him?"

"I liked him—at breakfast, anyway. He offered me a job, once. When it was time for my military service, he said he could get me a special placement—make me one of those boys in the meteorology platoon, the ones with the locked briefs full of photos and the tightly gasketed assholes. I wanted to be an astronomer like my father and stay away from politics, so I said no. I knew I'd been ~~that sure~~ stupid as soon as the shooting started."

"Why didn't you say before?"

"It's habit. I tried hard not to use that connection, because I didn't approve of what he was doing. I don't know the man well enough to be much use to you, anyway."

"You could front for us, though," Jon said. His words tumbled over each other, as always when his thoughts were racing. "If Vitek is being watched by the Net, maybe he can't just call Singer in and interview him. But he could have breakfast with you again without alarming anyone."

"I met his chief of security a few times," Genady said. "He's another Slava, a man named Lavrens Tausis. I never could tell which side he was buttered on, though he and his jefe seemed pretty tight."

"Tausis," Singer repeated thoughtfully. A feeling of distaste came with the word. Tausis had been an obstacle in Gero's way, but Singer could not tell if he had been so out of active opposition, out of loyalty to the governor, or out of loyalty to himself and his own territory. At any rate, he had not been in Gero's pay.

"If nothing else, I could talk to other Slavas," Genady offered. "I know the family connections."

Singer nodded. "Yes, come with us."

With Lyn and Saldivar, that made as big a team as he cared to slide past the border outposts. Numbers would not help with what he planned to do.

6

Their pilot set them down in a sandy blowout amid thorn scrub and dry grass at the eastern edge of the Open Zone. She had been curious about their destination but glad enough to take off once they disembarked. The border looked empty, but it was never safe. Jon shivered as he looked around, though the wind was already several degrees warmer than it had been on the coast.

"This landscape is depressingly familiar," he said. "If I haven't been here before, it was somewhere just like it."

"Out of the wire and into the briers," Saldivar said, shrugging his shoulder to feel the reassuring weight of his rifle against the strap.

"Now what? Are we walking to Jefferson?" Lyn said.

"Not yet." Singer smoothed the sand at his feet and drew a map with a stick. "There was a firebase not far from here. You remember, Palha? They picked us up after we came in from the Dust with Makho."

"I'm not likely to forget."

"Maybe they'll remember us, too."

"If we walk out of the Open Zone, they'll smoke us off before they stop to find out who we are," Jon protested.

"Can't smoke us if they don't see us," Singer said.

"This is not a game," Jon said. "They have weapons! We got away from the Somostai and the Nupis and now you're going to get us shot by our own people."

Singer's eyes gleamed with anticipatory pleasure. "This is a game. The weapons make it better."

Janet shoved Jon surreptitiously. "Relax, J.L. Old age is making you querulous. Look, if you wanted your gallbladder removed, you'd have to trust me. I'd have fun doing it, too. That's my game. Negotiating armed men and minefields with a whole skin, that's Singer's game. Smooth out."

Singer continued as if he had not been interrupted. "We'll go southeast and get as close as we can to the firebase before evening. Then we'll find cover for you to sleep in, and I'll go in and talk to the Delh'tani. I'll call you in when it's safe."

They fell into a squad pattern as if they had always traveled that way: Singer leading, Saldivar bringing up the rear, with Lyn and Genady watching right and left and Janet and Jon in the middle, carrying most of the baggage. Singer led them on a route that wound around the edges of dunes and sandhills, avoiding the crests and concealing their footprints in the shadows. By evening they were closing on a line of broken buttes that rose up to a higher plateau. Singer paused to sniff the air. The wind was blowing up from the heated sand toward the cooler air above. Nothing came down to him from the plateau. He let the others take a rest while he worked his way around the bluffs till he found a trail broken by booted feet. To Delh'tani eyes it would have been nearly invisible, but it had been used at least a handful of times.

"They're up there," he said, returning to the scrap of shade that sheltered the others. "Go on south as far as that stand of brush and set up camp when it gets dark. Do not camp near any clear trails—like that one. Do not light any fire. The smoke will rise straight up to them. They are blind and without noses, but the Dust teaches some lessons even to Delh'tani."

"And what will you be doing under the nonexistent noses of these Delh'tani?" Lyn demanded.

"When plenty of shadows are hanging on the thorns, Palha and I will go up and pay the soldiers a visit—see if they remember us."

"The two of you against the whole firebase?"

Singer shrugged. "No fighting. I'll just go quietly in and take a look at them. If they seem friendly, we'll talk. Do not move from here till I send them down to you."

They concealed themselves under the eaves of a thorn thicket. They still had plenty of water for the night, and Singer assured them that they would be riding down to Jefferson before they needed more. He worked the sand into a comfortable depression and dozed while they set up camp.

When the sunset wind had died away and the shadows were gathering, Singer took Palha and climbed the bluff. Singer smelled it before he saw it: fuel for the machines, smoke from the guns, and the strange nose-wrinkling perfumes of a dozen kinds of not-metal and not-cloth. The camp smelled of sweat and shit like any camp of armed men, but those natural, familiar scents were drowned by the warning stranger smells.

The camp was laid out in a familiar form, much like the one where Singer had lived with the Mobile Force when he had been a soldier for the Delh'tani. The airfield stretched out eastward, with the camp built at the edge of the plateau and a line of lights and fences defending it. They crept in from the far side until they could not go any farther without stepping into the light.

I want you to stay here and watch for me. Tell me if you see them moving. Don't get into any trouble. Run away if you have to, but don't fight. He could feel Saldivar stubbornly opposing him. *Don't you trust me, andri?*

Of course I trust you! The answer was fierce and solid as a fist.

Then wait for me. Believe I can get out of this without blood. Believe and hold back your hand.

Saldivar reached forward without ruffling the sand, found Singer's arm, and gripped it. *Don't let me down.*

Singer waited on the edge of the light, listening before he proceeded. It was hard to see the guards in the darkness behind the spotlights. He picked them out eventually by tiny shiftings in sand and shadow and then reached out for their breath and heartbeat and for the small, ever-changing perceptions and traces of thought that rose from them like body heat. Once he had them placed in his mind, he eased back into contact with Saldivar. He had to keep Palha's perceptions at some distance as he juggled his awareness of the guards, but he knew that Palha would alert him if anything dangerous happened behind his back. He slid forward, belly down, making no more sound than a snake.

Knowing the position of each guard, he found a way to slip through their overlapping fields of vision, as he would have slipped through a minefield. Once he sensed alertness and alarm and let himself sink limp and still against the sand, so flat that he could feel the wind piling miniature rills of sand against his back, beginning to bury him. The guard's attention shifted, his alarm subsided into boredom, and Singer moved swiftly to the next line of shadow.

Close in to the fence he could move more easily, for the guards had their eyes on the distance. The boundary was marked by the usual rolls of Delh'tani wire with sharp edges. He found a place where drifting sand had forced the coils apart slightly and jack-knifed himself neatly through the narrow gap. One arm brushed the edge of the wire below his sleeve, and the sting told him he was cut. He froze for a moment just inside the fence, pressing his hand against the cut till the skin had healed over. Checking Palha's sight for any sign that he had been perceived, he withdrew delicately from his watch on the guards and reached into the camp ahead to find anyone who was waking there. He was searching for an alert mind that would give him some clue to where the base commander lived. He found nothing definite but made a guess based on the camp layout and moved on toward the tents.

There were too many people still awake, so he found a pool of shadow behind a tent fly and waited till voices and movement had died down. That gave him a chance to watch the pattern of comings and goings. He noticed several tents that were better sited than others and surrounded by deck boards and railings. Officers came and went from all of them, but there was one tent where they stopped and saluted before entering. He watched patiently. Soldiers went into the other tents and did not come out. One by one the lights went out inside. In the one tent he had selected, all who went in came out again. He kept count. It was a long time before that light went out. Singer waited still longer before he moved. He waited till all the minds he could reach had relaxed into sleep and he could feel their dreams coming and going softly like the shifting breeze that came up from the desert.

At last he moved. As he crept toward the tent, he brushed the fringes of the inhabitant's dreams and linked himself into them so that he would know if any alarm penetrated the Delh'tani's sleep. The dreams were familiar. The stranger dreamed that he was moving through debated territory. The grass was a lush, lowland green like nothing in the northern plains, and the great trees reminded Singer of those he had seen in Palha's memories. The formation was familiar, however, and the uniforms, and the fear. Singer sent an image of himself to fall into line with the others, and the Delh'tani commander accepted him without question. The commander turned in his sleep, and Singer reached the back wall of the tent.

As he had hoped, the tent was open at both ends to let the wind blow through. He could see the sleeping man inside through the mesh that kept insects away. He ran his thumb and finger down the seam, unsealing it, stepped inside, and dropped noiselessly to the floor. The sleeper stirred at the touch of the cooler air that came through the opening, but if he was aware of Singer at all, he thought Singer was something he was still dreaming. Singer reached up and resealed the tent, then composed himself to wait.

I'm here, he said to Saldivar, and showed him the tent.

Great, and what happens when they find out you're there?

Saldivar was not happy. In his mind were pictures of Singer's torn body sprawled on the sand. Singer tried to erase them, but they would not go away.

If they try anything, then I will find out if I really can move faster than humanly possible.

Saldivar was quiet. Singer knew he was thinking about the moment when Singer had leapt to rescue Jon in the furnace shed and, farther back, the day they had all left North Fork together.

You were there, and then you were—somewhere else, Saldivar said finally. For the first time Singer saw what it looked like to someone else. He seemed to flicker, as if the observer had blinked without meaning to. The watcher's eye and mind immediately denied what they had seen. *When Lyn's vito was going down that time in North Fork—you moved us all from one place to another, like that. I was there, but I still can't believe it happened.*

I don't know how *it happened,* Singer said. *I do it, but I don't know how I do it, and that makes me afraid. Very much afraid. If this can happen, then the world is not the way I thought. I was in fear of my life when I did that. I have never tried it with a cold mind. It is like a jump into the dark. That is why I don't want to speak of it. I don't want anyone thinking that way—that I can get them out of trouble—because in truth I don't know if I can. I might kill us all next time.*

Hey, I feel better already, Saldivar said dryly.

I promise you one thing—if the Delh'tani try to shoot me, I will be somewhere else, by whatever way is quickest. So don't worry.

7

Dawn was coming. Singer heard birds beginning to stir in the brush on the far side of the camp, beyond the wire. His muscles were stiff with enforced stillness. He glanced down at the sleeper and was able to discern his face as a dim, pale oval. The man stirred and reached for his blanket. Singer felt the dream breaking up and fading out of sight. Just before the sleeper opened his eyes, Singer held up his hands, palms out, so the Delh'tani would see that he held no weapons. He heard a gasp as the man fumbled for his handgun. All traces of sleep were gone, and the Delh'tani's thoughts were racing like his heart.

"My name is Singer," he said softly. "I was with Marcus Kruger's Mobile Force. I'm here to ask a favor, not to cause trouble."

He could hear the tumult in the other man's mind.

Some crazy humper—relief that Singer was something familiar—*he could be dangerous*—*Kruger?!* *But Mack's been dead since last year*—and a shiver fleeting across the man's bare shoulders—*could he be*—

"Excuse me, but I'm not a ghost and not an assassin. I wish you'd lower the gun. Makes me jumpy."

By the quick back-and-forth movement of the man's head, Singer guessed that he wanted to make a light but not put away the gun.

"Tell me where the light is. I'll get it."

"Uh—just above the shelf to your right."

Singer's hand brushed smooth metal, and light bloomed out.

"I don't know your name, but I remember your face," Singer said. He was pleased that he had been right. "You gave us a ride back from the desert—what was left of us. You remember? You weren't a captain then."

"I remember that," the man said evenly. "You want to tell me what you're doing in my rack?"

"It's a long story." Singer lowered his hands and stretched his legs into a more comfortable position. "First of all, he's not dead."

"Kruger?"

"That's right."

"How do you figure that? He was poisoned by thornkiller— autoimmune reaction. Half his force died of it. He died in the ~~cooling~~ hospital—how could there be any mistake about it? Doctors aren't good for much, but they have been known to tell the living from the dead."

"He was supposed to die, but he got better instead. He was in trouble with the Net—he said they knew the location of prison camps holding our men. They said that was a lie and further- more it was restricted information. He had to run for it. So the Net put it out that he had died."

"Where is he now?"

Singer pointed with his chin. "Northwest. We liberated one camp already. He's working on the others."

"It was true, then," the commander said slowly.

"Yes, it was true. I was with him."

"That doesn't explain what you're doing here."

"He wants to bring the prisoners home. But they aren't supposed to exist, and he's been declared dead by the Net. They don't like to be wrong. He has to bring them down through the zone, and he could easily be fired on by anyone who saw him. He might need help transporting them if there are casualties. That's half of what I'm doing here. Someone had to know that he was coming, know to ask questions before shooting. You are the outpost closest to the route he'll probably take."

"Why did you hide out in my tent to tell me this?"

"Think about it. If I walk up from the Dust, I'm almost sure to be seen. Then either your people smoke me or I kill some of them. And then you're not my friend. This was the only way I could think of to come straight to you without making trouble."

"How did you do it?" the commander asked suddenly, as if he could no longer resist his curiosity.

"Crawled over the wire. Walked in."

"That's impossible."

Singer shrugged. "You could look for my tracks. They're probably gone by now, though. The wind was blowing all night."

Kruger's troops had been legendary as scouts and trackers, but it was hard for the commander to believe that even one of them could have eluded his security.

"One more favor I need. Five of my friends are camping down below. We walked out of the zone, but we can't walk all the way to Jefferson. Can we catch a ride down?"

"Friends of yours," the commander said, shaking his head. "This I've got to see." He started to put away the gun, then snapped the barrel up again. "I don't suppose you have any identification on you?" he asked.

"Nothing."

I should have him arrested, Singer heard him thinking. *Why do I believe him? Why does he seem so familiar?*

Someone rapped on the tent post and unsealed the front flap. It was daylight outside. A soldier entered.

"Sir, I—" He noticed Singer. "Excuse me, I didn't know you were with someone—"

He saw the gun and froze.

The commander rose out of bed and handed the gun to the soldier. "Mays, search this man and keep him under guard while I dress."

He stepped out the back of the tent, and Singer heard water splashing.

The soldier patted Singer down one-handed. Singer thought he could easily have held out a weapon if he had wanted to, but he had chosen to come unarmed, and Mays found nothing. Mays stood awkwardly pointing the gun in Singer's direction while Singer amused himself by working out several ways he could have taken him had it been necessary. He then tried to find ways of disarming the man without hurting him. That was more of a challenge.

The captain came back with wet hair and a smooth chin. He put on his uniform hastily, as if repossessing his authority.

"He's unarmed, sir," the soldier reported.

"Mays, do we have anyone here who used to be with the Mobile Force?"

"Slovo, sir—he's a cook."

"Go get him."

The captain took back his gun and sat down. He kept the gun in his hand but let it lie across his knee instead of pointing it at Singer.

"Make yourself comfortable. At ease."

He looked at Singer curiously. "Are you still in the Forces? Do you consider yourself under orders?"

"I'm supposed to be dead. Don't know what's the protocol for dead soldiers. Do we still have to salute?" He laughed. "I serve my Con-el. I'll cooperate with you. I haven't saluted anyone in a long time."

Mays came back with a thickset man in a T-shirt.

"Step outside," the captain said to Singer, motioning with the gun.

As Singer came out into the early sun, the thickset man's eyes widened.

"Do you recognize this man?" the captain asked.

"Sure. That's Mack's eyes and ears—I mean, he was Colonel Kruger's security liaison." His finger went unconsciously to his own face in a gesture Singer recognized, tracing the path of a vanished scar.

"Are you sure this is the same man?"

"Yes, sir. There aren't two like him. But—Singer had a scar. How'd you lose that?"

Singer smiled. "A very good surgeon."

Slovo smiled, too. "That's his voice. You couldn't fake it, sir.

Have him sing something. You'll understand." His face clouded slightly. "Is he in some kind of trouble?"

"You can get back to fixing breakfast," the commander said. "Dismissed."

The soldier walked off reluctantly, trailing behind him a cloud of doubt. *Where the hell did he come from? Did I get him in trouble?*

"Thanks, cofra," Singer called after him.

The commander realized he was still holding the gun and put it away. "You put me in a difficult position, Mr. Singer—if that really is your name. You're asking me for some very irregular actions—on the word of a shadow."

"Your decision," Singer said calmly.

"I want to see these friends of yours. I'll send a party for them. And there's a world of vicious shit waiting for you if you lead them into trouble."

Singer summoned Saldivar out of the sand on the way to the plateau's edge. The soldiers' faces registered shock and disgust when he appeared out of nowhere, inside their perimeter.

"Damn, I heard Kruger's people were good, but this is spooky," one of them muttered.

The others were still waiting where they had been told. Singer spotted a bit of fabric carelessly unconcealed, but the soldiers had to be told where they were. Even Genady was improving, Singer thought with satisfaction. He would make a Rider someday—but they were going back to the city. The soldiers were even more amazed when they came out of the brush, shouldering their packs.

The captain showed surprise, too. Maybe he had believed Singer in theory, but he had not really imagined the appearance of a whole squad of total strangers. He found it hard to take when Janet introduced herself as a doctor. She was still hollow-eyed and bone-thin, nearly swimming in a big coat sewn out of blankets. She had cut her hair in grief for her patients who had died in the final attack, and it hung in dark hanks around her pale cheeks. She did not wait for the captain's disbelief to subside. Sticking out her chin, she demanded to see the base medical officer.

After a talk with her, the medical officer was agitated enough to force his way into the captain's tent.

"She's a doctor, all right, there's no question about that, and if what she says is true, it is extremely important that you fly them down to the city immediately. We've been expecting something like this for years. Now it's finally here, and we aren't ready for it.''

The captain sent the rest of them out of the tent and had a talk with Janet and the doctor. He came out visibly shaken.

"Best I can do is send you to Jefferson with orders to get you a flight to North Fork from there. I don't have anything with the range to get to North Fork nonstop.''

"That'll do all right,'' Singer said. "Can we go now?''

"You're in a hurry.'' He looked off at the distant hills uneasily. "You're leaving me with some difficult decisions.''

"That's why they made you commander.''

"Do you really think he'll fly Marcus home?'' Janet asked as they rode down to Jefferson. Captain Galen had given them uniforms, money, and signed passes.

"He'll think about it,'' Singer answered. "I'm almost sure of him. More important, the word will get around now. Palha and Genady spun stories as fast as they could talk for the soldierfolk there. The stories will spread. The man named Slovo recognized me. He will tell the story of one of the Mothers come back from the dead. Someone will hear how we came in the night, unseen—ghost scouts with news of a lost army. And the bigger the story grows and the farther it walks, the more time they'll take to think before they shoot when they see Makho coming. Whatever their commander does. But I think he will help Makho. One polvorado does not turn his back on another.''

8

The captain had given them a signed request for transportation that would have allowed them to take the next available spaces on a flight from Jefferson to North Fork. Instead, they got off the truck on the dirt access road that ran past the farms toward town. People did not walk there for pleasure, but it was common enough to see small groups of soldiers hitching their way to the field to catch a flight or into town for a drink.

They passed work details of civilians coming back from their shift in the fields and were passed by truckloads of troops on their way out to the Dust. No one took any notice of them as far as they could tell.

"I thought the civilians here would look good after what I've been seeing," Janet said. "They look like prison inmates. Pale, bad skin tone. I'd like to check them all for anemia and malnutrition."

"Don't stare at them, Janney," Saldivar said. "People remember eye contact."

"What's our objective here?" she asked. "Are we trying to be seen, or not to be seen?"

Singer was so used to staying under cover that it was hard for him to walk down the middle of a paved street in daylight. With every step he felt that they were getting away with something that couldn't last. But he understood better than before how the Delh'tani did things.

"Be seen," he said. "Can't create rumors if you can't be seen and heard."

"You could walk me to the hospital and hold Petersen down for me. That would get their attention."

Singer suppressed a shudder. "I had so much trouble walking out of that place last time I was there that I prefer to stay away from it. Take us where there are people, and a phone, but no golpos."

"The Bucket," Jon suggested. "That storefront around the corner from the hospital. There was a good mix there of ducks, polvos, and civilians."

The place had damp cool air and was filled with the smell of chah. They had only a little money among them, but Janet ordered drinks for everyone and plates of fried and spiced Delh'tani food that smelled good even to Singer.

"Lighten up," Lyn said, when she saw him watching how fast her glass emptied. "Grab time to celebrate, in case we have to go back to being ghosts before the day ends."

Janet took the glasses back to the bar to be refilled. The bartender waited for her to pay before handing them back. She leaned over the bar to give him a better look at her face.

"You're hurting my feelings, Ojo! Isn't my credit good anymore? I suppose I left a small tab behind when I went missing, but I thought we were friends."

The bartender's professionally friendly expression went stone cold, and the color drained from his face. "It can't be."

"Why not? Don't tell me I've been declared dead. That would mean I don't have a tab here anymore."

He flinched as Janet reached for him, but she seized his arm and held it firmly.

"See? I'm here. And look over there. Remember how I used to come in here and drink and cry about Jon? Remember how I used to say crazy things about going out to the Dust and getting him back?"

The bartender saw Jon seated at the table. He felt for the glass he had filled for Singer and drained it himself. "Kristo! Welcome back, doctor. Where the hell have you been?"

"That's what I'm telling you. We've been out in the Dust, and beyond. We're not the only ones who are coming back. Big changes are coming. Ask Jon. He'll tell you. I have to use your phone for a minute. Just put it on my credit, since I still have it."

The bartender did not want to let her go, but she towed him over to the table where Jon was sitting and left Jon and Lyn to answer his questions. She remembered where the phone was. It had a door that shut, barely, once Singer, Janet, her backpack computer, and the beer were crammed into the booth together.

She tried calling the hospital. For a moment, she could not remember the code that had once come to her fingers without conscious thought, but slowly it came back to her. She asked for Petersen.

"He's in conference. May I leave your code for him?"

"No. Just tell him Dr. Logan called. I'll try to call back. Wait—I have some material he needs to see. Put me through to his desk."

She explained to Singer as she plugged her computer into the phone. "I can leave him the notes I got from Nasri in Solidari: the course of the epidemic, the mortality rates, and the analysis of the Somostai antibiotic, as far as they had gone with it. That should put the fear of God into him. He's going to want badly to hear from me again. I'll have to find a way to see him in person."

"Slide over and let me have the phone," Singer said. "And send me Jon and Genady."

Janet started to pack up her computer.

"Leave that; I need it."

"What do you mean? You don't know how to use this."

"I do now. The fingers are clumsy, but the mind understands."

Reluctantly she let him have it. "Take care of it. You know that's like your lending out your best sword to some amateur."

A growing crowd had gathered around the table to hear the stories Lyn and Jon were telling. Saldivar had encountered some polvorados who had once served with Kruger, and was huddled with them, speaking rapid, intense Spanya. Janet had trouble pulling Jon away. When she sat down in his place, she was immediately besieged with questions.

"Why did you interrupt me?" Jon grumbled as he and Genady squeezed into the booth with Singer. "I was just making some progress. There's a woman here who works as a tech at the communications center. She wouldn't give me the name of her contact, but she's sending for him. I found out that several of the people I used to know are in detention. Apparently Janney sent them contraband information, and some of them got caught distributing it."

"I need you here because I have to make some calls, and I want you to listen and advise me. I have many names here, and I know what Gero thought of them, but I need to know what your friends thought. Genya, you call Vitek first. That is most important."

* * *

They left The Bucket hurriedly, in the back of a trash truck, after the bartender received an anonymous call informing him that the golpos were on the way to disperse the crowd that by then had spilled out into the street, as the word spread that people missing and presumed dead had returned with tales of life beyond the Zone and news of many others returning soon. The noise made clear that the golpos were not having an easy time of it.

The truck dropped Janet, Jon, and Lyn at a prearranged rendezvous with Jon's contacts and two of Janet's friends, surgical paras who had agreed to smuggle her into the hospital to see Colonel Petersen. Singer, Saldivar, and Genady rode on out to the edge of town. Vitek's security chief had promised to send them a ride. While his eyes ceaselessly scouted the scrub at the road's edge, Singer followed Janet anxiously in his mind. He still did not trust Petersen, and he would worry until she returned to him, safe and sound.

9

Janet heard the receptionist's voice out in the hall as she sat in the chief of medicine's familiar office.

"There's a Captain Logan to see you, Colonel Petersen."

"That's impossible," Petersen said. "Completely out of the question. You've misheard the name." The loud, pompous voice had remained the same.

"She said she was sorry to have kept you waiting, so I thought you must be expecting her. Shall I tell her you're busy?"

"Never mind. I think I'd better deal with this myself."

Janet recognized Petersen's stoop-shouldered walk as he

pushed the door open impatiently. He barged into the room with his head thrust forward, his mind on something else as usual.

"Now just what do you—" His eyes focused on her, and he stopped in midspeech with his mouth slightly open. He turned pale.

"Heyo, Doug."

His hands came up involuntarily as if to ward her off. It dawned on her that he thought she was a ghost. Nothing else would explain the fact that he was not dressing her down for insubordination.

"I'm still alive," she said. "I don't know why everyone has so much trouble believing that. It's not very flattering."

"What—but—Janet!" he observed. He cleared his throat, glared at her, and started over. "Logan, get up off that desk and explain yourself!"

"I'm sorry, but that would take too long." She slid off his desk and moved to get the desk between them. He had not yet thought of calling security. He was still too surprised. She wanted to say what she had come to say and leave before he could recover.

"Remember that casualty we had words about just before I left? The one the Net wanted to take to PCOM and interrogate? He was a native, Doug. There are people living on this world already. I've seen them.

"And remember those indigenous diseases you used to worry about? I've just come from Solidari. I hope you read that memo I sent you. There's plague in Solidari, Doug. A vicious respiratory infection. They tried all the standard antibiotics, and none of them worked. We got this from the natives."

She held out the blue glass jar full of dried, shredded vegetation.

"They administer it as a tea. It cut the death rate down to about twenty percent. I think it would work better intravenously if you could isolate and synthesize the relevant compounds. They grind up the whole plant, but my opinion is that it's a fungus on the plant that really does the work. You need to start now if you want to be ready by the time the disease works its way over here. Maybe it won't hit us this time—but I'd hate to take that chance, wouldn't you? Sooner or later we will encounter it.

"We also need to send a mercy mission to Solidari. They are in pathetic condition, and those who don't snuff it from the plague will soon die of exposure and secondary infections. Nobody who calls himself a doctor could possibly see what's happening there and walk on by. Furthermore, they are an ideal test population for this antibiotic and whatever vaccines you can come up with. I can get you blood samples with antibodies, but I won't until I know that you aren't going to turn me over the way you did that casualty. Kiss ass to North Fork this time and you could be kissing it good-bye. This bug is more vicious than any shark you ever saw."

"But—" he said.

"That's your problem. You're good at politics. Use it for something. Look, Doug, just check this out and you'll see I ain't shitting you."

She shoved the jar at him so that he had to take it or let it fall to the floor. He cradled it protectively in his arms as he cradled the secret she saw in his thoughts. His heart leapt at the chance even while his mind told him this was preposterous. He wanted the possibilities that lay in the jar. He wanted to go back to medical research, the reason he had come to a strange world. For the first time Janet realized just how much Petersen hated running a military hospital. She had never bothered to read his voice and posture before, disliking him too much to care. Now it seemed very obvious as she watched disbelief and excitement struggling for control.

She wanted to stay and see how the struggle came out, but it seemed like a good time to leave. She had checked the room for an escape route before planning her meeting with Petersen. She knew that just to the right of the window there was an array of solar collectors with a convenient brace. She swung the window open, got onto the sill, and gripped the bracket. Before Petersen reached the window ledge, she had lowered herself to the roof of the story below and dropped to the ground. She fleetingly recalled a time when she would have considered the descent dangerous. She glanced up once as they hurried away and saw Petersen leaning out the window, his face a blur, his arms still clutched around her gift. He shouted something that she could not quite make out, but her lingering link with him brought her the words he intended: *And quit calling me Doug! That's still Colonel Petersen to you, Logan!*

Singer, Saldivar, and Genady walked slowly along the road to the airfield. Jon's contacts had confirmed one thing about the governor: No one knew him. He never openly opposed the military commanders, yet he withheld cooperation from them in subtle ways. His security chief was another puzzle. He had sometimes traded information with representatives of the opposition, but they did not know where his loyalties lay, so they kept him at arm's length.

"Are you sure it's safe to walk up to Vitek's boys?" Saldivar said, as if he had been following Singer's line of thought.

Singer had followed Genady's call to Vitek a few minutes later with a call to Tausis, the security chief. Singer had billed the calls to accounts owned by Gero and never closed because no one still alive knew they were there. He had guessed that Tausis would chase down the codes for those accounts and be disturbed.

"Vitek sincerely wanted to see me. He was curious. He needed me as an excuse to get you and Singer in. But he also wanted to see me," Genady said.

"Sure, but why?" Saldivar said. "Maybe he sincerely wants to shut you up."

"My father liked him. He ate at our house. I can't believe he'd have me killed."

"Sometimes the left eye winks while the right eye aims the gun."

Singer recalled his conversation with the security chief. "When I called Tausis, his governor already had called him. So I know they are together on this. And the contact site and people Tausis proposed were known to Jon's friends and had been used before without problems.

"I told him I knew many things the Net alone had known, but that I was not with the Net. I gave him a heavy hint that if the Net found me, I'd be gone before he could hear those things I know. As I read his voice, he wanted badly to get hold of me before they did. I don't think he'll turn us over."

"Maybe he's just eager to get hold of you, period. Snuff you."

"I think not," Singer said slowly. It would be hard to explain what he had heard in the distant voice. There had been a note of eagerness, of hope, that he thought would not be kindled by the mere wish to trap and kill a spiller of secrets. He was betting his life on that sound, betting that Tausis and his master really wanted the news he carried.

They had reached the point where they had been told to wait, and seated themselves where they could watch the road without being seen. Concealed in the brush, close to the earth, Singer relaxed his vigilance for the first time that day. He unlocked the new things he had seen in the bar before they had to leave, and examined them at leisure. Men and women had talked to Jon and Genady, wide open, the faces of their lost ones clear at the surface of their minds. Some of those faces Genady had recognized from the camp where he had been held. Most of them Singer had never seen, but he committed them carefully to memory. He knew they were important. The news that somewhere those faces might still be alive had made the listeners angry and brave enough to act.

He began to search for them beyond the memories of their friends, in whatever place they might be in the present: clothed in rags, trudging, limping, riding double on horseback, with Kruger, coming home. *Makho!* he cried, and he knew that he was seeing Kruger in truth. A great crowd marched with the Asharya. He could smell the dust of their passing, though he could see little because it was night.

Where are you? Kruger asked immediately.

We're in Jefferson already. We begged a ride from Galen at Firebase Flathead. You remember, he gave us a ride once before, when we came out of the Dust with the Mobile Force. Steer that way as you come south. I told him you were coming. I don't think he'll fire on you.

Jefferson already! There was envy in Kruger's thought as he jounced through the dustcloud on horseback. *We're moving slowly. I kept them going after dark, because we're in a hurry and we're harder to spot at night. They can't move fast, though. These people are not in good shape, but they are alive. Hazzan must have given the orders as he promised. We walked into the first of the camps. It was deserted. The Nupis had walked out. We picked up the survivors, and we're heading south, toward the other camp marked in this area.*

That's good. Be careful, Makho.

He felt the Asharya worrying.

We're safe here, at the butt-end of nowhere. You're the one walking into a minefield, Kruger said.

Singer was interrupted by Genady shaking him.

"Wake up!"

A van with the registration number Tausis had given them came up the road. It pulled off, cut its lights, and waited.

"Last chance to bug out," Genady said.

"No. I'm throwing the bones on this," Singer said. "But resist if they try to separate us. That could mean trouble."

They ran down the sandy bank and climbed into the van. The driver and guard inside wore Dust goggles that covered most of their faces, and they spoke little. The van was cleaner and more comfortable than any truck or moto any of them had traveled in, but Singer did not find it pleasant. It reminded him of the clean comfort of the PCOM building, hiding the permanent cells and the interrogation center.

They rode a type of aircraft different from the vitos and the slow, heavy transports Lyn flew. It shot nearly straight up into the air, high above the clouds where the atmosphere was too thin to breathe, and descended again in an arc like an arrow shot after a high-flying bird. This flight was hard for Singer to endure. When he had first come to the place of the Delh'tani, he had ridden in such a flying machine, not knowing what it was or where he was going. He remembered the curved gray-painted metal walls, the faint sharp smells of metal and fuel, the vibration of engines, and he remembered also the sickening tumble to earth and the split metal blooming into a cloud of fire.

He reached back to check on the others again. Janet greeted him but avoided full contact. She and Jon were bent over Jon's equipment, occupied with problems in clandestine communication. Their minds hummed swiftly and harmoniously, working together.

Hey, I've got time for you, cofra, Lyn said. *I'm on standby at the moment.*

He felt the edgy bite of adrenaline in her. *What's happening?*

Wouldn't we all like to know. The golpos who were sent to The Bucket got pinned down inside. Every time they tried to come out, people threw rocks at them. The shock squad came and arrested a truckload of people, and now there's talk that a crowd is about to take down Jefferson detention. Jon says the antis didn't start this. It's like spontaneous combustion. People are mad. The antis would like to see detention come down, because a lot of their people are in there, but they're scared the army will come in if they push it too far. Turns out Jon's friends don't have to make the wave. They're just trying to ride it. I don't like being stuck in here. I want to be out where it's happening.

Stay there! Singer ordered her, alarmed. Then he realized that giving her orders would be no help at all.

See this, he said, showing her the flying machine and letting her feel the edginess that echoed her own. *It is fearsome and strange. I want to get off.*

She grasped enviously at his vision. *You have the luck. I've always wanted to fly a hi-rider.*

She stayed with him most of the way, watching and enjoying, forcing him to notice all the details of the flight and teaching him what they meant. She kept him too busy to feel any fear.

The flight was short. Much sooner than he expected, the aircraft hurtled down out of the sky to meet earth again. As they screamed earthward, he felt her attention waver.

They've done it, she said, returning. *Reports coming in that detention is breached, and they're taking people out. We're being moved again, to try to pick up with some of the escapees. Check you later.*

They were met on the airfield with more politeness, more clean surfaces. Singer saw Genady pushing his fingers through his hair as if they could comb it flat. Clothing that had seemed comfortable and adequate among the rocks of the mountains and the half-stripped dead was now revealed as threadbare and dingy next to the looks of the soldiers in their smooth, pressed uniforms.

They sped through parts of North Fork that neither Singer nor Saldivar had ever seen and passed a checkpoint to approach the governor's house. He met them himself at the door, shadowed by a big, well-groomed man in uniform, who Singer assumed was Tausis. Vitek peered at them without recognition for a moment. Then he actually saw Genady. His face changed, and he embraced Genady warmly. Singer felt his real affection for the younger man and was relieved on Genady's account. Yet he also recognized the bearing of a leader. All the governor's actions had a kind of public grace—no foolish grimaces, no ugly tears, but only what would seem smooth and admirable if anyone were watching. Makho had the heart of the pallantai and could appear before them just as he was without fear of losing their love. The governor ruled through the good opinion of his people and, to keep it, had to hide his heart sometimes.

Vitek shook hands with Singer and Saldivar somewhat less cordially, measuring them with his eyes.

"Well, Lav, there's no doubt about it. This is my young friend, and he is most definitely alive. Thank you for getting him here so quickly. I'd like some time to visit with him and his friends undisturbed, if you could keep everyone out for a while."

"Sir, a word . . ." Tausis looked grave.

"Speak up."

Tausis drew the governor away from them and spoke softly, but Singer could still hear him.

"Sir, the background checks—you know the tall one had charges against him. Would you like me to make them comfortable elsewhere while you talk with Captain Cherny?"

"That won't be necessary. I have complete confidence in your security arrangements."

Tausis obviously took that as a rebuke, but he withdrew.

Resting one hand on Genady's shoulder, the governor turned to Singer and Saldivar. "Introduce me, Genya, and tell me the whole story. It takes a weight off my heart to see you well."

Singer listened while Genady tried. The governor took them to his private quarters, where food had been laid on a table, along with the hot black medicine drink the Delh'tani preferred to tea, and the brown Delh'tani version of chah. Singer ate cold meat and fruit, ignoring the bread, which he found inferior as always. He felt his whole body humming with the exhilaration of enough food. He hardly needed the chah, but it was excellent, so he worked on it while Genady sweated over his tale, and handed Genady a glass when the Delh'tani appeared to be getting confused.

The governor had turned pale a short distance into the story. Singer watched while his face fell from easy happiness into anguished disbelief. By following his eye movements, Singer discovered where the monitor was probably concealed. The governor could not help glancing that way, as if wondering what the hidden watchers were making of the news that shocked him so much.

The governor let Genady stumble on to the end, leaving many things unexplained. When Genady fell silent, Vitek sat staring until Singer offered him chah, too. He accepted and tried to smile.

"It's not that I don't believe you, Genya, but this is very difficult to grasp. Mr. Singer, your record—I took the liberty of looking it up since Major Tausis told me your name—your record states that you enlisted in a transient camp near Camara, on Delta, arrived on Ship 3, served as a scout in the Mobile Force, and eventually became an aide to Colonel Kruger. If I understand Genya correctly, none of that is true."

"I work for the Con-el still. But he tells me he is a general now. Promoted when he retired."

"Yes, of course. I had forgotten. But Mr. Singer, according to my records, General Kruger died shortly after retirement, in the hospital in North Fork."

"The records lie."

"He's alive, all right," Genady said. "And a⟨ ⟩ tight heavy. I wish I'd been with the Mothers. I wouldn't have ended up in a Nupi wire farm."

"You'd have been dead, cofra," Singer said gently. "Palha and I are the only ones left. Maybe one or two more in a camp somewhere, if we can ever find them."

"You haven't answered my question, Mr. Singer."

"You haven't asked a question. And you can stop calling me 'mister.' This is a word that means nothing much to me."

"Are you human or not?"

"I am born of earth. This earth. You are the strangers here."

"But you look so much like us. There's no difference that I can see."

"My friend who is a doctor tells me that we are very much alike. But there are some changes, small but important. She says we might think of ourselves as cousins. I say more shame to you if you kill us like animals when you can't tell the difference between us and you."

"What do you mean, kill you? We signed a nonintervention treaty with the Union to leave the natives strictly alone. In fact, no one outside the very highest levels of clearance even knows that aliens—natives—exist. Better that way for everyone."

Singer laughed. "Is that what you think? Listen, you keep secrets from your own people, and others keep secrets from you. Tony Gero knew the real treaty, approved by those who ruled you on Delta. It was an agreement to stay away from us. Until we could be killed. You approved the order that killed my people. I can show it to you."

The governor stared at him. "Either you are crazy or I am. I never signed such an order."

"Let me use your desk."

Vitek watched in disbelief as Singer turned on the desk and accessed restricted clearance. "How did you get those codes?" he asked coldly.

"Tony Gero. He had everyone's codes. Did you think the Net was only for catching other fishes? You're just another minnow to them."

"Why would Gero give you this information? How do you know him?"

"He did not mean to give me anything. I met him in the interrogation rooms. He thought he could get something for nothing. My people have a story song about the one we call the Soul-eater. He is the one who dreams he can take and give nothing back. In the end he cannot keep what he stole. A bolder gambler wins it all away. It's a good song. We teach it to children. You should hear it sometime."

He had been searching and scanning while he spoke. "Here. Read this yourself. There's more, but this is the copy with your name on it."

Scanning it, Vitek looked relieved. "Yes, I signed this order, but it had nothing to do with indigenes. This was an order for a surveillance flight over the Open Zone."

"Before and after pictures included. Is this surveillance?"

Vitek looked and said nothing.

"Those were my people," Singer said. He did not look at the pictures himself. He had to keep his head clear for dealing with this man. Instead, he looked at Vitek and read the paling of his skin, his quickened breath, the skin of his hands cooling down and sweat starting on his palms and behind his neck. Singer moved closer as the governor stared at the screen, close enough to smell the man's fear and the sour taste on his breath. Vitek did not want to believe, but he was believing.

"You said there was more," Vitek said. "Where is it?"

"Paper," Singer requested. He wrote the rest of the numbers and letters carefully and a little clumsily. He saw them clearly in Gero's memory, but it was his own hand that had to write them, and he was unaccustomed to the task.

He waited while the governor read doggedly through file after file. Vitek maintained a straight face. Singer admired it. But the governor had not learned to keep control of his feelings. His humiliation intensified and thickened till Singer felt he could put out his hand and grasp the ugly substance of it. Vitek was not only angry at the Net for their betrayal. He blamed himself bitterly.

Singer noticed that he stopped periodically to copy sections of the file.

"Why do you do that?"

"I don't know where this came from. I don't know what will happen to it after I read it. If someone is monitoring access to these files, they might wipe them or move them. I want a copy, if only to assure myself I have not completely lost my mind."

"Already done," Singer said. "My friends sent a copy to one who would know how to pass it on. It is loose in your system somewhere."

Vitek stopped reading and let his hands fall from the pad and rest on the edge of the desk. "Wonderful," he said. His lip twisted as he spoke, as if he had smelled something foul. "Some unknown group of people knows more about what has been happening here than I do."

He turned a dark, hurt gaze on Genady. "Genya, I must ask you this. These friends of yours—they are people who are wanted for questioning by the police, people who have caused great destruction, who may have killed. Genya, are you, son of my old friend, a part of some movement trying to destroy my government?"

"I've been in a prison camp all year, courtesy of your government. Not in a position to do any conspiring even if I'd wanted to, and I never wanted to set myself against you, Uncle.

"I'll say this, though. These people are my friends. I trust them with my life. Whatever you do to them, you'll have to do to me also, so think about it. You can't handle me with kid gloves while you let others suffer. I said no to that when I went into the Forsas, and I won't swallow it now. I don't want to oppose you, Uncle, but the people who put me in prison are my enemies. The people who killed my friends are my enemies. The people who want to take away from me all that I hoped to do with my life are my enemies. If you put yourself on their side, you're not on my side. How can it be any other way?"

"What do you expect me to do?" Vitek asked.

Genady noticed the sandwich in his hand and bit off and chewed another large mouthful. "I'm not in a position to expect anything. But if you are the honorable man who ate at my father's table, you'll declare an end to martial law. Negotiate peace with the Nupis while you still can. Give us a chance to make this world our home instead of an armed transit camp. Treat Singer's people with decent respect, and they'll show you around."

"It's not that simple," Vitek said heavily. "Respect. You haven't shown much respect for our laws."

"My Con-el is a man of law, and I respect him," Singer said. "He uses the law to rule himself and to give justice. For Gero, law is only another kind of weapon. Respect for his law means death to me. What is your law? Is it a shield for you to hide behind? Or does it protect me, too? These are things I must know before I give you my respect."

Vitek turned abruptly to Saldivar. "What about you? I don't hear you saying anything."

Saldivar cleared his throat. "I'm from the Tregua. We have nothing to say about what happens to us. We have no place. Not on Delta, not here. I have a place now, but you didn't give it to me. Ask me for loyalty and you're wanting something for nothing."

"I need some time." Vitek looked from one to the other of them. "I'd like you to be my guests at least till tomorrow."

"Meaning you don't want us to talk to others about these things," Singer said. "You were afraid to let us in, now you're afraid to let us out. For my part, I'll stay. The food is good."

Vitek pushed a button, and a very young man in a plain uniform entered the room. "Jesky will show you your rooms and get you anything you want. Call me anytime."

His eyes rested on Genady, though he did not try to embrace him again. "It's good to see you again, Genya. I mean that. Whatever you think."

10

They followed the young man to a suite of rooms, sleeping places with a common area stocked with more food and drink. Soft blankets had been provided, as well as clean clothing, soap, and towels. The mild, sweet smell of soap filled the rooms, bothering Singer like a sound that could not be turned off. It masked other scents, as luxury and courtesy masked the true intent of the people who lived in this place.

"What do you think he will do?" Singer asked Genady.

"I don't know. I think he's upset. He hates surprises. He'd like to make this unhappen, but he does have a conscience. It won't let him discount you till he finds out if you're telling the truth. He'll be looking at those records, cross-checking everything, and maybe calling some people to try to worm a corroboration out of them. Deal with people. Negotiate. That's how he works."

"What else do you know about him?"

Genady shook his head. "Not much. He's a hard man to know. I know what he likes to eat for breakfast."

Then he thought of something and smiled. "I remember one thing that might interest you, though I don't know what use it would be. He likes music. Strange music—serious stuff and old stuff, really old. Historical. He listens to it constantly. He's as bad as the polvos and their boxes."

That intrigued Singer. "I want to hear this."

Saldivar smiled at him, and he remembered that the first time he had seen Saldivar, Palha had been plugged into a box, listening to music Singer could not hear. He remembered saying to himself, *If I knew his music, I would know the man.*

He tried the door and found that it was not secured. He left the room and wandered through the house, his bare feet soft and soundless on the carpets. It was a very big place for one man. He soon found that Vitek was not alone in the house. Certain rooms had closed doors, with men seated outside them who looked at him closely but did not challenge him. He guessed that they had already been told of his presence and wondered if Vitek had told them or if there was another authority in the house.

He could hear music playing somewhere, very faintly. Following the sound, he found himself outside another closed door, but one without a guard. He opened the door, standing to one side. No one attacked him or challenged him, so he entered. The room seemed empty till he located Vitek seated in a high-backed chair with his back to the door. Singer was startled that a man in such a position of power had so little care for his own safety.

He wanted to learn about Vitek more than he wanted to speak with him. He sat down quietly on the soft carpet and listened to the music. Voices sang, but not like Medicine Shirt and the other singers that polvorados favored. A feeling of peace and delight touched him like cool water as the music sank into his senses. He perceived clarity and order, simple like sunrise over green hills but playful, too, like the ripple of countless currents blending in the changing surface of a clear stream. He forgot all about Vitek and listened only to this singer who was right next to him, telling him things that could never be explained in any other way. The voice was young, young enough to be his beshani, and yet she must surely have been old to understand so well. Horizons opened before him, as if he rode the wind higher and higher and looked over the world's shoulder, beyond the edge and then beyond that again. Music opened in his mind as a lover's touch opened unknown worlds within a single skin.

It ended, and the silence was broken by an exclamation, a clumsy step. Vitek stood above him, startled but trying to regain control of himself.

"What—what are you doing here?"

"Who is that?" Singer said. "When can I meet her?"

"Who?"

"The singer."

Vitek looked more confused than ever. "Good heavens, I don't know. I suppose the name is on the label. Somebody back on Delta."

"No, not just she who sings this. I mean she who made the music first." His heart sank as he realized that the wonderful singer might still be in that far-off place they called Delta, but surely there must be some way to send a message.

"He. The singer was a woman, but the composer was a man." Vitek said the name, but as usual, the awkward Deltan syllables conveyed no music to Singer. He puzzled out a translation with the help of Gero's memory and some of Kruger's words. "Wolf-walker"—and "Loved by the Mountain Spirit."

"Loved he must have been, certainly," Singer murmured. "But where is he? I want to talk to him."

Vitek looked down at him strangely, almost with compassion. "This music was old when my people left their first home. He's been dead for more than a thousand years."

"A thousand years." Singer found it hard to grasp. The music had been so close to him. He grieved as if this Wolfwalker had been a friend, someone he could have known. How could he be dead when his music was so full of life? Yet there had been sorrow in it, too. The singer had fallen from his first brightness young, like the pallantai.

Singer looked up and met Vitek's eyes again. "Then I don't understand."

"What don't you understand?"

"You. Your people. You had this music for a thousand years, and still you are—as you are."

Vitek laughed, an unhappy sound. "You are a strangely intense young fellow. What would you expect? Music doesn't change anything, you know."

He turned away so that Singer could not see his eyes, but Singer was sure that he had understood.

"You'll have to excuse me. I'm busy."

"I'll stay awhile. You should have someone to watch your back."

Vitek glanced back at him. "If I wanted a guard, you're not the one I would have chosen."

"Maybe when you finish your studying there, you'll change your mind."

Vitek went back into the inner room, and Singer heard him talking to his desk. Bored, Singer closed his eyes and reviewed the wonderful music. He could not recall all of it as well as he wanted to. He thought of Hilurin and felt very sad that Lurya had not been there to hear it. The old singer would have understood it better than anyone.

For the first time since the destruction of the Rock, Singer truly wanted to live a long time, not to fulfill his responsibility to his people but because he saw something ahead of him that he passionately wanted. That music had been only a fragment from a treasure he could hardly imagine and would never touch unless the Delh'tani let him live. He wanted it. He wanted it so much, he could hardly breathe.

Then a thought came to him unbidden, piercing him like a knife or like one of those blades of light the Delh'tani used to pierce holes in steel. He could have lived out his life in the pallantai, perhaps died young, perhaps grown old as the Singer for the Rock, among the people he had always known, and never heard this music. He might never have felt the power of his own gift if the fear of death had not forced him again and again to make a desperate leap. If some power made it possible to go back, which way would he choose? His heart burned with the unanswered question.

He wanted that music back again. His fingers drummed on his knee, but there was nothing to drum with, and he laughed at himself for thinking he could drum in the governor's room. He wondered if he could recall it well enough to learn, to keep it with him even if he never heard it again. He set himself to the task. It helped him forget his need to move and run; it helped him endure the waiting.

Singer's humming under his breath did not disturb Vitek's concentration at first. Gaining confidence in the way the song went, Singer began to voice it aloud. Only then did the governor pause and let his hands sit idle on the desk. He stopped seeing the screen, which was packed with unwelcome news, and listened to that voice.

Singer knew the archaic syllables only by their sound, with no idea of their meaning, so he got a good many of them wrong or forgot and had to fill in with nonsense sounds. The music was right, though. Vitek heard him stop, correct the phrasing, and go on, patiently shaping the song till it pleased him. The Deltan forgot that he was listening to someone he had called an alien and a criminal. He heard the pain of longing and the anguish of a divided heart working with repeated patient effort toward something else, something that came through in brief flashes of effortless beauty. The voice seemed to question him, searching him as it searched itself.

Singer searched in the harmonies for a resolution of his questions about Vitek. Gero had not liked this man. But where was his true self? Singer had not yet touched it. *You loved this music or you would not carry it from world to world, old as it is. But how can you love it and not let it reach you? How can you deny the power even while you long for it?*

What is the thing you love, Delh'tani? Why do you listen to this music when no one is here, though you pretend it means nothing? Where is the love that you have hidden and betrayed?

He felt Vitek's attention first, then saw that the governor had turned in his seat and was looking at him.

"What do they say?" Singer asked. "I know about the music, but what do the words say?"

"It's an old lingua without modern descendants—not on Delta, anyway. I don't remember the lyrics. The songs are about love."

Vitek rose from his chair again and paced around the room while Singer watched him quietly. He knew that Vitek was lying because he could hear the words still sounding in Vitek's memory and knew that the governor understood their meaning.

"What do you know about music, anyway?" Vitek asked. "I would not expect you to study the preflight Terrans—either as an alien or as a scout for General Kruger's Mobile Force."

"Among my own people I have a name for music."

"Oh, of course. Singer. I thought that might be a nom de guerre only. You're called the same thing in your own language?"

"I had a war name, but Singer is the one that stuck."

Vitek turned on Singer abruptly. "How can I know that 'your own people' even exist? How can I tell this is not an elaborate hoax?"

"When Makho—when Kruger brings the prisoners home, everyone will know. Or you can call the Union contact I gave you and begin to talk of a truce. They will know who we are.''

"And what if I don't? What if I simply refuse to alter my course? *If* Kruger is alive and if he has rescued some prisoners, they'll come back, anyway. If it's true that the Union is experiencing an epidemic, so much the better. They'll be reduced to helplessness, and our colony will be secure for the first time since the landing. I don't need you or your advice.''

"So it seems now," Singer said wearily. "What will you do when hundreds of soldiers come back, convinced you betrayed them, led by a man your government tried to murder? What will you do when the sickness in Solidari comes here and you have no medicine to stop it? What will you do when the Union orbital platform drops a dying vengeance on you or when the new ship comes in, full of Union soldiers who think you killed their people? Then what?''

"Those are long-term problems. Far from certain. What's certain is the situation I have to deal with now.''

Vitek did not turn away from Singer as he had before. Instead he kept his eyes on Singer's with unnatural fixity, as if challenging him. Or, Singer thought suddenly, as if there were something he wanted to say and could not. Singer glanced quickly around the room. He could not spot the monitor, but it must be there, just as in the other place. The Net was watching Vitek.

"Let me put it to you from my viewpoint," Vitek said. "Even if everything you say is true, it could be far better if you allowed the authorities to decide how it can best be used. And I couldn't say this to Genya—he never chose to comprehend political realities—but you are alone. It would be easy for you to vanish until the problem is settled.''

Singer decided to take a risk. "It would not be safe to assume that," he said carefully. "It would not be safe at all to assume we are alone.''

"Are you threatening me?" Vitek said. "I'm not worried. My security is very good.''

Singer could not miss the twist of irony in that statement, though he thought it would not be heard by the other listeners, wherever they were.

"Not quite good enough," Singer said. "Ask them what happened in Jefferson Detention. Did they tell you about that?''

The reaction was greater than he had expected. Vitek's eyes narrowed, almost flinching, like a cat's at a feinted blow. Singer saw fear, almost panic, in them.

"What happened?" Vitek said. It was an effort for him to keep his face straight, and his eyes betrayed him, flicking irresistibly toward the hidden monitors.

Singer shrugged. "Ask them. They must know by now. Maybe they don't tell you everything, no?"

Vitek rose abruptly. "I don't wish to seem rude, but my time is very limited. I really can't talk anymore. We'll see you at breakfast, hm?"

Jesky appeared at the door, and Vitek courteously but firmly escorted Singer toward him.

Singer followed the orderly. He had intended to provoke a response, but he could not define what he had seen. Vitek had been getting rid of him, yes. He had been suddenly afraid. Yet there had been no hostility in his bearing—almost as if he feared for both Singer and himself. As if Singer had been about to say things the hidden listeners should not have heard. There was only one conclusion he could draw from that. If Vitek feared his own security, he was keeping secrets from the Net.

11

As Singer entered his own room again, Jesky closed the door behind him. Singer immediately tried the door again to make sure it was not locked.

"I hope you're listening," he said softly. "There will not be a locked door or a restricted file in the Blue Zone within three days. Jefferson is the beginning."

"What are you talking about?" Genady asked.

"I'm talking to *them*," Singer said.

"Vitek wouldn't let them bug our room," Genady said. Then a pained expression crossed his face. "Well—maybe he would."

"I think they did not ask," Singer said.

"He should have known, anyway. He was responsible." He leaned his head on his fist. "I liked it better at the wire farm. I knew my enemies there. What did he tell you? Anything?"

"Nothing." Silently he said, *Nothing I want to tell you now. He was afraid.*

They agreed to keep watches in the night. They could not assume their safety. Singer agreed silently with Saldivar to give Genady the third watch and let him sleep through it. He was too confused to be alert.

Singer had just fallen asleep when he felt Saldivar nudging him. *Someone coming.*

Even as he woke, he was stretching out into the darkness and he immediately found Vitek. The governor tapped at the door for courtesy's sake but did not wait to be let in. He carried a small handlight.

"How's everything?" he whispered. "Oh, I see he's asleep. Too bad. Well, we can talk in the morning. Don't wake him."

He tapped his lips for silence, as if playfully, but the look he gave Singer was anything but playful.

He knows they're listening, Singer thought.

"Are you comfortable here? Good. You know, this room has a balcony. Maybe Genya didn't show you. If you want fresh air—but maybe it's too cold for you. No? Well, let me show you."

He opened the doors for them, and they stepped out with him into the dry chill.

"Tell me what happened at Jefferson," he said as soon as the door clicked behind them. "Keep it quiet and face away from the building. We're looking at the stars and talking about the weather."

"If they haven't told you yet, then your security is too good."

"There was a disturbance in Jefferson. I know that. It was hardly news; just a bar brawl that got out of hand."

"Check again. Angry people broke down the doors at the detention center and turned loose the prisoners, including those who first heard the story we told you. I hear a rumor that army units are moving in. Your own people will be firing on each other, soon."

Singer smelled Vitek's fear, even in the cold dry air.

"The army can't move without my authorization. I will never give it."

"Can't?"

Vitek flung his hands out in a gesture of despair. "If you have any influence with whoever started this, for God's sake tell them to throttle down. If they give the Net an excuse, we will lose everything."

" 'We'? Who is that?"

Before Vitek could answer, boots thundered on the floor inside. In his concentration, Singer had not heard them coming, but as the door opened and they came through, he felt them: armed men in great haste. Killing was not the first thing on their minds, but it was never far from the thoughts of any armed man. His Thanha self smelled the hot foretaste of blood while the Gero memories assessed the probabilities: *It's a coup against Vitek, or else they think you're an assassin and they're trying to save him. Either way you're dead unless you strike first.* He heard Genady cry out, waking—had he been hurt?—and saw the governor turn toward the sound in time to collide with the troops as they came through the balcony door. There was a moment of confused struggle, plenty of time for Singer to see himself and Palha dead and bleeding on the ground and to see all the ways he could prevent that bare-handed. The Gero memories screamed at him to do something, called him the worst kind of fool, wasting his one chance with Vitek, while his Thanha body ached to spring, to move. He froze and refused to act at all, his thoughts frozen, too, in turmoil. It was the best he could do.

The soldiers knocked Vitek down, and one of them jumped on him, but not to harm him. The soldier covered the governor with his body as if he truly believed that Vitek was in danger. More roughly, the others pushed Saldivar and Singer against the wall and searched them, then pushed them back through the open door to lie on the floor inside.

Genady must have struggled. His shirt was half torn off, and his arms were clipped behind his back at the elbows and wrists.

"What is the meaning of this?" Vitek demanded, straining to get his mouth out of the carpet. "Take those off."

The soldier in command looked confused and unhappy. "Please, your Excellency, let me explain."

"Explain, and bleeding quick." Vitek struggled to stand up, and the soldier hastily squatted down next to him, motioning for him to stay put.

"Sir, I was ordered to secure your person because you are in danger. There are disorders in the city, and sniper attacks have been reported. I was sent to make sure you were not in an exposed position. Begging your pardon, sir, but no one is beyond suspicion when we're talking about terrorism.''

"He's family," Vitek said. "Son of an old friend. Practically my godson.''

"I'm sorry, sir.''

"At least take off the arm restraints. You're pulling his arms out of their sockets." Vitek made an effort to speak calmly.

The soldier hesitated.

"Am I still the governor, or am I not?" Vitek did not raise his voice, but he intensified it and brought it to bear like a beam weapon on the soldier. "You've thrown me to the ground, roughed up my family and guests. Before you ignore a direct order, you'd better answer that question. If I am still the governor, then I order you to report yourself to Colonel Patel for insubordination. If I am not the governor, I suggest you call the colonel here and let him tell me that. You have no orders to personally depose me—do you?''

"No, sir. Nothing like that. My orders are to protect the governor, sir.''

"Good. Then you can do as I ask. I've known this boy since he wore diapers. I'll let you know when I need him hog-tied.''

Reluctantly, the soldier nodded to the man watching Genady, and the arm restraints were released. Genady took a long, painful breath. It was hard to breathe with arms clipped together at the elbows.

Vitek relaxed very slightly. "Continue your explanation.''

"Well, sir, we are to escort you to the secure area till conditions return to normal. Those are my orders.''

"Nonsense. This is not the time to hide in a bunker. Order a motorized guard ready and have Major Tausis sent here at once.''

The soldier looked more embarrassed than ever. She was saved by the arrival of another smooth, clean officer in uniform.

Vitek rose immediately in spite of the soldier's move to restrain him. "Patel, what the hell is this?''

"A very serious situation, I'm afraid. We have reports—''

"Come down to my office and we'll discuss this. Flash Jefferson security and get Tausis for me.''

"I'm afraid that won't be possible," Patel said solemnly. "Major Tausis was killed by a sniper half an hour ago.''

Total silence fell in the governor's mind as well as in the room. Singer tried to get hold of what Vitek really felt about the dead colonel but found it difficult.

"How did this happen?" Vitek asked simply after a minute.

He might have been asking about a malfunctioning machine by the sound of it, but behind his words, in his heart, slow music began to play. The music held an iron beauty of wrath and woe and no hope at all. It was the music that Singer listened to.

"He was walking on the grounds. He was shot. An antigovernment sniper, we assume. I have parties combing the area within range now, but they have not reported finding anything."

His words struck a small flare of suspicion in Vitek. *Why didn't I hear it happen? Why didn't I hear an alarm? Why didn't they rush him to the hospital?* He did not say any of those things, but the words were so close to the surface that Singer heard them.

"Where is he?" Vitek asked in the same dead-quiet voice.

"He's in the emergency room. In the bunker. But Vitek—"

"I want to see him. And get those wrist clamps off my godson. Come with us, Genady."

He charged out of the room, leading them, as if he were going of his own free will. Patel tried again to stop him when they reached the security area, but the governor pushed him aside with a contemptuous look.

The body was hardly recognizable. Tausis had been shot in the back of the head. His smashed skull was partly concealed by bloody dressings. The force of the impact had left his face swollen, blue, and distorted.

"Why—" Vitek closed his eyes for a moment, then forced them open. "Why wasn't he taken to the hospital? Why didn't you do something for him?"

Patel shrugged. "There was no point. I'm sorry. The hospital could not have done anything that our in-house medic did not do. He could not have been revived."

Singer reached out to touch the dead hand. It was stone-cold already. Tausis could tell him nothing. Then he remembered that there were those who could read a corpse like a book, make it tell secrets. He reached again and touched the warmth of Zhanne.

She was right beside him, yet she was also somewhere in the darkened city; they must have reached North Fork some hours earlier. He smelled night-cooled air blowing over hot paving and, under that, a dark-green smell of water. She had to be somewhere near the irrigation tanks. That meant they were south of the airfield, not far from the communications center.

Ugh. She looked through his eyes with sorrow and disgust.

He felt her hand go out to turn the bloody head and reluctantly obeyed the impulse.

They're lying, she said flatly. *See the angle of entry?* He did not see; there was a brief struggle to fit his perception with hers, and then the smashed ruin of bone and tissue suddenly focused for him and made sense.

The projectile entered at his occiput and tore a path upward and out here, above the left temple. No sniper did that unless he was lying on the ground. Don't suppose they'd let you extract the projectile—no, I guess not. But a high-velocity sniper slug would have blown his head up. This wound is consistent with a small-caliber handgun at close range.

Her attention left the wrecked face, to Singer's relief, and focused on the dead man's hand. Singer picked up the hand, wondering what he was supposed to see. Dark marks scored the skin of the inner wrist and the edges of the wrist bones.

See that? Check above his elbows.

Singer slid the sleeve up the dead man's forearm and found similar marks.

They had him clipped and didn't take the restraints off till after he died. So the marks never had a chance to go away. I hope this man was not a friend of yours. He was shot in the head from behind, with his hands tied behind him. Murdered.

No. Not a friend. Nevertheless Singer felt angry and shaken, the feeling overlaid on Zhanne's, resonating like a chord.

Are you all right there? I see security with guns, and I don't like it.

We're with the governor. I think they're going to lock us up again, but that doesn't matter. For his protection, they say. Tell Jon to get his friends in place before the Net provokes an incident and shuts down the city. I think the governor is being put in the cooler by the Net, but I can't be sure yet.

Get sure. And be careful.

I'm being as careful as I can, isé. No fighting. We're here to protect Vitek, not to make trouble. That's your job. Now I need to concentrate.

He felt her turn away from him and got a brief flash of the place she was in. Then she was gone. He let the heavy cold weight of Tausis's hand fall to the table.

The brief examination had taken only a few moments. One of the soldiers pushed him back from the table.

"Hands off."

Singer yielded, stepping back. As he did, he spoke Zhanne's

words aloud, while they were still fresh in his mind. He watched the guns rise to cover him, the watchfulness rise in Patel's eyes.

"Are you a doctor?" the colonel asked.

"I've seen more head wounds than you're ever likely to. I'm familiar with snipers, too."

"Polvorado," Patel said scornfully. "Keep quiet till you're asked to speak."

But Singer had aimed his words at the governor, and they were taking effect. He saw the line of sweat at the back of Vitek's neck, his shoulders going rigid as his hands clenched tightly at his sides.

"I want to see the doctor who attended him," Vitek said.

"I'm sorry, but that won't be possible," Patel said, overriding the governor's anger. "Tausis is dead. I must assume his function as security chief, and I will secure this area whether that suits you or not. I must respectfully request that you remain in this area until I receive a condition upgrade. I'm leaving a detail here to protect you. They have orders to honor any reasonable request. I regret the inconvenience."

He waved Vitek away from the others.

"Clip them," he said to the soldiers.

Vitek seized Genady's arm, pushing himself between the soldiers and his nephew. "No. Absolutely not. My family and guests will not be subjected to this indignity."

"We're only seeking to protect you."

"Such a disgrace is too high a price to pay for my life."

Again Singer found double meanings in the words. So, apparently, did Patel, for he backed down.

"Watch them," he ordered a pair of his guards, and departed with the rest.

Vitek held Genady's arm a little longer. "I'm sorry about this."

Genady turned away, stretching his wrenched arms. Vitek dropped onto the nearest seat.

"He was my friend," he said to no one in particular. *I sent him to find out what happened. I thought I could trust him. Why was he killed if he was not my friend? Unless there was a sniper. In that case, I can't know about Tausis—or Genya, either. Something is different about him. Maybe he has been turned, become an agent of the antis. Did he bring his friends here to kill me? But if that's true, then why not kill me? Why talk about music instead? They want something from me. More likely they're Net agents. What do they want me to admit? And how much does Genya know?*

Singer heard him pacing off the boxes in his mind, unable to find a way out. Gradually the arguments and counterarguments became indistinct and died away, and the deep-toned, ominous music returned.

Singer listened with half his attention while he kept an eye on the guards and watched Genady roam restlessly about. The room was comfortably provided with all the necessities, like the rest of the house, but it was still a bunker. There were no windows or openings. The air blew in through ventilators. From the damping of all sound and the feel of the air, Singer knew the walls were thick and deeply buried.

Saldivar struck the wall with his fist. "Underground again. ▓▓▓▓ When I get out of here, I'm going to go up to the top of the biggest hill I can find and climb the tallest tree on it and live in the top of the ▓▓▓▓ tree."

Genady found the video panel and turned it on. "I want to see what's happening."

The news selection showed military security parties searching empty storage buildings, a warning of dangerous prisoners escaping from Jefferson Detention. Then the picture cut to crop statistics and a weather report.

Vitek tried the other channels and slapped the panel in silent exasperation.

"Get used to it, your Excellency," Genady said. "That's how it is for the rest of us. Lies, more lies—and then the weather."

Singer reached for Janet again. As soon as he touched her, he knew that she had been traveling and was still in motion. She was working on something with Jon, so closely linked with him that Singer could see and hear him clearly. The video broke into a report on improvements in the irrigation system and returned to a view of the square outside the governor's house. The image quality was inferior, but they could see running figures chased by golpos. A crowd milled about, spilling into the street, and smoke smeared out from homemade bombs hurled toward the house. Singer let Zhanne look over his shoulder.

That's a lie! That isn't happening—it's synthetic! Jon became incoherent in his excitement and simply imposed another image over Singer's sight, so strongly that Singer momentarily lost contact with the bunker and felt himself out on the street with Jon and his sister.

The crowd was real enough and far bigger than the one on the screen. But there was no chaotic movement and no violence. They swayed back and forth with locked arms, chanting. At the moment when Singer listened, they were chanting Vitek's name. The golpos charged an arm of the crowd at intervals, and the margins would withdraw like an animal cringing from an attacker, but the total mass of the people never retreated.

Singer felt Jon's exaltation. *It's working. The antis have called out their people. There's a general strike for an end to martial law. And we've been spreading rumors about returning prisoners and about an outbreak of native disease. Half the doctors are out protesting, too.*

Jon dodged and ran as a cylinder spraying mist shot toward them. A girl with a cloth tied over her face scooped up the can with a fishnet and threw it back across the street. Then she staggered and fell, and others dragged her away into the crowd. Singer felt the edge of panic under Jon's excitement.

Lyn locked arms with Janet, bracing her against the surge of the crowd.

"Did you catch him?" Jon shouted to her. "Did you catch Singer? I saw the video he's watching. It's synthetic. They're broadcasting a fake riot. You know what comes next! They're manufacturing an excuse to counterstrike."

More. Singer showed them the bunker, the guards. *The governor's a tight-coiled man. I haven't been able to read him. Maybe he's on our side—or wants to be, thinks about it. Whatever he is, he's not a fish for the Net, and they're tired of it. They haven't made up their minds to smoke him yet, but they are close to it. Tell your friends: keep demanding to see Vitek. Keep up the pressure. Force their hand.*

"Force it the wrong way and they'll smoke you, too," Jon said.

Singer smiled inside their thoughts, reckless and happy, to face down their fear. *That won't be so easy.*

"What are you grinning about?" Genady asked.

Singer reoriented himself as he recognized the bunker again; he swiftly checked the guards, then finally answered Genady. "Because I think something will happen soon."

"Is that good?"

Singer smiled again. "Yes. I'm bored."

Vitek sat up and looked at him. "Who are you?" he asked grimly. "Who are you to make jokes about being bored while a good man is getting stiff on a table next door and God knows what is happening to my city?"

Singer gestured to the video. "Rest your heart. What you see is not happening."

"What do you mean?"

"I have a friend who knows how to construct such a picture. It's a lie for the eyes. Only ones out there with violent hands are the security forces. Your people stand on the street and call your name. Why don't you answer them?"

"I'm not in a position to answer anyone."

Clever he is, Singer thought, and stubborn. When cleverness fails, he falls back behind a stone wall. He trusts no one, but he's getting desperate. There must be a way to get inside.

He returned to the music, trying to find an answer there, but something disturbed him, distracted him. The vague unease suddenly resolved into something tangible: a smell, a hot, stinging scent that set off every alarm in his body. He put his hand up to the ventilator. The air coming in was only faintly warm, but it would be warmer soon.

The Gero memories scanned through the possibilities and panicked. *They've sabotaged the ventilation system. They're going to torch the house—eliminate the governor and blame it on the crowd. Has to be an inside job because no ordinary fire would damage this bunker.*

The memories screamed at him in panic. They could not find him a way out. *Shut up,* he said to their useless advice. He took a long deep breath and dropped into the familiar cool timelessness of Thanha readiness.

"Vitek—Governor—is this bunker hardened against air attack?"

"Yes, certainly." Vitek was startled.

"So it has its own ventilation system to protect against fire and poison and such things?"

"Yes."

"Then someone has disabled your system. I think they are burning your house, Governor."

That got the attention of the guards.

"There would have been an alarm," said the nervous soldier.

"Can't you smell it?" Singer asked.

The tall one shook his head, but the nervous one looked worried.

"Maybe should check it out," she said.

"The major said don't open the door."

She hesitated, then ordered them all to the far corner of the bunker. "Your Excellency, would you please go sit over there so you'll be safe if anything comes in this door? And the rest of you chucks, get down on the floor and put your hands back of your heads. Now don't move or Pasco will splatter you across the wall."

Singer heard her opening the door. There was an exclamation, and the door slammed shut again. A moment later the smell of smoke reached him.

"Shit, Pasco, he's right; there's smoke in the accessway. What do we do now?"

"Stay put," Pasco said. But doubt crept into his voice as he began to understand the situation.

"There's smoke in the fucking ventilator, you butthead," she cried. "Something's happened up there. We're going to fry if we can't get out of here."

"Not fry," Singer said calmly. "There won't be any air to breathe in a few minutes. You will choke. Then I guess just dry up like meat strips on a smoking rack. Probably not burn."

Singer could hear the tall guard breathing faster. Panic was beginning to seep out into the room like the choking gases.

"We have to get out," the tall guard repeated. Singer heard sounds of rummaging, doors opening and closing, and guessed that the guard was going through the storage lockers.

"Pasco, you can't get out that way. There's too much smoke. Listen to me!"

The other mumbled something in a muffled voice.

Singer stole a quick look from under his raised arm and saw that the guard called Pasco had found a breather mask and was headed for the door.

"Pasco!" The nervous guard could not stop him. He plunged out into the smoky passage and disappeared.

"Shit, oh, shit," she moaned. She hesitated on the threshold as if she would go after her teammate, but scorching fumes poured in. She slapped the lock, and the door slammed shut again. She backed away from it, coughing uncontrollably.

"Get down on the floor," Singer called. "It's better here."

She dropped down. Her rifle dragged on the floor beside her, so Singer risked raising his arm to feel the air. Above his head it was getting warmer.

"I'm going to turn over," Singer said. "Not much point in shooting me now if I move, no?"

He reached out for Genady and Palha. He touched them, embracing them in his mind so they would be at his fingertips any time he needed to move. Vitek was another matter—and the

guard? She would add another variable to the dangerously unstable structure he was trying to balance. As he turned over, he
saw her white, scared face, red-eyed and runny-nosed. He would
not have left a horse in a burning stall even if it belonged to his
enemies.

"There is a way out," he said. "Come closer."

They crawled toward him.

"You have to calm down before I can show you. It won't be
easy."

"I am calm," the guard choked. "Get me ██████ out of
here."

"There's plenty of time. All the time we need. Here—grab
my hand."

She clutched him with tense, wiry strength.

"Don't scam her," Vitek said quietly. "There's no way out.
I should know."

"Who would do this to you?" Singer asked.

"The antis," the guard said promptly. "They're rioting out
there. Didn't you see the video?"

"I didn't ask you. I asked the governor."

"I have no way of knowing," Vitek replied.

Singer! It was Jon's loud-and-clear channel, guided and rein-
forced by Janet. *Get out of there. It's burning. Armored trucks
coming. We have to get off the street. Hurry!*

I'm gone. No fear till you hear from me.

"I'm giving you one more chance to tell me the truth," he
said conversationally to Vitek. But the governor was running
programs in his head. Singer could hear them clearly, even over
the music.

*This whole thing could be a setup. Maybe they're all acting,
and once they get a statement from me, they'll strike the set and
haul me away for further interrogation.*

"I can't tell you anything," Vitek said. The fumes forced
tears from his tightly shut eyes. Black smoke was pouring from
the ventilators.

"Dakko—the hell with it, then," Singer said.

He gathered them up like string wound around his fingers in
an ever-tightening pattern. With one swift gesture he jerked the
string loose, and the pattern snapped into another form.

12

From lung-searing air and blinding smoke in a cramped room, they had transferred instantly to infinite space and air so clear and cold that it seemed for a moment like no air at all. It was still half-dark. They rolled over and over on a bumpy, coarse surface that was not paving and not carpeting.

"Grass!" Vitek exclaimed incredulously.

They picked themselves up from the various points on the slope where they had come to rest.

There was a heavy pause in which Vitek, Genady, and the guard tried to make sense of their situation and failed.

Singer took advantage of the moment to send a message south with the wind for Janet. She felt very far away, not because the distance mattered but because his attention was held in the place where he stood, and so was hers. There were no words in the message, only a caress of cool wind and the feeling of sky and space around them, so she would know they were all right and far from the fire.

"All right—I'll say the obvious," Vitek said at last. "Where are we?"

"Home," Singer said.

It grew lighter moment by moment, revealing slope on slope, crest on crest of rolling empty grassland stretching away to the south. Wind rushed across the vast plain and hissed in the grass. Somewhere in the distance, muted beneath the wind music, there was one other sound, irregular and rhythmic, the rush and rumble of water over rock.

"Home. This was my home." He pointed with his chin

downhill to the east. There was enough light to show, like a dark sprawled shadow, the tumbled pile of black rock below them.

"What is this place?" Vitek asked, and shuddered. He groped desperately for a logically acceptable explanation. "What—you drugged me and took me out of the city. How long has it been?"

"No time at all. No drugs. We had to leave swiftly, so I took you to the one place I knew I could find without thinking. My default setting." That was the Gero memory, and it wrung a surprised laugh from him even as he said it.

"That's impossible," Vitek said. He looked back and forth from Singer to the desolate plains, and Singer could hear his thoughts stuttering, unable to calculate a change too big to fit his pattern.

"Yes. All the thoughts you have are true. All those things could happen. A single man could destroy your refinery or your orbital shuttles and make you scratch a living from the ground with sticks. The knowledge I have now shows me precisely where to strike at you. I don't even need to go there."

Vitek grasped at a conclusion. "Shoot him," he said to the guard.

But the guard's knees had failed her, and she was sitting in the grass gasping, her hands clenched into white-knuckled fists. Saldivar crouched down beside her and spoke to her quietly in the polvorado dialect, trying to calm her.

Singer laughed again. "I brought our clothes this time, but I think I forgot her rifle, Governor. Besides, I could be gone before a shell reached the place where I am."

He saw on the governor's face the horrified realization that Singer could simply be elsewhere, leaving them with no way to get home.

"Do you want to go home?" Singer went on. "So do I. Men like you make their own circuits where the power runs. To go another way is unthinkable when you sit in the middle of the pattern. You can't see another way. But that pattern is small. The world is big. I brought you here to show you that world. Now you taste a little sip of the bitter medicine you poured for me when you broke my world and shattered my heart and made me seek another path for my life."

There was silence, broken only by the wind voices.

"If you're going to kill me, I can't stop you," Vitek said heavily. "You want revenge for that order I signed, I suppose. At least spare Genady and the soldier. They never harmed you."

Genady was shocked and shaken himself, but he tried to reassure the governor. "Vitek, he's my friend. He's not here to hurt anyone. Just listen to him."

But he, too, looked at Singer fearfully. Singer knew that fear. They could accept him as one of themselves only as long as he did not shock them with his differences.

"I saved your life. Back there you are a dead man. Why would I give you another life if I wanted to kill you? Put away your fear and try to think straight. I am not your enemy."

"Then why did you bring me here? What are you trying to do?" Vitek seemed to be near the end of his endurance.

"I want you to look. Down there are the bones of my people scattered in the grass. I want you to see the place where the world ended. You sent me out naked to look for another life. Now I'm returning the favor. It's a kind of revenge, I suppose— the only kind I can have."

"It's a damn good revenge if that's what you want. My city is burning, and I'm not there. Everything that I tried to do will be wasted."

"Lying and bargaining with liars? Letting the Net use you while you turned your back and closed your eyes? Too bad to waste that."

Vitek did not flinch from his scornful look. "What do you expect me to say? I lied when I had to, and I let the Net use me when I thought I could get something back. I made bad deals. I sold your people along with my own. You can't tell me what to regret. I used the only weapons I had. I kept some possibilities alive. I kept the Net off the backs of the same people who wanted to throw my ass out on the street. If I hadn't cooperated, they'd have chosen someone else. Someone without the guts or the brains to resist in any way. What choice did I have?"

The words were bitter and tough in his mouth, not false but chewed over so many times that the taste sickened him. As he spoke, Singer felt the buried thing inside Vitek, the thing that he had chained and weighted and fed with music to keep it quiet as it struggled to get free. It called him closer.

"You have a choice now."

Vitek shook his head, backing away. "It's too late. Your presence destroyed the only choice I had. You alarmed the Net, and now they are systematically wiping up my city."

"Don't say those words to me—too late! My people are bones and ashes down there, and I have waded in blood and fire to get to your nice house in North Fork. Too late—are you dead? You don't look dead to me."

Singer grabbed for the Delh'tani leader to stop him from moving any farther away. He touched Vitek just over the heart as the buried thing finally broke the surface.

Freedom, said Vitek's heart.

And the music poured back into Singer with the touch, washing over him in a wave of sweet relief. He had not been wrong. Vitek had a true self embedded somewhere in the trap he had built. Yet Singer still could not open the trap.

A terrible hunger for the truth burned Vitek, but still he would not let Singer in. Singer could have torn down his defenses, could have crushed and overwhelmed the Delh'tani and rifled his mind like a wrecked storehouse. That would have been Gero's way. It would get him the facts he wanted, but it would solve nothing. Force could destroy but not create. No force could make the Delh'tani's choices for him.

The iron music strode on, and Singer kept his balance by clinging to its structure. *Freedom? Stretch out your hand and take it. Take it.*

Vitek still resisted. *No. It's another trap. Something hidden.*

A memory came back to Singer: Siri, too, had mistrusted him. *There is a darkness in you, young one, like the darkness running before a great storm.*

Frustration tensed his skin and made the short hair on his neck stand up. *I don't have time for this! I don't have time!*

He let go of Vitek. "How do I make you trust me?" he asked aloud.

"You can see what I think," Vitek said. He was not calming down. He was panicking, his heart racing so fast that it stumbled over itself.

"Yes, all right," Singer shouted, wrung with frustration. "I can't help hearing the things you are shouting out loud. The things I want, the things I need, those I can't see because you won't let me. Yes, I could take it whether you wanted or not. But ask yourself why I don't do that. Why don't I take all your memories and kill you now? How can I see what you think when you are not thinking!"

Vitek stared at him, breathing hard. "Why?"

"It's like this: I can do to you whatever I don't mind living with. Forever. I don't forget easy. I can kill you and live your death forever, like the Rock lives in me, forever burning."

"I don't understand."

"You never will. Not from inside the box."

He held his hands out, palms up.

Slowly, as slowly as a man running in a dream, Vitek reached out to touch him.

The first thing Singer knew was that the music was a song for the dead. It strode inexorably on, and Singer moved with it, keeping the balance, allowing Vitek to take what he could and make of it what he would. The governor was not content to see what Singer had been doing in North Fork. His need moved back and back in time, toward the moment Singer never wanted to taste again. It took all his strength not to strike and not to flee. He felt Vitek's hand tremble in his grasp as the scattered stones below stood tall again and fell again, burning—or was it he who trembled in the fire of memory?

Vitek bowed under the wall of fire that had swept Gero to his death. Short, bald, oversoft from too much sitting, he sank beneath the weight, he bowed, he sank to his knees as the firestorm swept through Singer's heart and his. But he lived. On his knees to Singer's dead, he cried out without any defense.

The music broke up in his mind, in confused lament, its beautiful form shattered.

> *Whatever is hidden shall appear,*
> *No wrong remain unpunished.*
> *The wicked confounded, cast into devouring flames,*
> *. . . begging, kneeling, my heart crushed to ashes,*
> *tearful that day*
> *when the guilty man rises from the ashes to be judged.*

He flinched from Singer and trembled, finding himself inextricably woven into Singer's awareness, unable to hide.

If you brought me here to punish me, avenger, I am punished. My people are killing each other, and North Fork is burning. I'm lost.

Singer held on to the governor while he hunted for something in Vitek's mind that would explain what he wanted to say. There was a treasure of music there that made him tremble again with desire, but he stopped with the first thing he found that might work.

Listen: Within these walls no betrayer hides. For we forgive our enemies. If you cannot learn this, you are not worthy to be human.

He had the words wrong; he knew that. They came kindly to him, for they sounded like Kruger's mother tongue, but he did not have time to understand them fully. But the music that came with them was easy and sweet and could be pointed like an arrow straight into the governor's heart.

"What you just saw killed Tony Gero. I took from him everything he knew. Then he taught me some things he did not know himself. This is one of them. There's no victory in revenge for me. I cannot separate your fate from mine."

He leaned on Vitek, forcing the full weight of that, the heavy bitterness, down his throat after the sweet music.

"I do not say this to you because I like to say it. I did not wish to be your friend. But I have no choice. What is it you call my world? New Hope? If you will not trust me, nothing new will happen here. This is the end."

Vitek straightened himself up slowly, still grasping Singer's hand for support.

You can trust me, Vitek. You know me now. I, too, made fool's bargains. I kept myself alive with the weapons of my enemy, though they burned my hands. I know what it is to hide the truth within a lie and go into bondage for the sake of freedom. I know your songs, Delh'tani. I am not your enemy.

"Do I hear running water?" Vitek asked hoarsely. "I'm thirsty."

Singer led them to the river. It was strange and terrible to be in this familiar place and find it still empty—not a voice, not a single footfall to echo those which lived so clearly in his heart.

Vitek crouched down in the shallows, with the swift current rippling about his boots, and plunged his hands into the icy water. Thunder River flowed so fast that it was open in all seasons, but fragile flakes and droplets of ice formed wherever the current slowed and eddied. Vitek lifted water in his hands and splashed his face and head, gasping with the cold but repeating it till the soot and the smell of smoke were washed away. Before he drank, he straightened up, shaking drops from his hair and hands. He reached clumsily for Singer's arm.

I know what I'm doing. His communication was labored, almost all in words transmitted one by one as if in some ancient code, but he was talking. *I saw how they used to wash here after the fighting. I respect your custom. I admit my responsibility for what happened here. Will you let me drink from Thunder River?*

Singer searched him for certainty that he really meant it, that this was not a clever act, daubing the unpalatable with honey. Vitek's face shone fresh and raw like the new skin over a wound. Suddenly the landscape was no longer empty in Singer's perception. The old ones of the Rock stood all around him, looking over his shoulder, silently waiting.

Drink, he said. "Drink."

They all drank thirstily, washing away the dryness of smoke and fear. And he knew for certain that he had done the right thing. *This is how the Rock has always survived. We take the children of our enemies and make them our own. What was I when I came here? A son of the cityfolk—son of Hadhla, the Riders' enemy. They gave to me with both hands.*

Vitek splashed back to the bank. He stretched out a hand for Genady to help him up over the edge and kept the handclasp once he was up.

"Thanks, Genya. Thanks for giving me the benefit of the doubt. You saved my life."

He looked over at the guard, who still sat in the grass, wide-eyed. "What's your name, soldier?"

"Tyler," she stammered.

"On your feet, Tyler. These men are allies. They came to warn me of a coup attempt by Colonel Patel, and they have succeeded in rescuing us. Go get a drink, wash your face, pull yourself together. We have work to do."

He had set aside the strange circumstances and returned to his normal frame of reference. "Now what? Is it possible to go back to North Fork at some other location?"

"Possible. Maybe not the best idea. Let me check with my friends," Singer said.

He could feel how cold Janet's hands were. Her shoulders still jumped and trembled with fear.

It's nothing, she assured him quickly. *The governor's house burned like a straw stack. Then the golpos came after us and cleared the street with gas and rubber bullets. Not many casualties—it reminded me of back on Delta, that's all. We're in a safe house now. What comes next?*

He showed her the governor.

He thinks the Net was trying to smoke him. He wants to come back. Ask Jon's friends what they think. Can their people protect Vitek from assassination? Will they?

Janet conferred with others and waited while unknown voices argued. Singer could not follow it all.

They say it's better if he can get to Jefferson—I assume you're out in the zone somewhere. Jeff would be safer because North Fork is crawling with golpos now. We can come down and meet you. Will he go on the video and announce that the Net has attempted a coup and the police actions are illegal? Will he say he's in favor of ending the state of emergency?

Singer looked at Vitek for an answer and then realized that he had not heard the question.

"They want to know what you'll do if they help you. Will you declare an end to martial law and call off the security forces?"

"Wait a minute. You're communicating with North Fork?"

"Sure, like I did with you. Distance is not important."

"There are more of your people there?"

"No. There are more of my people, but my friends in North Fork are Delh'tani. Like you."

"Humans can do this? Could I do this?"

"You're going to have to find another word for your kind," Singer said gently.

"Sorry. Could I do this?"

"You already have."

"But over distance—if I were in North Fork?"

Singer shrugged. "Don't know. Zhanne could do this before I knew her, a little. I opened a door that was not latched. We have been together a long time. But you won't ever know what you can do till you have time to learn.

"Here's what I think: Whatever is in me must be in someone else, too. I did not come from nowhere. Maybe that is true for your people, too. Somewhere all the things that would make a person like me exist. Someday they will come together. Already have, most likely. So if you are thinking—or if one of your people thinks someday—that you could stop the changes by killing me, maybe you should think again. I learned in a hard school. You can't count on that next time. When the next one like me comes along, you might want to have me here. Killing me—assuming that you could—does not make you safe. Just the opposite."

He thought of Roishe as he spoke and of all the little shaved-heads scuttling around the Black City, some of them, maybe, more of Korro's experiments. The Delh'tani thought of Tony Gero and his talent for taking people apart.

"I see your point," Vitek said. He frowned as he considered other implications of Singer's question. "Are you telling me that the antis have control of broadcasting? They'd have to if they want me to make a statement."

"Don't know, but if they say so, it's true."

"Then tell them yes."

Singer relayed Vitek's decision. *But I'll talk with Makho first,* he added. *Everything must come together.*

We put in a call to Captain Galen at Firebase Flathead, Janet said. *You know, our friend. He says a long-range recon picked up Marcus about two days out.*

Good, Singer said. *Keep telling me where you are. And if you move, stay off the street. We're going to see Galen now. Expect a message soon.*

"Come close to me," Singer said aloud. "It's easier that way."

"So. We're going to—" Vitek swallowed. "We're going to—*travel* again? Would you like to explain how you do that?"

"Sure, I would like to. But I can't. It feels like a shaping of things, a changing of the pattern. *Here* is a configuration. Distance is a way of looking, not a thing itself." He shrugged. "Maybe with practice I will understand. Or maybe one of you Delh'tani will give me the words someday. I do not like to trust in arts I do not understand—or ask you to trust them. But remember, for me the first time I flew was as bad."

He reined them in as he spoke, like a starter for a race, calming all the horses for a moment's stillness before the leap into action. He had them all in hand, and then he leapt.

13

They landed softly on sand, up on the plateau by the firebase. Singer straightened up slowly and waved his hands, empty, so the watchers would know that he wanted to be seen.

"Don't move. Let them come and get us. That way they will not be so nervous. I do not want any shooting. These are polvorados and not your tame house soldiers."

They sat down and waited. In a few minutes a light vehicle came surging over the sand toward them.

"Remain seated," the speaker instructed them. "Put your hands on your head."

The moto trained its pod gun on them, and two soldiers jumped out with rifles ready. As they approached, one of them recognized Singer, Saldivar, and Genady.

"You again!"

"Yes. We have brought someone back with us. It is important for us to see the captain right away. He would want that."

The soldier looked at Vitek, and his eyes widened. "My orders are to take you there, anyway. Get in."

The captain was waiting for them, on his feet and looking ill pleased. He ordered the sentry to keep everyone away.

"There has been a lot of confusion in this area lately. I hope you're here to clear it up."

Then he saw Vitek.

"Good afternoon, Captain." Vitek held out his hand in the formal gesture. "I am Vitek Karoly. The governor."

"Holy shit," the captain said. "Excuse me, your Excellency. If you really are Governor Karoly. I mean, where the hell did you come from?"

"Have you been watching the video lately?"

"Of course I have," the captain snapped. "I have nothing better to do with my time than check out the flix. That's why you sent me to this sandpile."

"Had you been monitoring," Vitek continued, keeping his temper, "you might understand why I am here if not how. There has been a coup attempt against my government. One of my aides was assassinated, and I was the target of another attempt. There is rioting in North Fork, and the governor's house has burned to the ground. I was supposed to be in it."

The captain sent a runner for his communications officer.

"I brought the governor here for refuge," Singer said.

The captain interrupted him. "Dakko, suppose this flippo story of yours turns out to be true—it is the governor, and the Net is trying to assassinate him. Why me? Out of all the places you could have gone, why pick on this particular pile of rocks and sand flies? I've got three companies of humpers and a couple of sandblasted vitos that are flight-ready on alternate Tuesdays only. What do you want from me?"

"Why: you are farthest north of any outpost," Singer said. "Closest to where I want to go. And you were straight with me when I came here before. What I want: provide transportation and support for General Kruger and his forces so the governor will have a bodyguard to protect him when he goes back to North Fork to declare an end to martial law. And use your uplink to contact Solidari so the governor can negotiate a truce with the Nupis. That's all."

Singer knew he had caught him. The captain had spent months thrashing in the sand, losing men to attrition and accident, picking off an occasional Nupi patrol for no discernible purpose. The possibility of definite and sweeping action glittered in his eyes like the reflection of water in the desert.

"I can't do that," he said. "I have no authority. You've got the wrong man."

The communications officer arrived, out of breath. "Yes, sir, the security forces have been called out in North Fork and Jefferson. The news channel says the antis have provoked violence and the governor is reported missing. His security chief was killed by sniper fire."

"What do you pick up from chatter?"

The communications officer started to answer, then looked at the strangers. He stopped and looked again at Vitek.

"Is that the man whose picture you saw in the news?" the captain asked.

"Yes, sir—that is, he looks like him."

The captain rubbed his eyes wearily. Singer moved closer to him and sensed the sting under the man's eyelids.

"Don't rub it," he said. "I can fix that if you want."

The captain looked at him dourly. "No, thanks. One thing at a time."

He pulled Singer aside. "One of my scouts overflew a column like what you described. Now we're getting calls on the radio. Talk to them; tell me if it's Kruger. I've seen him. If Marcus Kruger comes here and tells me this is the governor, I'll believe it."

Singer was not used to speaking to the Delh'tani machines, but as soon as he heard the small, faraway voice, he made direct contact, as well.

"Makho!"

"About time someone answered us. What are you doing there? You were in Jefferson last time we spoke."

"I have the Delh'tani Asharya here. The governor. We had to take them out of North Fork because the Net burned his house down. But everything is under control."

He heard an incredulous snort from Kruger.

"What about you?" Singer asked.

"We're ready to come in. The camp guards had deserted, just like the last one. There was an airstrip and hangar space for midsize cargo vitos. Looked like all the guards had climbed on one of those and just taken off. I don't know why they didn't take the rest of the vehicles. Probably couldn't fuel up. Their stocks were low. We had to estimate the optimax for number of trucks we could use and distance we could travel with them. We've got all the men, but they're not all fast on their feet. We could use a ride home. That's why I called."

"I'll get you your ride, Makho."

Vitek had been listening. "You don't need special orders to pick up on a distress call, do you?" he asked the captain.

"No, I don't."

"Dakko, then assist Kruger with all speed. When he gets here, he can identify me. We'll take it from there."

"I don't know that pickup was meant to apply to a small army."

"Stretch a point. I can assure you that no one in North Fork is paying the slightest bit of attention to Firebase Flathead. Nor are they likely to."

The captain shrugged. "No choice if they are really my cofras. I have to go after them. As soon as we can power up the vitos."

It was close to midafternoon when the first flights of prisoners arrived. Kruger was not with them. The pilots reported that he had refused to leave the pallantai. With at least three vitos working at any given time, the last flight, with Kruger on board, arrived on the plateau before midnight. They had dropped food and water for the two dozen Riders who had stayed to bring the horses along to the river. The trucks had been abandoned, their last drop of fuel drained. The new arrivals crowded every corner of the firebase. Medics and cooks worked late into the night.

Kruger leaned out of the vito, shading his eyes against the floodlights. Singer loped to his side and offered him a shoulder for support as he climbed down. The Asharya growled at him as usual, but without conviction.

"I want to see Vitek," Kruger said immediately.

The governor advanced toward them before the wash had died. "Colonel Kruger—excuse me, General Kruger—allow me to express my great happiness at seeing you alive. I attended your funeral, you know. You'll find my speech on record. It was quite laudatory.''

"I don't doubt it," Kruger said. "Words are cheap."

Having made his speech, Vitek found himself temporarily at a loss. Kruger's appearance had changed a good deal. He was strong and darkly tanned; what remained of his hair had grown long and was braided behind him for riding. Little of his original gear remained, though he had salvaged the insignia from his uniform shirt and wore it on a vest of black coltskin embroidered with a border of golden flowers.

"I was told a number of things that were not true," Vitek said finally. "I received a report that you'd died in the hospital. That was the week of the PCOM fire—a week of many funerals. It would not have occurred to me to question your death. I knew you had been seriously ill for some time. How—how did you recover from Karpinski's syndrome? Was it a misdiagnosis?''

"No. But that's a subject for another day, Governor. That problem is a wolf shot and skinned. We have others still kicking at the spear's end. Meanwhile, I'd like a cup of coffee and something to sit down on that neither trots nor experiences turbulence.''

A knot of polvorados had already gathered beside the strip, watching Kruger. The captain came up to them, also watching the Asharya. When he got close enough, he saluted and held the salute till Kruger reluctantly returned it. The polvorados stood in silence with their eyes on Kruger till he had gone with the governor into the captain's tent.

"Welcome back, sir," the captain said. "I can't tell you what it means to see you here like this. My people are finding friends, relatives listed as dead for more than a year. To be bringing them home again—it's like a miracle.''

"This is the first time since I left Jefferson that I have been able to think of the Mothers and keep my head up," Kruger said. "We made the pickup. Finally. You took a chance for us. I won't forget that.''

"I take it that you admit this is General Kruger," Vitek interrupted.

"Hell, yes, it's him," the captain said without taking his eyes off the Asharya.

"General, will you certify for the captain that I am Vitek Karoly, the colony governor?''

"Oh, I have no doubt about your identity," Kruger said. "I didn't realize that was an issue. Captain, I recognize him personally, but for future reference, whatever Singer tells you, I will back up. I consider him completely trustworthy.''

''Now that we've established that, will you accept my orders?'' Vitek asked.

The captain took a quick look at Vitek. ''I don't know about that, but I'll take orders from *him*.''

Singer felt a chill in the air as Vitek considered that response.

''What about you, General—will you accept my authority?''

Kruger chuckled. ''Having second thoughts, your Excellency? You made me a general.''

''I had in mind an officer of the Deltan Consorso, not a freelance generalissimo. I heard the way some of those troops—if that's what they are, for I saw children, longhairs, all kinds of people out there—I heard the way they speak of you. They call you 'the Asharya.' What does that mean? Just what kind of sway do you hold over them?''

Kruger threw back his head and laughed. ''Well, I've been left for dead, poisoned, declared a criminal, fired, and buried in absentia by your government, sir. I agree that my status certainly requires regularization. But I can assure you that the sack of Jefftown is not high on my agenda right now. You're really worried about my title? You think I'm some kind of a caudillo? It means 'Grandfather,' your Excellency. You're welcome to call me Grandfather, too, if it makes you feel any better.

''Otherwise call me Marcus and skip all this crap. Titles don't mean a lot to me now. Singer has briefed me on the situation. Let's discuss what you need.''

While they talked, Singer quietly withdrew into himself and looked up Janet. He found her almost instantly. He was startled, as if he had tripped over someone he thought was far away. As he moved into her senses, he felt that she was moving, coming closer to him. The motion went in all directions, too free to be riding in a truck, yet he felt a vibration humming through her body.

Suddenly he realized that he was feeling the vibration with his own outer senses, as well. He jumped up and looked out through the tent door.

''They're here!'' he exclaimed.

The others, their conference interrupted, crowded up to look. ''What is it?''

''It's Zhanne,'' Singer said. ''She has stolen some vitos.'' He felt a surge of great pride, as if she had come home from a raid with a whole herd of horses.

He pointed to the place where he could detect the disturbance in the sky, but the others saw nothing. Kruger turned his head back and forth, trying to get a fix on the distant sound.

"Yes, I hear something," he said.

In a few minutes the vitos' running lights showed as bright specks, and the soldiers were looking and pointing. A short time after that a tight formation of three came roaring across the plateau and landed in clouds of dust that glowed pale in the searchlights. They were painted with the white stripes that meant a medical flight.

Singer sprinted down the field to meet them. Zhanne jumped down to him, beaming like Roishe after getting away with some piece of mischief.

"Petersen came through. We have the first batch of antibiotic—or should it be antiexobiotic? Oh, well, Petersen will think of something suitably stuffy. Pete-o-cillin, maybe. I was going to say it's hot from the vat, but actually it's still chilled from the freeze dryer. He isn't with us. He thinks he has isolated an antigen from a sample of my blood, and he's going nuts in his eagerness to find the bug itself and culture it out. Petersen's dream: meet interesting bacteria and kill them."

"Zhanne!" Singer cut her short with difficulty. "How did you do this? I couldn't think of a way."

"Look inside, paliao. You have all the authorization codes to cut orders. I saw them in there and salvaged them. Sorry, but to me it's like seeing a perfectly good tool just lying by the side of the road. You weren't using them, and I can. I convinced Petersen that you'd need emergency flights for the prisoners and that would be a good way to keep the vitos safe so we'd be sure of having them for a mercy flight to Solidari later. Mira!"

"You have crew?"

"Yes. They were on strike, anyway, and Petersen said he'd cut them orders to go. He amazed me. I didn't know he had it in him."

"Everybody has something in him. Give him a chance to use it, and you find out if he really means it. That's all."

"Yeah, maybe. Maybe that blow on the head I gave him did him good. Or maybe I just didn't understand what motivates him—bugs in large quantities."

"And you?"

"Me what? Oh—motivation."

He felt a flash of something too quick and complicated for words: her feeling for the systems she had been trained on. She loved them as he had loved the swift patterns of his sword.

I love you, my heart, and I love your people. I am a Rider, and I'll be one forever now. But madre'dio, it's good to be home. There's so much I can do, but I have to have the tools for it.

She was light on her feet, almost dancing in the curve of his arm in spite of her desert boots.

"*Ayei*, all right, then, isé," Singer said. "I'm glad you're here. There's another thing I need you for before we move out."

"What?" Quick alarm; she thought he meant more fighting.

"A night of dreams. But first we have to talk to Hazzan."

14

The captain met them at the end of the strip. "I don't have any fuel for you," he said.

"If you need fuel, let Makho speak for you. He owns many favors, no?"

Kruger was mildly startled. "That's true. I never lived to collect on some of them. Let me see who's stationed in this area and owns trucks. I shall rise from the dead and request to be fueled up." He grinned; the prospect obviously pleased him.

"Governor, I think it is time to call the Nupis," Singer said. "I will stand with you and greet them."

"Jon has a video link in place, and he thinks we can jam the news channel at least once. We can record whenever you're ready and transmit to the news at the auspicious moment. He doesn't know how long that window will last. It depends on how fast security catches up with us."

"Can we get face-to-face with the Nupis?" Singer asked.

Easy. Jon spoke simultaneously to Janet and, through her, straight to Singer.

"Do it," Singer said. "The Nupis are desperate. Seeing faces will help."

Hazzan still lived, but he had the look of a man who had been clinging to a cliff face all night.

"Thank God it's you," he said when he saw Singer, as if he had never played master to Singer's slave. He did not wait for Singer to introduce the faces behind him. Anxiety and isolation had burned away his caution.

"Where is Luis-Win?" Vitek asked immediately. "I can't negotiate with a commander for a planetary truce."

Hazzan looked to Singer in desperation. "You know our situation! Tell them this is not a trick, I swear it. Who will satisfy your leaders, to negotiate? The chairman is dead, as you know, and the senior officers—" He swallowed. "There was not enough medicine for all the sick. You knew that. The medical staff made a decision. They treated irreplaceable specialists first, then children and their parents. Then the young and strong. The officers—they are still waiting. I think that most of them will not survive."

Abruptly he stood straight and looked Vitek in the eye. "The medical staff decided. They were very angry. Dr. Nasri took responsibility for all of them. I could have given orders, at gunpoint, to change the procedure. I did not. If the Consorso leaders will negotiate only with Luis-Win and his staff, then there will be no truce. We will die here. And we will see you in hell."

"Commander Hazzan, I recognize you as the representative of the New Peoples' Union," Singer said formally. "General Kruger will accept my decision, and Governor Karoly will accept his."

"I just have one question for you before we begin," Vitek said. "If we reach a decision, are you able to carry it out?"

"Yes," Hazzan said slowly. "I believe that I can."

Kruger turned to look at Singer, and Singer nodded to him almost imperceptibly. Hazzan's face was naked with shock. He had no defenses left that would hide a lie.

"I am readying a medical rescue mission," Vitek said. "Three vitos with supplies and personnel. They can leave tomorrow or the next day. But these are my people. I must have your assurance of their safety before I order them to do this."

"I give you my assurance," Hazzan said.

Again Singer nodded. Hazzan had spoken with great confidence that time. There was no doubt in his mind that the medikhani would be received with honor.

"On our part, the truce will begin when your medical flight lands," Hazzan went on. "No more offensive action against your troops. But we will continue to defend ourselves. I cannot guarantee anyone's safety if we are attacked."

"Understood, of course," Vitek said.

Hazzan explained haltingly that he preferred not to enter into any binding agreements until the current crisis was resolved. He attempted to conceal from Vitek the fact that Solidari was in a state of complete collapse, but Singer and the others who had been there could hear that in the tone of his voice and the gaps in the things he said. Singer also recognized the gaps in the information Vitek gave to Hazzan and hoped that the Nupi was too distraught to notice the deception. They agreed to speak again when the medical flight had arrived and to decide on a formal process of negotiation at that time.

Vitek turned away from the blank screen. "Can I borrow a sweat rag?" he asked the captain. Singer noted that the governor had remained cool and calm till the transmission had ended. Then he had suddenly bloomed with sweat and the sharp smell of anxiety. Vitek had more control of himself than he knew. Singer thought he could learn very quickly not to be cold.

"I have to be there to keep my promise," Vitek said, mopping his neck. "I have to return to North Fork—or Jefferson, it doesn't really matter which, as long as I hold a center of command and population—and stay alive when I'm there."

"Jefferson is easier," Kruger said. He stared off at the tent wall in a way that told Singer he was visualizing maps and terrain, not seeing the people around him. "We need a unified force, and we can't mobilize the air transport to get us all to North Fork at once. I think I can get the trucks for Jefferson. But it's slow. It gives them time to get ready." He frowned and fell silent, figuring.

"Marcus, I hope you're not considering this in terms of a military offensive," Vitek said. "I will not exchange war with the Nupis for an internal conflict."

Kruger snorted. "Then I am afraid I cannot help you very far. If you forbid me to kill your enemies, I may as well stay here and picnic. I certainly shall not take my people weaponless against the Net. If I don't have your authorization to use appropriate force, I won't go."

" 'Appropriate force'! You're asking me to declare war on members of the Consorso. I can't do that.''

"All my troubles started with a file labeled 'Clausewitz,' " Kruger said. His voice grated as if he still had sand in his throat. "Maybe you should have read what he had to say before you took charge of this colony. The Net has tried to kill you. It sure as hell tried to kill me. A state of war already exists—has existed for years. A state of war between the government whose actions you sanctioned and those who were subject to its will. There is civil war for you, your Excellency—the worst and most pernicious kind. And 'war is such a dangerous business that the mistakes which come from kindness are the very worst.' "

Singer stepped between them. "My Asharya, listen." He listened himself, far back into Kruger's memory, to make sure he had it right. "Even in war there are different shapes, no? It can change. A change in policy changes things—'changes the terrible battle sword that a man needs both hands and his entire strength to wield and with which he strikes home once and no more into a light, handy rapier—sometimes just a foil for the exchange of thrusts, feints, and parries.' That's right, no? 'One point and one only yields an integrated view of phenomena.' " He stumbled a little over words familiar to his memory but not to his lips. "Makho, I had to give away my sword. It's not kindness I advise you. I look for that one point. Let me try.''

~~~~~, get out of my head. How can I argue with you when you turn my own thoughts against me . . . Kruger's anger trailed away as he realized that he was demonstrating what Singer had just suggested.

Singer continued as if there had been no reaction from the Asharya. "I can show you a way to enter Jefferson without a blow struck, but it is not without danger. There is maybe more risk to Vitek's people than to our own.''

The flat white light in the tent and the heat of lights and bodies blocked his sense of the time. He stepped out for a moment to look at the stars and get a breath of the air. Night was far advanced, but they still had a few hours till dawn, and he still could not hear any hint of the trucks coming.

"You cannot leave till Makho's trucks get here, in any case. Give me the night to work in and decide in the morning,'' he said.

"I don't like this,'' Kruger said. He and Vitek stared each other down, measuring.

Makho! Singer said, pleading. *Let me try this. You know I will be straight with you if I see that it will not work. I will not give up lives to the governor's wishes.*

Kruger shrugged. "Well, he has been right before. Let's sleep on it."

"Yes," Vitek said wearily. "I need to think."

"You can rest in my tent if you want," the captain offered. "My bed's probably the only one in camp that isn't in use."

They returned to the captain's sleeping place, leaving Singer, Saldivar, and Janet in the communications tent.

Janet stopped Singer before he could begin to explain. "I think I understand. But I'd like to try something more obvious first. We have a list of prisoners and their next of kin. I can send this down to Jon and have him flash them all. The message will appear to come through proper channels but will have no return numbers. It will be another mystery to occupy their minds."

"What will you say?"

"What do you want me to say? The name and the news that they are coming home. A message to meet them on the access road from the north."

"That's good." Singer thought for a minute. "We need the airport blocked with bodies, too. So send to the kin of the wounded that they should meet them at the airstrip. The families and the friends they tell should fill up the strip."

She began sending the list of names to Jon.

"We're going to jam the morning news and send them Vitek's little chat with the Nupis instead," Jon sent back by way of acknowledgment. "Let them try to explain that. But I'll cut the bit about Luis-Win, with your permission. No point in encouraging the hardshells to go for a decisive solution. Let them think the old turtle is still snapping."

"That's good," Singer said. "The dream will come. Then the sign to prove it. I think few will resist both."

"What are you talking about?" Jon asked suspiciously. He was deftly editing his recording as he spoke, and he resented being distracted from the technical niceties. Singer recognized the same pleasure in expertise that he had seen in Janet.

Dreams, Janet said gently. *A kind of singing. Another kind of calling, because print and flix won't reach them all.*

"I'll help."

You sure? Openness and tight rapport with even one stranger made Jon's skin crawl. He needed more distance than any brother Singer had ever known.

Yes, I'm sure. The speaker was silent. Jon's answer came in the heart language. *I speak loud and clear, you know that. I'm strong. And the stronger we are, the better the chances, no? I want to be with you.*

For once, instead of closing himself off again as soon as he had spoken, he waited, rested, pressed as close to them as palm against palm.

They left the radio to the puzzled communications officer and went in silent agreement toward the nearest tent full of prisoners. On the way they passed a group huddled on the flatbed of a truck under a makeshift awning.

Might as well start here. Singer leaned over the truck bed and reached toward the first sleeper. Slowly, cautiously, he began to weave himself into the man's mind, as he had done with the captain, so that his presence, when finally recognized, would cause no alarm. When he felt safe, he looked around for the sleeper's name.

Silvio Masyk, he told Janet. She found in her list the name of his next of kin—not really kin; he had no one closer than a woman he had once lived with.

Singer made him an offer: courteous and respectful, like the palms-up Thanha gesture of greeting. He was ready to leave if Masyk rejected him, but the sleeping Delh'tani reached out with longing for his company and willingly shared his memories of the woman who had been his friend.

That was the easy part. The hard part was finding that woman among so many, finding that one particular flavor in the stew of Jefferson's streets. Singer despaired of it. They were too far away. There were too many of them. They were strangers. Janet steadied him.

She's as close as Jon. As close as we are. Think you are walking through the tent and looking for her.

Jon had been busy at his desk again. *She moved back to the farm.*

The dark green smell of the water tanks came back to Singer then. The window in the barracks was open, though the night was chilly. The woman wanted air fresher than the stale warmth of the barracks. She slept fitfully. She was a heavyset, strong-armed woman. Her face was sunburned, and she frowned as if still squinting against the glare, though the sun was gone. Masyk smiled in his sleep when he saw her face.

Lia, he said wistfully. *Lia, I'm coming home.*

The woman woke up with a gasp, stretching out her arms to nothing. She looked around, bewildered, and then began to cry.

The woman in the bunk next to her woke up, too, and turned to her in sympathy.

"What's wrong?" Singer heard her say. "What has happened?"

At first she could only cry and shake her head, but at last she replied. "Silvio. He was right there, I swear, as close as you are. He reached out his arms to me and called my name. He said, 'I'm coming home.' "

She faded from Singer's awareness as she came wide awake, and he returned to the darkness beside the trucks. The sleeper next to Masyk was a thin brown woman. Her name was Erminia Honas. She had a little brother.

Ayei, *there are hundreds*.

So many names, each with its warm, aching weight of memory and desire. For a moment he wanted to run into the cool empty darkness, but he braced himself and touched her hand, pacing his breath to go lightly like the rise and fall of her gaunt ribs.

From each sleeper they took the faces to go with the names in Janet's memory. They hunted for those kindred and friends down the streets Jon knew and spoke into their dreams the lost names. One by one they hunted them down and breathed fire into the ashes of memory. It was a long journey through the dark, empty streets of the colony, through years of sorrow. Singer was lost in the procession of their memories. His hands knew the stained and crumpled garments that held all those dreams, but to his inner eye the dreamers appeared as myriad lights in tangled constellations, slowly turning around each other, drawing and repelling in a dance that bound them all. He might have wandered with them endlessly, but his hearth was around him to bring him home. The cold dew weighed on his body and pulled him down through fathoms of sleep till he could feel Palha's hands shaking him awake. All over Jefferson he felt the pang as they woke up to the white, ghostly morning, hearts pounding, faces wet, reaching out for hands that vanished as they touched.

Singer shook with cold and confusion, clinging to their hands. He knew who they were, but for a moment he could not remember their names.

I dreamed of Mama, Papa, Jon choked. *It's been years since I could see their faces. I dreamed they were coming home.*

He cried in Janet's arms, though it was Saldivar who held her. *Dio, what a fool,* Jon said at last, wiping his face on his sleeve. *I'm a big boy now. Too old. That was far, far away. Just then it came so close.*

They have to come close, Janet said. *It's why we came here. They died on Delta, and they were buried in prison. We had to come here to set their memory free. When we're free, they can live again. In us.*

There was a long silence from Jon. *Day's coming,* he said shakily. *I have to get ready.* He turned his attention to setting up for the broadcast, and his presence faded to an occasional touch.

Singer sorted himself out from them slowly. The growing light helped by giving back to the trucks and the brush and his own body their distinctive outlines and shadows. He looked around at the tents and the huddles of sleepers in trucks and under ponchos and sheds.

"Are we finished?" he asked Janet.

"Yes. We did everything we could."

They walked slowly toward the open area by the cooks' tent. Singer longed for the heat of crackling sticks and glowing coals. Heaters were not like hearth fires, but at least they might get some hot water for tea. He shook his head to clear the buzzing in his ears and then realized that it was the sound of trucks laboring up the steep, winding road.

By the time they reached the captain's tent, Kruger was awake. He took the cup from Singer's hand and swallowed a gulp, then grimaced. Firebase Flathead could supply neither tea nor honey. The cup held hot sugar water.

"What's the matter with you? You're shivering."

Hilurin took Singer's hands. "I dreamed of strangers all night. You should have asked me to help." As he spoke, he urged Singer's body to warm itself. Hilurin took the cup away from Kruger and thrust it back into Singer's hands. "Drink it. And sit down."

Singer rested himself gratefully on Kruger's cot. "I dreamed with the strangers, Lurya. It can be done. They will be waiting for us on the road."

"Who?" Vitek still sounded groggy. His eyes were swollen from the smoke of the preceding day.

"Your people. The story has been running free in the colony for days—the story of how the lost are coming home, the warning to meet us on the road. They'll be there. If we can get to Jefferson, they will protect us."

15

The Deltans loaded up as soon as the trucks were ready. They crowded into the trucks as if they were mounting a drive to reinforce some besieged position. They took their weapons, rations for a couple of days, and their sleeping bags—nothing more. A couple of fuel tankers and a water truck followed them. The frailest and the feeblest of the prisoners stayed behind to catch up later by vito. That was a taste of sadness to Singer; they would have taken a chance of dying on the way to get home sooner, but they yielded and stayed behind because they knew they would slow down their friends. It was hard for them to have come so far together and be separated at last.

The Riders had left most of the horses behind. They had to climb into the trucks with their Delh'tani stranger brothers. After they had been packed together hour after grinding hour, their nerves fed on the strangeness of it till they were in a fever, ready to burst out with some kind of violence. Singer feared for them. He remembered riding that terrifying edge for days when he had first come among the strangers. He traveled among the trucks all day, jumping down when they slowed for hills or drifted sand and swinging up onto the packed bed of the next to talk and joke with his people and calm them.

They stopped for a few minutes before dark to let the soldiers eat and stretch their legs. Kruger had arranged a safe radio link with a light colonel he knew at a base closer in so they could talk to Jon without Singer's intervention. Singer himself made contact with Jon at intervals to sample his mood and see the city through his eyes. Through Jon, he could feel a mood of reckless excitement building in Jefferson, as well.

When the trucks started up again, Singer vaulted into the moto where Vitek was riding with Kruger and Hilurin and respectfully commandeered the space behind the seat for himself. He needed a place where he could stretch out. He was traveling restlessly among their dreams when he was stabbed awake by the sound of vitos coming. Hearing that sound in his sleep was like hot wax dripped on his flesh. He curled awake, already scrambling for cover. They swept by low to the ground, fanning everyone with their wake of hot air. The leader had the cabin lights on so they could see his gunners waving and shouting.

"Welcome home, cofras!" the loudspeaker said. "We'll be your escort tonight. Tell Mack no accidents on this run. We're going all the way with you."

Singer heard Kruger on the radio to his friend. "Where did you get orders for this kind of thing?"

"Who gives a flying fuck for orders? What can they do to me? Send me for a luxury vacation at Dusty River? Didn't you watch the news this morning, chuck? This war is *over*."

The vitos paced them all night long, patrolling from one end of the column to the other. They were patched, battered machines, paint scoured off by sand and fire. They hugged the ground to minimize detection, scudding along like a grim gray wolf pack.

Most of the convoy stayed awake after that. The presence of more flying machines raised the Riders' state of excitement yet higher, but it reassured the Deltans. Sleep was no longer possible for Singer, so he sat up and listened to the talk.

"It doesn't mean much," Kruger said to Hilurin. "The real threat is from bombers up above. They could unload on us before the vitos got a sniff of them." Like the other Delh'tani, though, he was moved and happy because his brothers were with them. Singer could tell that by his voice.

"It's too late for that," Singer said. "We are too close to inhabited territory. The strike would be seen. People would come to the site and find the results. There would be no way to hide who did it, and the people would never forgive. The Net does not now have any leader who could force such a decision and carry it out."

"You're very sure of that," Vitek said.

"I am gambling for bones on it—no, what is that in Delh'tanhi? Betting my life. I bet also that the Net heavies in North Fork have not yet understood what is happening here. They have rioting and strikes in the cities, and this morning's news flash. Till this morning they believed you dead. Now they will believe that you are still somewhere in Jefferson. They will not know you are here even if they finally grasp the nature of this convoy.''

"I hope you're right," Vitek said. "But I notice that you still haven't answered my question.''

"You didn't ask me a question.''

"Singer always knows more than he'll tell," Kruger said, rescuing him from trying to explain.

It was still dark when they hit the main access road into Jefferson. They had come down out of the dunes. The plain was so flat that they could see all the way across to the refinery towers. Their lights still shone. The sky over Jefferson was brighter than the surrounding darkness, but there was no sign of the fires and burning barricades reported in North Fork. Yet as they came closer, some difference in the approach bothered Singer.

Suddenly he knew what it was. There were lights where they had never been before.

He ran head-on into Janet's focused sending, and he knew what the lights were. A sea of people blocked the streets and spilled out into the road and along the embankments. They held lights—as small and wavering, and as numerous, as stars in deep water: handlights, candles, dismounted lights from buses and trucks, burning sticks. The security forces had tried in vain to disperse them. The armed men were swallowed and forced to move with the crowd. They were eerily silent. Their breathing and their footsteps merged into one ever-varying rhythm like the motion of some great beast.

I think every man, woman, and child in Jeff is here. Her voice was hushed, too, even in his mind. She was holding herself together on pure nerve and nothing else. No battle had ever terrified her like this. She was singing with fear like a plucked string, but still she walked steadily past the police in their riot gear, on toward the darkness.

I'm walking for my parents. I'm walking for all of them, she said fiercely. Because he was looking with her eyes, he could not see her, but he remembered the small, guarded light he had seen in her eyes the first time she had leaned over him in the hospital, before they had shared any language.

Zhanne. It is shining. It was shining all around them now. In her heart he saw her calling up her own dead to walk with her:

the young scared faces, bloody and smashed or pale as leached sand, their futures draining out in bright ribbons or dark lines.

You're not the only one who ever failed to save them, she said. *Singer! Listen, if something goes wrong, then bury me like a Rider. Make a song for me and keep something of mine to wear. Just don't ever think for one second that I had any regrets. I love you, andri. You'll never know how much.*

"I know, barasheli. Yes, I know. Because I know that life is no good unless we live in hope. I'll make a song for you, and I'll wear your ornaments around my neck. But I won't be around to bury you, my heart. Bury your hope and you're as good as dead. Look! We can't die—we're already on the Heroes' Road. Starfires all around."

He opened his eyes and knew he had spoken out loud. Kruger and Hilurin had heard him, and Saldivar, and Lyn. The trucks met the first lines of vigil keepers. The lights swirled and danced as the people carrying them turned around and jogged beside the road, keeping up. A shout of welcome started next to them and ran like a wave up the road ahead till it doubled back on itself and the sound crashed and roared like surf. Suddenly Singer knew it was time to bail out.

"We must leave the trucks," he told Kruger with his mouth close to the Asharya's ear. "Let the crowd carry us. That is safety—but I'll stay close to you and Vitek. I will take you to Jon."

All around them the prisoners had the same idea. People who had waited a long time to welcome them swarmed over the trucks and persuaded them to come down. Riders and Deltans alike were dancing away into the darkness. The security police forced their way through the crowd—or perhaps the crowd simply avoided them, allowing them a planned path—but the trucks were empty when they arrived. And as they stood bewildered, their arms were pressed to their sides by the crowd. A few shots went overhead or into the ground, one or two gas pods popped open, causing a momentary eddy in the flow of people, but the weapons vanished into the darkness and their owners were borne to the ground by irresistible force. They surfaced again in torn T-shirts, with bruised ribs and broken fingers, to cling to the trucks like sailors shipwrecked in an unfriendly sea.

The crowd flowed back like a tide. They repossessed enough trucks to carry those too weak to walk and to carry Kruger in triumph to the end of the road. The trucks slowed to a walking pace to avoid running down their escort in the dark. Messengers came down the line on bicycles to report that the airfield was secured and a sound system was waiting for the governor to speak. When the trucks came out onto the flat paving of the field and the spotlights hit them, a roar went up around them that rattled their bones like artillery fire.

"Quiet, please! The governor is going to speak."

Jon and his impromptu crew repeated the message many times before the crowd quieted. They finally got the stage lights on line, and Vitek was illuminated, standing on a platform improvised from containers and skids. The bleak white light made him look plainer and more featureless than ever, a short, round-faced, balding man. He waited patiently for the mutter of surprise and curiosity to die down. At last it was quiet; they could hear the wind fluttering across the mike.

"Fellow citizens, I have some brief but important announcements to make," he said. "Please don't say anything until I'm finished. I want you all to hear this.

"I have received a communication from the New Peoples' Union in Solidari requesting medical assistance and opening the possibility of peace negotiations."

A surge of voices rose in spite of his request, and he waited for it to pass before continuing.

"I have decided to send assistance as soon as possible and will pursue negotiations as speedily as prudence allows. You should be aware that the Union colony is experiencing a serious epidemic of an illness apparently native to this world. We will benefit greatly from the chance to stop the epidemic before it reaches our area. The Union has shared resources for a possible cure with us in return for our assistance now. That alone could save countless lives.

"My second decision concerns our current state of war. While negotiations continue, I am declaring a unilateral cease-fire. Since we will no longer be at war, I revoke the state of martial law which has been in effect up to this point."

The voices swelled louder.

"The results of this decision will be far-reaching and complex. It will take time to resolve all issues, and I ask you to be patient. Be assured that we will return to a peacetime condition as soon as possible.

"I have asked General Marcus Kruger to return from retirement and accept a temporary position as commander of space and ground forces. He will oversee the return of our forces to their normal relationship with your elected representatives.''

This time the commotion took several minutes to die down.

''I am aware that news releases listed General Kruger as dead. This was an error I will not attempt to explain at this time. His condition was very serious, but he has made a complete recovery. General Kruger.''

Kruger stepped out into the light. The crowd greeted him first with astonished silence, then with a roar of approval that started in the back where the polvorados stood and spread forward among the civilians.

''Thank you, your Excellency,'' Kruger said. ''I have only one thing to say—no, make that two things. First: I am completely satisfied that the governor's course of action is correct and wise. I have sources very close to the situation confirming that. Second: to the brave fighters who have endured to this hour of homecoming, well done. And to our friends and allies from the north, who made it possible, thank you and welcome.''

The governor took the microphone again.

''My final announcement will surprise most of you. You may have noticed unfamiliar faces among us. They are, as General Kruger has said, our friends and allies. It seems that others have been living on this world before our arrival. These brave men and women—for I must call them that now that I see their faces—have fought side by side with General Kruger to free the prisoners and bring them home. Please welcome them and let this night be the beginning of a long history of cooperation between our peoples.

''There are many things I could still say and much work that must be done before the hopes we have raised tonight can become a reality in daylight. Tonight, however, it is time to go home—for all of us. Officers will be stationed at Hangar one to assist any of the returnees who have not found next of kin and to arrange lodging for the allies. We will want to interview all the returnees, beginning tomorrow, to learn the fate of your comrades who are not with you. Announcements will be sent over the news channel tomorrow regarding these arrangements.

''Thank you for your attention. And now, let's go home.''

He stepped down. There was total silence for a long minute. Then someone started singing ''New Home.'' The song had always been something of a joke, victim of countless scatological revisions, first casualty at any drinking party. They sang the original words this time. The sound reverberated from hangar walls and vibrated in Singer's bones. It spread out into the black, starry sky that arched over their small lights and sank into the ground beneath their feet.

It will always be here, Singer whispered to Janet. *Even when they think it is silent. Earth and sky have witnessed the first time they call this home.*

Kruger's men surrounded the governor like a breakwater. One of the returned soldiers made his way through the crowd to the place where Genady stood with Singer and his friends.

"Please come this way—he wants to see you."

Genady thought about it. "Is that an order?" he asked.

The soldier shrugged. "How the hell would I know? Mack says not to turn him loose in this crowd—he's afraid someone from the Net or one of the regular staff people might shoot him. So if you want to talk to him, you'll have to go over there. Do what you want. It's no slice off mine."

"All right, I'll come," Genady decided.

Vitek had sweated dark patches into his suit. The soldiers would not let him take it off because the light shirt underneath made too good a target.

"Genya," he said, grasping Genady's hand. "Since I'm your next of kin—I was hoping you'd come home with me. Your friends are welcome. There's room."

Genady slowly shook his head. "Sorry. My place is with the others."

Then he laughed. "Besides—where are you going to put us? Your house burned down. Look, Vitek, why don't you rack with us? You're a civilian, but we could overlook that. Maybe we'll all be civilians again someday."

Vitek's eyes started to smile back but hesitated. "Is that safe?"

Singer grinned and did not answer. Genady looked around, seeing the faces of those he had fought his way out of the camp with. To Vitek they must have looked fierce and wild. To him they were familiar and comfortable.

"You'll have to make up your own mind about that," Genady said. "As far as letting anybody else get to you, though, these chicos are a better shield than a ship's hull."

"Take us wherever the Asharya is staying," Singer said to the soldiers.

Kruger had taken over the main barracks, between the airfield and the hospital. When they arrived, Singer looked around and approved the Asharya's reasoning. To sleep elsewhere and leave the regular soldiers to brood on the sudden changes and chew over rumors would leave open the possibility of rebellion. By immediately taking up residence among them, he had made his authority felt. In addition, he had given his ad hoc force a chance to mingle with old friends and tell their stories over and over again till firsthand accounts of what had happened in the north spread through all the Forces.

He saw Janet leaving as they were going in. She had changed back into her duck whites again and looked as she had when they had first met. It hardly seemed possible that that had been less than a year before.

"We're equipping teams to fly out to Solidari," she explained rapidly, barely pausing to greet them. "I just checked the final flight roster with Kruger. Lyn is down on the field waiting for us." Her eyes unfocused slightly for a moment, and then she smiled. "She's in a hurry—I've got to run. We'll be out of here before daylight. I don't know how long we'll be there, so call me, dakko?"

Jon shifted from foot to foot in an agony of indecision. He wanted to go back to Solidari with Janet and film the first peaceful contact with the Nupis. Equally, he wanted to stay and witness the transition to a civilian government in the Green Zone.

"You can't be in two places at once, Jon. Stay here. You'd just be in our way. If you need to know what's happening, link up with Singer and be with me. I'll show you whatever there is to see."

"It's not good enough," Jon said gloomily. "I know you. I won't get anything out of you but close-ups of bronchial tubes and endless injections."

"Try Lyn, then. She'll scout around for you."

"Lyn!" Jon shuddered in mock horror. "I'd rather stick my head in a blender."

Janet grinned. "She heard that. You'd definitely better stay here."

Jon knotted his thin arms around her shoulders. "I'm scared to let you out of my sight," he admitted.

"I know what you mean. But the war's over, J.L. We have to start living like it."

"Dakko, J.L." He let go reluctantly.

They found Kruger. Singer approved again when he saw that the Asharya was keeping Hilurin close by his side, where a Singer had to be when important decisions were being made. He had to smile at the sight of Hilurin in clean, neatly pressed fatigues, but Lurya wore them with the same disdainful grace

with which he had once worn the court clothes of Erech Tolanh.
His fine, narrow features contrasted with Kruger's broad cheek-
bones and heavy brows; Hilurin's hair was silver, and Kruger's
was iron-gray. They could have been brothers all the same.

"I brought you another refugee," Singer said.

"What about you?" Kruger said. "Where are you going?"

"My Con-el, you know I do not like to sleep within walls,"
Singer said.

"Seriously—what are you up to?"

"There is a chance, small but still possible, that what's left
of the Net will try to stop this peace from happening," Singer
said. "Gero might have chanced it if he were here. The easiest
way would be to strike down one or both of you, creating confusion and delaying the decisions till it is too late. I will have a
better chance to smell such an attack in the wind if I can be
outside watching for it."

Kruger made a dismissive gesture. "I assure you this has all
been discussed and planned for. I hope you were on my staff
long enough to expect that."

Singer fidgeted silently.

"All right, all right, if you're not worn out yet, you have my
permission. But for heaven's sake, be careful."

16

The nearest perimeter guard knew Singer by sight and passed
him and Saldivar through the wire fence. It was little more than
a boundary marker, not designed to keep out anyone who really
wanted to come in. The guard saw Singer shaking his head.

"It's not just us. The old man has people spotted up on the
roof and other places. It's covered."

Out in the darkness Singer sensed someone moving. More than one—there must have been dozens of them milling around in the shadows beyond the wire.

"Who is that?" he asked.

"It's the civilians," the guard said. "Nothing I can do about it. They aren't on the base."

As Singer watched, small fires were kindled in the dark. He moved toward the nearest, making as much noise as he could so his sudden appearance would not startle anyone.

"Heyo," he greeted the fire tender, squatting down beside him.

"You can't force us to leave," the man said evenly. "This is city property, and I'm a citizen."

"I don't want to run you off. I only want to know why you're here. I work for Kruger. I'd take it personally if anyone made trouble tonight."

At that the man turned and offered his hand. "Well, that's different. In that case we're on the same side. Half of Jefferson is here to make sure nothing happens to Kruger or the governor. People have brought their children along. We're going to stay all night. If they want a war, let them start right here."

Singer looked out over the flat, sandy plain. From the lights of the barracks to the runway lights of the airfield, the ground was dotted with small fires, each surrounded by shapes that the wind-whipped flames revealed and then relinquished to shadow again. Singer smiled slowly. The wind was with him. He had chosen the right way.

"My name is Singer," he said to the man sitting by the fire. "This is my friend Saldivar. We'll be staying all night, too. If there's any trouble, send for us."

They spent what was left of the night wandering among the fires, pausing to talk for a minute, to share stories or a drink. Singer dipped into the thoughts and dreams of those he passed and found nothing false there, no hint of a threat to those he protected. The desert stars shone molten-bright, like sparks from a glowing forge. The sandy earth had been the forge where they had all been hammered and seared. Now the foundry was quiet. The finished steel waited for the day to show whether it was good enough for the job.

"This is like old times," Saldivar said. "When you were Kruger's boy and we used to visit around with the Mothers to catch what was smokin'. You remember?"

"I remember."

"If the war is really over . . ." Saldivar said. Spoken, the thought hung tight and fragile as a thread stretched across the path, one that might trigger an ambush. He made an effort and pushed on against the threat. "If the war is really over, what are we going to do?"

"Breathe," Singer said, turning his face into the wind. "I could spend a month or two just breathing easy. But not here. I want to go north. I want to go where it smells green, where I can lie in the grass and listen to the river."

He took Saldivar's hand and turned it palm up, uncurling the fingers that had knitted just a little crooked, thoughtfully tracing the scars.

"I want to take you home with me. You've never been, not really. I miss the little children, and the mothers, and the old ones laying down the law. I miss cold nights by the fire and hot summer afternoons when there's no sound but the weavers' shuttles and the horses swishing flies."

His voice sank so low that Saldivar could hardly hear it. "I know I have started something that can't be stopped. Maybe the old days will pass away and the Riders will find a different way to live. I want to go home with you for a while before it changes too much."

Saldivar returned the handclasp silently, but his question was not put to rest, and after a moment he spoke again. "I mean, what are we going to do for a living? Your people got their paychecks for soldiering, too. What do we do when that's gone? I can't see you as a farmer."

Singer laughed. "Farming is good work. I don't spit on it anymore. But I'm a Thanha horse. I don't think I can pull a plow. We might help Zhanne for a while. There will be plenty of people who need healing. And Makho will always have use for us. He is an Asharya, Palha. People will always look to him, and he will take the burden for them, whether he thinks so now or not."

He watched the sky for a while, long enough for a handful of shooting stars to trail their brief flares across the zenith.

"I have an old promise to keep. Once I promised Dona we'd go to the far places we had never seen. I have already journeyed far from that night—farther, maybe, than he could have imagined—but that promise is still unkept. When your people and mine agree to share this world together, there will be many who seek the new places. There will be work for people like us, who know the weather and the way of things far from cities. Dona and I meant to go together. Now you and I must go instead.''

Singer felt Palha's tight shoulders relax under his arm. Saldivar did not care at all how he made a living. He needed to know that he and Singer would still be together when they had ceased to be sword arm and shield arm.

"There's a lot you never told me about Dona," he said. "A lot of things I'd like to know."

"Memory is something a warrior does better without. That's another job for peacetime—to remember Dona and all of them as they should be remembered. To tell the stories."

"I'd like that," Saldivar said. "I want to leave something behind me, you know? I want it to mean something that I lived. I remember so many who didn't. It's like they never lived at all. Just gone. I want to make something that will stay. I spent my time blowing things up. Never learned to make anything. That's what I want now. A road with my name on it is a good start. A road going somewhere they could never go before. A good road. So even if they don't know who I was, someone will look at it someday and say, 'This is a good road. Man that made it must have been a good man.' And they'll say my name."

They had come around in a wide circle and returned to the first fire by the gate. The same man was sitting by the fire. He waved to them, and they sat down gratefully and stretched their feet toward the coals. Singer felt as if he might be dreaming. He could not remember a night like this, out of earshot of the wounded and dying, a night without blood and fire. Even sleep had not closed the door on the sound of the death cries and the smell of burning.

The fainter stars had faded on the eastern horizon. It would be dawn soon. The part of him that had been a Net chief calculated the odds while he dozed by the fire. By dawn, the time of decision would be passing. If the Net and the military chiefs wanted to hold their power, they would have to move soon.

The distant sound he remembered from a hundred nightmares snapped Singer out of his drowsy wondering. Saldivar caught his alarm and sprang upright.

"What is it?" The man beside them scrambled up, too, looking around wildly for the danger. Singer waited motionless, listening, and in a few minutes everyone heard it, coming from the direction of North Fork. All around them startled exclamations sounded as the crowd roused.

"They're coming," Singer said. He was almost relieved that

it had happened at last. "The Net maintained a private field next to the PCOM building, good enough to scramble a flight of vitos without going through the main field."

"Kristo, the children," the man groaned. "I can't believe the bastards are going to do this."

Singer guessed and second-guessed. It was impossible to know for sure. He did not think the military heavies wanted the hatred they would incur by firing on the civilians; nor would they want to kill hundreds of soldiers to get at Kruger and Vitek. It was more likely they would try to land assassins. Yet there was no way to predict what the pilots would do in the crunch. They might decide to improve their odds by softening up the target whether it was good policy or not.

The man beside him moved as if to run toward the threatening sound in the sky and ward off the attack.

Singer gripped his arm. "Wait."

At last he heard what he had been waiting for: torn air in the wake of rockets going up as the vito flight passed the airfield. The sky over the airfield flickered and glowed like a false and temporary dawn. The air shook with concussions huddling one on top of another. A rain of glowing fragments sprinkled down, some of them windblown to the edge of the encampment. A thin lament of children crying drifted to Singer on the same wind, but they were cries of fear, quickly hushed, not of real pain. He realized that he was bruising the man's arm and let go.

He sat down again, huddling close to the fire, wanting its warmth but finding unwanted visions in the coals.

"Belser, Simko, Solinas, Argon . . ." he murmured. He could not remember all their names. There had been too many for him to reach before the rockets.

"What's he saying?" their companion asked Saldivar.

"The names of the teams on those vitos, I think," Saldivar said shakily.

"I hoped this night could pass without any more dying," Singer said. "That was too much to expect. I warned Makho this could happen, and he had the defenses ready. I told them to stop. They wouldn't listen. Maybe they couldn't hear."

"Is he all right?"

"He's all right," Saldivar said. "Come on, cofra, I think it's over. Everybody's awake now. They don't need us here." He coaxed Singer away from the fire.

"See you around," he said over his shoulder to the man who stood frowning after them. "You never learn, do you?" he added to Singer when they were out of earshot. "You tried to talk to those chucks."

"It was worth a try," Singer said. He remembered how they had felt, falling, and stumbled.

"Fuck it. It's not worth it," Saldivar said. "Not if you're going to hurt for every fuckhead who tries to kill you. Fuck them all."

"No. Every life is worth it, Palha. I have to believe that. Because I've seen where the other road goes."

He shuddered, leaning into the living warmth of Saldivar's arm. "Pain is just pain. It passes. The bad thing is going dead inside so you don't feel anything."

"Fuck them anyway." He heard the helpless anger in Saldivar's voice. *How many nights, how many years of peace before he's all in one piece again?*

"Maybe never," Singer said gently to the unspoken question. "It doesn't have to be perfect, paliao. I'll take whatever I can get. Thanha live with scars. As long as you can take me as I am, I'm satisfied."

Saldivar did not say anything, but Singer did not need words from him. He had what he needed.

They found Kruger also awake, reading the flash reports from the airfield and from North Fork and a message from the medical mission. Singer was amused, tired as he was, to see that Deltan clothes now bothered the Asharya, too. Kruger had shed his jacket, loosened his sleeves, and unfastened his shirt. The open shirt revealed that he was still wearing two or three of his ornaments around his neck, and when he turned his head, a glint of gold showed that he had forgotten to take off his ear stones.

"They shot down four vitos," Kruger said. "Two others were restrained on the ground at North Fork. We had casualties but no kills. I don't have a medical report on how bad it was. The vitos had full crew plus strike teams. No survivors are reported."

"I know," Singer said wearily.

"Sometimes you know more than is good for you. What I want you to find out tomorrow—no, today—is who authorized that flight."

"Dakko, my Asharya." He gave Kruger an elaborate salute.

Kruger gave him a sharp look. "Of course I'm not going to have them killed. What do you think I am? The rule of law has returned, as of 2200 tonight. Whoever they are, they are now citizens who must be tried and convicted before they can be punished. As they will be. But not by assassination. Nor would I have sent you to do the job in any case. I'd as soon use Siri's sword to pound rocks. I am not the fool you apparently think me.''

Singer tried to speak, and the Asharya shut him down.

''You put me in charge of this mess. Now I am in charge. You appear to be in danger of forgetting that. Get some rest and don't come back till your mind is working again.''

Saldivar resented those orders till he saw Singer suppressing the urge to smile, a lopsided expression that made his face almost foolish with relief. He had needed someone to order him to stop, and Kruger had understood that perfectly.

''I am tired,'' Singer said apologetically to Saldivar. ''If I could just sit down for a minute . . .''

He took Kruger's discarded jacket, wadded it up for a pillow, and lay down in the corner with his head against the wall. He was unconscious in seconds. Saldivar sat down next to him, thinking he would not sleep but would rest his feet till he was needed.

He was still resting his feet when he saw Singer walking toward him with someone he did not recognize following. He recognized Singer at once, though there was something odd about him. His face was much younger, but the scar that marked it had not been healed. He wore an old, threadbare pair of trousers and no shirt or boots. His bare back and chest showed terrible scars, still fresh. The boy who followed him had strange, pale eyes that seemed not to focus on anything, and he clung to Singer as if he were blind and could not find his own way. The sight of him sent a chill through Saldivar.

''Get rid of him,'' he said to Singer.

''This is Anh'ton,'' Singer said. ''Don't worry about him, Pavlito. He can't hurt you.''

It was rainy season, but Singer did not seem to notice the mud around his bare feet. He did not belong in the camp. Saldivar knew that, but he did not know how to get him out.

''I'm sorry,'' Singer said. ''I never really sleep anymore. I travel around.''

''We have to get out of this place.''

''Run for it,'' Singer said.

''They'll shoot us!''

Singer grinned at him. ''Not if we move fast enough.''

Singer seized his hand and made a running leap. Saldivar saw

the wire coming up at them and thought they would rip into it
for sure, but they made it up and over and landed on a hillside
covered with long grass that caught at their feet. Saldivar's foot
knocked against something on the ground. He looked down and
saw a skull. Singer's eyes were fixed on the horizon.

"Keep moving," he said.

They ran faster and faster in a circle of green that stretched
unchanging from edge to edge of the sky. The strange-eyed boy
ran behind them like a shadow. *We'll never get out,* Saldivar
thought, despairing. But Singer was not trying to escape anymore. He was running for the joy of it, dancing on the green
ground. A thunder of hooves ran with them, invisible horses
with manes like blowing clouds, and they were running, flying,
dancing in the sky, till they rounded the shoulder of the world
and the stars beyond it dazzled them with their brightness. Saldivar turned and looked back and saw the world they had left
hanging almost within reach, shining like a perfect jewel. He
reached out for it, longing, but could not quite touch it. It was
small enough to float within his reaching hands, but it was not
cold like a jewel. It was warm, beating like a heart.

He turned to share the wonder with Singer. As he did, the
sense of amazing lightness and freedom faded. He found himself stiff and cramped, leaning against the wall beside Singer.
He suspected that he had been sleeping with his mouth open.
Singer woke instantly and gracefully.

"I'm sorry," he said. "I don't really sleep anymore. I travel
around."

He looked at Saldivar and smiled, as if he could still see in
Palha's face the wonder of that jewel of light they had dreamed
together.

"You won't go back to the camp anymore. It's finished. That
was another world."

17

Day came and passed without further incident. Night followed, and nothing broke their sleep. And on the next day still nothing happened. At first the fighters lived in waiting, perpetually keyed up to face a challenge that never came. At last, by imperceptible stages, there came a stand-down in the soul. They began to forget. They went out at night unarmed and walked into their rooms afterward without checking for intruders.

Singer and Saldivar followed Kruger wherever he went, mostly traveling with Vitek. They spent endless hours waiting while the elders held conference—negotiating, discussing, planning. From those conferences came the orders that changed the colony. Fuel was diverted to transport and work vehicles. Returning soldiers went to work extending and planting the fields and building family housing for the civilians who had been living in barracks. All around them work went on at a feverish pace, but they had nothing to do but talk. At last Singer began to wonder if they were really needed in the city. He started to raise the subject with Hilurin. The old man was smiling before Singer could finish a sentence.

"Yes," he said with his hands on Singer's shoulders. "Yes, you should go. Your Con-el and I have an excellent understanding. I can be his Singer for a while. Go to your beshani and be happy."

"I had in mind to do some work for a change," Singer said. He was on his dignity, but it was no use with Hilurin.

"Oh, no doubt you will find something to put your hand to wherever you are—but give up thinking ahead for a little while.

You may have forgotten that you are only a young one yet, but I have not.''

He put his hand on Singer's head as he used to do when Singer was still an inch or two shorter than he was, but Singer's hair had not yet grown, and Lurya had to reach up to his shaved skull.

"I think I will not be young again," Singer said. "The time has passed."

Hilurin held him tight, sudden tears in his eyes. "I know it, little brother, I know. It was a long, hard road to travel in one year, and the price was hard and dear. Isé, sweetness, my little heart, if an old man's love could do good like a medicine, you'd be whole now."

"It does good, Lurya," Singer said hoarsely. "You were nothing but good to me, ever. I'd pay the whole price just to have seen you again."

Hilurin kissed him and turned him loose. "Go, then. Enjoy what peace you can."

Singer got Palha and flew back to Solidari, where they joined Janet and Lyn and worked hard in the hospital sixteen hours a day. Singer concentrated on learning from Zhanne and the other doctors how the inside of a body really worked. It kept his mind filled with amazement and left him no time for evil memories.

When the medical emergency in Solidari was stabilized and the survivors were able to feed themselves again, Singer and Saldivar worked their way up the coast to the Iron City by ship, another new experience. The changing colors and voices of the sea were another amazement, though Singer agreed with Palha that horses were preferable because you could get off them occasionally.

In the Iron City they were joyfully reunited with Bone, Olmalik, and Selem and other friends. Morne was there, too. The Riders Kruger had left behind were staying near the city until spring. Parties came down to visit when the word got around that Singer was there. Bone had been in charge of scavenging in the Somostai fortress; he had salvaged enough stores to get the refugees through the spring. Ex-blackrobes and cityfolk worked side by side with the farmers, planting and herding, while Bone and his cadre carefully cataloged the records they mined in the city. They had started the work of clearing out the rubble from the mines and foundry, but it would be some time before they could produce iron and coal again.

They were with Bone when word came that the new Union

government was ready to sign the peace treaty. It was early summer, and a great celebration was being planned for the ceremony. Kruger sent transportation for them, and they went down early to help prepare. They took Bone with them. Singer hoped the medikhani in Jefferson could fix the ex-slave's eyes in time to see the day.

The doctors let him sit with Bone while their light knives reshaped his eyes. Bone clung to his hand, trembling, till the Delh'tani drugs put him to sleep. Singer was there when he woke up and there again when he opened his new eyes for the first time.

"Blue-eyed Death," he said slowly, wonderingly, staring at Singer's face. "If this is what you bring, I don't mind it. I should have died before. But the face you wear among the Somostai is so different, I didn't know you for a friend. Now I understand."

He still held on to Singer's hand. "Don't keep so many regrets. The old things have to die to make room for the new, and it's worth it sometimes. Oh, it's worth it."

His mocking smile crumpled. "Will it hurt my eyes if I cry? Will it?" he asked frantically.

"I don't think so," Singer said. "Though you never cried at the sight of death before."

"Ha, very funny," Bone said, but he was smiling again. "This joke is getting tired. Death has a new occupation; maybe he should get another name."

"Death and Bone go together, don't you think?"

"Yes, very true, but your friend Genady has been teaching me such marvelous things. The beautiful thoughts of the sky-fathers. I thought perhaps to honor my poor self with their glorious names. Newton Khalileo Bone. How does that sound to you, Singer?"

Bone's eyes had healed by the day of the celebration. As darkness fell, he lay with the rest of them in a dry, grassy field north of the Jefferson airstrip and watched the stars come out. Singer thought Bone must surely close his eyes sometimes but could not remember ever catching him that way. Those eyes had been wide with wonder ever since they had healed, and they still seemed too big for his starved face. He lay head to head with Genady, back in a running argument that involved much finger pointing at the spangled sky. They were trying to work out conventions for constellations and star names. Since each was upside down from the other's point of view and they were both more than slightly drunk, useful conclusions were a long time coming, but the two men were enjoying the process.

"Please to remember I am now author of paper," Bone said with drunken dignity. " 'Preliminary Proposal for Mapping Project, Nuvospera Northern Hemisphere,' author Newton K. Bone, so show respect."

"*Second* author!" Genady replied in outrage. "My name comes first on that proposal."

Lyn reached out a long leg and dug her bare toes into Genady's middle.

"Peace, chicos," she murmured sleepily. "I'm resting. Came all the way from Solidari this morning, you know."

Genady pushed the foot away. "That's not your only reason for being tired."

Lyn sat up and looked around. "Where's Marcus?" she asked. "He said he had to stay in North Fork for a couple of hours to make the ceremonial rounds with the governor, but he promised he'd be here before midnight."

Singer scanned the scene by moving from one set of eyes to another without opening his own. The night was balmy and mostly clear, with long flags of high cloud moving swiftly with the gusting wind. Down on the airstrip a video screen had been set up so everyone could see the signing of the treaty, which had taken place early in the morning in Solidari. As a courtesy and a sign of good faith, Vitek had flown to the Union Zone for the actual ceremony. Now the speeches were all over, and the screen showed only the celebrations happening in Solidari and in North Fork.

Good smells of spices and frying onions, barbecued meat, coffee and liquor floated over the field. Children's voices could be heard calling and shrieking in wild games played long after bedtime. The sounds of guitars, fiddles, flutes, and drums came and went as small groups of dancers formed and broke up. Already Singer could hear Thanha tunes being blended with the Delh'tani music. The crowd had begun gathering early, waiting to see the governor's on-screen, official declaration of peace. All the time Lyn had been flying Vitek and the delegation home again, people had been celebrating. A lull had come, but Singer felt that the night was not over. The whole great crowd still waited for something.

At last he found the touch he had been looking for. Lyn saw him smile with his eyes shut.

"He's here?"

"Yes, he's coming. Lurya is with him. See?"

The approaching lights set down to the west of the people-jammed main field on an auxiliary pad.

Ayei, *Singer!* Hilurin greeted him. *Now we see if Marcus and I still have any skill as scouts.*

The vito was mobbed almost immediately. The cheers and shouts sounded loud even from the hilltop, but they died away again when it became apparent that Kruger had slipped away.

Singer opened his eyes then, in time to see them coming—a couple of plainly dressed old soldiers trudging up the hill, inconspicuous among the shadows and ignored by the revelers.

"I could use a drink," Kruger said mildly when he had recovered from being greeted en masse and sequentially. Genady silently held out his flask, and the Asharya swallowed half the remaining contents without flinching. He sighed and folded himself down onto the ground before taking another drink.

Janet relieved him of his jacket and began to rub his shoulders.

"Ah, God. Thank you. Yes, all is well. The treaty is signed and enshrined, and Hazzan by all appearances is well in control in Solidari. It seems the hostilities are truly ended. Vitek sends his regards and heartfelt regrets. He would be with me if he could but is forced to attend an official dinner and dance. He's wearing a stiff suit and sash now and dancing the corredera with military widows."

He reached back and caught Janet's wrist. "Come around here where I can see you, Doctor, and give me something to make me feel better. Dios, I feel like celebrating."

Genady reclaimed his flask.

"I haven't quite finalized the analysis on this stuff, Marcus," Janet said. "I wouldn't drink any more of it till you give the speech."

Kruger freed his mouth long enough to advise a destination for speeches and those who listened to them.

Janet shook her head regretfully. "Such language."

"No more speeches," Kruger said more clearly. "They don't want speeches, anyway."

"No," Hilurin said. "But they are waiting for something."

"They're setting up live sound equipment down there," Jon said, craning his neck to see. "Looks like they're serious about it."

"Reminds me of Landing Day celebrations in Heimat," Kruger said. "But we used to have fireworks. Maybe they're waiting for the fireworks."

"No fireworks," Saldivar said decisively. "We had enough fire from the sky for a lifetime."

"Landing Day," Janet said. "I'd forgotten about that. Forgot about all that stuff. We used to fish for rojos in the inlet and grill them and squeeze fresh limeade, and Tia Rita made this wonderful frozen custard with coconut milk in it."

A taste of creamy snow ran across all their lips.

"What will they call this a long time from now?" she mused. "I never thought of that. We'll be history someday. They'll come out to the airstrip and barbecue. What will they call it, when they remember? Treaty Day? Peace Day?"

Singer had been dozing blissfully with his head on Hilurin's knees and his feet across Saldivar's lap. Suddenly he sat up and brushed the grass bits out of his hair. "Homecoming. They'll call it Homecoming."

"Oh?" Kruger said, amused. "You're a prophet now?"

Singer shrugged. "I just know. Also, I'm going to make a song about it. They'll remember. That's what they're waiting for. Come with me, Lurya; now you'll see if I've learned anything. You can help me out if I get stuck. You, too, Palha. I need you to drum for me."

He jumped up onto the platform, and the answering roar told him that he was right. They handed him the Delh'tani thamla, hanging the strap around his shoulders like the gift of an ornament. He would have to make it good, good enough to remember for a lifetime and beyond, but he thought he was ready to try.

He paused with his hands caressing the thamla and felt the wind touch him, waking its music within him as if his limbs were strung with silver. He looked up and saw the Sky Road stretched gloriously above him like a broad necklace of silver embracing the whole world, like a pathway marked with bright beacons. Below him he saw firelight and starlight reflected in the eyes of the crowd that gathered around him, ready to dance. It was Homecoming. He felt the unseen companions close to him, as if they, too, were waiting to share the music. He took a deep breath, and he sang.

Epilogue: Homecoming

The world spun on, and the stars danced their slow, elegant figures while the small two-legged beings sorted out their affairs. On the surface of Nuvospera the people forestalled sickness and fed famine. Then they began to think about the next long step in the dance. Riders and cityfolk participated as observers when the resupply shuttles leapt up to visit and reassure those who spun on their platforms high above the world. They returned with a wonder in their eyes and voices that was handed on from person to person, down the roads and around the fires, till all the people of Nuvospera had seen it. The young ones gathered to meet the skyfolk teachers and learn the ways of steel and fire, the numbers on paper and, in the magic mirrors, the webs of wire and glass that carried invisible fires. They prepared themselves for the great journeying, to ride the Sky Road and to see its glory with their own living eyes.

And so it happened that there were watchers waiting when more battered travelers fell in from the stars at last. Riders, cityfolk, Consorso, and Union together gathered them in, greeted the astonished landing crews, and decided with them how and when to wake their freight of sleeping armies.

The colonel tried to swallow, but there was nothing in his mouth but a foul taste. It was dry as paper. He had a name, but it did not seem particularly relevant. All the instruction he had received before the long sleep had to do with his function when he was awakened. Other memory had gone as dry as his mouth. He was just another colonel, one more in the long line. There was supposed to be something different about him, he felt. The difference was like a sore spot in his mouth. He worried at it, though he had a feeling he would not like it when he figured out what it was.

He had volunteered to go off-world.

He wriggled and screamed in silent denial. That could not be it. He would never have done anything that crazy. But the simple statement brought a cascade of others, building up till the picture was so clear that he had to believe it. At that point he managed to utter a groan. He heard someone coming toward whatever it was that he was lying on, and in a panic he forced his eyelids open. It felt as if they were tearing like rotted cloth.

The face that looked back at him had a friendly expression but frightened him anyway because he could not figure out what kind of face it was. It looked female, and because of the bright, curious eyes and the gentle curve of the mouth, he thought at first that she was just a girl. But she was dressed in duck whites and had diagnostic equipment clipped to her vest and belt. He searched in vain for insignia he recognized. How could he tell if she was friendly or hostile? That was the big worry—the possibility that they might be intercepted and awakened by pirates of the opposing forces who would try to force vital information from them.

She touched the pad he was lying on, and it raised his head a few inches. She handed him a squeeze and helped him get the tube in his mouth.

"Drink slowly," she advised. "You want it to stay down."

It had no taste and did not even feel wet at first, but cold and sharp like a knife. As his throat opened up, he drank faster and the taste came through: a hint of chemical saltiness with a fruity, sickly-sweet overlay.

"Lousy," he croaked.

"Sorry." She shrugged. "It's good for you, but we haven't figured out how to improve the taste any. Got you talking again, though. How do you feel?"

"Lousy," he croaked again.

"You remember where you are?"

"Colonel Carlos Nagoya, ship *Justicia*, United Forces of the Deltan Consorso." He ran out of breath by the end of the sentence and could not recall his identification code.

"Colonel Nagoya, I myself am well aware of our location and of all matters relating to you personally. I have fully accessed the ship's files on you and all your command before commencing revival procedures. I was not requesting information or initiating interrogation. That was a simple, doctor-type bedside-manner question intended to determine your state of mind. Obviously your synapses are still rusty.''

She loaded a charge into her skinjet and pressed it against the inside of his elbow before he could pull away. She spoke and moved with a swift skill that told him she was older than she looked. As she gave him the shot, he saw a blue mark like a tattoo on the heel of her hand, a circle with a triangle inside. The same mark was sewn as a patch on her vest.

''I am Dr. Janet Logan. I've been assigned to supervise the revival of crew and passengers. You're the first. It's an honor you will learn to appreciate later.''

''Doctor? What rank? What forces?''

She looked at him strangely, so that his heart skipped a beat again with the fear of the unknown.

''Before I explain that to you, there's something I want you to see. Try to sit up—slowly! You should be able to walk now.''

She turned and spoke rapidly with a man who came forward and helped Nagoya to his feet. Some of the words were Delteix, but not all. The man wore a coverall with the same triangle-in-a-circle patch, but Nagoya could not tell if it was a uniform. The man himself was dangerous even if the doctor was not. He had a rock-solid steadiness and control that Nagoya recognized even in his dazed state. He was obviously more than a mere para. As he turned, Nagoya saw that his dark hair was worn long, braided close to his head and wrapped in a club behind. He could not be a soldier, then. Or could he?

As Nagoya tried to rise, he felt himself suddenly lurch into the air. The scant contents of his stomach nearly lurched on ahead of him. The man steadied him. He realized that, of course, he was in zero gravity or close to it. He had been trained for this, but he seemed to have forgotten how to deal with it. He allowed the doctor and her assistant to tow him along. They passed through a cylinder that he recognized as a docking tube and into another, wider space. The dark-haired man took up a position Nagoya could only regard as a guard post.

There was another man in the room. He was sitting in the air with his legs crossed, but his arms and shoulders made it clear that he was tall. His clothes did not resemble a uniform in any way: loose trousers and a sleeveless shirt made of some rough material. Over that he wore a utility vest like the others, but the vest was thickly covered with patterns and patches that Nagoya could not sort out without staring. This man, too, wore his hair

long and intricately braided. A silver chain with a white pendant
floated around his neck, taped to his chest to keep it out of the
way. He wore a red stone the size of a man's thumbnail as an
earring, and he had the bluest eyes Nagoya had ever seen. He
smiled but did not speak.

"This is Singer," the doctor said. "Over there, Paul Saldivar." She indicated the dark man. "Both from Marcus Kruger's
own barhedoni. That means nothing to you now, but it will.
They are here especially to greet you."

"Kruger?" Nagoya croaked. "Kruger is here?" It was a name
from another life. *My old commander. Swore he'd get off Delta,
and he did. I got bumped from that flight. Just stubborn and
stupid enough to get on the next one, years later. But I never
thought he might still be alive.* But maybe he was not. Nagoya
said nothing. Who knew what kind of trick they were trying to
pull?

"The situation here has changed since you launched," the
dark, steady man said. This time he spoke clear Delteix, but his
accent sounded low to Nagoya, not what he would have expected
from an important man. The discrepancy put Nagoya on guard.

He revised his estimate of who those people were. Probably
the dark man was in charge of the woman doctor. He must be
some kind of security, or he would not be present at a first
interview. But he was not sure of the blue-eyed man. He was
big enough to be meat, but he did not dress the part.

"Pablo and I are originally Consorsans," Logan said. "There
are Union citizens working in orbital, as well. You can question
them if you wish. We're no longer at war."

She glanced briefly at the man called Singer, then turned back
to Nagoya and smiled. "Yes, I know your suspicions are
aroused. You think this is a trap. Let me remind you again that
I don't need any information from you. I already know everything there is to know about you and your ship. Please note that
I have not asked you to answer any questions. All I want is a
chance to share what we know with you."

"Explain," Nagoya said. His throat ached again, and he could
have used another drink.

"We'll take you through to orbital presently and brief you
there," the doctor said. "Some members of your wake-up crew
will be there. But there is something you should see on the
way."

She offered him her arm, pushed off with her toes, and floated
him to the wall. The shutter slid back, and the unfiltered sunlight

of space flooded in. He saw that they were docked within a large configuration of construction in progress. With his nose to the glass, he could just see the engine section of the *Justicia* gleaming in that light. It made him feel oddly homesick.

Then something moved outside. He forgot all about the ship. His stomach lurched again, and his mind flailed in complete inability to analyze what he was looking at. At first they showed up as bright specks. They came closer, tumbling and spinning but always in formation.

At last they came close enough for him to make out detail. He was relieved to see that they were just people, after all—humanoid in form, anyway, he corrected himself. Their pressure suits bore no resemblance to the stiff, uniform white outfits he was used to. They were flexible and multicolored like the pelts of strange animals, and the helmets were adorned with beast faces, starbursts, and other symbols he could not identify.

They flashed past the window, using the nearby structural elements to alter the trajectory. Most of them were not using safety lines, though he saw the line feeders bouncing at their belts. He saw them kill momentum at the hull of a cylinder across from him, open a hatch, and dive through one by one. The last hit too hard and bounced off but was snagged by a teammate and neatly tucked inside. Then they were gone.

He looked to the doctor for an explanation. Was that what she had wanted him to see?

"Who was that?" he asked.

"Just a construction team. Mostly Rider kids, some vets to boss the outfit, a few bright greens and blues, bored with gravity. By their flashes, I'd say those were mostly Wild Brother barhedoni"—that word again, he thought—"with a couple of Hilt Star heavies. Hilt Star trains a lot of electronics assemblers."

She smiled impishly, as if his bewilderment amused her.

"There are a couple of dozen groups up at any one time. Hilt Star, Sun Arrow, Double Lightning—it's a great, great honor to be recruited for one of the sun hearth barhedoni."

"But what are they *doing*?"

"Carrying out the mission, of course. Our original mission. To live on Nuvospera and use its space as a way station. To get back out to the stars and find our longparents. Step one is building a really adequate orbital facility and using that to launch the communications and power satellites we need. Oh, we're also making observations as we build. I have a couple of friends on that project, too. Their data are being sent back to Delta—probably passed you in transit! After that we build ships."

"I was sent here to fight a war," he said. He stared at her with something entirely new expanding, growing inside him, making him feel truly weightless for the first time—hope, freedom, possibility. Nonconsumables. Too big ever to be used up.

She pointed back at the window. He realized they were slowly turning, relative to the stars. A crescent of blue light grew slowly at the edge of the glass and grew and grew into a disk that filled all his sight. It was jewel-blue and dappled green, ocher and umber and snowy white. Before he knew what he was doing, he had his hands pressed to the glass on either side of his face, as if he could reach out—up, down, or into—and take that treasure into his hands.

The tall man spoke for the first time. His voice was soft, and yet it sounded through and through Nagoya, ringing inside his head.

War's over, Singer said. *Welcome home.*

ABOUT THE AUTHOR

ANN TONSOR ZEDDIES spent the first three summers of her life on a mountaintop in Idaho. She wanted to be a cowboy but decided to be a writer instead when she found that the frontier had moved off the planet. She grew up in Michigan. She now lives in Kansas with her husband and four children: one son in college, one son in first grade, and two teenage daughters in between. She still has a horse, three cats, too many books and not enough time. She is a student of Tae Kwon Do and hopes to test for her black belt soon.